Kate Hardy has always loved books, and could read before she went to school. She discovered Mills & Boon books when she was twelve, and decided that this was what she wanted to do. When she isn't writing Kate enjoys reading, cinema, ballroom dancing and the gym. You can contact her via her website: katehardy.com.

Allie Kincheloe has been writing stories for as long as she can remember, and somehow they always become romances. A Kentucky girl at heart, she now lives in Tennessee with her husband, children, and a growing menagerie of pets. Visit her on Twitter: @AllieKAuthor.

Also by Kate Hardy

A Nurse and a Pup to Heal Him
Soldier Prince's Secret Baby Gift
Mistletoe Proposal on the Children's Ward
One Night to Remember
Fling with Her Hot-Shot Consultant
A Will, a Wish, a Wedding

Also by Allie Kincheloe

Heart Surgeon's Second Chance

Discover more at millsandboon.co.uk.

FOREVER FAMILY FOR THE MIDWIFE

KATE HARDY

A NURSE, A SURGEON, A CHRISTMAS ENGAGEMENT

ALLIE KINCHELOE

MILLS & BOON

First Published in Great Britain 2020
by Mills & Boon, an imprint of HarperCollins*Publishers*
1 London Bridge Street, London, SE1 9GF

ISBN: 978-0-263-27991-7

This book is produced from independently certified FSC™ paper
to ensure responsible forest management.
For more information visit www.harpercollins.co.uk/green.

Printed and bound in Spain
by CPI, Barcelona

FOREVER FAMILY FOR THE MIDWIFE

KATE HARDY

MILLS & BOON

To Julia Williams and Chere Tricot,
with love and thanks for their patience and kindness
when lockdown made writing very difficult!
Xxx

CHAPTER ONE

'I'M NOT HAVING you touching my wife.'

The words were audible right across the ward.

The raised voices weren't just going to upset the poor mum-to-be in that room, they were going to upset all the other mums-to-be within earshot. And none of them needed the extra stress during labour. Rebecca knew that the head of midwifery was in a meeting with the consultants, so she was probably the most senior person on the ward at that moment—meaning that she was the one who needed to deal with this. She walked swiftly over to the room, preparing to calm everything down.

'Everything all right?' she asked sweetly, knowing perfectly well that it wasn't, but also knowing that going in and shouting just as loudly wasn't going to help anyone.

'No, it isn't.' A stocky man stood in front of the bed with his fists clenched. 'I'm not having *him* touching my wife.'

'Him' being the midwife. Rebecca hadn't met Nathaniel Jones yet, as she'd been on leave for the last two weeks since he'd joined the maternity team at Muswell Hill Memorial Hospital, but she knew he was one of the very few male midwives in the country. And this situation needed to be de-escalated as fast as possible.

'Let me introduce myself,' Rebecca said. 'I'm Dr Hart, obstetric registrar. Why don't you come over to my office, where it's a bit more private, and we can discuss it?'

'What, and leave *him* here with my wife?' the man demanded.

'Mr—' This couple hadn't been to any of her clinics, and one of her colleagues had done the ward round this morning, so she didn't know their names. She glanced at the whiteboard above the bed, where the words 'Ruth Brown' had been written, and hoped that her assumption wouldn't make things worse. 'Mr Brown. Your wife's on our ward right now, and our priority is to keep her comfortable and the baby safe,' she said calmly.

'I'm fully qualified,' Nathaniel said gently, 'and Dr Hart is right—your wife and baby are our priorities. Just to reassure you, I had to deliver forty babies before I could qualify, and I've delivered a few more since then. Your wife is very safe with me—my job is to listen to her and help.'

'It's not that. I'm not having a man looking at her…' Mr Brown gave a jerk of his head. 'Down there.'

Oh, for pity's sake. This was a maternity unit! But she bit back her impatience; telling the man he was being an idiot would only put his back up even more and make things worse. 'While you and I have a chat, are you OK for Mr Jones to take your wife's temperature, blood pressure and pulse rate, and keep a check on the baby's movements?'

'I suppose so,' Mr Brown admitted grudgingly.

'Good. Let's go to my office,' she said, giving Nathaniel a reassuring smile. 'We'll be back in a minute,

Mrs Brown.' She led Mr Brown to her office and closed the door to give them privacy.

Clearly she'd meant well, but Nathaniel was a little bit irritated that Rebecca Hart had swept in to deal with a situation he was perfectly capable of handling himself. He really hoped she wasn't the sort of doctor who felt the need to pull rank on a midwife; he'd worked with that sort before and in his view the mum's needs should come before everything else. Or was she like one of his tutors, feeling that men had no place as a midwife?

He took a deep breath to stem his irritation and turned to Ruth Brown. 'Mrs Brown, I'm sorry about that,' he said.

She grimaced. 'I should be the one apologising. Mike was so rude to you.'

'Hey. That's not important. *You* are,' he said. 'And I'm guessing your blood pressure isn't going to be great, so either I can regale you with some terrible jokes or you can do some breathing exercises to help you relax a bit before I put the cuff on your arm.'

As he'd hoped, she laughed and looked less awkward. 'I'll do the breathing. Mike doesn't mean to be rude. We had a scare a couple of weeks back, when I couldn't feel the baby moving. And he's a typical bloke—can't say what he feels, so he gets cross instead. Oh, present company excepted,' she added.

Nathaniel laughed. 'Fair point, and I don't think I'm an exception. I don't know many men who are good at talking about their feelings. Right. Let's try that blood pressure...'

'I've never heard of a bloke being a midwife,' Mr Brown said, his mouth twisted into a sneer. 'What's he doing it for—so he can look at women down there?'

'No. There are several hundred male midwives across the country, and they do it for exactly the same reason our female midwives do their job—the same reason that I, as a senior doctor, do my job. To deliver babies safely,' Rebecca said, keeping her voice cool and even.

'It's not *right*, a bloke being a midwife,' Mr Brown continued, his face flushed with anger.

'Nathaniel is qualified and he's experienced,' Rebecca said. 'If I was in labour, I'd want someone like him to look after me. A trained midwife, who'd be able to spot the signs of any problem right in the early stages and could sort it out before it became an emergency.'

'I suppose,' Mr Brown acknowledged. 'But I still don't want him looking after my wife.'

'Would you have a problem with your wife being seen by a male doctor?' she asked.

He looked surprised. 'Well, no.'

'It's the same thing,' she pointed out gently. 'Just a different title.'

He shook his head. 'Midwives aren't doctors.'

Midwives were just as important as doctors, but this wasn't the right time to have that argument. She needed to deal with the immediate situation first. 'I can talk to the midwifery team to see if anyone else is available to look after your wife,' she said. 'But I can't guarantee there will be.' She could see fear in Mr Brown's face. Was it fear that was driving all this? 'Is this your first baby?' she asked gently.

He nodded.

'It's exciting, because you can't wait to meet your baby, the one you've felt kick and seen on a scan; but it's also really scary, because you see all these awful things on the internet. All the horror stories of things going wrong.' She'd just bet Mr Brown was familiar with 'Dr Search Engine'—and she really hoped that he hadn't seen fit to share his findings with his wife.

'Yeah,' he admitted. 'Ruth couldn't feel the baby moving, a couple of weeks back. I drove her here so fast I got stopped by the police. But when I told them why, they escorted us in with their blue lights going.'

'And everything was all right?' Well, obviously, or she wouldn't be in labour. But he was talking now and Rebecca wanted to keep that going.

'We had a scan and the baby was kicking.' A muscle tensed in his jaw. 'But the doctors said the baby's a bit small for dates. That's why they wanted Ruth to come in today and be induced.'

'So you came in first thing this morning?'

He nodded. 'We had a different midwife when we came in. She said she was going to do this membrane sweep thing.'

'That's an internal exam, which separates the membranes of the fluid-filled sac around the baby from the cervix, releasing the hormones that kick-start labour,' Rebecca said, sure that the midwife had already explained the process but wanting to make completely certain that Mr Brown understood what was happening. 'I assume her labour hasn't started yet?'

'No. And *he* said he'd insert a pessary. In her…' He paused, looking embarrassed and cross.

'Your first midwife probably—' *definitely* '—told you that might need to happen if Ruth's contractions hadn't started within six hours,' she said gently.

'I didn't really take it all in,' Mr Brown admitted. 'I was just worried about Ruthie and the baby.'

'OK. When we induce labour, if the membrane sweep

doesn't work then we'll insert a tablet of the prostaglandin hormones into the vagina.' Rebecca chose her words carefully, keeping everything as impersonal and cool as possible. 'Sometimes it takes a second tablet before labour actually starts. Right now, I think you need someone experienced looking after your wife. Someone who understands about the scare you had during pregnancy, and how worrying it is to have your labour started for you instead of it all happening naturally. You need someone who's going to keep a really good eye on your wife and the baby. Someone who sees her as a mum-to-be and understands her worries—and yours, too. If anything, I reckon Mr Jones is going to be able to help you a bit more than a female midwife could because he'll have a better idea of what goes through a bloke's head.'

Mr Brown shuffled in his chair.

Clearly he was still focusing on the idea of another man looking at and touching his wife's vagina. So she was going to have to embarrass him slightly. 'I can assure you, Mr Jones won't be looking at your wife in the same way you do,' she said, as kindly as she could. 'Just as if, say, you had a lump in your testicles and I was your GP and needed to examine you.'

This time, his face went a very deep shade of crimson.

'I'd examine you, because that's my job,' she said, 'but I wouldn't be looking at your body in the same way that your wife does. I'd see you as my patient—someone who's worried, who has a symptom on a part of his body and who needs my help. There wouldn't be anything at all sexual in the way I looked at you, just as there's nothing sexual in the way Mr Jones looks at your wife. He'll simply be following the procedures, just as a female midwife would.'

'I guess,' Mr Brown said.

'If a female midwife isn't available and you're really concerned about the propriety of having a male midwife, we can arrange for a chaperone,' she said. He'd said earlier that he wouldn't object to a male doctor, so maybe this was the best way to make the point. 'And if any of our male doctors need to see her, we can also arrange for a chaperone for them if that would make you feel more comfortable.'

She waited for him to think about it.

Eventually he looked at her. 'I'm making a fuss over nothing, aren't I?' he asked.

'You're worried about your wife and the baby,' she said. 'But you're also worrying about something that isn't an issue, so that's one burden you can choose to take off your shoulders and make your life a bit easier.'

He took a deep breath. 'All right. He can do it.'

'Thank you.'

'And we don't need a chaperone.'

Relief flooded through her. She smiled. 'Rest assured, all the staff here will treat your wife—and you—with the utmost dignity and respect. But I'd also like to remind you, Mr Brown, that the hospital has a zero-tolerance policy. Our staff have the right to care for our mums-to-be without being attacked or abused, physically or verbally.'

He shuffled in the chair again. 'I owe that bloke an apology, don't I?'

Yes, he did. 'That's your call,' she said, still keeping things calm.

'I'm sorry. I just—I panic, sometimes. I'm used to...' His voice tailed off.

Used to blustering and shouting at his juniors at work if things didn't go quite according to plan? She knew the type. But this wasn't a battle worth fighting. She'd dealt with the important bit so Mrs Brown would get the care she needed. 'OK. Shall we go back and see how your wife's doing?'

He looked shamefaced. 'Ruth's going to kill me.'

'As she's being induced, I think she might have something else distracting her,' Rebecca said with a smile. Mr Brown needed distracting, too, given an important job to stop him overthinking things and getting upset and shouty again. 'And I'm pretty sure she'd like you to do some hand-holding. To chat to her and keep her mind off the wait, because this bit of an induced birth can really get boring. She'll need you to rub her back when she's having a contraction, or get her some really cold water, or fetch her a sandwich when she's getting hungry—that sort of thing.'

'Yeah, I suppose.'

'Shall we go back?'

He nodded.

She escorted him back to the ward where Mrs Brown was waiting on the bed with Nathaniel sitting on the chair next to her, the curtains drawn round them. She was chatting to Nathaniel, clearly completely at ease with him.

Mr Brown walked over to the bed. 'Sorry, mate. I was in the wrong,' he muttered, holding his hand out to shake Nathaniel's.

'You're all right,' Nathaniel said, shaking his hand. 'First babies can do that to you, especially when you've already had a scare and your wife's being induced, and you feel a bit helpless because she's the one going through it and you're not really sure what you can do to make things better.'

Clearly Mrs Brown had filled him in on the situation,

Rebecca thought. And Nathaniel was handling this brilliantly, empathising with a scared dad-to-be.

'Yeah,' Mr Brown said.

'You're such an idiot, Mike. Nathaniel's been really good,' Mrs Brown said. 'So are you going to stop making a fuss now and let us get on with having this baby?'

Mr Brown nodded, looking hangdog.

'You could go and get your wife a cup of tea while I sort out the prostaglandin,' Nathaniel suggested, clearly sensitive to what one of the big problems had been.

'I will,' Mr Brown said. 'Can I get anything for you?'

Nathaniel smiled. 'I'm fine, but thanks for asking.'

'I'd like a chicken salad sandwich on wholemeal with that cup of tea, please, love. I'm starving,' Mrs Brown added.

When Mr Brown had left, Mrs Brown said, 'Mike doesn't mean to be an idiot. He's just...' She wrinkled her nose. 'A bit old-school, I suppose.'

'I've reassured him,' Rebecca said. 'I think he realises now that medics don't see their patients in a sexual way, so he won't worry any more.'

Mrs Brown rolled her eyes. 'Open up, ground, and swallow me now,' she said. 'I'm so sorry.'

'There's no need to apologise. A lot of dads-to-be feel like that, at first. It's all fine. Let's concentrate on you and the baby,' Nathaniel said. 'Now, let's get you comfortable and see if we can get this labour up and running.'

'I'm going to back to my paperwork before my clinic. Call me if you need anything,' Rebecca said.

'Thank you,' he said, though there was something in his eyes that said he had no intention of calling her. She suppressed a sigh; the last thing she needed was a team member with a chip on his shoulder. There wasn't room for egos in this job. Their mums-to-be and babies always came first.

The afternoon ward rounds and clinic took up most of the rest of her day. She was just finishing some paperwork when there was a knock on her open door. She looked up to see Nathaniel standing there.

'Dr Hart.'

Normally she would've suggested first-name terms and asked how he was settling in to the team, but his attitude earlier had irritated her. 'Yes, Mr Jones?'

'I thought you'd like to know that the Browns had a healthy little girl, two point six kilos.'

'That's great news,' she said, pleased. 'Thanks for telling me.'

He smiled. 'They both want her middle name to be Natalie, after me.'

Only a few hours ago, Mr Brown had been yelling that he didn't want Nathaniel anywhere near his wife, and now he wanted to call his daughter after their male midwife?

And then it hit her: she'd steamed in and assumed he needed help to defuse the situation. He could've done it perfectly well himself.

'I'm sorry,' she said.

He frowned. 'Why?'

'When I came in earlier, during the shouty bit. Of course you could handle things.'

He smiled at her, then, and a tingle ran down her spine. A tingle she suppressed ruthlessly; even if he wasn't involved elsewhere, as a single mum she wasn't interested in dating.

'Mike Brown *was* disturbing the ward. I can see where you were coming from,' he said.

'All the same, I think we might have got off on the wrong foot.'

He gave her an assessing look. 'You must be due a break. Let me buy you a coffee.'

'Thanks for offering,' she said, 'but there's really no need. We're a team on this ward and we support each other.'

'All my midwife colleagues are either with a mum or they've finished their shift and gone home. I've just delivered a baby and right now I really want to babble about how amazing it is, to someone who actually gets it.'

'And I'm the only one around?'

'Pretty much.' He gave her another of those smiles that made her stomach swoop, and it unsettled her. She wasn't used to reacting like this to someone.

'Coffee and cake. My shout. And you can let me babble about babies.' He gave her another of those incredibly winning smiles.

Part of her resisted. This man was charming—and she knew from personal experience that charming was fun for a while and then slid into heartbreak. On the other hand, he was her new colleague, they'd started off on the wrong foot and she wanted to smooth things over between them. 'OK, but only if I buy.'

'Dr Hart, it's coffee. No strings,' he said gently.

Which made her face feel hot with embarrassment. 'Sorry,' she mumbled.

'By the way, what did you say to Mike Brown?' he asked, sounding curious.

'I pointed out that if I was a GP looking at a lump on his testicle, I'd see him as a worried patient, not a sex object, and you wouldn't be leering at the business end of his wife because your job was to deliver the baby safely and make sure she was OK during labour. Or something along those lines.'

He grinned, his dark eyes crinkling at the corners, and Rebecca noticed how long his eyelashes were. 'I wish I'd seen his face when you said that.'

'Patient confidentiality,' Rebecca said, knowing how prim she sounded but unable to stop it.

'He really squirmed, didn't he?' His grin broadened. 'To be fair, I would've squirmed, too. Let's go get that coffee.'

She saved the file, logged out of the computer system and walked with him to the canteen.

'How do you like it?' he asked.

Coffee. He was talking about *coffee*. For pity's sake, why was she reacting to him like this? She never flirted. Not since Lucas. And she wasn't going to start flirting now. 'Skinny cappuccino, no chocolate on top, please.'

'OK. Cake?'

'I'm not really a cake person,' she said. 'Though thanks for the offer.'

'Something savoury?'

'Just coffee's lovely, thanks.'

Once he'd ordered their coffee—and cake for himself—they found a quiet table.

'I was away when you joined the team. How are you settling in?' Rebecca asked.

'Pretty good—the staff are all lovely, here,' Nathaniel said. 'I trained at the London Victoria, but I've always liked this part of the city, so when the job came up I applied for it.' He paused. 'How about you? Have you been here long?'

'Two years. I trained at Hampstead,' she said. And she'd loved it there. Until Lucas had crashed his motorbike three and a half years ago, leaving her a widow with a year-old baby. Riding too fast—but not to get home to her. He'd been going too fast because he'd loved the thrill of speed. Because he'd liked taking risks. And either he hadn't seen the icy patch, or he'd thought himself invincible, or maybe both. The end result was the same.

They'd had to airlift him to his own emergency department.

Losing a patient was always tough. But when that patient was a colleague as well, one who was charming and popular with everyone no matter what their qualifications or status… The accident had broken his team as much as it had broken Rebecca. And she hadn't even had a chance to organise the funeral before Fate added another nasty twist. She'd assumed her missed period was because of the stress of the situation; she hadn't even considered she might be pregnant. Being rushed into the same emergency department where Lucas had died and learning that she'd had an ectopic pregnancy—losing one of her fallopian tubes as well as the baby—had been almost too much to bear.

She shook herself. Not now. She'd had three and a half years to get used to being a widow. Three and a half years of learning not to wrap Jasmine completely in cotton wool, not to worry every second they were apart, and not to overcompensate and try to be both parents. Moving to Muswell Hill had really helped her, and Jasmine loved her nursery school. 'Being a male midwife is a fairly unusual career choice,' she said. 'What made you pick midwifery?'

'I used to be a building site manager,' he said.

Site manager to a midwife? That was quite a career change. 'Just as well Mr Brown didn't know you worked on a building site, leaning down from the scaffolding and whistling at every passing woman,' she said. 'He'd have worried even more about letting you near the business end.'

Nathaniel laughed, a rich, deep sound that set those tingles off again. 'That's horrible stereotyping.'

'A bit,' she agreed. 'But whenever I've walked past scaffolding that's what the builders always do.'

'You're blonde and you're pretty. Of course they'll whistle at you.'

She felt her face go pink. 'I wasn't fishing for a compliment. I meant they whistle at *every* passing woman.'

'Not all of them do. Some builders prefer men,' Nathaniel said.

Was that an oblique way of telling her that he was gay? 'OK,' she said carefully. 'So what persuaded you to change careers?'

It was a story Nathaniel was used to telling. 'Fell off a roof,' he said cheerfully. 'Broke my back. I spent four months in hospital.'

'Ouch,' she said. 'And I imagine you must've needed a ton of physio when you left hospital.'

He nodded. 'It gave me a long time to think about what I really wanted to do with my life. Whether I had the nerve to work on a site again, whether I could make myself go up a ladder to check something.'

'Did you?'

'Let's see. Work in an air-conditioned hospital; or be on a site in all weathers, from frost and snow to rain or blazing sun, knowing I'd maybe make it to forty before arthritis started making my job a lot more difficult every day?' He spread his hands. 'It was an easy choice.'

Though not all of the choices had been his. It had been Angela's choice to end their engagement. It had taken him a long time to come to terms with the fact that the love of his life hadn't stuck around when he'd needed her most. Eventually he'd worked out why: she'd agreed to marry Nathaniel the site manager, the man whose career was doing nicely. She hadn't signed up to nurse him through a broken back, not knowing if he'd ever be able to walk again and they'd spend their entire marriage with her as his carer. Even though he understood it, he still found it hard to forgive. And even now he resented the fact that she'd ended their engagement so fast, not even waiting a couple of weeks to see if there were any signs of recovery.

To dump him so swiftly: had she ever really loved him in the first place? Was he that hopeless a judge of character when it came to relationships? The whole situation had really knocked his confidence in himself, and he hadn't had a serious relationship since, not wanting to get close to someone else and risk discovering that he wasn't enough for her, either. He kept his heart under wraps and his relationships short.

Not that he was going to tell Rebecca Hart anything about that. It wasn't relevant to his job. Or to what she'd asked him.

'I wanted a job where I'd make a difference,' he said. 'Where I'd make people's lives better. The nurses on my ward got me through those first rough weeks, and it made me realise how amazing they were. I wanted to be able to do that for someone, too.'

'Nurses are amazing,' she agreed. 'So did you start training as soon as you were back on your feet?'

He nodded. 'I left school at sixteen, so despite having my site manager's qualifications I had to do a year's access course at the university before they'd accept me to do a BSc in nursing.' He smiled. 'I loved the course. I was going to work in the Emergency Department, because that was my favourite placement. But then, in my final year, my best friend's wife was pregnant. Jason was away on business and Denise's family was in Paris, celebrating her aunt's sixtieth birthday—they thought it would be fine to go because all first babies are late and take ages.'

'Right,' Rebecca said, rolling her eyes because she clearly knew how much of a myth that was. 'So I'm guessing she went into labour early?'

'Yes. Her best friend was meant to be her backup birth partner, but she was a junior doctor and was in Theatre when Denise went into labour. Obviously she couldn't just walk out of the op, so Denise called me in a panic. I thought I'd just be there for the first stage of labour and Jason would be back in time for the birth, but it was a quick labour and he didn't make it to the hospital until Sienna was a couple of hours old. It was the most amazing thing in the world, being there when my goddaughter took her first breath.' He grinned. 'The first thing Sienna did after being born was an enormous poo, and my first job as her godfather was to change that nappy.'

Rebecca's blue eyes twinkled. 'Ah, yes, the joys of the first nappy. So even the meconium didn't put you off wanting to be a midwife?'

'Nope. In a weird way, that decided me. Looking at her face, seeing those first few moments, I knew Maternity was where I wanted to be. Which meant I was just about to graduate in the wrong subject.' He wrinkled his nose. 'Well, ish. My degree gave me good foundations for midwifery. After I graduated, I did the eighteen-month short course to become a midwife. I was the only man in my year group, but most people accepted me.'

'Most?'

'One of my tutors didn't really take to me,' he admitted. 'In her view, men shouldn't be midwives because they can't have babies.'

Rebecca winced. 'That's unfair. And also not true—are you going to say heart surgeons can't do their job if they haven't had heart surgery themselves? And what about women who can't have children? That's not a valid reason for them not being midwives.' She looked cross. 'I hate that kind of prejudice.'

And that really gratified him, at the same time as it made him realise that he'd misjudged her. She hadn't stepped in earlier to pull rank; she really had intended to help and be supportive.

He shrugged. 'I guess it helped prepare me for any parents-to-be who thought the same as my tutor did. I learned to come up with some solid answers. But here I am. I qualified, I love my job, and it's such a privilege to help women through one of the most intense and emotional experiences of their lives.'

'Do you get many dads reacting to you the way Mr Brown did today?' she asked.

'One or two. A couple of women have said they didn't want a man delivering their baby—ironically, they ended up with sections and a male surgeon,' he added, rolling his eyes, 'but normally, once people get over the surprise of me not being a woman, they're fine about it. Not many go from nought to shouty in two seconds, the way he did.' He smiled at her. 'What about you? Why did you choose Maternity?'

'It was my favourite rotation,' she said. 'That first moment after the birth, when all's still, and the baby opens their eyes and looks at you, and you see all the wonder of the universe in their face.'

'Those tiny fingers and tiny toes,' he said. 'I *love* babies' feet. And the way babies grip your finger.'

'The softness of their skin,' Rebecca said. 'Even if they're a late baby and a bit overcooked, or an early baby covered in vernix—they're just *beautiful*.'

And that look of joy on her face took his breath away, transforming her from the slightly starchy doctor he'd first met to the most gorgeous woman he'd even seen. His spine pricked with awareness of her.

'I think,' Nathan said, 'we're on the same page.'

'I agree.' She smiled. 'Thank you for the coffee, Mr Jones.'

'Nathaniel.' He waited a beat. Was she going to stay all starchy and formal? Or would she…?

'Rebecca.'

Only then did he realise he'd been holding his breath. Which was crazy.

'I'm afraid I need to get going—but welcome to the team.'

'Cheers,' he said, and deliberately stayed to finished his own coffee.

He was so aware of the brilliant sky blue of her eyes, and the way her hair—even caught back in a ponytail for work—looked like sunlight on ripened cornfields. The shape of her mouth.

Although he'd dated a few times since the end of his engagement, there hadn't been anyone serious and it had been a long while since he'd felt that instant zing of attraction. He'd just been going through the motions, doing what everyone expected of him.

He hadn't been able to help himself glancing at Rebecca's left hand as they chatted. No ring, though that meant nothing nowadays. For all he knew, she could be in a committed relationship but hadn't formalised it. Though he wasn't going to ask any of his colleagues if she was single; the last thing he wanted was to put either of them under the focus of the hospital rumour mill.

She hadn't flirted with him; but he hadn't been able to stop himself flirting a bit with her.

He was really going to have to be careful.

CHAPTER TWO

NATHANIEL MANAGED TO keep himself in check the next day, more by luck than judgement because his path didn't actually cross Rebecca's. But on Thursday he had a patient who worried him. It should've been a routine thirty-four-week antenatal appointment, but Josette Kamanya's blood pressure was a bit high for his liking. And his worries increased when he tested her urine sample and the dipstick showed the presence of protein. Her BMI was more than thirty-five, she'd had high blood pressure before getting pregnant, and this was her first baby; an alarm bell began to ring in the back of his head. Particularly when she admitted to having had a few headaches recently. 'But that's all just a part of pregnancy, isn't it?' she asked.

Yes, but the symptoms were adding up to something he really wasn't happy about.

'Mrs Kamanya, would you mind if I had a look at your feet?' he asked.

She looked surprised but nodded and slipped her feet out of her shoes.

'Your ankles and feet look a little bit swollen to me,' he said. That was another sign that worried him.

'It's probably just because I've been walking about a lot and it's been hot for June,' she said.

He wasn't convinced. 'What about your hands and fingers?' he asked gently. 'Have your rings started to feel tight or anything like that?'

'I guess they have, in the last couple of days,' she admitted.

The alarm bells in his head grew a bit louder.

'Have you felt any pain in your tummy or under your ribs?'

'No.'

He smiled. 'That's good. Have you had any feelings of nausea, or actually been sick?'

'No, thankfully,' she said, looking relieved. 'That was all over weeks ago.'

'Glad to hear it. Going back to those headaches you mentioned—have you noticed any flashing lights, or any blurriness in your vision?'

'No. I don't get migraines or anything like that,' she said. 'It's just a headache that's been a bit hard to shift.'

Nathaniel still wasn't happy. Often women with pre-eclampsia felt perfectly fine and it was only the urine test and blood pressure result that indicated there was a problem.

'Has anyone in your family ever had pre-eclampsia?' he asked.

'I don't think my mum had any problems when she had me. I'm an only child, but I can't remember any of my cousins having a problem, either.' She looked at him, biting her lip. 'Is something wrong?'

'I think,' he said, 'you might have a condition called pre-eclampsia, but I want to talk to one of the doctors. Would you mind if I brought someone else in to see you?'

Her eyes widened. 'Is there something wrong with my baby?'

He held her hand. No medic could ever promise that everything was going to be a hundred per cent fine, but he didn't want her worrying. 'It's not that. If I'm right in my suspicions and you have pre-eclampsia, it's a very common condition, and we're used to treating it. You're in absolutely the right place and we're going to look after you both,' he said.

'All right,' she said, but she still looked anxious.

'I'll be back really quickly. Have a sip or two of water, and I'd like you to try some breathing exercises for me while you're waiting.' Those at least he knew would help. 'Rest your hands at the bottom of your rib-cage so your fingertips are just touching,' he said, and she followed his directions. 'That's perfect, Mrs Kamanya.' He smiled at her. 'Breathe in for a slow count of five, and your fingertips should move apart. Now breathe out for a slow count of five, and your fingertips should come back together again. That's brilliant.' He smiled again. 'I'd like you to do fifty breaths in and out like that, and I'll be back before you know it. Is that OK?'

'All right,' she said, clearly worrying but trying to be brave.

The only one in the doctors' office was Rebecca. Given their talk the other day, he hoped she'd be supportive rather than trying to take over or dismissing his fears; though it didn't help that the little flare of attraction grew brighter when he saw her. 'Reb—' He stopped himself. They'd been on first-name terms the other day in the canteen, but she might prefer formality on the ward itself. 'Dr Hart, can I ask you to come and see one of my mums, please?'

'Rebecca,' she said. 'I prefer working on first-name terms.'

'Nathaniel,' he said.

'What's wrong, Nathaniel?'

Weird how hearing her use his given name for the first time made a little prickle go all the way up his spine. He shook himself. He was here for his mum-to-be, not himself. 'I think Josette Kamanya might have pre-eclampsia.' He gave Rebecca a quick rundown of the case. 'She's had high blood pressure since before she was pregnant, and according to her notes this is the first appointment where she's had protein in her urine. But I've just got a funny feeling about it.'

'You're probably right. I always trust a midwife's instinct,' Rebecca said.

Good. So this wasn't going to be another power struggle. He'd been right in his revised assessment of her. 'Thank you.' He walked with her to the antenatal clinic room. 'How are you doing, Mrs Kamanya?'

'I just did breath number fifty,' she said.

'Perfect timing, then.' He introduced Rebecca swiftly.

'Mr Jones is a little bit concerned about how you're doing, so he asked me to come and see you, Mrs Kamanya,' Rebecca said.

'So what exactly is this pre-eclampsia thing, Dr Hart?' Mrs Kamanya asked.

'It's a condition that affects mums and babies and often starts after the twenty-week mark. It's quite common—about one in twenty mums has it—so don't get too alarmed,' she reassured Mrs Kamanya. 'Usually our first clue is when you have high blood pressure and protein in your urine. We think it's to do with the blood vessels in the placenta not developing properly, so the placenta doesn't send as much blood as it should do to the baby.'

'Is the baby going to be all right?' Mrs Kamanya asked.

'You and the baby should both be just fine, but if we don't keep a close eye on you and treat you then there is a risk of you developing complications,' Rebecca said.

'What sort of complications?' Mrs Kamanya asked.

'There can be a problem with your blood clotting, or you could go on to develop a condition called eclampsia, where you might start having fits. You're also at a higher risk of having a stroke,' Nathaniel explained. 'Which I know sounds scary, but if we start treating you now all the risks go way down.'

'So I agree with Mr Jones that we need to keep an eye on you and the baby,' Rebecca said. 'I'd like to do some blood tests to check your liver and kidney function and make sure your blood's clotting properly. I'd also like him to monitor the baby's heartbeat—which won't hurt either of you; we'll give you an ultrasound so we can take a closer look at how the placenta's doing; and we'll give you a blood test to check levels of a hormone called placental growth factor, which will help me diagnose whether this is pre-eclampsia or not. Is that OK with you?'

Mrs Kamanya nodded.

Rebecca checked the notes Nathaniel had made. 'Your blood pressure's a bit on the high side for my liking, so I'd also like to give you some medication to lower it. It's safe for pregnant women to take, but you might have some side effects.' Between them, she and Nathaniel ran through the side effects.

Mrs Kamanya bit her lip. 'I really don't like the idea of taking medication while I'm pregnant. And I'm worried that it might hurt the baby.'

'It's your choice,' Rebecca said gently, 'but without the medication there's a risk that your blood pressure could go up further, and that's more likely to cause complications which will be more of a risk to the baby.'

'So there isn't really a choice.'

Rebecca took her hand and squeezed it. 'You can change your mind at any time, Mrs Kamanya. It's fine. This is all about making you comfortable and keeping you well. Plus we'll be here with you, so if you decide to have the medication and you start to feel any side effects, you can tell us and we can do something to help—including giving you a different medication.'

'You'll be here with me?' Mrs Kamanya's eyes widened as she took in what Rebecca had said. 'Do you mean I'll have to stay in hospital?'

'For a couple of days, yes,' Rebecca said. 'We'll see how things go. It might be that we send you home in a couple of days under strict instructions to rest, and to call us straight away if you're worried about anything. But, like Mr Jones, I'd be happier if you were admitted for the next couple of days so we can keep a close eye on you and the baby.' She paused. 'There is one thing. If you do have pre-eclampsia, and we can't get your blood pressure to settle, we might need to deliver the baby a bit earlier than planned.'

'But I'm only thirty-four weeks pregnant!' Mrs Kamanya looked shocked. 'That's way too soon.'

'We'll see what the tests say,' Rebecca said, 'but if we do have to deliver the baby early, we'll make sure you have steroids to help mature the baby's lungs and minimise any risks to both of you. The main thing is that we look after you both properly.'

'I've had my labour bag packed for weeks—everyone at my antenatal group has—but I never dreamed…' Mrs Kamanya shook her head. 'I can't have the baby yet. I just *can't*.'

'Try not to worry,' Nathaniel said. 'I know that's easier said than done, but you're in the right place.'

'So why did I get pre-eclampsia? Is it something I did wrong?' Mrs Kamanya asked.

'It's nothing you've done. We don't know the exact causes,' Rebecca said. 'The risk factors include having high blood pressure and a family history of pre-eclampsia—not just your family, but including if your partner's mother had pre-eclampsia—or if you have an autoimmune disease such as lupus or antiphospholipid syndrome.'

'I don't have a family history and neither does Andras, as far as I know. And I don't have any other diseases. I've felt perfectly fit and well.' She bit her lip. 'Will the baby be OK?'

'The baby's going to be just fine, because we'll be monitoring you both,' Nathan reassured her.

'Will I get this pre-eclampsia again, if I have another baby?' Mrs Kamanya asked.

'You're at a greater risk of having high blood pressure and developing pre-eclampsia in your next pregnancy, yes. But it doesn't mean that you'll definitely get them, just that the risk will be a bit higher and we'll keep a closer eye on you,' Rebecca said, squeezing her hand. 'We're going to look after you, and it's your job to get plenty of rest.'

'I'm not very good at resting,' Mrs Kamanya said ruefully.

'Me, neither. I was a total nightmare during my pregnancy. And the worst thing was when people nagged me to put my feet up and *rest*.' Rebecca rolled her eyes and grimaced. 'It drove me crazy and I used to remind them that "rest" is technically a four-letter word.'

During her pregnancy?

Rebecca had a child?

Again, Nathaniel found himself glancing at her left hand to double-check. Definitely no ring. Was she still in a relationship with the father of her baby, or was she a single parent?

There was absolutely no way he could ask without being rude. He'd have to think of a tactful way to broach the subject.

'But, much as I sympathise with you and I'd hate it if I were in your shoes, I'm afraid I'm going to have to tell you to rest,' Rebecca continued, smiling at Mrs Kamanya. 'Is there anyone we can call for you to go and fetch your things?'

'Andras—my husband—is in meetings all day.' Mrs Kamanya shook her head. 'If I call my mum she'd never stop fussing over me and it'd drive me mad, being wrapped in cotton wool. My best friend's a teacher so she can't just ask for time off whenever she feels like it.' She grimaced. 'And my mother-in-law would start wringing her hands and making it all about her.'

'That kind of drama makes it hard for anyone to rest,' Rebecca agreed.

Nathaniel wondered if she was talking from personal experience, or from what she'd observed on the ward.

'Perhaps we can call your husband or your best friend during their lunch break, and they can bring some things in for you this evening,' Nathaniel suggested.

'That would be good. Thank you.' Mrs Kamanya bit

her lip. 'If I do have to have the baby early…that doesn't mean I have to have a section, does it?'

'We might be able to induce you,' Rebecca said, 'but I think it's a good idea to prepare yourself for the possibility of having a section. But it's really not as bad as you think. Women recover much quicker nowadays than they did twenty years ago. You're not going to be stuck at home for months, unable to drive and having to rely on everyone else to lift things for you.'

Mrs Kamanya didn't look convinced.

'Maybe we can get one of the mums here who's had a section to come and have a chat with you and tell you what it's really like,' Nathaniel said. 'That way, you won't be guessing and worrying and making it scarier than it really is.'

'I suppose,' Mrs Kamanya said.

'Nathaniel will get you booked onto the ward, and I'll get everything written up so we can run the tests,' Rebecca said.

'And we're here to answer any questions,' Nathaniel said. 'Not just us—all the midwives and doctors on the ward. We'd all much rather you asked us whatever you want to know than just kept worrying in silence.'

Rebecca smiled at her. 'As Mr Jones said, try not to worry. You're in good hands with him.'

She was completely different from how she'd been the other day. And Nathaniel liked the fact that she put their mums first. He liked *her.*

But he couldn't get involved with her. Even if she didn't have a partner, she had a child; she had commitments. The little voice in his head added a sharp reminder: he hadn't been enough for Angie, back in the days when he was getting on in his career, so what made him think that a junior midwife could be enough for a successful senior doctor? He needed to put a lid on his attraction to her.

He sorted out the blood samples Rebecca had asked for, organised an MRI and set up the cardiotocography to measure the baby's heartbeat and keep a trace for the file. Then he took Mrs Kamanya through to the ward and got her settled in, organised the monitoring he wanted done for the rest of the day, and asked Gurleen, who was on the reception desk, to get in touch with Mrs Kamanya's husband and best friend.

When his clinic was over, he dropped in to the ward to see how Mrs Kamanya was doing. Rebecca was there, sitting next to the bed, talking to her and making her laugh.

He blinked in surprise. 'I didn't expect to see you here.'

'It's my lunch break,' Rebecca explained. 'And I remember what it was like to be told to rest and being desperate for someone to take my mind off things.'

'Distraction is good.' Though he hadn't expected this sort of kindness from her. Then he made the mistake of meeting her eye, and the attraction he'd been trying to suppress turned into a hot, heady pulse. Oh, for pity's sake. Now wasn't the time or the place.

'Dr Hart's been so kind,' Mrs Kamanya said.

He opened his mouth, intending to say something anodyne, but what came out was, 'Don't tell her this, but she's my favourite out of the doctors on the ward.'

Oh, no. Earth, open and swallow me now, he begged silently.

Rebecca shocked him even more. 'Don't tell him this,' she said in a stage whisper, 'but he's as good as a woman when it comes to being a midwife.'

And she gave him the cheekiest, cheekiest grin—one which turned that flicker of attraction into a raging fire in an instant.

If someone had picked them both up right now and dropped them on a deserted island, he would've kissed her until they were both dizzy.

But this was work, and they needed to concentrate on their mum-to-be. 'Is there anything I can get you, Mrs Kamanya?' he asked.

She shook her head. 'Thanks, but I'm fine. That nice woman on reception talked to my husband and my best friend. Andras is going to move one of his meetings so he can go home and fetch my labour bag, and my best friend's coming in straight after school finishes so she can take over—well, babysitting me, I guess.' She rolled her eyes.

'That's good,' Nathaniel said.

'And, meanwhile, we're talking sudoku,' Rebecca said with a smile. 'Want to join us?'

He held up his hands in a surrender gesture. 'Number puzzles are not my thing at all. If it was a pool table, you're on. Or a quiz team where someone else gets to do the literature questions and I can do sports, TV and music. But those?' He nodded at the magazine. 'Count me out.'

'Nice pun, Mr Jones,' Mrs Kamanya said, laughing.

'Quiz team,' Rebecca said thoughtfully. 'We can always use someone good for the ward quiz team. We have a monthly quiz in the pub with Paediatrics and the Emergency Department—and we're a bit overdue a win.'

'Are you asking me to join the team?'

Oh, for crying out loud. Why had he opened his mouth? He'd practically purred it at her, as if he were teasing her about asking him on a date. This was nothing of the sort. It was a team thing.

But she didn't look awkward or embarrassed. She just smiled. 'Yes. But you'd better be good, or you'll be buying everyone cake to make up for it.'

'That,' Mrs Kamanya said, 'sounds like an excellent idea.' She gave Rebecca a high-five.

This was a side of Rebecca he hadn't seen. Playful, fun. And he really, *really* liked it.

'Let me know when the next quiz is and I'm in—as long as I'm not on duty,' he said.

'Sure,' she said.

That smile made his heart feel as if it had done a backflip. An anatomically impossible backflip, but a backflip all the same. 'I'll see you both later,' he said.

At the end of his shift, Nathaniel checked in with Mrs Kamanya again; her best friend was with her and she seemed a lot more settled. And then he headed for Rebecca's office. She was clearly finishing off some paperwork.

'Hi,' he said.

She looked up from her computer. 'Hi.'

'I just wanted to say thanks for all your help with Mrs Kamanya today,' he said.

'That's what I'm here for. To support my team when things get complicated.'

Yeah. He'd definitely misinterpreted the way she'd come in to bat his corner with Mike Brown.

Her smile was warm and inviting, and even though he'd had every intention of keeping his distance he just couldn't resist asking, 'Do you fancy grabbing a pizza with me after work tonight?'

'I… Thank you for asking, but I have commitments,' she said, clearly choosing her words carefully.

'Your partner would be welcome to join us, of course.' Oh, way to go, Nathaniel. Subtle. *Not.*

'No partner,' she said.

And that changed everything. If she didn't have a partner, there was no barrier to them getting to know each other better. 'Then maybe we could have that pizza another evening?'

She took a deep breath. 'It's kind of you to ask me—' Kindness hadn't even been in the running order of reasons why he'd asked.'—but I don't date.'

So it wasn't personal? Not like Angie. And that gave him the courage to say, 'May I ask why?'

'I'm a widow,' she said, 'and I don't want to get involved with anyone.'

Rebecca was very young to be a widow. Though Nathaniel wasn't going to be crass enough to ask what had happened. Plus it was none of his business. But he still wondered why she didn't date. Was she still grieving for her husband? Did she think nobody would match up to his memory? Or had her marriage been unhappy and she didn't want to get involved in another potentially difficult relationship? Not that he could ask. That was way, way too intrusive.

'I'm sorry,' she said. 'I have a daughter who's almost five, and she comes first.'

'Of course.'

'I'm not looking to date anyone,' she said. 'But friendship—that's a different thing. I'm happy to be friends.'

'Friends,' he said, deliberately keeping his voice neutral and non-judgemental.

'I'm sorry I can't offer you anything else.'

So was he. But he wasn't going to blank her just because she'd turned him down. 'Friendship is fine by me,' he said. And, wanting to make her feel more comfortable, he added, 'Maybe we can do the pizza as a team thing.'

She smiled. 'That'd be good.'

'OK. See you later,' he said, and left before he could make even more of an idiot of himself than he already had.

Rebecca stared out of the door after Nathaniel.

It was the first time anyone had asked her out since Lucas.

Six and a half years.

In some ways, it was flattering; in others, it was terrifying. No way could she risk dating again. She had Jasmine to think of; and her daughter would come first. Always. And, apart from that, she'd learned her lesson well. She'd married someone gorgeous and charming, someone who'd swept her off her feet and they'd got married six months after they'd first met. Not long after their first anniversary, she realised she'd made a mistake; Lucas was an adrenalin junkie who didn't get enough thrills even from his high-pressure job, and he'd put his need for adventure before everything else. The thrill of thc chase had worn off very quickly for him, to the point where he seemed to prefer the company of his friends to hers, and she'd been seriously considering leaving him when she'd found out that she was pregnant.

The news had meant she'd stayed, wanting to give their baby a chance to be part of a family. Lucas had promised to change. She knew he'd tried—but he'd been so bored by domestic life. He'd hated the day-to-day grind of life with a small baby, with the nappy-changing and the crying and the lack of sleep. Even when Rebecca had sent him off climbing at the weekends with his like-minded friends, it hadn't been enough; he'd felt guilty about leaving her to cope with the baby on her own. And that guilt had come further and further between them, leading him to do more and more reckless things.

Including buying the expensive motorbike that had ultimately claimed his life.

Rebecca sat back in her chair, no longer seeing the words on her computer screen.

She hadn't been enough to soothe Lucas's restlessness, and nor had fatherhood. Even if he'd survived the crash, even if he'd been able to go back to work afterwards and back to riding his motorbike, she was pretty sure that she and Jasmine wouldn't have been enough for Lucas. He'd needed more than their little family unit: he'd craved the adrenalin rush of danger. She'd suspected that Lucas had also found female distractions elsewhere since she'd fallen pregnant—though she'd never asked, never accused, because she hadn't wanted to rock the boat. Not when she was heavily pregnant, or sleep-deprived with a newborn, and too tired for a fight. Though she had been starting to think that maybe she and Jasmine would be better off on their own. That Lucas needed his freedom much more than he needed a family.

She'd actually planned to sit down with him that night and suggest it. She'd fallen asleep on the sofa, waiting for him to come home.

And then the police had called round to see her and everything had changed…

She didn't want to risk her heart again. To risk falling for another Mr Wrong, especially when she had her daughter to consider. Yes, Nathan seemed a nice guy; but charming men could always seem to be whatever you wanted them to be. Who was to say he wouldn't change, the way Lucas had, once she'd given him what he wanted?

Plus, if he wanted children of his own, what then? She'd lost one of her fallopian tubes as a result of the ectopic pregnancy. Even getting pregnant again might be an issue, and if she did conceive then her risk of having another ectopic pregnancy was greater than average. Was it fair to get involved with someone who might want kids of his own when she might not be able to give him a family?

So it was better to stay single. To keep her heart intact. To focus on the important things in her life: her daughter, her family and her job.

Saying no had been the right thing to do.

And those wistful 'what ifs' trying to fight through her heart were just going to have to stay buried.

CHAPTER THREE

NATHANIEL WAS OFF duty on Friday, which gave him plenty of time to brood. Going for a run didn't help; he couldn't settle to watching a movie, so in the end he cleaned his flat, deciding that his least favourite chore suited his mood. Why had he been so stupid, giving in to that mad impulse to ask Rebecca out? Why hadn't he waited, let them get to know each other a bit better first? Even though he'd covered over the immediate awkwardness by suggesting that they did the pizza as a team thing, he knew he'd rushed it.

Would she give him a second chance, maybe a bit later? Or had he ruined it for himself by asking too soon?

And why was he asking her, in any case?

'I need my head examining,' he told Leo, his Bengal cat.

Leo patted Nathaniel's hand with his paw.

Nathaniel smiled. There was probably more sense in his hand right now than there was in his head. Rebecca had already told him she didn't date. Even if she changed her mind, he didn't do serious relationships. Angie had dumped him while he'd still been up to his eyeballs in painkillers. He didn't want to get involved with someone, lose his heart to her and then discover he wasn't enough for *her* to love, either.

Yet he couldn't stop thinking about Rebecca. He didn't really understand why. He hadn't even liked her when he'd first met her. He'd thought she was the sort who pulled rank and interfered. But how she'd been with one of their higher-risk mums, listening and even spending her lunch break with Mrs Kamanya to cheer her up, had shown him that Rebecca Hart had a kind, soft heart.

Plus she was gorgeous. All that straight blonde hair she kept tied back for work, and eyes the colour of a summer sky.

Why was it getting to him just now? It wasn't an anniversary or anything like that. And he knew what his big sister would say when he turned up with flowers and a punnet of those candyfloss grapes she'd been scoffing for England since getting pregnant. He could even hear Charlotte's voice echoing in his head: 'Nate, you're thirty-four years old. Young, gorgeous and single. The world should be your oyster.'

The life he had now wasn't what he'd planned at all. Nine years ago, he'd been looking forward to a summer wedding with everyone dancing at the reception in a rose garden; he was doing well at work; and he'd been thinking about the two kids he and Angie were going to have—a boy first, then a girl.

And then he'd fallen off a roof.

One little slip and his whole word had shattered.

No wedding and no babies.

The nearest he was going to get were his goddaughter, his niece-to-be, and the babies he delivered on the ward.

He told himself he was fine with that. He *liked* the

new life he'd made for himself. He had a close family, great friends, and a really rewarding job.

'So why, this week, doesn't it feel enough?' he asked the cat, who just stared at him with huge green eyes.

He wasn't still in love with Angie. He'd been hurt and angry and desolate for a while, but he'd finally come round to thinking that she'd done them both a favour. If she couldn't stick around when the going got tough, at least they didn't have two kids whose lives would be ripped apart in a break-up.

But it had also left him unable to trust. Unable to trust himself—how had he managed to pick someone so wrong for him?—and unable to trust that whoever he dated might really love him. Or had the problem been him, all along? If he hadn't been enough for Angie, how could he be enough for anyone else?

Enough brooding, he told himself. He needed to go and buy flowers. And he'd try to get Rebecca's smile out of his head. He really needed to stop wanting things he couldn't have.

Rebecca curled up on the sofa with a mug of tea. She really wasn't following the plot of the film she'd been trying to watch. Mainly because she couldn't get Nathaniel Jones out of her head.

Should she have said yes when he'd asked her out? She knew what her best friends and family would say. At the age of thirty-four, she was still young enough to have fun, and she shouldn't spend the rest of her life in mourning for Lucas.

She could almost hear her little sister's voice. 'You need something for you, too. You're more than just Jasmine's mum or my sister or Dr Hart. You're Rebecca, too. And it'd be good for you to have a night off. This guy didn't ask you to marry him, he asked you to go out on a *date*. There's a difference.'

But there was a good reason why she'd said no. Lots of good reasons. The first of which was that she'd made a huge mistake with Lucas. She'd loved him, but she shouldn't have married him in a rush like that, and she didn't want to make the same kind of mistake in any future relationships. She didn't want to end up with someone else who didn't think she was enough. It wouldn't be fair to Jasmine, either.

And even if she did find someone who loved her for herself, who wanted to make a future with her and be a stepdad to Jasmine, there were other hurdles. Supposing he wanted children and she couldn't have them?

No. She'd made the right decision in turning him down.

Though she couldn't help wondering, what if? What if she'd said yes? What if she'd let herself have a nice evening, got to know him better and then decided if she wanted to repeat it?

Dating.

Opening herself up to a relationship again.

It was a terrifying proposition.

It could be so easy.

But she would be opening herself up to a world where she could get hurt again. A world where she'd be found wanting. A world where she'd fail.

It was too much of a risk.

Yes, Nathaniel Jones was cute; his dark eyes had the longest lashes she'd ever seen on a man. His mouth was beautiful. Then she wished she hadn't thought about his mouth, because her thoughts immediately rushed on to the next stage—wondering what his mouth might feel like against hers.

For pity's sake. She was thirty-four, not fourteen. Mooning over a good-looking man wasn't the sort of thing she should be doing.

But all the same she found herself thinking about Nathaniel later that night, going over and over the same questions. Had she been too hasty in turning him down? Should she have agreed to go out with him? Could she take the risk of dating again?

On Monday morning, Nathaniel was in the middle of writing up notes when Rebecca came to find him. 'I know you're rostered on the labour ward, this morning, Nathaniel, but I was wondering how many ECVs you'd done?'

An ECV or external cephalic version was a procedure used to turn a breech baby in the womb. 'I've seen a couple, but not actually done any myself,' he said. 'Is that what you're doing today?'

She nodded. 'If you'd like to assist—or even do the ECV yourself, if my mum's happy for that to happen—you'd be very welcome.'

'I'd love to.' And it warmed him that she'd thought of him.

'Great. I'll come and find you at half-past ten, and maybe you can do the initial checks for me and talk my mum through the procedure.'

'You're on.'

She was as good as her word and came to find him at half-past ten. 'So you're clear on how the procedure works?'

'Yes.'

'Great. You take the lead, and I'll be there as backup.

I've already checked with the Ridleys and they're both quite happy for you to do the procedure.'

Nathaniel had already arranged for a colleague to look after his mums-to-be while he was working with Rebecca, so he followed her to the consultation room.

She introduced him to the couple sitting on the bed. 'Mr and Mrs Ridley, this is Nathaniel Jones, who'll be doing the procedure this morning.'

'Nice to meet you, Mr Jones,' Mrs Ridley replied, smiling.

'Nathaniel, this is Mr and Mrs Ridley. Mrs Ridley's thirty-six weeks right now and the baby's decided to stay feet-first.' Rebecca smiled and gestured to him to take over.

'Lovely to meet you both,' Nathaniel said. 'It's really common for a baby to be feet-first or bottom-first in your pelvis during pregnancy, but most of them have turned head-down by this point. I'm assuming you've both already talked this through with Dr Hart and you've decided to have an ECV in the hope the baby will do a somersault in the womb, so he or she will be born head-first rather than feet-first and you're more likely to have a normal birth?'

Mrs Ridley nodded. 'Dr Hart's warned us there's a fifty-fifty chance of it working, and if it doesn't work then I'd like to try for a vaginal breech birth. I'd rather not have a section, though I realise that might have to happen if we can't make a normal birth work.'

'Some babies are stubborn and turn all the way back again a few days after they've turned head-first,' Nathaniel said. 'And there's also a small chance that we might have to deliver the baby today, if we're not happy with the baby's heartbeat afterwards or if there's any bleeding from your placenta.'

'We're prepared for that,' Mr Ridley said, indicating a labour bag.

'Great. And I'm also assuming that you don't have pre-eclampsia, you're not having twins, the baby isn't small for dates, you haven't had any recent bleeding and your waters haven't broken,' Nathaniel said, mentally ticking off all the criteria.

Rebecca's approving smile meant he'd remembered all the contraindications for the procedure.

When Mrs Ridley nodded, he said, 'So what happens now is we'll do a scan to confirm the baby's position and the position of your placenta, as well as the amount of amniotic fluid.' He smiled. 'Then I'll check your blood pressure and your pulse, and check the baby's heart rate. Once we're happy everything's as it should be, Dr Hart will give you a small injection to help relax the muscles in your uterus. The medication won't affect the baby, and there's no risk to you or the baby, but it might make you feel a bit shaky and you might be aware of your heart beating a bit faster.'

'The medication wears off in three minutes,' Rebecca added, 'but it increases the chance of us turning the baby successfully.'

'Can I just double-check your blood group?' Nathaniel asked.

'A positive,' Mrs Ridley said.

'Excellent.' As her blood type wasn't rhesus negative, he knew that meant they wouldn't need to give her an injection of anti-D to stop antibodies forming against the baby's potential rhesus positive blood cells.

The scan confirmed that the baby was breech, and Nathaniel was happy with the position of the placenta and the amniotic fluid level. He checked Mrs Ridley's blood pressure and pulse. 'Perfect,' he said. And the baby's heartbeat was absolutely fine, too.

'Between us, we're going to persuade the baby to do a forward roll,' Rebecca said. 'The whole thing should take about ten minutes, and it might be a little bit uncomfortable. But it shouldn't be painful, so if it hurts you need to tell us immediately and we'll stop.'

'Got it,' Mrs Ridley said.

Rebecca prepared the syringe. 'You'll feel a sharp scratch,' she said, and administered the injection. 'Try to relax your tummy muscles for us, Mrs Ridley.' She turned to Nathaniel. 'So now you put your hands on Mrs Ridley's abdomen, under the baby's bottom, and gently manipulate until you feel the baby starting to move forward. Mrs Ridley, are you comfortable?' she checked.

'I am,' Mrs Ridley confirmed.

'Mr Ridley, you're doing OK?'

Nathaniel liked the fact that Rebecca was considering the feelings of everyone in the room. Her calmness and capability meant that everyone was relaxed, even though this wasn't a hugely common procedure.

Rebecca directed his movements quietly, and then he felt the baby shift under his hands and do a forward roll.

'Oh!' Mrs Ridley said, sounding surprised. 'I felt the baby turn!'

'And you should feel quite a bit more comfortable, now the baby's head is no longer under your ribcage,' Rebecca said with a smile.

'Oh, I do,' Mrs Ridley said feelingly, rubbing a hand along her ribcage.

'We're going to do another scan now,' Nathaniel said.

'And then we're going to monitor the baby's heart rate for about thirty minutes, to check the baby's comfortable.'

'That's amazing. And it's so much easier not having the baby's head pushing under my ribs,' Mrs Ridley said.

The scan and the monitoring were both satisfactory, to Nathaniel's relief.

'It's all good,' Nathaniel said. 'You're free to go home now, and we'll see you back here in a week. But if you get any vaginal bleeding, or your waters break, or you get painful contractions, or the baby doesn't move as much as normal, then I want you to call us straight away.'

'We will,' Mr Ridley confirmed.

Once the Ridleys had left, Nathaniel turned to Rebecca. 'Thank you. That was amazing.'

'You're welcome. You did a great job—you were calm, you explained everything well, and you did the movements perfectly.'

'I appreciate you giving me the chance to do the ECV myself.'

'Pleasure.' She smiled at him. 'I guess I'd better let you get back to the ward.'

'I guess. Catch you later,' he said.

Rebecca watched Nathaniel leave the room. He'd been really good, calm and reassuring. All the way through the half-hour monitoring after the ECV, he'd chatted to the Ridleys to make sure they were both relaxed and comfortable. He was patient and kind with their parents-to-be, and in a weird way that made Rebecca feel safe with him. As if she could rely on him and he wouldn't let her down, the way Lucas often had.

Not all men were like Lucas.

So maybe she could take a risk.

Maybe she could ask him out for a drink.

Tomorrow, she promised herself, and got on with writing up her notes.

CHAPTER FOUR

REBECCA DIDN'T ACTUALLY see Nathaniel on Tuesday or Wednesday, because their shifts clashed, and on Thursday morning she came in to overhear Amara, one of the younger midwives, who was married to their newest junior doctor, saying to Nathaniel, 'Tanvir's gone down with that gastro bug. There's no way he's going to be able to do the abseil on Saturday.'

She knew Tanvir had organised a team of ten to abseil down one of the buildings in Central London, to raise money for a new scanner for the ward.

'If we don't have the full team, the organisers might not let us do the abseil,' Nathaniel said. 'Maybe I can persuade them to let one of us do it twice. Or…' He looked at Rebecca. 'Dr Hart.' He gave her the sweetest smile. 'How are you with heights?'

She stared at him. 'You're asking *me* to step into Tan's place?'

'It's only a few minutes out of your day. You'll have the most amazing views over the city.'

'And that building is a hundred times my height.' She shook her head. 'Tan asked me a month ago when he first organised it. I said no then, and I'm saying no now.' She couldn't quite believe this. 'I had no idea Tan had talked you into it.'

'My very first day on the team,' he said with a smile. 'And he talked me into being his second in command, so as he's sick it's up to me to fix this.'

'But you hurt yourself falling off a roof. How can you *possibly* offer to walk off the edge of a roof and go down the side of a really tall building, after *that*?' The idea was horrifying.

'My back's all fixed, now.' He shrugged. 'And mentally I'm doing OK. It'll be good for me. I know there will be ropes and a lot of safety requirements, so there's nothing to worry about.'

It sounded to her as if she'd just met another Lucas. Her late husband would've loved the thrill of walking backwards over the edge and then abseiling as fast as he could down one of the biggest structures in London; the sponsorship money and what it would do for the ward would've been incidental to him.

Surely Nathaniel could see the risks, the way she did? Or had she been the one out of step, rather than Lucas?

'Sorry. I can't do it. I've never abseiled before,' she said.

'It's easy. Just don't look down, and think about the money it'll raise for the ward.'

'You're asking me to abseil down one of the tallest buildings in London,' she reminded him.

'With safety ropes,' he pointed out. 'I'm not suggesting you walk a high wire between buildings without a safety rope—or even a little rope off the ground, without a net.'

At least he was acknowledging the need for safety. But it wasn't enough. She shook her head. 'It's still a risk. I'm a single mum. I can't take that kind of risk.'

'When Tan first asked me, I said no,' Nathaniel said. 'All I could see were the risks. I remember what it feels like to fall off a roof. I remember what it feels like to land. And I've pretty much avoided heights ever since. But then I thought about it. This is a really good way to overcome those lingering fears. I'll have to walk over the edge—but I'll be in a safe environment. So it helps me and it helps the ward. Double win.'

Oh. So he *did* see how terrifying it was. And he was trying to face his fears. Move on.

Was it time she did the same?

Take a risk.

'Can I think about it?' she asked.

'Sure,' he said. 'I'm going to call them during my break this morning to see what our options are.' He paused. 'Tell you what. Have lunch with me, and we'll talk about it then.'

'Aren't you on the labour ward this morning?'

'Nope. That's Amara. I'm on clinic,' he said. 'So. Lunch. And you can talk babies to me.'

Was he flirting with her? The way he'd said it, it was as if the words meant something completely different. The base of her neck felt hot. 'I'll come and find you,' she mumbled. 'Better get to my own clinic.'

She managed to put Nathaniel out of her mind during clinic, but then it was lunchtime. When she went to find him, he'd just finished writing up notes.

'Lunch is on me,' he said. 'Not because I'm trying to make you feel beholden to me, or to guilt you into agreeing to do it.'

No, but she suspected he intended to charm her into it. And she'd learned the hard way that charm wasn't enough. It faded and left resentment in its place. 'I'd rather go halves,' she said.

'Is it that scary, someone buying you a coffee and a sandwich?' he asked.

Yes. 'No,' she fibbed.

'Well, then. Let me buy you a sandwich, and we'll talk babies.' He smiled. 'There aren't any strings.'

'Just abseiling ropes.'

'Yes, but the sandwich isn't dependent on that. It's just lunch, Dr Hart.'

She knew he'd deliberately used her title rather than her first name, to remind her of their formal working relationship. Making a fuss would be ridiculous. Plus part of her really did want to have lunch with him, get to know him a bit better. She gave in. 'All right. Thank you.'

In the canteen, she chose a tuna salad sandwich on seeded wholemeal bread, and a skinny cappuccino. He kept the conversation to work, but she knew she owed him an answer about Saturday. 'What did the abseil people say?' she asked.

'We can still go ahead, but I need to give them the name of a replacement team member.'

And if she took too long giving him an answer, that wouldn't give him enough time to find a replacement for Tan. It was too short notice.

'Why are you doing the abseil?' she asked.

He shrugged. 'To raise money for the scanner. To feel part of the team.'

Which was fair enough, but worry still nagged at her. 'I know you said to Amara that your back was fixed, but isn't it going to be tough for you to face heights again?'

'Abseiling is a completely different situation from doing a roof inspection,' he said. 'Yes, it scares me, but it'll do me good to face that last, lingering fear.' He paused. 'So have you had a bad experience with heights, then?'

'No. I'm just aware of the risks.' The sort of risks Lucas had taken. The sort of risks that had literally made him crash. 'The idea of just one little rope being between me and a huge drop… That makes my palms sweat.'

'You'd be on a safety line and you really couldn't fall,' he said. 'I know what you mean about sweaty palms. I'm scared, too. But I weighed up the risks before I said yes. And we need that scanner. So the way I see it is you have to ignore the scary stuff and just get it done.'

Ignore the scary stuff and just get it done. Which wasn't the same as being a risk-chaser. It was about being confident, not over-confident and cocky. Taking calculated risks. Ignoring the voice in your head that made you miss out on things. And that confidence drew her even more. 'That's pretty good advice for life in general,' she said thoughtfully.

His eyes were kind as he said, 'Sometimes it's easy to overthink things.'

Since Lucas, she knew that she had a tendency to do that. Maybe she should take Nathaniel's advice. Be brave. Ask him out. Her skin suddenly felt a bit too tight, but she ignored it. What was the worst that could happen? If he said no, she'd back off. And if he said yes… Actually, she wasn't going to think about that, because it was even scarier.

'You're right. Sometimes it's easy to overthink things. And sometimes you think about it again afterwards and realise it should've been simple. Like—' She took a deep breath to steady her nerves. 'Like going out for a pizza with someone.'

That got his attention. He met her gaze head-on, and

his dark eyes were warm and sweet, with a hint of sultriness. 'A pizza.'

Stop overthinking it, she told herself. *What does it matter that you haven't dated anyone except Lucas for six and a half years? What does it matter that you've never asked someone out before? This is a simple yes-or-no question. A first step. Do it.*

'Uh-huh.' She cleared her throat again. 'That pizza you suggested last week. Would you—are you—could we—?' Oh, for pity's sake. Since when was she so inarticulate? Keep it simple. 'Could we do it?'

The corner of his mouth quirked. 'That sounded like a proposition, Dr Hart.'

She felt the colour flood through her face. 'It…' she croaked.

His grin broadened. 'Sorry. I was teasing you. It was irresistible. Of course I know you were talking about pizza.'

Though he'd made it sound like sex.

He'd made her think of sex.

He'd made her think of things she'd shut down for years. She couldn't speak, just nodded.

'I'd love to have pizza with you.' He paused. 'Are we talking as a team thing?'

She shook her head. 'Just…'

'Good friends?'

She dragged in a breath. 'I haven't dated anyone since Lucas died. I've never asked anyone out. I'm…' She shook her head. 'I don't know how to do this.'

'But you *did* do it. You've thought about it; you ignored the scary bit and did it,' he said. 'And, yes, I'd like to go out with you. Very much. Which isn't something I'm used to feeling, either.'

Funny how that made her feel better; though at the same time she wondered why someone as nice and as gorgeous as Nathaniel Jones was single. Had someone broken his heart? 'OK. When's good for you?'

'I can be flexible.' He paused. 'What about you? Would an evening be a problem?'

'No. My mum or my sister will be happy to babysit.' She smiled wryly. 'Actually, my sister will be thrilled as she's been nagging me for ages to date again.'

'I know how that feels,' he said. 'My big sister is always on my case.'

'Little ones can nag just as much, believe me,' she said feelingly.

So they'd both been nagged to date someone.

And their pizza—even though it would be low-key and casual—was going to be a proper date. The fact made her feel ridiculously shy, as if she were a teenager all over again. Considering she was the one who'd asked him out, the shyness was even more ridiculous. She got a grip on herself. Just. 'Are you free on Monday evening?'

He took his phone from his pocket and checked his diary. 'Monday evening's fine.'

'OK. I'll book a table and text you the details.'

'What's your number?' he asked. 'Then I'll text you so you've got my number.'

She recited it, and a couple of moments later her phone pinged with a message from him.

And that was it.

They were officially going on a date.

And, instead of being scared by it, she found that it made the world feel weirdly brighter. It made *her* feel brighter, too. Encouraged. Empowered.

'All right,' she said. 'I'll do the abseil.'

'You really don't have to. I can find someone else,' he said.

'No, you're right. Of course it's safe. The people who set things up do that every day. They do a ton of checks.'

'And think about it this way: they'd be terrified at the idea of delivering a baby, which you do without batting an eyelid,' he said.

'I guess. OK. And my daughter won't have to see it. She has a swimming lesson in the morning—Mum was going with me, but Dad can go in my place.'

'Aren't you going to have anyone with you to cheer you on?' he asked. 'I'm bringing my sister and her wife.'

'I could ask my sister,' Rebecca said.

'Thank you. Though I meant it about no pressure.' He gave her another of those smiles that made her heart flip. 'Excuse the pun—no strings.'

'I definitely don't want strings. I want nice, solid ropes.' That was how she'd wanted her relationship to be, too. Strong and solid. But the supports had turned out to be flimsy. She shook herself. 'But you were right. I need to face the fear.' She didn't want Jasmine to grow up being a thrill-seeker like her dad; but she was starting to think that going too far the other way and wrapping her in cotton wool would cause just as many problems. Doing something that scared her, in a safe environment, was a good way to help her find the right balance.

The rest of the day flew by; Rebecca booked the table, that evening, and texted the details to Nathaniel.

Meet you there at seven.

He texted back.

Looking forward to it.

So was she.

But they had the abseil to get through, first.

Friday went by incredibly quickly.

And then on Saturday morning she met Nathaniel, along with the rest of the team, in the centre of London. Between them they had quite a throng of supporters, all armed with cameras.

'Saskia, this is my colleague Nathaniel, who's just joined our team. Nathaniel, this is my sister, Saskia,' she introduced them swiftly.

'Delighted to meet you,' he said, shaking her hand. 'And this is my sister, Charlotte, and her wife, Robyn,' Nathaniel said, indicating a heavily pregnant woman who looked so much like him that even without the introduction Rebecca would've guessed that was his sister, and a slender woman with a kind smile. 'Guys, meet some of my new team.' He introduced his family to everyone on the Muswell Hill Memorial Hospital's team. 'I guess we'll see you all back here at the bottom.'

'Good luck, Bec!' Saskia said.

And then Rebecca was heading for the top of the building with the rest of the team, to have her harness and helmet fitted. She and Nathaniel were the first two to walk along the metal openwork pathway next to the security fence. Suddenly it felt a very, very long way up. Even the tops of the tallest buildings across the city seemed a long way below them.

Why on earth had she ever thought that this was a good idea? Had she been temporarily insane when she'd agreed to join the team abseil?

Obviously her fear showed in her face, because Nathaniel asked softly, 'Are you OK?'

No. She was incredibly nervous and even the thought of what she was about to do made her hands feel sweaty. 'Fine,' she fibbed. 'You?'

'Fine.'

The calmness in his voice and his smile made her feel very slightly better.

'It's going to be OK,' he said. 'There are lots and lots and *lots* of layers of security. It's safe, or they wouldn't let you do it. We're not the first team to go down today.'

No, but they were the first of *their* team.

'You've got this,' he said. 'I've seen you in Theatre performing a C-section. If you can deliver a baby and sew all those layers of muscle and skin back together in that short a time, and so neatly, then you can do this one tiny little abseil. Ten minutes, that's all it'll take. You can do *anything* for ten minutes, Rebecca. Anything at all. And that's all this will take. Ten minutes. You've got this.'

If this was how he talked his mums through contractions and breathing, no wonder he was so popular on the ward, she thought. He was calm and reassuring, and—more importantly—she believed what he was telling her.

She trusted him.

'OK,' she said.

Though her nerves came back when she stepped up onto the platform and the woman from the event team clipped her carabiner and safety rope on. She was vaguely aware of Nathaniel standing next to her, going through the same safety checks, but she was even more aware of the open space behind her. The sheer drop. And she was going to have to walk backwards over the edge…

'Now your gloves. They're thick enough to handle the

rope and protect your hands,' the woman said. 'I'll talk you through it.'

Rebecca could feel clamminess on her face and the racing of her heart. 'OK,' she said.

'I want you to go to the outer edge and hold on to the bar. You're not going to fall, and you'll be perfectly safe,' the instructor reassured her.

Every step felt as if her feet were made of lead. She was shuffling rather than picking her feet up.

'Now put both your hands on the rope.'

'Let go of the bar?' Her voice sounded as quivery as it felt.

'You're clipped on. You won't fall,' the woman told her. 'Both hands on the rope, lean back, and keep your shoulders back—it should feel like you're sitting down, but your legs are out straight instead of bent.'

Her movements felt slow, as if they were going through treacle, but finally Rebecca managed it.

'Now lift the rope up. It'll feel heavy to start with, but it gets easier.'

It definitely felt heavy.

'As you go down, the rope will be lighter so you'll go faster. But you're in control of your speed,' the instructor continued. 'When you push the rope up through your hands, you'll start to go down. Take your time. There's no rush.'

No, but she was dithering so much that she was holding everyone else up. She glanced to the side, expecting that Nathaniel would be long gone—but, to her surprise, he was there, waiting for her.

'Hey. I thought we could do this together,' he said.

'OK.' She was aware that she was talking through

clenched teeth. How could he be this calm and sanguine, all this distance up?

'Rebecca? I want you to start going backwards now. One foot at a time. You'll feel a ledge beneath your feet,' the instructor said.

Slowly, slowly, she got her feet to move. The rope's weight made her arms ache.

'Spread your toes to keep your balance, and take another step,' the instructor said. 'Over the ledge. You can do it. Remember there are people waiting for you at the bottom to help you, and you're not going to fall because we've got you. Take your time, enjoy the views, and think of all the money you're raising.'

One step. Over the ledge.

Rebecca was terrified, but she made herself do it.

Then there was a clicking sound that made her panic. 'What's that?' she asked. 'It's clicking. Does that mean something's going wrong?' Her blood was roaring in her ears.

'It's just the rope going through the pulley. The clicks mean it's working and you're safe,' Nathaniel said. 'Come on. One step at a time. Down we go. Wave to your sister. Make her proud of you.'

She managed it. Just. Then she made the mistake of looking down. And it was a long way down. A long, long, *long* way to fall. Why had she ever thought that this was a good idea? Why hadn't she just said no? 'Oh, my God.'

'Don't look down,' he said. 'Look across to me. See me smiling at you.'

He was smiling, all the way up here, even though he'd fallen off a roof and broken his back. And that confidence warmed her. Boosted her. Nathaniel Jones was amazing.

He'd hurt himself—very badly—yet here he was, up here with her, facing his fears and raising money for the ward.

If he could do this without shaking, so could she. Because he knew what it was like to fall from up high, what the crunching of bones sounded like, what the shock of impact felt like.

'One more step,' he encouraged. 'Take a little step, and push that rope up. You just have to travel one hundred times your height, and then you'll be back with your feet on the ground.'

A hundred times her own height hadn't sounded so bad, on the ground. Now she was actually up here, it was terrifying.

'You're doing great,' he said. Just as if he were encouraging one of his mums through a contraction. 'You've got this. Baby steps. Down we go. Push that rope up.'

And, gradually, the earth began to move a bit closer. Down they went.

'Look at me,' he said.

She did so. How warm and sweet and soulful his brown eyes were. How beautiful his mouth was. Why hadn't she noticed in the time they'd been working together? Nathaniel Jones was every bit as gorgeous as a heart-throb movie actor, and she wanted to look at him a lot more than she wanted to look at the view.

'You can do this. Keep going. Push that rope and take another step,' he encouraged.

Just as the instructor had said, the rope gradually felt lighter and lighter. And either she really was going faster, or she felt a bit less scared than she had at the top, because suddenly they were whizzing down and she was actually enjoying it—to the point where she could risk looking out, and the city looked beautiful instead of much too far away. Finally, she understood why people liked an adrenalin rush. Right at that moment, she felt as if she could conquer the world.

She glanced across at Nathaniel. Just then, it felt as if there were only the two of them, suspended in space. Floating.

Was this how it would feel if she danced with him? As if she were walking on air, weightless?

He was looking right back at her, and there was a bloom of colour in his cheeks. Was he thinking the same thing? she wondered. Thinking about how it would feel to be in each other's arms, their mouths just a touch apart, on the brink of a kiss?

For a second, she couldn't breathe.

'OK?' he asked.

Yes. No. She didn't have a clue. 'I feel…' She shook her head, unable to articulate it. 'This whole thing…'

'It's pretty amazing,' he said, his voice husky.

So was he. Again, her breath caught. 'You're pretty amazing,' she blurted out.

'Takes one to know one,' he said, and her heart skipped a beat. Was he saying he thought she was amazing, too?

'Let's finish this,' he said. 'You're doing brilliantly. Wave to your sister and smile.'

And this time she could look down. She could see Saskia standing there on the ground at the front of the spectators, waving madly.

She waved back and grinned.

'Well done. Keep going,' he said.

Down they went, step by step, the rope clicking, until finally they were at the bottom; there were people helping her touch down and unclipping her from the ropes.

Nathaniel was standing next to her, having just taken off his hard hat, gloves and harness.

'We did it.' She flung her arms round him and held him close. 'Thank you. If you hadn't talked me down…'

'You would still have done it,' he said. Though he was holding her just as tightly, as if he didn't want to let go of her either.

She looked him straight in the eye. Suspended in mid-air, she'd thought his eyes were dark and soulful. Close up, she could see that there were little flecks of gold and green in his dark brown eyes. Like little bits of sunlight. And his mouth was beautifully shaped, only a few centimetres from her own; his lips were slightly parted. She felt her own lips parting, felt herself rising up on her toes ready to touch her mouth to his.

And the rush she felt when their lips met was even stronger than the rush she'd felt as she'd abseiled down the building. Here, with Nathaniel kissing her, the rest of the world fell away. It felt as if they were alone on the top of a cliff with the sun shining down and the sea lapping against the sand, far below.

Except it wasn't lapping.

It was *clapping.*

She opened her eyes in shock and pulled back.

Dear God. She'd snogged the face off Nathaniel Jones in front of her sister and quite a few of her department. And now everyone was *clapping.* How were they ever going to live this down?

She risked a glance at Nathaniel.

Those gorgeous eyes still had those green and golden flecks—but he looked slightly dazed, as if she hadn't been the only one carried away by the rush of the abseil.

Except it wasn't the abseil. It was *Nathaniel* who'd

made her feel this rush, this thrill of pleasure. That kiss. The feel of his heart thudding against hers. The warmth of his body.

What was she going to do?

What was *he* going to do?

She didn't have a clue. She had no idea what to do, what to say, what to…

He recovered first. 'It's so long since I did anything like abseiling, I'd forgotten what a buzz it gives you. I think my last lingering fear of falling might just be over. Thank you for sharing the moment, Dr Hart, and I apologise for getting carried away.'

He was going to take the blame?

Gallant, but she couldn't quite let him do that, it wasn't fair. She'd been the one to instigate it. 'And I think my fear of heights might be cured, too. You're right. It's easy to get carried away—and I apologise, too, Mr Jones.'

Please don't let anyone work out that she was lying though her teeth.

That kiss might have started out from relief at being back on solid ground, but it definitely hadn't ended that way. The end of that kiss had been about desire, pure and simple.

And she hadn't been alone. He'd kissed her back.

'I, um—I need to go and collect my daughter,' she said.

'And I think we both need to reassure our sisters,' he said.

'I…um—see you Monday.' And she fled before she could say or do anything else stupid.

Though of course Saskia had seen everything.

'I assume that was the guy you're seeing on Monday night when I'm babysitting?' she asked, fanning herself.

'Whoa. Mr Darcy, eat your heart out. I think any woman would want to snog him.'

Rebecca groaned. 'Sas. Please don't tease. I feel… Oh, my God. I snogged him in front of everyone.' She put her hands to her face in horror. 'How am I going to face the rumour mill at work on Monday?'

'Just tell them it was the adrenalin rush from the abseil,' Saskia suggested.

'We already did.'

'Good. You've probably nipped it in the bud. If you haven't, then just brazen it out and make them give you extra money for sponsorship.' Saskia raised an eyebrow. 'I haven't seen you look this flustered since you were a teenager.'

'I don't think I've *felt* this flustered since I was a teenager,' Rebecca admitted. Except maybe in the early days with Lucas, but she hadn't had any responsibilities to worry about back then. Now, she did. She couldn't afford to be flustered.

'It'll do you good to be flustered,' Saskia said. 'You need some fun.'

Fun? Rebecca wasn't quite sure this was fun. It was scary. Nathaniel was the first man she'd dated since Lucas. The first man in years who'd put her in a spin. And she didn't know whether that was going to be a good thing or a bad.

Later that evening, once Jasmine was asleep, Rebecca was about to text Nathaniel to thank him for talking her through the abseil when her phone beeped with an incoming message.

You were very brave today.

She typed back, wanting to be honest,

I was very scared. Thank you for talking me down.

And they were going to have to talk about what had happened afterwards.

Sorry for...

Except she wasn't sorry for kissing him. Not in the slightest.

Sorry if I've made it awkward at work.

He texted back,

We both got carried away by the rush of the moment.

Meaning that the kiss hadn't affected him and she was setting herself up for disappointment already?

Her phone beeped again.

At least, that's all they need to know.

Meaning that kiss *had* affected him the same way that it had affected her. Feeling better, she texted.

Looking forward to Monday.

She added a kiss and sent it.

She didn't have to wait long for an answer.

So am I. x

That kiss at the end made her feel like a teenager all over again, fluttery and excited.

Monday was going to be…

Fun, she reminded herself. *Keep it light. Enjoy it instead of worrying.*

CHAPTER FIVE

WHAT DID YOU wear for a first date? Jeans were a bit too casual, Rebecca thought; on the other hand, a little black dress would be a bit over the top, given that they were only going to the local pizzeria. She didn't want to seem too keen, but she also didn't want to look as if she hadn't made any effort. In the end, she settled for a pretty summer dress and wore her hair loose.

Her sister, who adored Jasmine, was babysitting, and Rebecca was relaxed as she walked out of her front door; but her nerves kicked in with every step she took towards the restaurant and by the time she reached the pizzeria her fingers were tingling with adrenalin. Was she doing the right thing? Was she really ready to date again? Why did even the prospect of dating Nathaniel make her feel all at sixes and sevens?

This was simply having a casual dinner together in a restaurant she knew well; there shouldn't be anything intimidating about it. Yet it was hard to make herself open the door.

Nathaniel was already there when she walked into the restaurant and confirmed that she had a table booked. He stood up when she reached him, and she rather liked his old-fashioned manners.

'Hi,' she said.

'Thanks for coming,' he said, smiling. 'You look lovely.'

'Thanks. So do you,' she added shyly. He was wearing a smart-casual burgundy shirt and dark trousers, teamed with suede shoes—very different from the navy scrubs he wore on the ward. Here, he wasn't a midwife, another member of her team on the ward: he was a man. The man she'd kissed after the abseil. *The man she was starting to date.* And she wasn't sure if that made her more scared or thrilled.

'What would you like to drink?' he asked.

'A glass of red wine would be nice,' she said.

'I'll join you. Shall we order a bottle?'

'Sure.'

'Chianti OK with you?' he checked.

'That'd be lovely.'

Once they'd ordered their wine and pizzas, with salad and dough balls to share, Rebecca's nerves flickered again. It was so long since she'd dated that she'd forgotten the etiquette. Why on earth hadn't she looked up some tips on the internet, first? Her social skills seemed to have deserted her entirely.

At least work would be a safe topic of conversation. 'How was your day?' she asked.

'Brilliant. I had a first-time mum in, everything went almost completely according to her birth plan, and the dad cut the cord and bawled his eyes out.' He grinned. 'I love days like this. How about you?'

'I did a section,' she said, 'after the poor mum had been in labour all night. She was gutted, but the baby was starting to show signs of distress and she was exhausted.'

'You did the right thing, then.'

'Yes.'

Silence spun between them. Oh, help. Had they exhausted work as a topic? What now? She was about to make an anodyne comment about the weather when he surprised her by asking, 'What made you change your mind about going on a date with me?'

Because she couldn't get him out of her head. Not that she wanted to admit that. Not yet. 'It was time I started dating again,' she said instead. Though she knew she needed to tell him about what had happened to Lucas. 'Just so it doesn't become the elephant in the room, I'd better explain about my husband. He was a doctor in the emergency department, and…' She paused. 'Let's just say Lucas liked an adrenalin rush. He used to ride a motorbike. One night, he hit a patch of ice and crashed. Nobody else was involved, but he didn't survive the accident.'

'I'm sorry,' he said. 'That must have been hard for you.'

'It was.'

'How old was Jasmine when he was killed?' Nathaniel asked.

'Just over a year.' She bit her lip. They'd been dark days indeed. And she'd been so grateful for her family's support.

Losing her husband in a crash, when their daughter was only a year old. Rebecca would've had to be strong for the little girl, rather than letting herself grieve. No wonder she didn't date, Nathaniel thought.

'I'm sorry,' he said again.

For both their sakes, he should stop this now. Tip it back over the line into friendship.

The problem was, he didn't want to.

She was the first woman who'd intrigued him this

much since Angela. He really wanted to know where this could go.

He didn't want to explain about Angela, because he didn't want Rebecca to pity him. But maybe there was a middle ground. She'd mentioned that Lucas had been an adrenalin junkie; Nathaniel could at least assuage that fear.

'Just so you know, despite the fact I fell off a roof and I was OK about doing the abseiling on Saturday, I'm not a thrill seeker. But I haven't been in a serious relationship for a while.'

'You've been busy changing careers,' she said. 'There isn't much time for fun when you're juggling shifts and lectures and everything else.'

It was technically true; just nowhere near the whole truth. But it was enough for now. So he smiled and said, 'Yes.'

She spread her hands. 'I'm so rusty when it comes to dating. I'm totally clueless about etiquette.'

He rather liked the way she'd admitted that. And the way she wrinkled her nose was oh, so cute.

'What are we even supposed to talk about?' she asked.

'On our first date? I guess we'd talk about what we do for a living, and then what sort of things we like,' he said. 'You and I already know about each other's work. So I'll start the next topic: are you a dog person or a cat person?'

'Neither,' she said. 'I'd love a dog, but I don't have one because it wouldn't be fair when I'm not home very much. You?'

'Cat. I have a Bengal cat called Leo—because he looks like a mini leopard.'

'Seriously?'

'Seriously.' He took his phone from his pocket and

flicked into the photographs before handing the phone to her. 'Here you go.'

'Oh—he's very pretty,' she said, sounding surprised. 'He really does look like a mini leopard.'

'And he's a total sweetheart. He kind of thinks he's a dog, so he'll sit or he'll do a high-five if you ask him to,' Nathaniel said with a grin. 'He's ten, now. And he kept me sane when I was recovering from the accident. He stayed right by my side. And he used to miaow when I was doing physio, almost as if he was telling me to keep going. As if he was counting the reps for me.'

'That's really cute.' She smiled and handed the phone back.

'OK. What kind of music do you like?'

'Anything I can sing to, but I guess I like the eighties stuff my parents used to play when I was a kid,' she said. 'You?'

'Classic rock. That's my dad's influence. He used to play in a band.' He thought about it. 'Best film ever?'

'It's a Wonderful Life,' she said promptly. 'Followed very closely by *Love, Actually.*'

Interesting choice. Films with a bit of darkness but a lot of happiness. Was that what she was looking for—the happiness after the darkness she'd had to endure so young? 'So you're a Christmas fan?'

'It's purely coincidental that they're both Christmas films. It's the happy endings I like,' she said.

She wanted a happy ending.

This was their first date. He couldn't guarantee anything. But he'd do his best to make today happy for her.

'How about you? What are your favourite films?' she asked.

'The Empire Strikes Back,' he said. 'Followed by *Raiders of the Lost Ark.*'

She smiled. 'I'm guessing that's influenced by your dad, again?'

'Absolutely.' He spread his hands. 'Do you prefer sea or mountains?'

'Sea,' she said promptly.

'Me, too. Cheese or chocolate?'

'Cheese.'

'Chocolate,' he said. 'Which is also the answer to what's the best ice cream ever.'

'No, that's salted caramel,' she said. 'Favourite food?'

'Jamaican,' he said. 'My best friend's parents are from Jamaica. His mum makes the most amazing run-down stew.'

'Run-down stew? What's that?'

'Fish,' he said, 'stewed with coconut milk, tomatoes and spices until it falls apart. Served with dumplings. Her fried dumplings are like nothing you've ever tasted. They're amazing.' Bits of him knew he ought to shut up now, but his mouth wasn't running with the programme. 'Actually, Rita taught me how to cook them. So maybe—if you decide you'd like a second date with me—I can cook stew and dumplings for you. Leo will be pleased, because it'll mean he gets fish.'

Part of Rebecca loved the idea of a man who could handle domestic stuff—someone who could cook, instead of forgetting to order takeout and leaving everything to her. But part of her worried. Eating dinner at his place would be much, much more intimate than eating in a crowded restaurant. It was too big a step for her to take right now.

'I...can we take a rain check on that?' she asked, biting her lip and feeling awkward.

A rain check.

Nathaniel realised he'd tried to take this too fast. Their food hadn't even arrived yet, and he was asking her for a second date? Ridiculous. No wonder she'd backed off. Time to keep things light.

Except the little insidious voice in the back of his head—the one that had plagued him in his hospital bed, after Angie had dumped him—whispered, *She's just trying to be polite. Why would a successful, clever, beautiful woman like her want to date you? She's out of your league and there's no way you'll be enough for her—just like you weren't enough for Angie.*

He took a sip of wine to distract himself. He'd silenced that voice of doubt before and he'd do it again. Technically, Rebecca had asked him out. Which she wouldn't have done if she was simply being polite. This was a first date, and first dates were always awkward.

'Sure,' he said, trying to be kind and not let her guess how horrible he felt right then.

Their pizzas arrived then, and he kept the conversation light—about books, favourite holidays, and cake.

And then her fingers accidentally brushed against his as they reached for a dough ball at the same time. It felt as if he'd been galvanised. And, when he looked at her, he could see it was the same for her.

'Sorry,' she muttered. 'I...'

He guessed that she was finding this as awkward as he was. Her situation made dating a minefield.

'Me, too,' he said. 'This dating thing is hard, particularly when you're a single parent. I'm not going to push you into doing anything you're not ready for.'

'Thank you.' She looked relieved, and he had to suppress another whisper of insecurity.

'Perhaps we can be kind to each other,' he said. 'See where this takes us.'

Be kind? That sounded as if someone had been less than kind to him. Had someone broken his heart? Rebecca wondered. Though asking felt too intrusive, right now. And she was grateful that he was being understanding rather than pushy.

'Being kind sounds perfect to me,' she said.

When they'd finished their pizzas, they lingered for a coffee, and then Nathaniel suggested walking her home. 'The long way round. Via the park—I haven't had time to explore much, since I moved here, but it looks nice.'

'It is,' she said. 'Whether it's all the blossom on the trees in spring, or the roses in summer, or the trees in autumn—actually, it's even nice in winter. And Jas loves it there. I'm sure your goddaughter would, too.'

'Perfect for kids to run around. Do you have a garden?'

She nodded.

'You're lucky. My flat has space for a couple of pots of herbs on the kitchen windowsill, and that's it.'

He grew herbs on his windowsill? 'So you like cooking?'

'I found it relaxed me after a day at work, when I was still in the building trade,' he said. 'And then, when I was stuck in bed and waiting to see if I could walk again, looking at recipes and planning how I was going to tweak them was one of the things that kept me sane. There's only so much sport I could stand watching on TV.'

'I'll bet. It must've been really hard for you.'

'I got through it.' He shrugged. 'The only other choice was to give up.'

And he clearly wasn't the sort to give up easily, or he wouldn't have got back to walking again and then switching careers completely. 'I guess,' she said.

As they walked through the park, his hand brushed against hers a couple of times, sending tingles through her. The third time, he let his fingers curl round hers; it wasn't demanding or a gesture of possession, but gave her more of a sense of promise.

The more she was getting to know Nathaniel, the more she liked him. He was sweet, funny and romantic. And walking hand in hand through the park with him made her feel like a teenager again—though carefree and light of heart, rather than socially awkward.

She remembered that moment after the abseil when she'd kissed him. How she'd forgotten everything and everyone around them, only aware of the feel of his mouth against hers and the way her blood had surged through her veins.

Would he kiss her tonight?

Would it make her have that floaty feeling all over again?

Anticipation tingled through her as they reached her gate.

'My sister's babysitting,' she said.

'If it was my sister babysitting,' he said, 'she'd start grilling you the second you walked through the door.'

'Saskia is a psychologist,' she said. 'So, yes. There would be grilling.' She had to be honest. 'Professional-level grilling. So I know it's rude not to invite you in for coffee, but…'

* * *

'It's fine. I understand. Goodnight, Rebecca. And thank you for a lovely evening.'

So he wasn't going to kiss her. He'd said earlier that he wouldn't be pushy. She liked the fact that he'd kept his word; though, at the same time, part of her was disappointed. Because she'd been itching to kiss Nathaniel Jones again ever since he'd taken her hand in the park. She'd wanted to feel like a carefree teenager again. 'Goodnight, Nathaniel. And thank you for seeing me home.'

He was still holding her hand. 'I'd really like to kiss you goodnight,' he said, his voice as soft and smooth as melted chocolate. 'But that's going to be your choice.'

The heat in his eyes made her knees weak.

'Yes,' she said.

'Good,' he said, and dipped his head.

It was a sweet, gossamer-light kiss, brushing her lips just enough to make them tingle. A kiss full of promise—a promise that next time the warmth would scorch into flame. Just as it had after the abseil, making her head spin and the rest of the world vanish.

'Goodnight, sweet Rebecca,' he whispered.

'Goodnight.' Her voice sounded as wobbly as her knees felt.

'I'll wait here until you're safely inside. See you at work,' he said.

Despite her wobbly knees, she managed to walk to her front door without tripping over, then turned to wave at him. He lifted his hand in acknowledgement, then turned away.

She opened the front door with a smile on her face. This evening had been a revelation. With Nathaniel, her spirit felt so light, not weighed down with worry. Yet, at the same time, she had the feeling that he understood the fact that she had responsibilities; he was taking things at a pace that suited her, rather than rushing her the way Lucas had.

Later that evening, Rebecca's phone beeped with a text from Nathaniel.

Really enjoyed this evening. Thank you. See you tomorrow. N x

I enjoyed it too. R x

On impulse, she added,

So what wine do I bring to go with fish stew and dumplings?

Then she panicked and deleted it, replacing it with,

See you tomorrow. x

He sent a smiley face back.

She couldn't remember the last time she'd felt quite this light of heart. Her lips tingled as she thought about that kiss, so sweet and so full of promise. And she really, really wanted him to kiss her again.

The next morning, when Rebecca did the ward rounds, she really wasn't happy about Josette Kamanya's blood pressure. She sat down next to her and took her hand. 'Despite the medication, your blood pressure still isn't down enough for my liking, Mrs Kamanya. I think we've got to the point where we need to deliver your baby to keep you both safe.'

Mrs Kamanya's eyes widened. 'I'm only thirty-five weeks. Surely it's still too soon?'

'If it makes you feel any better,' Rebecca said gently, 'around eight per cent are born before thirty-seven weeks. I'd like to give you steroids to mature the baby's lungs, and give you a section tomorrow. Your husband can still be there during the delivery, holding your hand, and he can still cut the cord, so your birth plan isn't *completely* out of the window.'

'But what happens then?' Mrs Kamanya looked pinched with fear.

'We'll have someone from the neonatal team in with us during your delivery, and they'll take the baby in to the Special Care Baby Unit at first, just while he or she needs a bit of extra help feeding, breathing and staying warm. Then, when the baby's ready, they'll move him or her to the neonatal unit.'

A tear rolled down Mrs Kamanya's face, and Rebecca squeezed her hand. 'I know it's not what you wanted, and I'm sorry about that, but I promise you it's going to be fine. You'll still be able to feed the baby yourself and you'll still be able to do a lot of the care. It really won't make a huge difference that the baby's a little bit early.'

Just then, Nathaniel walked through the ward and came over to them.

'Good morning,' Rebecca said.

'Morning,' he replied, smiling.

The heat in his eyes made her pulse skitter, and she had to take a deep breath to tamp it down. Right now Mrs

Kamanya needed her to be professional, not distracted by her emotions.

'I can see that everything's not OK. How are you doing, Mrs Kamanya?' he asked.

Her voice wobbled. 'Dr Hart says we need to deliver the baby tomorrow.'

Nathaniel sat on the opposite side of the bed to Rebecca and took Mrs Kamanya's other hand. 'To keep the baby safe, because your blood pressure's still higher than we'd like it to be. But I can tell you I've seen Rebecca operate, and she's *magic*.'

'I just wanted everything to…' Mrs Kamanya dragged in a breath. 'To go like I planned it.'

A natural birth, with just gas and air—the thing most of their first-time mums wanted. And most of them ended up screwing their birth plan into a ball and throwing it in the bin. 'Babies are notorious for disrespecting birth plans,' Rebecca said. 'I'm not sure I know anyone who actually had the kind of delivery they planned—and that includes me.'

'You?' Mrs Kamanya looked surprised.

'Absolutely. As an obstetrician, I should've known better, but I hadn't quite finished packing my labour bag when my daughter decided she was ready to come into the world,' Rebecca admitted. 'Jasmine was two weeks early—and she's nearly five now and bright as a button.'

'The same thing happened with my goddaughter,' Nathaniel said. 'She's four. Sienna decided to be born while her dad—my best friend—was on a business trip in Scotland. Denise went into labour early and I ended up being her stand-by birth partner. I fell in love with seeing babies delivered, and that's why I became a midwife. I love those first moments after a baby's arrived into the world—they're really special.'

Rebecca rather thought that Nathaniel might be special, too, but didn't voice it aloud. 'I agree. Those first moments are so precious. I remember every single baby I've ever delivered, and I never get tired of newborn cuddles.'

Mrs Kamanya gave them both a wobbly smile. 'So what happens now?'

'What we'll do today is give you two steroid injections, twelve hours apart, to mature the baby's lungs,' Rebecca said. 'Then we'll deliver the baby tomorrow morning.' She squeezed Mrs Kamanya's hand again. 'So the good news is, you're not going to be like the mums who are hot and tired in the middle of summer and wishing their baby wasn't nearly two weeks late. You'll be able to see your baby tomorrow.'

Mrs Kamanya bit her lip. 'But if the baby's in Special Care, doesn't that mean I won't be able to hold the baby or do anything?'

'You can hold the baby and do lots of things,' Nathaniel said. 'Though your baby will look a bit different from what you'd expect from a newborn. He or she'll look a bit thinner, the skin will be quite red and maybe there'll be a bit of down on the baby's face, though that'll change quickly as the baby grows.'

'The baby will be in an incubator at first,' Rebecca said, 'but you'll soon be able to do what we call "kangaroo care". If you wear a front-opening top and dress the baby in a nappy and a hat, you can hold the baby against your chest and wrap your top round you both. You'll be skin to skin, which helps your baby maintain a healthy body temperature and also helps you and the baby to bond.'

'What if they need to put tubes and wires on the baby?' Mrs Kamanya asked.

'You can still do the kangaroo care,' Nathaniel said, 'but you just need to stay near the machines. And you can stroke the baby, make eye contact, talk and sing to the baby, and the baby can hold your finger, just as if your baby was full-term.'

'You might be able to breastfeed the baby, too, if that was what you'd planned,' Rebecca added. 'The nurses can help you, though if the baby can't quite latch on you can still express milk so you can feed the baby through a tube from her nose to her stomach.'

'Do you want us to call someone to be with you today?' Nathaniel asked.

Mrs Kamanya nodded. 'I really want Andras here.'

'I'll go and call him now,' Rebecca promised, 'and I'll come back to let you know when he'll be here.'

'And I'll stay with you for a little while—my clinic doesn't start for another ten minutes,' Nathaniel said.

After his clinic, Nathaniel was in the staff kitchen, making coffee, when Rebecca walked in.

'Perfect timing. Coffee?' he asked.

'Love one, please. Though I've got about three minutes to drink it,' she warned. 'My clinic was running late this morning, and I'm in Theatre this afternoon.'

'I'm on it.' He dissolved the coffee in boiling water, added milk, then added cold water so she could drink it straight down.

'Thank you. You have no idea how much I appreciate that,' she said.

Funny how her smile made his heart skip a beat. The warmth, the sweetness… And his mouth tingled as he remembered kissing her, the previous night.

He wanted to kiss her again, but here in the staff kitchen really wasn't the right place. Besides, he wasn't entirely sure how she felt about it. She'd texted him to say she'd had a lovely evening—but she hadn't said anything about a second date.

Play it cool, he told himself. *Take it slowly.*

'How's your morning been?' he asked.

'Good. Yours?'

'Good. Actually, I need to catch you up on one of our mums. Mrs Ridley was in clinic this morning.' He smiled. 'You'll be pleased to know the baby hasn't decided to turn back the other way and his head's nicely engaged in her pelvis.'

'That's great news,' Rebecca said with a smile. 'So she's thirty-seven weeks, now. Hopefully we'll see her in a couple of weeks and it'll be a nice easy delivery, to make up for all that discomfort.'

'They've got their labour bag packed, and Matt's done a test run several times so he knows exactly how long it takes to get here.'

She laughed. 'Bless. It's lovely when the dads get really involved.'

Was it his imagination, or was there a faint bit of wistfulness in her eyes? She hadn't said much about her marriage, but she'd mentioned that Lucas was an adrenalin junkie. In his experience, that didn't go well with the demands of a baby. Had her husband maybe not supported her during her pregnancy and when Jasmine was tiny?

It was none of his business, and it would be way too intrusive to ask. Better to keep everything impersonal and work-related. 'Yeah. It's lovely when the dads are really part of it,' he agreed.

'Righty—it's off to Theatre for me. Catch you later. And thanks for the coffee,' she said.

'Pleasure. Catch you later,' he said.

Rebecca administered the second dose of steroids on the Tuesday evening, and Mrs Kamanya was her first mum due in Theatre on Wednesday morning. Mrs Kamanya's husband, Andras, was there to hold her hand; Rebecca introduced them both to the anaesthetist, who took them through consent for the operation, and she explained exactly what was going to happen. Then she went to scrub in and prep for Theatre; she was pleased to see that Nathaniel was on the team.

The operation went smoothly, Mr Kamanya cut the cord, and Nathaniel was there to check the Apgar score once the baby was delivered.

'I'm pleased to say you have a healthy little girl,' he said. 'She weighs two and a quarter kilograms, and she's forty centimetres long, so she's doing very nicely.'

Both parents had happy tears running down their cheeks.

'Can we hold her for a minute?' Mr Kamanya asked.

'Of course, but then she's going off to Special Care to warm up.' Nathaniel handed the baby, wrapped in a blanket, to Mr Kamanya.

'Our precious little girl,' he whispered. 'Look, Jose. She's perfect.'

'Our precious little girl,' Mrs Kamanya echoed.

Rebecca could see moisture in Nathaniel's eyes when he took the baby back, ready to hand her over to the neonatal team. He really cared, she thought. And he had a proper emotional connection with their mums, which made him good to work with.

She finished sewing Mrs Kamanya back up. 'We'll keep you in the recovery room next door for about half an hour, just to keep an eye on you and make sure everything's as it should be, then we'll sort out a wheelchair and get you to the Special Care Baby Unit so you can be with your little girl,' she said. 'You're doing really well. Have you decided on a name, yet?'

'Kayleigh,' Mrs Kamanya said.

'That's a lovely name,' Rebecca said. 'I'm going to go and scrub out, now, but I'll pop in to SCBU to see you after my shift.'

'Thank you.' Mrs Kamanya reached out and squeezed her hand. 'You've been so kind.'

'You're very welcome,' Rebecca said.

Later that afternoon, she visited SCBU to discover Mrs Kamanya sitting with the baby doing kangaroo care.

'Well, Miss Kayleigh, you look very settled with your mum,' she said with a smile, stroking the sleeping baby's cheek very lightly, then turned to the Kamanyas. 'How are you both doing?'

'Besotted with my wife and my daughter,' Mr Kamanya answered. 'I'm still a bit scared of holding her, because she's so tiny, but the way I feel about her…' His face was filled with pride.

'Me, too. Mr Jones came in to see us earlier,' Mrs Kamanya said. 'I still can't believe how lovely everyone is.'

'We've got a good team,' Rebecca agreed. 'We all love babies and we want our parents to have the best possible experience. And we're all here to help if you've got any questions, however small or silly they might seem. We'd all much rather you asked than held back and were worried about something.'

'That's good to know,' Mr Kamanya said.

'I'll pop back in tomorrow. But it's good to see her doing so well,' Rebecca said.

'That's what Mr Jones said,' Mrs Kamanya remarked.

Rebecca was beginning to think that she and Nathaniel were very much on the same page. So could this thing between them actually work—or was she hoping for too much?

CHAPTER SIX

NATHANIEL WAS ALREADY with a mum in the labour suite when Rebecca got into work, the next day; she had clinic in the morning, then visited Mrs Kamanya in the SCBU during her lunch break.

'How's it going?' she asked.

'Kayleigh's getting stronger, hour by hour,' Mrs Kamanya said. 'She's not quite able to latch on, yet, but I'm expressing milk for her.'

'That's good. And she'll get there when it comes to latching on,' Rebecca reassured her.

'Mr Jones popped in to see us this morning, too,' Mrs Kamanya said. 'Before his shift. He brought me a croissant—we'd been talking about them the other day, and he said pain au chocolat is the best breakfast, but I voted for croissants. I didn't expect him to do something so lovely.' She smiled. 'He's such a sweetie, isn't he?'

'Yes,' Rebecca said. She was beginning to realise that Nathaniel was a man who paid attention to the little things that mattered to people, and acted on them. He was the reliable type.

Not like Lucas, a little voice whispered in her head, and she silenced it. She'd dated Nathaniel once. There was a long, long way to go before she could consider anything major.

She eventually caught up with him mid-afternoon.

'Guess what? I delivered a baby boy, this afternoon. And Nathaniel's going to be his middle name. Reee-sult!' He grinned and gave her a high-five.

'On a post-delivery high, are we?' she teased, to take her mind off the fact that the way his eyes crinkled at the corners made her knees go weak.

'Absolutely.' His gaze held hers. 'So come and celebrate with me?'

'Sorry. I have ward rounds,' she said. Though she didn't want him to think she was pushing him away. 'Maybe some other time?'

'How about,' he said, 'I cook for you?'

'Would this be your famous run-down fish stew?' she asked, remembering what he'd said on their date.

'Rita's run-down fish stew,' he corrected. 'Yes.'

A second date. Except this one would be much more intimate. Nathaniel was offering to let her into his space. Could she be brave enough to say yes, and let him closer to her?

She thought about it. Part of her was wary; she'd worked out that he'd been hurt and he'd said he hadn't been in a serous relationship for a while. Did that mean he wouldn't be able to commit if things started to get serious between them? She didn't want to take a risk on her heart—or Jasmine's. She needed someone who was stable, strong and committed.

But another, more insistent part of her wanted to get to know him better. How else could she find out whether he was someone who'd stick around when things started to get tough or someone who'd vanish at the first hint of things not being perfect?

Saying yes would mean pushing the boundaries a bit—for both of them. 'OK. Thank you. I'd like that.'

'Tonight?' he suggested.

'I can't do tonight, but maybe tomorrow night, if I can get a babysitter,' she said. 'Is it OK to let you know later?'

'Sure.'

At the end of her shift, Rebecca collected Jasmine from her parents.

'Mummy! I drawed you a picture today,' Jasmine said. 'It's a dinosaur.'

A pink diplodocus, with what looked like a glittery silver bow round its long neck. Rebecca smiled. 'It's beautiful, darling. Look how well you've drawn his neck. We'll put that up on the fridge as soon as we get home.'

Jasmine beamed and hugged her.

'Can you go and put all your things in your bag and say goodbye to Grampy, while I have a quick catch-up with Nanna?' Rebecca asked.

Jasmine nodded and scampered off.

'Mum, I know it's a massive cheek, but if you're free could I ask you to babysit for me tomorrow night?'

'Babysit? Of course I can.' Caroline looked pleased. 'Is this a date?'

Rebecca squirmed. 'Yes, but it's really early days.'

'I'm glad you're finally moving on. Lucas wouldn't have wanted you to be alone—just as, if you were the one who'd had the accident, you wouldn't have wanted him to spend the next fifty years mourning you.'

'I know,' Rebecca said softly. 'But we're just taking it one step at a time.'

'I just want to see you happy again, love,' Caroline said gently.

'I *am* happy, Mum. I've got the best family in the world, my friends are great, and I love my job.'

'I know, love. But you also need time to be *yourself*,' Caroline counselled. 'You're still young. And you know your dad and I will babysit any time you need us to. So will Saskia.'

'I love you, Mum,' Rebecca said, hugging her.

'Love you, too. Let me know what time you need us tomorrow.'

'I will,' Rebecca promised.

Jasmine chattered all the way back to their own house, and helped Rebecca make the gnocchi with mozzarella and tomato sauce, rolling the balls of dough down a fork and giggling. Moments like these were so precious, Rebecca thought, making memories that could help her daughter through any tough times in the future. She hoped that Jasmine would always associate the scent of basil with a sunny late afternoon in their kitchen.

Once they'd eaten, and done the bath and bedtime routine, Rebecca read a last extra story and hugged her daughter. 'Time for sleep, now,' she said gently. 'Sweet dreams. Love you to the moon and back.'

'Love you to the moon and back twice,' Jasmine said.

Rebecca curled up in a chair with her phone and texted Nathaniel.

Babysitting organised. Let me know your address and what time.

He replied with the details almost straight away.

Seven o'clock was just about perfect; it meant she

could make lasagne for her parents and Jasmine tomorrow afternoon.

OK. I'll be there. Should I bring red or white wine?

No need. Just yourself.

She called him. 'I can't just bring myself. You're cooking for me. It feels rude not to bring something.'

'It's fine,' Nathaniel said.

'No, it's not,' she said. 'If you don't tell me, I'll bring a bottle of red and a bottle of white.'

'It's a spicy stew, so wine doesn't really go with it. Really. Just bring yourself,' he said again.

'OK. I'm not going to fight with you,' she said. But she also didn't intend to turn up empty-handed. If he didn't want her to bring wine, she'd bring something else. 'See you tomorrow.'

Rebecca had a half-day on Friday, so she was able to pick up Jasmine from nursery at lunchtime and take her to the park. The weather was perfect, sunny and bright but without being too hot. She thoroughly enjoyed pushing Jasmine on the swings, helping her on the climbing frame—Jasmine's favourite thing—and watching her come down the slide, then walking through the rose garden on the way home.

They took a detour to the high street, where they bought strawberries and salted caramel ice cream for pudding, and Rebecca bought some things to take to Nathaniel. Back at their house, Jasmine gave her teddies a tea party in the kitchen while Rebecca made lasagne.

'Everything's prepped, Mum,' Rebecca said when her parents arrived. 'Lasagne's in the oven, salad and strawberries are in the fridge, and Dad's favourite ice cream is in the freezer.'

'Wonderful. Thank you. Now, off you go and have a good time,' Caroline said.

'You look so pretty, Mummy. Just like a princess—no, like a queen,' Jasmine said.

'Thank you. I'm going to have dinner with one of my colleagues from the hospital,' Rebecca said. It wasn't a lie—just not the whole truth. 'Be good for Nanna and Grampy.'

'Don't rush back,' Caroline said. 'Your father will fall asleep in front of the TV, and I brought my crochet with me.'

'See you later, Mum.' Rebecca kissed them all goodbye, then headed for Nathaniel's flat. It was a nice evening, and he was only a twenty-minute walk away. The flat was in a purpose-built development; seeing the small square of grass and nondescript shrubs at the front reminded her what he'd said about envying her having a garden of her own.

She took a deep breath and rang the bell for his flat.

The intercom crackled. 'Hey, Rebecca. I'm on the second floor. I'll buzz you in.'

When he hung up, she heard a buzz and then the front door opened. She closed it behind her and climbed the two flights of stairs; as she reached the landing, she saw him standing in one of the doorways.

'Welcome,' he said, and ushered her inside.

The door to her left was closed; she guessed it was his bedroom. 'The bathroom's just here, if you need it,' he said, gesturing to the second door, and then shepherded her into the living room. There was a small kitchen at one end, with a bistro-style table and two chairs set next to a large window; the main living room area was just big enough for a sofa and a TV. There were no books in evidence, and she guessed that his music and films were all streamed digitally.

Everywhere was scrupulously tidy.

'You said not to bring wine, so I brought you these,' she said, and handed him a brown paper carrier bag.

'You didn't have to, but thank you,' he said, looking inside. 'Oh, wow. Posh chocolates. I love these. Thank you. And basil.'

'You said you had enough space for herbs on your windowsill, and I know you're a foodie,' she said.

'And you can't beat fresh basil for pesto, pasta sauce or ratatouille—thank you.' His smile broadened as he took the final thing out of the bag: a pink corduroy mouse. 'I assume this is for my flatmate?'

'Of course.' She smiled. 'It's filled with catnip. I've never had a cat, so I have no idea whether he'll like it or not.'

'Oh, he will,' Nathaniel assured her. 'Come and meet him.'

Leo had draped himself across the back of the sofa.

'Leo, come and make friends. This is Rebecca and she's the reason why you've got fish for dinner tonight,' Nathaniel said to the cat.

Leo purred and allowed Rebecca to stroke him; she was surprised by how soft his fur was.

And the cat seemed thrilled with the toy mouse when Nathaniel gave it to him; Leo immediately started throwing it about and pouncing on it.

'Something smells lovely,' she said.

'I hope it tastes all right,' he said.

'Is there anything I can do to help?'

'Thanks for the offer, but it's all sorted.' He glanced at his watch. 'It should be ready in about ten minutes. If you'd like to take a seat, I'll get you a drink.' He gestured to the neatly set bistro table. 'Would you prefer coffee, beer, or something soft?'

'If you've got any sparkling water, that'd be lovely, thanks,' she said.

'I have,' he said, and took a bottle from the fridge. He poured the contents into two glasses. 'Ice? Lime?'

'Both, please.'

He added the lime and ice to the sparkling water, then handed a glass to her. 'Cheers,' he said, and clinked his glass against hers.

He put the chocolates on the worktop, the pot of basil on his windowsill, and smiled at her. 'OK. I'm afraid I have to be boring now and do things.'

'Are you sure I can't help?' she asked.

'I'm sure. Just chat to me,' he said, and took a bowl out of the fridge. 'The dumplings—I made them earlier,' he explained.

'So you're going to boil them?' she asked, noting the large pan of water coming to a simmer on the hob.

'I'm going to fry them,' he said, 'which probably sounds as if it'd clog your arteries, but actually they're very light and fluffy—at least, they are when Rita makes them. It's a while since I've made them.' He took a skillet out of a cupboard, added oil and set it to heat. While the dumplings were cooking, he added dark green leaves to the water. 'Cavolo Nero,' he said. 'You need something strong to stand up to the spices. I hope you like it.'

'I like all vegetables,' she said, 'with the exception of really large Brussels sprouts.' She grimaced. 'Or even the small ones, if they've been cooked to a mush.'

'Sprouts are only edible, in my view, if you shred them and stir-fry them with ginger, chilli and garlic,' he said. 'Mushy veg…' He spread his hands. 'Not in my kitchen.'

'I see you have a few drawings on the outside of your fridge,' she said.

He smiled. 'Feel free to have a look, if you want to. I imagine you get the same kind of thing brought home from nursery.'

'Your goddaughter drew them?' she asked.

'Yes. Every month she gives me a picture she did especially for me, with varying amounts of glitter. She's hugely into dinosaurs at the moment.'

'So's Jas. Whenever I ask her what she wants to do at the weekend, if it's raining she always wants to go and see the dinosaurs in the Natural History Museum,' Rebecca said, smiling.

'Sounds like fun,' he said, smiling back. 'Grab a seat, because I'm serving up.' He flicked into something on his phone, and music started playing from a speaker on the windowsill. 'I hope you'll like this—Dad's a part-time musician, and this is the kind of stuff he used to play all the time when I was a kid.'

Indie music from the nineties, the sort of thing her own father played. 'I used to hear a lot of this in the car, too,' she said. 'It brings back lovely memories.'

'I'm glad.' He brought two plates over to the table.

'Cheers.' She lifted her glass in a toast. 'Thank you for inviting me.'

'Thank you for coming.'

She took a mouthful of the stew. 'Wow. This is amazing.'

He looked pleased. 'Glad you like it.'

They chatted easily through dinner, and Rebecca

learned that Nathaniel had never set foot in a gym but had played rugby at county level before the accident. 'Obviously contact sports for me are spectator-only, nowadays.' He shrugged. 'But I'm lucky. I'm not going to moan about missing sport. Not after months of wondering if I'd ever be able to even walk again. I can still kick a ball round a park with my goddaughter. I'm luckier than a lot of people.'

She liked the fact he focused on the positives.

'What about you? You do gymnastics? Roller skating? Champion swimmer?'

She laughed, enjoying the twinkle in his eye and the absurdity. 'No. Saskia and I did ballet when we were kids, and I did aerobics classes before I had Jas. I don't really get time for any of that sort of thing, now.' She smiled. 'But that's fine. I get to have fun with her in the park, going for a walk and seeing what we can find, and pushing her on the swings.'

'Sounds good,' he said, and for a moment there was wistfulness in his eyes.

And she could imagine him pushing a child on a swing or walking with a toddler and pointing out butterflies and bees and flowers. It made her heart feel as if it had been squeezed. Did he want more from life than she'd be able to give him?

Nathaniel wouldn't let her clear the table, but brought over a bowl of summer berries and a tub of very posh salted caramel ice cream. 'I know it's a bit of a lazy pudding, but I remember you said it was your favourite.'

Again, she noticed, he paid attention and remembered the little things. Lucas would've remembered her dream holiday destination or her dream car, but even after they'd been married for a year he'd still put sugar in her coffee despite the fact she'd never taken it. 'It's my dad's, too. Actually, that's what he, Mum and Jas are having for pudding tonight.'

'Great minds think alike, then,' he said lightly.

He did at least allow her to help with the washing up, before making them both coffee and leading her into the living room. Although there wasn't a fire, there were some shelves opposite the sofa, and the middle one contained framed photographs.

'Can I be nosey?' she asked.

'Sure.'

She walked over to the shelves. There was a photograph of Charlotte and Robyn's wedding, with Nathaniel looking handsome in top hat and tails; there was a second photograph of him in top hat and tails with a man of similar age, clearly at another wedding, but she couldn't see a family resemblance between them.

'My best friend, Jason,' he said, 'at his wedding to Denise.'

There was photograph of Nathaniel wearing a gown and mortar board at his graduation, with his parents; and another of him holding a baby in a very pretty white dress. 'Is that Sienna?' she asked.

'Yes.' He smiled. 'I can't wait to be an uncle. It'll mean I get double the drawings on my fridge.'

There was another of Sienna as a toddler, with Leo sitting on her lap. 'That's cute.'

'Yeah. She loves Leo—and he adores her. Whenever Jason brings her over, he always sits with her.'

The final photograph was a picture of an older couple at sunset, smiling broadly, with a city spreading out behind them. She recognised them from his graduation photograph. 'Your mum and dad?' she asked.

'Yes. Suzanne and Mark,' he said. 'It was their ruby wedding, last year. Charlotte and I sent them to Paris for the weekend—that's where they went on their honeymoon.' He smiled. 'They had a fine time pretending they were twenty-one again, wandering around in Montmartre and the like. We bought them tickets for the Eiffel Tower at sunset—and apparently there's this *guinguette* by the Seine, a kind of open-air bar which serves food and people can dance as well. So they went dancing, had something to eat, did the Eiffel Tower, got someone to take a photograph and sent it to Charlotte and me, then went back dancing until midnight.'

'That sounds like the sort of thing my mum and dad would do,' she said, smiling.

Clearly Nathaniel was really close to his family. She liked that; Lucas hadn't been that close to his parents, and it was only when he'd got married to her and she'd made the effort to stay in touch with them that his family had become closer. He'd always been a bit bored by family gatherings, unless they were barbecues when he was in charge of the grill; and she'd ended up going to see her own family alone, most of the time, fibbing to them that Lucas couldn't get the time off work to join her while knowing that he was off somewhere getting his adrenalin fix. And she'd always quietly envied her friends with partners who were happy to do the domestic stuff and were close to their families. Sure, they wouldn't have the excitement of being whisked away to Rome or New York for the weekend; but they had something much more important. A solid foundation to their marriage.

'Come and sit down,' Nathaniel said, and drew her back to the sofa.

Leo stretched out along the arm of the seat next to

him, and Nathaniel slid his arm round Rebecca's shoulders. She leaned in closer, and then somehow his mouth was brushing against hers, sensitising the skin and making her want more.

Kissing Nathaniel held just the same excitement as kissing Lucas once had, except there was something underpinning it. Something safe. Something cosseting. Something that made her feel special and treasured, made her feel as if she was wanted for *herself* rather than just the thrill of the chase.

When he broke the kiss, she opened her eyes. His pupils were huge, making his dark eyes seem almost black, and he laid one hand against her cheek.

'I'm calling a halt,' he said.

'It's over?' The words were out before she could stop them, and she was furious with herself for sounding needy.

'Oh, honey. I didn't mean *that*.' He stole another kiss. 'I mean, I'm calling a halt to the kissing, because I don't want this to be rushed.'

'Oh.' That put a very different complexion on things.

'No pressure,' he said, 'but I like you—a lot—and I'd like to keep seeing you.'

'But you said you didn't really do serious relationships.' She frowned, confused.

Oh, his stupid mouth. Nathaniel groaned inwardly. Well, he was going to have to tell her now. At least some of it. Because she'd practically asked.

'I used to be engaged. She called it off.'

'I'm sorry,' Rebecca said. 'That must have hurt you a lot.'

He could see she was trying really hard not to ask

any more, and he appreciated that. On the other hand, he didn't want her leaping to conclusions, thinking that either he or Angie had cheated.

If he told her the truth, he didn't want her pitying him. 'No pity, right?' he asked.

Her expression was full of sympathy rather than pity. 'I promise. I've been "poor Rebecca", and I hated it. I won't do that to you.'

He hadn't considered that, but it gave him the confidence to tell her. 'Angie and I—I thought she was the one. But she signed up to marry a building site manager.'

'She didn't like your career change?'

He winced. 'We didn't get that far.'

Her blue eyes widened as she clearly worked it out for herself. 'She broke it off after the accident?'

He looked away. 'We didn't know if I'd be able to walk again.'

'Hang on. She dumped you before you found out whether you would actually recover from the accident? That's *heartless.*' She sounded furious on his behalf.

'It was honest. If I hadn't recovered and we'd gone ahead with the wedding, then she would've felt trapped and we would have both been miserable.'

She rolled her eyes. 'You're a lot more reasonable than I would've been, in your shoes.'

'There isn't much point in being anything else.' He shrugged. 'Yes, I was hurt and angry at the time, and I resented her for dumping me while I was still in hospital—but, when I think about it, maybe that was better than facing up to a lifetime with someone who didn't want to be with me.'

She flinched, and he frowned. 'Rebecca?'

'I…' She blew out a breath. 'You've been honest with me. I should be honest with you, too. My marriage wasn't great. Lucas felt the same way as your Angie did—trapped.'

He stared at her, shocked. 'I'm sorry. I didn't mean to bring bad memories back for you.'

She shook her head. 'It's not your fault. I don't broadcast the fact that I wasn't enough for my husband.'

Exactly how he'd felt, after Angie left. That his judgement was off—that he'd been too stupid to realise that he wasn't enough for her.

He wrapped his arms round Rebecca. 'So we're kind of the same, but different.'

Her laugh was rueful. 'Yeah. Jasmine wasn't planned, but I was thrilled when I found out that I was pregnant.'

And Lucas wasn't?

He realised he'd spoken aloud when Rebecca said, 'He said he was pleased. But, as I got more and more round, he felt more and more trapped. Broken nights and the demands of a small baby, bogging you down in domesticity when you want to be out there doing extreme sports and getting your adrenalin fix…' She wrinkled her nose. 'It didn't help.'

'It's hard on all of you,' he said, 'when you want different things.'

'I don't want to make that mistake again,' she said.

'Completely understandable. I don't want to make another mistake, either.'

He paused. 'Except something about you makes me want to keep dating you.'

She looked at him. 'I kind of want that, too.'

'But?' She hadn't said the word, but it was written all over her face.

'I'm not ready to introduce you to Jasmine as anyone other than my colleague.'

'I understand that completely,' he said.

'And there's the risk of gossip at work.'

'Which usually lasts about a week and then everyone starts talking about something else,' he pointed out. 'But we can keep this just between us, if that makes you more comfortable.'

'It does at the moment,' she said.

'OK. We have all the time in the world. No need to rush.'

How very different from Lucas and the way he'd swept her off her feet.

With Lucas, she'd always felt as if she were walking on a tightrope with nothing to break her fall. With Nathaniel, her pulse still raced when he kissed her and her heart felt as if she were doing acrobatics, but there was a safety net—Nathaniel himself. He made her feel giddy as a schoolgirl, but at the same time he made her feel grounded and safe, in a way that Lucas never had. As if she had someone on her side, someone who'd be there in a crisis to support her and help her—and not just assume that she'd be happy to take the full burden of sorting everything out.

'I'd like that,' she said. 'So what do we do now?'

'Given that your ex liked doing risky stuff, I'm assuming you're not that keen on surprises?' he said.

'No.' She appreciated the fact he'd worked that out for himself. 'I like to know what I'm dealing with.'

'How about a half-surprise?' he suggested. 'Monday night, I'd like to take you out. It's something I think you'll like. If I can get tickets tomorrow, then you'll need a coat and someone to babysit until about eleven p.m. If I can't, then I'll have a rethink and come up with some alternatives and run them by you.'

'All right. That'd be lovely.'

'Good.' He stole a last kiss. 'It's raining, so I'll drive you home. Or I can call you a taxi, if you'd rather.'

She glanced over to the kitchen window and realised there were raindrops spattered against the glass. 'Since you put it so nicely, thank you. A lift would be nice.'

He kept the conversation light all the way to her house. 'See you at work on Monday.' He kissed her lingeringly, and even though it was still raining his kiss made her feel as if it were the middle of the day, with the sun shining brightly. How was it that he could make her feel that kind of warmth, that kind of brightness?

'Monday,' she said, and kissed him one last time before climbing out of the car. She turned to wave at him just before she opened her front door, and he blew her a kiss.

Cute.

Nathaniel Jones was seriously cute.

And she was going to have to be careful, or she'd be in danger of losing her heart to him completely.

CHAPTER SEVEN

REBECCA DIDN'T REALLY have time to think about Nathaniel on Saturday—Jasmine had a swimming lesson and then a play date with her best friend from nursery, giving Rebecca a chance to blitz the house and catch up with laundry. But she did check that Saskia could babysit on Monday, and texted him to let him know that babysitting was fine.

Sunday morning was spent making Eton Mess and brownies, and then they headed off to her parents' house.

But when she checked her phone on Sunday evening, there was a message from Nathaniel.

Got the tickets I wanted. Will pick you up at eight. Bring a coat and wear something warm. I'll bring chairs and blankets. xx

She had absolutely no idea what he had in mind; clearly he wanted to keep it a surprise. But he had at least told her information she needed to know.

Thank you. Am intrigued.

She wrinkled her nose, then added,

Where are we going? Xx

Out. xx

That was the reply, followed by a smiley face.

OK. She'd stop asking and let him enjoy making the surprise.

See you tomorrow. xx

Rebecca was in Theatre the next day when he was on a break, and he was in a delivery suite during her break, so she didn't get to see him until he picked her up at eight.

When he rang her doorbell, Saskia beat her to answering the door.

'Hey. Nice to meet you properly, Nathaniel. I'm Saskia,' she said.

'Nice to meet you, too,' he said, shaking her hand.

'Enjoy your evening.' She glanced at the bags slung over his shoulder. 'Are you taking my big sister on some kind of picnic?'

'Oh, no,' Rebecca said, 'because I've already had dinner and you didn't warn me not to.'

'It's not a picnic. Wait and see,' he said.

She rolled her eyes. 'Man of mystery, are we?'

He glanced down at his jeans and light sweater. 'I really should've dressed all in black and worn dark glasses.'

Saskia laughed. 'He's not going to tell us what you're doing tonight, Bec. Have fun, you two. I have a date with a good film and a mug of hot chocolate.'

Rebecca still didn't have a clue what they were doing until they reached the park and she saw the signs. 'We're going to a pop-up cinema showing of *Dirty Dancing*?'

'Is that OK?' he asked.

'I love that film. Especially that bit where Patrick Swayze rescues Baby from her parents.' She smiled. 'Great choice. Thank you.'

'Good. We have fold-up picnic chairs—borrowed from my sister—a fleecy blanket, and I was planning to get us hot chocolate.'

'Let me get them,' she said.

He shook his head. 'My idea, so I'm paying. But you can message your sister to tell her you're doing the same thing—except outdoors.'

Now she realised why he'd told her to wear something warm and bring a coat. While he was getting hot chocolate for them, she texted Saskia.

Pop-up cinema. Dirty Dancing! Xx

The reply came immediately.

Good choice. Keeper! Xx

'OK?' he asked when he came back.

'Very. Thank you,' she said.

There was something incredibly sweet and romantic about sitting in a picnic chair next to his, with a fleecy blanket tucked round them, holding his hand under the blanket and holding a cup of hot chocolate in her free hand, watching the sky darken as the film started and a few faint stars begin to appear above them. No pressure: just warmth and a sweetness that made her heart feel as if it had done a somersault.

She'd seen the film a few times with her mum and her sister, but she still enjoyed it: everything from the music to the dancing. Nathaniel wrapped one arm round her shoulders during the second half, when the air was beginning to get chilly, and she leaned her head against his shoulder, feeling warm and cherished. This really was the perfect evening.

The final scenes of the film came onto the screen, and the whole of the audience chorused the iconic line before watching Johnny and Baby's show-stopping dance, ending with that triumphant lift. And it felt so right, so natural, to turn to Nathaniel when Baby and Johnny were still in the centre of the dancing crowd, leaning into each other for a kiss in exactly the same way as the couple on the screen.

Her eyes closed as Nathaniel's mouth touched hers in the lightest, sweetest, gentlest kiss. And then, as the kiss deepened, it felt as if fireworks were going off inside her head. Huge starbursts, bright and sparkling, the sort that lit up the whole sky in silver, white and gold.

Shaking, she broke the kiss. 'Nathaniel,' she whispered.

He looked as dazed as she felt. 'I… You…'

There were no words.

So she just laid her palm against his cheek and kissed him again, until she was dizzy with need and desire.

And then she realised that everyone around them was standing up, packing up their chairs and their blankets.

Her face heated. 'Sorry.'

'I'm not. I like it when you kiss me.' He kissed the tip of her nose. 'But we'd better go. Your sister's expecting us back. And everyone else around us…' He gestured to the people streaming past them.

Between them, they packed the fold-up chairs back into their carry-cases and put the blanket back in the tote bag. He slung all the handles over his shoulder, then took her hand. 'I'll walk you home.'

It turned out to be quite a slow walk home, punctuated by a kiss under every fourth lamppost, but finally they reached her front door.

'Goodnight,' he said. 'And thank you for coming to the film with me.'

'I loved it,' she said honestly. 'Thank you for making it a *nice* surprise.'

'So you'd trust me if I wanted to surprise you in future?'

She didn't even have to think about it. She already knew. Nathaniel was a man who thought about things, who noticed little details and paid attention instead of muddling through. She trusted him. 'Yes.'

He kissed her again. 'Good. I'll see you at work tomorrow.'

'And maybe we can synchronise our off-duty,' she said. 'I'm on a late on Friday.'

'So am I.'

'Maybe,' she said, 'we can have breakfast together.'

'Do you have somewhere in mind?'

She nodded. 'It's a bit of a trek, but we can get a bus and the Tube.'

'It sounds like somewhere you've been before?'

'I haven't, actually, but I've planned to take Jas there for a while. I thought maybe we could scope it out together.'

He smiled. 'I'd like that.'

'I'll sort out the details and tell you tomorrow,' she said.

He kissed her one last time. 'Goodnight.'

'Goodnight,' she said, and quietly let herself into the house.

* * *

The next morning, Rebecca got up early to make the batter for pancakes, chop fruit and lay the table for breakfast; by the time she came downstairs again after helping Jasmine get ready for nursery, Saskia was in the kitchen and had made coffee.

'Here you, go, Big Sis,' Saskia said, handing Rebecca a mug of coffee just the way she liked it.

'Angel. Thank you.' Rebecca heated oil in the pan and busied herself cooking pancakes while Jasmine poured a glass of milk with Saskia's help.

'Where did you go last night, Mummy?' Jasmine asked.

'I went to the pop-up cinema with a friend from work.'

Jasmine looked confused, 'What's a pop-up cinema?'

'It's a cinema outside in the park,' Rebecca explained.

'That sounds so cool. Can I go with you next time? Please?' Jasmine added swiftly.

'It'd be a bit too late for you, darling. You'd be asleep before the film had started.' At the disappointed look on Jasmine's face, she said, 'But I read there's going to be a floating pop-up cinema in the summer, showing films every morning. Maybe we can do that.'

'If it's *The Little Mermaid*, I'm so coming with you,' Saskia said. She broke into a chorus of 'Part of Your World', and Jasmine joined in.

'We'll make it a girly day,' Rebecca promised, 'and take Nanna with us.'

'Can we have popcorn?' Jasmine asked, spooning fruit onto her pancakes.

'Absolutely. Or we can make a special picnic,' Rebecca said.

'Did you have popcorn last night?' Jasmine asked.

'No. But we did have hot chocolate. Now, finish your pancakes and go and clean your teeth,' Rebecca directed.

'I'm glad you had a good time last night,' Saskia said when Jasmine had gone upstairs to clean her teeth.

'I did—and thank *you* for making it possible.'

'So are you seeing him again?'

Rebecca nodded. 'Though we're taking it slowly. I don't want to make the same mistake I did with Lucas.'

'Sensible,' Saskia agreed.

Between them, they cleared up in the kitchen; then Rebecca hugged her sister goodbye at the front door, took Jasmine to nursery and headed to work.

The day was incredibly busy, with ward rounds and two full clinics, so she didn't get to see Nathaniel, even briefly. Though she called him later that evening, after Jasmine had gone to sleep.

'Hey. Had a good day?' he asked.

'I did. I thought you'd like to know, Mrs Ridley was in my clinic today,' she said. 'The baby's still head-down, so hopefully she'll get the birth she wants.'

'As much as a baby will let its mum plan a birth,' he said, and she could practically hear the smile in his voice.

'How was your day?' she asked.

'Clinic, and a mum who got to five centimetres dilated at the end of my shift—so I'll miss out on the birth,' he said.

'But you can still get your baby cuddle if she's on the ward tomorrow,' she said. 'About breakfast on Friday—I need to take Jasmine to nursery, first. Can I meet you at nine at the bus stop outside the park?'

'That sounds good,' he said. 'Is there anything I need to know beforehand?'

'Only that it's my idea so it's my bill—and you can't argue, after yesterday evening.'

'All right. I'll see you tomorrow,' he said. 'Sweet dreams.'

And she had the feeling they might be of him. 'Sweet dreams,' she echoed.

On Friday morning, Nathaniel was at the bus stop at ten to nine. Although he tried to appear as if he was casually browsing the internet on his phone, he felt keyed-up. Nervous. This would be their fourth date—and his relationships hadn't progressed this far in years. And he had the nasty feeling that Rebecca could really matter to him—that she could break his heart.

Maybe he should be sensible and back away now, before either of them got hurt.

Yet something about her drew him. She was warm and sweet and kind. OK, so he'd once thought that about Angela and got it very wrong… But Rebecca wasn't Angela. Just as he wasn't Lucas. And maybe, just maybe, they'd be enough for each other.

While he'd been brooding, she'd somehow managed to walk up the road without him noticing her. She was dressed casually in faded jeans and a stripy T-shirt, and she looked so cute that his heart did a somersault.

'Good morning.' She greeted him with a smile. 'I hope you're hungry.'

'Starving,' he said, smiling back. 'So where are we going?'

'To see some lavender fields,' she said.

He frowned. The ones he knew about were hours away. 'But we're both on duty at half-past one.'

'I know, but we've got plenty of time.'

'You're telling me there are lavender fields in London?' he asked, surprised.

'There are indeed,' she said.

They took the bus to Finsbury Park Tube station, then headed out on the Victoria line.

At the station, she consulted her phone. 'This way,' she said, and it turned out to be a five-minute walk to a park. He still didn't quite see how this was a lavender field, until they turned a corner.

'This is lovely,' he said. 'I had no idea that this was here.'

'I know there are bigger lavender farms outside the city, but I saw an article about this the other day and I thought this'd be a nice place to take Jasmine. She loves butterflies. There's a fabulous butterfly house opening in Notting Hill next year, and we've already been to the ones at the Horniman Museum and London Zoo. I wanted to take her somewhere a bit smaller than Kew but where she'd still see lots of butterflies.'

'This looks perfect. My goddaughter loves butterflies, too.' Should he take the risk? Push their relationship one step further? 'Maybe we can take the girls together, sometime,' he suggested.

'Maybe.'

He could see the wariness in her face. 'What's worrying you about the idea?' he asked, trying to be gentle.

'It's still really early days between us,' she said. 'Sorry, I don't mean to be horrible, but I'm not quite ready for you to meet Jasmine properly, yet.'

'Fair point,' he said. Time to back off. He didn't want her to be so far out of her comfort zone that she wouldn't see him again. She had more to lose than he did. He really shouldn't be letting himself get involved with someone whose life wasn't as free as his own; yet she drew him.

'Let's go have breakfast before we walk round the lavender,' she said.

'OK.' They headed to the café and found a quiet table. 'So are you going for the full English breakfast?' he asked.

'Not when there's a cranberry, Brie and bacon toasted sandwich with my name on it,' she said. 'How about you?'

'Coffee and a bacon sandwich, with brown sauce, please,' he said.

'Brown sauce?'

'Bacon butty and brown sauce. Builder's best breakfast,' he said with a grin.

To his relief, the slight clowning around seemed to relax her again.

The bread was fresh granary, the bacon was smoked by a local butcher and cooked to the perfect crispness, and the coffee was excellent.

'It doesn't get better than this,' he said. 'Good choice, Dr Hart.'

'You're welcome, Mr Jones.'

He kept the conversation light until they'd finished and headed back out into the park.

Walking through the lavender brought back memories for him. 'The scent of lavender always makes me think of my grandparents,' he said.

'Were you close to them?' she asked.

He nodded. 'They still live in the same little cottage by the sea, and there are these huge pots of lavender by the front door. Mum and Dad have moved near them so they can keep an eye on them, but I remember growing up in London and going to stay with my grandparents in the summer holidays. Charlotte and I would spend hours building sandcastles and collecting shells. Even when I was a moody teen, I liked staying there—I'd take their dog for a long walk on the beach and just let the sea work its magic.' He smiled. 'It's Gran's birthday this weekend, so I'm going down to see them and my parents.'

'You mentioned their dog,' she said. 'I thought you were a cat person?'

'I like both,' he said, 'but with my working hours it's easier to have a cat.'

'Fair point,' she said.

'Grandad was a builder. He used to let me help mix the mortar if he was building a wall for someone locally, and he taught me how to lay bricks.'

'Is that why you became a builder?' she asked.

'A chip off the old block, you mean? Probably.'

'Do you miss building?' she asked.

'Sometimes,' he said, 'but I love what I do now even more than I used to like building. I thought Grandad would be disappointed in me not carrying on in his footsteps, after the accident, but he told me to follow my heart—and he also said that it would be a lot easier on Mum, not having to worry about me every time I went to work, in case I fell off another roof.'

She squeezed his hand. 'I think all parents worry about their children, no matter how old their children are.'

'I guess.' He blew out a breath. 'Funny, I thought by the age of thirty-four I'd be settled with kids. Yet here I am.'

'Did the accident affect your fertility as well as breaking your back?' she asked, her voice very gentle.

'Thankfully that wasn't an issue. The only thing that's

held me back is not being able to trust that I've met the right person.'

And now it made him ask himself: was Rebecca the right person?

He felt drawn to her in a way he hadn't felt drawn to anyone since Angela.

But it wasn't going to be easy, because he knew she'd been hurt and she had trust issues, too.

'Do you want children?' she asked.

He might as well be honest about it. 'Yes. I'd like to be a dad, at some point in the future. I love being a godfather and I'm really looking forward to being an uncle, but I want the day-to-day stuff, not just the fun stuff. I want to be there for bedtime and breakfast.'

So now she knew for sure: Nathaniel wanted children.

Would being a stepfather be enough for him, or did he want children of his own? She only had one working fallopian tube, which might cause problems if she tried to conceive in future. But she wasn't ready to tell him about that. Not yet. Instead, she said, 'It isn't all fun, being a parent. There are times when it's really hard, when your child's upset and nothing you can do or say can fix it. Or times when they're angry and throw a hissy fit, and you get judgemental comments from random strangers who either never actually had a close encounter with a toddler tantrum or they've blocked out the memories.'

He smiled. 'I remember Sienna's tantrums. There was one day last summer when Jason and I took her to the funfair on the South Bank. She was overtired and overhyped, and I said no, she couldn't go on the merry-go-round again because she'd already done it three times. She screamed her head off. The *looks* we got. In the end,

Jason hauled her over his shoulder and walked away, and I said cheerfully to everyone I passed that my goddaughter got her temper from my best friend and not from me.'

'Jasmine's done that before, too. In the middle of the supermarket,' Rebecca said, 'when I'd said no to sweeties. I ended up apologising to everyone round me and feeling like the worst parent in the world. But one woman was really lovely and helped me put my shopping through the till and got Jas to clap along to a song. She said she still remembered what it was like when hers were that age, and she wanted to tell me that it really did get better—just like someone had once done for her.'

'That's a lovely thing to do,' he said. 'I'm prepared for toddler tantrums and teenage moodiness. I'm close to my parents and my sister, and one day I want to share that closeness with my own children.' He looked at her, his eyes filled with questions. 'What about you? I know, in the circumstances, it couldn't happen—but did you ever want more than one child?'

Yes, she had. But how badly that had gone wrong. She couldn't help flinching.

'Sorry. I didn't mean to be intrusive and upset you,' he said, as if he realised he'd accidentally trodden on a sore spot.

'It's not you. I grew up with a sister, so I always thought that if I ever had children I'd probably have two,' she said.

She didn't want to talk about that lost baby, but she knew she ought to give him some kind of explanation. And he'd shared his broken engagement with her, so she knew he wouldn't pity her if she told him the truth about her marriage.

'As you say, Lucas's accident made that decision for

me,' she said. 'But, if I'm honest, things had started to go wrong between us even before I got pregnant. I have to be fair to him: he *did* try. But it wasn't the life he really wanted, and the cracks started showing pretty quickly. If he'd been with us for the toddler tantrum stage, I don't think he would've coped.'

'I'm sorry,' he said.

'So am I,' she said. 'I'm sorry Lucas didn't have the chance to walk away and live the life he really wanted, and I'm sorry I didn't give Jasmine the little brother or sister I know she'd dearly love to have. But at least I have Jasmine, and she makes my world a better place.'

That was what he wanted, too. A partner and child to complete him. A family to love.

His break-up with Angela had made him think he'd wanted too much. But maybe he hadn't.

Though it was too soon to think about that where Rebecca was concerned. This was only their fourth date. Way, way too soon to think about families and potential extensions.

'Look—butterflies,' he said, as much to distract himself as anything else. And it seemed to work, because she changed the subject.

He kept the conversation light as they walked round the parkland. 'This really is a nice park—lots of grass for the kids to run around on, a playground, pretty flowers and all that lavender.'

'It's the perfect place for a four-year-old girl to spend an afternoon,' she agreed. 'I'm definitely bringing Jas here.'

Even though he'd intended to keep a tiny bit of distance between then, her hand accidentally brushed his as they walked, and he ended up linking his fingers with hers, moving closer until they were properly holding hands.

And he just couldn't shake the image that flickered into his head: Rebecca walking beside him, Jasmine running just in front of them, and the kind of glow in Rebecca's face that came with the end of the first trimester...

On Saturday morning, Nathaniel sent Rebecca a photograph of the lavender outside his grandparents' front door, plus one of what looked like a massively long, sandy beach. The message said:

You'd love it here.

The nearest she got to the beach right now was the local swimming pool for Jasmine's Saturday morning lesson. She replied.

Looks gorgeous.

And it was weird that she missed him.

She'd known him a month: hardly any time at all. Yet, weirdly, she felt as if she'd known him for years.

No rushing, she warned herself silently. She knew he still had his own issues to work through. The woman he loved had dumped him when he'd needed her most, and he hadn't let anyone close since. He might not let *her* close, either; and it would be stupid to start letting herself want what she might not be able to have.

The following Monday, Nathaniel had a case which concerned him.

Priya Kapoor was a first-time mum. He'd checked her height, weight, blood pressure and the foetal heart rate, and all was fine. He'd checked the baby's growth and the size of Mrs Kapoor's uterus. The blood test results from her twenty-eight-week test showed that her iron levels were normal.

But he wasn't happy with her urine sample.

'So you're thirty-one weeks, Mrs Kapoor,' he said.

'Yes.'

'There isn't any extra sugar or protein in your urine sample,' he said, 'but it's quite dark. Can I ask, are you finding it hard to keep fluids down?'

'No, and I'm drinking plenty, especially as it's been so warm lately,' she said.

'How have you been feeling?' he asked.

'Absolutely fine,' she said with a smile, but he noticed that she was rubbing the skin on the back of her hands. He couldn't see any sign of a rash, but it worried him.

'How about your hands?' he asked gently.

'My mum says it's hormones,' she said. 'She says all pregnant women get itchy hands.'

'Itching is common in pregnancy,' he agreed. 'And yes, it's down to hormones. Your mum is right about that.'

'She says I need to wear loose cotton clothes, and use unperfumed soap and aqueous cream,' Mrs Kapoor said.

'Again, she's right,' Nathaniel said. 'Oat-based soaps and creams can also help. Tell me, do your feet itch as well?'

She nodded.

'And do you find it's less itchy at particular times of day?'

'Most of the time I can cope with it in the day, but it drives me mad at night,' she admitted.

Just what he'd hoped she wouldn't say. 'Is the itch anywhere else?'

'My hands, my feet and the backs of my legs. And I don't understand why, because there isn't a rash or anything.'

'I'd like to do a blood test today,' he said, 'to check your liver function. There is a condition called intrahepatic cholestasis of pregnancy—ICP for short, or you might hear it called obstetric cholestasis. It causes severe itching, especially on your hands and feet. Usually, bile acid flows from your liver to your gut to help you digest food. If you have ICP, the bile acid doesn't flow properly and builds up in your body,' he explained.

'Is that dangerous for the baby?' she asked.

'I don't want you to worry about this, but ICP is linked to increased risks for the baby,' he said. 'If the blood test shows you do have ICP, we'll need to induce labour at about thirty-seven weeks. And I want to see you twice a week between now and then to check your liver function and monitor the baby.'

She bit her lip. 'Is it something I did wrong?'

'No—and it's quite common. One in about a hundred and forty women get it, though it's twice as common in women of Asian heritage,' he added. 'It does tend to run in families, so it might be worth asking your mum if she was ever diagnosed with it.'

Mrs Kapoor looked worried. 'Can you give me anything to stop it?'

'I'm afraid the only treatment is delivering the baby,' he said. 'Can I ask you a really personal question?'

'OK.'

'Have you noticed that your poo is paler than usual?'

'That's not what I was expecting you to ask,' she said, 'but yes. Is that another symptom?'

'It can be,' he said. 'So we might need to give you a vitamin K supplement to make sure your blood clots properly.'

'Is it—? Will it mean the baby's sick or...worse?' she asked.

'There is a small risk of stillbirth in the late stages of pregnancy,' he said, 'but please don't worry. We'll monitor you and the baby very closely, and we're here if you're worried about anything at all. I should have your blood test results back on Thursday, so I'd like you to come to see me at clinic—and, depending on the results, maybe have a chat with one of the doctors about your options.'

'A blood test.' She swallowed hard. 'I hate needles.'

'I'll be gentle,' he promised, 'and, before I do anything else, I want you to tell me all about the nursery you're planning for the baby.'

By the time she was halfway through, he'd done the blood test.

'I didn't even feel that!' she said.

Because he'd distracted her. 'Good. Mrs Kapoor, I can't give you a definite diagnosis until I get your bloods back, but I think it's very probable that you have ICP. And I know it's a lot to take in, so I'm going to print off a leaflet for you, plus I'll give you the number of the local support group—it often helps to talk to someone who's been through it and understands how you feel.'

'OK. Thank you.'

'Try not to worry,' he said, 'and we'll see you on Thursday.'

He saw Rebecca towards the end of his shift. 'I know I always seem to grab you for complications,' he said.

She spread her hands. 'Which is how it should be. We're a midwife-led unit and the doctors are here for the stuff that needs medical intervention.'

'I might need to borrow you on Thursday afternoon,' he said. 'I've got a mum who might have ICP. The bloods are due back on Thursday afternoon—if it's what I think it is, I might need you to have a chat with her.'

'It's my admin afternoon, so let me know the time of her appointment and I'll make sure I'm there,' she said.

CHAPTER EIGHT

FOR MOST OF the week, Rebecca and Nathaniel were rostered on different parts of the ward. On Tuesday, he called her in to see one of his mums-to-be when the tocograph reading suggested the baby might be in distress. 'I'm not happy with the baby's heart rate, and the labour's been pretty long. I want a foetal blood sample.'

It was the best way of checking that the baby was getting enough oxygen. 'OK. Have you talked the mum through the procedure and explained that it won't hurt the baby at all, or do you want me to do it?'

'Already there and we have consent,' he said.

'Great.' Once Nathaniel had introduced her to the mum-to-be and helped her to lie on the left side with her right leg supported, Rebecca inserted an amnioscope and draped the perineum to ensure a sterile field. Once the baby's scalp was visible, she cleaned it with sterile water, added a thin layer of petroleum jelly, sprayed local anaesthetic and took a sample. She handed the capillary tube to Nathaniel for testing before taking a second sample, checking that the baby's scalp wasn't bleeding, then helped position the mum more comfortably.

'The oxygen levels are fine,' Nathaniel said.

'That's really good,' Rebecca said. She reviewed the

tocograph results and sat down on the edge of the bed, holding the mum's hand. 'I'm happy for you to continue labour as it is, but we'll keep the baby monitored continuously. I'd like to put you on a drip to help with your fluid levels, and keep you lying on your left side for a while—what that does is reduce the pressure of your womb on a major vein in your body, so there's good blood flow to the placenta and your baby.'

The mum looked worried. 'So I don't have to have a section?'

'Not necessarily,' Nathaniel said. 'You're almost fully dilated. I know you want a natural delivery if you can, so we'll see how things go—though we might need to help you with delivery, with a ventouse cap or forceps.'

'If the monitoring or any future blood sample tells us that the baby's really not coping well, or the assisted delivery doesn't work,' Rebecca said, 'then we'll have to do a section. But Nathaniel will support you and work with you to try and get you the birth you want, so hopefully next time you see me it'll be on the postnatal ward and I'll get to have a cuddle with your gorgeous little one.'

The mum looked slightly reassured. 'OK. Thank you.'

'Come and get me if you need me,' Rebecca said to Nathaniel. 'I'll get the anaesthetist on standby, plus someone from the neonatal unit.' If things didn't go according to plan, they'd need to move quickly and move the mum to Theatre.

Half an hour later, Nathaniel rapped on the open office door. 'She's fully dilated, but I'm not happy with the baby's heart rate. Mum's consented to assisted delivery, and she knows it means an episiotomy. We've talked it all through and she'd prefer a ventouse, but she's prepared for forceps if you think it's better, and a section if we have to.'

'OK.' She followed him into the room and examined the mum. 'I'm happy for us to give the ventouse a try,' she said. 'I know Nathaniel's already talked it through with you, but I also remember how tough it can be to take things in during labour, so I'll run you through the procedure again and answer any questions either of you might have.'

While she talked the parents-to-be through the procedure, Nathaniel got everything ready and called the anaesthetist, the neonatal specialist and Tanvir, Rebecca's junior.

'It feels like Piccadilly Circus in here,' the mum said, clearly trying to smile.

'Hopefully we won't need them,' Rebecca reassured her, squeezing her hand, and introduced her to everyone.

'It's belt and braces, that's all. But you've got this,' Nathaniel said.

Rebecca sorted out the pain relief and did an episiotomy before attaching the vacuum cup to the baby's head.

During the next couple of contractions, she used gentle suction to help pull the baby out while the mum pushed.

'That's great. You're doing really well,' Nathaniel encouraged.

And finally, the baby arrived. There was the heart-stopping moment before the first cry, and then the baby started pinking up nicely.

'Gorgeous. Well done,' Rebecca said, moved as always by those first few minutes.

While Nathaniel and the neonatal specialist did the newborn checks, everyone else congratulated the new parents and left to get on with the tasks they'd put aside. Nathaniel handed the baby to the mum for skin-to-skin care; Rebecca delivered the placenta and then repaired the episiotomy.

'Well done. He's beautiful,' she said, stroking the baby's cheek.

She exchanged a glance with Nathaniel, seeing that he was as moved as she was by the first few precious minutes of life. And how excellent he'd been, she thought, encouraging the mum and judging exactly when intervention was needed. It felt as if she'd worked with him for years instead of just a few weeks. As if she'd known him for ever. And that, she felt, was a good sign for the future.

On Thursday lunchtime, Nathaniel caught up with Rebecca in the staff kitchen. 'You know the mum I discussed with you on Monday? I've had the bloods back from the lab, and we're definitely looking at ICP. I've already ruled out hepatitis, and Epstein-Barr.'

'OK. What time do you need me in?' she asked.

'Half-past three,' he suggested.

She nodded. 'I'll be there.'

When she knocked on the door of the consulting room, that afternoon, Nathaniel it and introduced her to Priya Kapoor and her husband, Devendra.

'Nice to meet you both,' Rebecca said. 'I believe Mr Jones has already talked to you about the possibility of ICP, and I'm here to answer any questions you might have.'

Mrs Kapoor dragged in a breath. 'We looked it up on the internet. And it said if you have ICP there's a huge risk of a stillbirth.'

'There is a risk, yes,' Rebecca said gently. 'But it's not as huge as the internet claims. We intend to monitor you very closely. We'll check the levels of the liver enzymes and bile acid in your blood every week, give you a vitamin K supplement to make sure your blood clotting works correctly, and at your twice-weekly appointment we'll also monitor the baby's heartbeat, growth and amniotic fluid levels.'

'And that will mean we definitely won't have a stillbirth?' Mr Kapoor asked.

'Nobody can promise complete prevention of any risks,' Rebecca said. 'But if I'm the slightest bit concerned with any of your test results, Mrs Kapoor, we can induce your labour. And we'll monitor the baby's heart rate continuously during labour.'

'Is there any medication you can give Priya to stop the itching?' Mr Kapoor asked.

'Nothing reliable, I'm afraid,' Nathaniel said. 'But once the baby's born the itching will go very quickly, plus the high levels of bile acid and enzymes will drop back down to normal.'

'I know it's really worrying for you,' Rebecca said, squeezing Mrs Kapoor's hand briefly. 'And the itching makes it really hard to sleep, so mums find that very debilitating as well. Try to rest whenever you can. If you get to thirty-five weeks and you really feel you've had enough, we can deliver the baby early.'

'Doesn't that mean the baby will have to go in Special Care?' Mrs Kapoor asked.

'Yes, but you can spend as much time as you like with your baby, and you'll have the support of all the unit's staff,' Rebecca reassured her. 'We can take you to have a look round the unit, so it'll be familiar and less scary, if you like.'

'Thank you.'

'And we're here if you're worried about anything. Just

talk to us and we'll do our best to reassure you,' Nathaniel said.

'Do you have any questions now?' Rebecca asked.

'No. But it's a lot to take in. To think I'm going to have weeks and weeks of this terrible itching…' Mrs Kapoor grimaced. 'I'm hardly getting any sleep as it is.'

'Cool water, calamine lotion, aqueous cream—try the one with a little bit of menthol—and loose cotton clothing will help,' Rebecca advised.

'Thank you.' Though Mrs Kapoor still looked downcast. Rebecca could understand why—the prospect of having to put up with that unbearable itching for months. If only she had a magic wand or a drug that would help. 'There aren't any clinical trials I know of,' she said, 'but I'll ask around. And if I hear of anything that might help, I promise I'll call you.'

Days like this, when she couldn't make much of a difference, were really frustrating; but it got better towards the end, when Josette Kamanya popped down to tell her that she was going to be taking Kayleigh home in the morning.

Over the next few days, both Nathaniel and Rebecca were rushed off their feet at the ward and ended up working with completely different mums. But although they barely saw each other at work, they video-called in the evenings after Jasmine was asleep, and they'd taken to messaging each other links to songs they thought each other would like—obscure indie music bands from Nathaniel and singalong pop from Rebecca. It had become a kind of game, trying to follow each other's choices with something appropriate, and Rebecca loved it because it made her feel young at heart again.

On Thursday evening when Nathaniel called, he said, 'I've got some news for you. Mrs Ridley came into the delivery suite this morning.'

Rebecca remembered the mum who'd had ECV. 'How did she get on?'

'A textbook delivery, which I hope made up for the bumpy pregnancy.'

'That's wonderful. But, come on, you can't tell me a tiny snippet about the delivery and skimp on the details,' she reminded him. 'Tell me all.'

'She weighed just over three and a quarter kilograms, had an Apgar score of ten, her name is Daisy, and they're both doing so well that they went home this afternoon.'

'Brilliant. It's always good to hear news like that.'

'Are you free this weekend?' he asked.

'Apart from Jasmine's swimming lesson on Saturday morning, I could be.'

'Could you have lunch with me on Saturday?' he asked. 'I don't mean just you; I'm inviting Jasmine as well.'

Introducing him to Jasmine would mean taking their relationship to the next stage. And although a part of Rebecca was pleased that Nathaniel wanted to meet her daughter properly, part of her went into panic mode. Was this rushing things? Yes, she worked with him so she'd got to know him pretty well, but she'd still only known him for a little over a month. And, yes, it wasn't like the way Lucas had swept her off her feet and into his bed within a weekend, but that still felt a little too fast.

'I'm not sure,' she said. 'Introducing you to my daughter as my friend from work is one thing, but introducing you as…' She stopped. What? 'Boyfriend' sounded too teenagery. 'Partner' sounded permanent—and that couldn't happen until they were both sure of each other, he'd met Jasmine properly and she was happy that Jasmine liked him.

'What do you have in mind?' she asked.

'Mum and Dad are coming to London to stay with me for the weekend,' he said. 'Charlotte's at the fidgety, fed-up stage of pregnancy, so we're going out for a picnic with her and Robyn. It would be lovely if you and Jasmine could join us.'

Meeting his whole family at once… She knew Nathaniel was close to his family; after the way he'd talked about them, she was pretty sure they'd be as easy to get on with as he was. But meeting his family was tantamount to making their relationship official. She wasn't sure she was ready for that.

'As friends,' he said, as if guessing what was holding her back.

It was tempting.

More than tempting.

But there was a massive hole in his plans. 'If your sister is anywhere near as observant as mine, she'll know we're not just friends.'

'She's not going to grill you. That's the benefit of meeting her at this stage of pregnancy,' he pointed out. 'She's a bit preoccupied.'

Meet his family. Introduce him to Jasmine. Take another step forward—a huge step forward.

'They're honestly not scary. My family's *nice*.' He paused. 'Were Lucas's family scary?'

'No. Actually, I still see his parents. I want to make sure Jasmine grows up knowing her grandparents.'

'Then ignore whatever's worrying you,' he said. 'Take your own advice. Come and have a picnic with us. Eat cake, enjoy the sunshine, and… I dunno, play I Spy with Jasmine?'

'That's one of her favourite games.'

'Let's do it. I promise you'll have a great time. Come with us,' he coaxed.

Ignore the scary stuff and get on with it. Which wasn't like Lucas's thrill-seeking: it was acknowledging there were problems, mainly in her head, and not shying away from them. 'All right,' she agreed. 'Just let me know where and what time. Can I make something for the picnic?'

'That'd be lovely. Mum's planning French bread, cheese, ham and tomatoes, and some nibbly bits.'

'Does anyone have allergies I need to work round?'

'Nope. I'm making chocolate brownies and sorting out the drinks. Is there anything Jasmine particularly likes?'

'Apple juice or water would be great. Thanks.'

'Sounds good.' She loved the fact he was so domesticated. Lucas would've bought something at the very last minute, if he'd remembered at all. Nathaniel was much more reliable. 'I can make some of my mum's cheese biscuits, hummus, and bring crudités and strawberries.'

'Perfect,' he said.

He texted her later that evening to say he'd meet them at half-past eleven at King's Cross.

On Friday night, Rebecca and Jasmine made the dough for the cheese biscuits and baked them on Saturday morning so the biscuits could cool during Jasmine's swimming lesson. While they were baking, Rebecca whizzed together some hummus, chopped celery and carrots into sticks, hulled a couple of large punnets of strawberries, and packed everything in boxes ready to take with them.

And at twenty-five past eleven they were walking down to King's Cross. It was the perfect day for a picnic, with bright sunshine and just the lightest breeze.

Nathaniel was already there; in faded jeans, deck shoes, a T-shirt bearing an old nineties band logo and sunglasses, he looked utterly gorgeous. Rebecca's heart felt as if it had done an anatomically impossible somersault, and it turned into a triple when he smiled and said, 'Hi. Thanks for coming.'

'Hi.' She smiled back. 'Jas, this is Nathaniel, my friend from work who invited us on the picnic. Nathaniel, this is my daughter, Jasmine.'

Nathaniel did a formal bow, then took Jasmine's hand and shook it solemnly. 'I'm delighted to make your acquaintance, Miss Hart. And you have a very pretty name—like the princess in *Aladdin*.'

Jasmine went pink with pleasure. 'I love that film. The genie's so funny!'

'Me, too. Shall we go and meet the others?' Nathaniel said. 'Everyone else is already at the boat.'

'Boat?' Rebecca asked, mystified. He'd told her they were going on a picnic. Given that they'd arranged to meet at King's Cross, she'd expected a walk along the canal, perhaps, or a wander through Camley Street Natural Park.

'Did I forget to tell you the picnic is on a boat? Sorry.'

Just like Lucas. Forgetting the important details.

She pushed her impatience aside. She wasn't being fair. He was probably just as nervous about her meeting his family as she was.

He looked awkward. 'I apologise. I should have asked. Do either of you get seasick?'

'No,' Rebecca said.

'Good,' he said, sounding relieved, and led them down the canal path towards a small modern boat. 'One of the guys I used to work with had got to the stage where his knees were protesting every time he laid a floor, so he decided to switch careers and started a hire-boat business. The engine's electric and the boat itself is made of lots of recycled stuff.'

'That's pretty amazing,' Rebecca said.

'He's one of the good guys—he wants to make a difference. Luckily for me, he had a cancellation this week and I was on his waiting list. And it means we can *really* distract Charlotte. On a boat, she's forced to sit and relax.'

Three women were sitting in the middle of the boat, round a table, and a man wearing a captain's hat was seated at the helm. Rebecca recognised his parents from the photographs in Nathaniel's living room, and his sister and sister-in-law from the abseil.

'Rebecca, Jasmine, this is my mum and dad—Suzanne and Mark—my sister, Charlotte, and my sister-in-law Robyn,' Nathaniel said. 'Everyone, this is my friend Rebecca from work and her daughter, Jasmine.'

'Nice to meet you,' Rebecca said, shaking everyone's hand in turn as they got onto the boat.

'Hello,' Jasmine said shyly, clinging to Rebecca's side.

'Where would you like the picnic food, Nathaniel?' Rebecca asked.

'I've put everything else here in the locker,' Nathaniel said, taking the bag Rebecca offered him and stowing it with the rest of the picnic stuff. 'Jasmine, you need to wear a safety jacket,' Nathaniel said, and deftly helped her to put it on before checking it was secure.

'And your hat,' Rebecca added.

She ended up sitting next to Nathaniel; although he

didn't hold her hand, he slid his foot next to hers under the table, the pressure just enough to tell her that he wanted to hold her hand but he would let her set the pace.

'I'm so glad we're doing this,' Charlotte said. 'I'm getting so fed up, staying at home and just waiting for the baby to arrive.'

'I guess if anything happens this afternoon, at least we have a midwife and an obstetrician on board,' Robyn said.

'Don't talk it up,' Suzanne warned with a smile. 'We don't want even a Braxton-Hicks while we're in the middle of the Regent's Canal!'

Everyone laughed. As the conversation went on, Rebecca felt very much part of the group and accepted by Nathaniel's family; she really liked the closeness and the banter.

The scenery was utterly gorgeous. The banks of the canal were lined with trees, and narrowboats painted in pretty colours were moored at the sides, with pots of pansies and marigolds on their roofs. Some of the narrowboats were clearly cafés; one stretch of the waterside seemed to have a collection of boats offering various different crafts for sale, along with a bookshop and a floating beauty parlour.

'We need to come back here on foot,' Mark said, spotting a narrowboat with a record shop.

'You and your record shops,' Suzanne said, smiling at him.

Nathaniel got Jasmine playing I Spy, and proceeded to cheat horrendously, making her laugh even as she protested. Rebecca warmed to him even more, liking the fact that he had the patience to entertain a little girl.

The thought slid into her mind: what a fabulous father he'd make.

And he'd said he wanted a family…

On the one hand, it gave her confidence that this thing between them might work out—that he could be a father to Jasmine. On the other, it terrified her. What if he wanted more children and she couldn't have any?

She damped down the fear. Not now. They were meant to be having a day out. Family time. Fun.

'Look—we're right on the edge of London Zoo,' he said.

'I like the zoo,' Jasmine announced. 'My favourites are the penguins. I love watching them waddle, and then seeing them swim.'

'I like penguins, too,' Nathaniel said. 'And swans—look, there's a gorgeous one over there. And a duck, with a whole row of ducklings following her.'

Jasmine peered over the side of the boat. 'They're so cute!'

'How many are there?' Nathaniel asked.

And Rebecca watched, fascinated, as Nathaniel drew her daughter out, so the little girl forgot her initial shyness and chattered happily to him.

'I know a song about swans and ducklings,' Mark called from the helm.

'Just be grateful Dad didn't bring his guitar,' Nathaniel said with a grin. 'That's why I let him drive today. He can't drive the boat and play guitar at the same time.'

Did that mean Nathaniel's dad was a terrible musician? Rebecca wondered. Yet Nathaniel had said something about his dad being in a band. But then Mark proceeded to sing 'The Ugly Duckling', and encouraged everyone to join in.

She nudged Nathaniel. 'He's really good,' she said.

'I know. Years back, his band played the university circuit,' Nathaniel explained. 'They still play the local pub once every couple of months, but if you get Dad started on music you're never going to get a conversation about anything else.'

'Warning heeded,' she said. 'Though I don't mind talking music.'

Lunch was idyllic, moored in the shade of a tree; it was exactly the same sort of afternoon Rebecca was used to spending with her own family, full of chatter and laughter and warmth, with everyone sitting round the table in the centre of the boat and passing drinks, plates and platters. She very much liked Nathaniel's sister, who was straightforward and down to earth; Robyn, who was a little shy; Suzanne, who reminded her of her own mother; and Mark, who was full of terrible dad jokes and she could see him getting on very well with her own father.

'I need the recipe for these, Rebecca, please,' Charlotte said after her first cheese star. 'They're the best thing I've ever tasted.'

Rebecca smiled, pleased. 'My mum makes them for every family party—and I think my gran gave her the recipe. They're really easy to make. Jas helped me.'

'They're amazing.' Charlotte took another, then grinned at Robyn. 'As I'm eating for two, I think I should have your share.'

'If it stops you huffing and puffing about waiting for the baby to arrive, you can have mine as well,' Nathaniel teased.

On the way back to King's Cross, Jasmine busied herself with the colouring book and pencils Rebecca had brought with them. Charlotte fell asleep with her head on Robyn's shoulder, Suzanne was taking a turn at the helm under Mark's direction, and Nathaniel whispered in her ear, 'Turn to face me.'

She did, and he stole a quick kiss. When her eyes widened in shock that he'd taken such a risk, he said softly, 'Nobody's paying attention, I guarantee that nobody saw that, and you look seriously cute right now so I couldn't resist.'

He looked seriously cute, too. And Rebecca manoeuvred her bag to hide the fact she was holding his hand all the way back to King's Cross.

'Thank you for a really lovely day,' she said, when they alighted.

'I had a really nice time. Thank you,' Jasmine said, and gave Nathaniel a hug.

He scooped her up, spun her around so she squealed in delight, and kissed the tip of her nose before setting her back on her feet. 'I had a lovely time, too, Princess Jasmine. It was really nice meeting you. Your mum tells everyone at work about you and that you're really good at baking. And now I know she's right. Those cheese stars were so yummy.'

Jasmine beamed at him, clearly pleased, and she didn't stop talking about her new friends all the way home. Later that night, Rebecca called Nathaniel. 'I really enjoyed today. Your family is utterly lovely.'

'They are.' He paused. 'You and Jasmine fitted in perfectly.'

'I felt as if I'd known everyone for years,' she admitted.

'They liked you, too. And, in case you're worrying, as far as they're concerned, you and I are just good friends.'

No expectations, no demands. He'd shared his family with her.

Maybe she should be brave and offer to let him meet

her family, too. 'Perhaps you can come and meet Mum, Dad and Saskia—properly, I mean,' she said. 'We could have a barbecue in my back garden, the next weekend you're off.'

'I'd like that,' he said. 'Let me check my off duty.' There was a pause, while she assumed he was checking dates on his phone. 'I'm working for the next two weekends, but I'm off duty the weekend after.'

'The Sunday, then. If that works for you.'

'It does. I'll put it in my diary now.' He paused. 'But in the meantime I'd like to go somewhere with you. I don't mind where we go or what we do—I just like spending time with you.'

'That's how I feel, too,' she admitted.

'Are you free any evening this week?'

'Friday,' she said.

'I'm on an early, so that's fine for me.'

'It's a date,' she said. 'See you tomorrow. And thank you again for today.'

'My pleasure. See you tomorrow,' he said.

CHAPTER NINE

NATHANIEL HADN'T SAID where they were going on Friday. He'd texted Rebecca on Thursday, saying,

It's dressy. I'll pick you up at eight.

Then he'd added,

Oh, and eat lots of carbs for dinner.

Why? she'd asked in her reply.

Can't tell you without ruining the surprise. Humour me. xx had come the answer.

Going out that late meant that she was able to have dinner with Jasmine and Saskia—pizza, to fulfil Nathaniel's recommendation about carbs—and Saskia did her make-up.

'I can't actually remember the last time you got dressed up like this,' Saskia said.

Rebecca wrinkled her nose. 'Are you sure this isn't too over the top?'

'It's a little black dress, Bec. You can't get more classic than a little black dress, heels and pearls, with your hair up,' Saskia said. 'Very Audrey Hepburn.'

'The last time I wore this dress, I was out with Lucas.'

'Who probably left you in a corner all night while he worked the room,' Saskia said. 'At least Nathaniel won't do that.'

'Considering you've only met him briefly, a couple of times, you seem to know him rather well.'

Saskia grinned. 'Psychologists know everything.' She gave Rebecca a hug. 'And, from the way you've talked about him, he pays attention—which is a good thing.'

Nathaniel rang the doorbell at eight on the dot.

'Go. Have fun,' Saskia directed. 'I have a book I'm dying to finish. Go.'

'You look gorgeous,' Nathaniel said when Rebecca opened the door.

'So do you.' She was used to seeing him in scrubs at work and smart-casual clothes on their dates—but tonight he was wearing a formal suit and tie. The formality emphasised his good looks. 'Where we going?'

'That's still classified,' he teased.

Clearly he could tell she was slightly antsy, because he took her hand, dropped a kiss into her palm and curled her fingers over the kiss. 'We're going out for cocktails, somewhere that will have the perfect view of the sunset over London.'

Which didn't tell her *exactly* where they were going, but it was enough to settle her worries about his surprise.

He held her hand all the way on the Tube, and all the way down the street.

'We're going to the Sky Garden?' she asked when they finally stopped.

'I booked us a table. One with a really good view,' he said.

'This has been on my list of places I wanted to go to for *ages*,' she said. 'Thank you.'

He smiled. 'Pleasure.'

When they walked out of the lift, she could see massive tree ferns and lush vegetation in a huge space filled with light. People were sitting at tables in front of the windows, drinking cocktails, and there was a band playing an acoustic set at one end.

'What would you like to drink?' he asked.

She could stick to something safe—wine, or Pimm's. But today she wanted to push the boundaries. 'I've never really done cocktails. Surprise me,' she said.

'Is there anything you really like or hate?' he asked.

'I'm not really much of a one for whisky,' she said.

'OK. I'll talk to the bar staff and bring back a surprise,' he said.

He came back with a glass topped with a paper umbrella, containing a drink that shaded from deep red to orange, reminding her of a sunset, and a copper-coloured glass that contained what look like ice and lime. 'Your choice,' he said. 'A Moscow Mule or Sex on the Beach.'

'I don't have a clue what's in either.'

'Try both,' he suggested, 'and you can tell me what's in them.'

'Ginger, lime, and…something else,' she said after trying the drink in the copper glass.

'Vodka,' he said.

The other was citrusy, tart and peachy. 'I really like this one,' she said.

'Vodka again—but with peach schnapps, orange and cranberry.'

'I think this could be my new favourite drink,' she said with a smile. 'Thank you.'

* * *

How pretty she looked tonight, Nathaniel thought, all lit up and sparkly. And he was pleased to see she was relaxing more with him, enough to dance with him when the light started to dim. They went back to their table to watch the sun setting over the city; the Thames turned into a ribbon of silver in the fading light, and then the city started lighting up beneath them, the top of the Shard brilliant white and St Paul's looking majestic.

They danced again, and Nathaniel enjoyed holding her close. She was warm and soft, and she smelled of vanilla and sun-warmed peaches.

Though he knew her daughter had a swimming lesson on Saturday morning. He wasn't going to be selfish about this. 'Come on, Cinders. I'd better get you home before the Tube turns into a pumpkin,' he teased.

'Yes. Though I really don't want tonight to end,' she said.

He looked at her, and his throat felt as if it were filled with sand.

Was she saying…?

'I don't want it to end yet, either,' he said. 'One more dance.'

'One more dance,' she agreed.

Except one more dance wasn't enough. He wanted her. Really wanted her.

'Rebecca,' he whispered. 'You could come back to my place for a nightcap.'

She pulled back slightly. 'A nightcap.' Her blue eyes were unreadable.

'Or I can see you home. No pressure.' He'd give her the choice.

'A nightcap sounds good,' she said.

And the world sparkled and spun with promise.

He held her hand all the way back to his flat. Leo gave a lazy miaow when they came in, but stayed in his basket.

'Nightcap.' He didn't actually drink that much. He rummaged in his fridge. 'Um. There's a bottle of champagne…'

She put her hand over his. 'I'm guessing you bought that to celebrate when your niece arrives.'

'I can replace it.'

'I don't want a drink,' she said. 'I want you to dance with me again.'

He connected his phone to a speaker and streamed some slow dance music.

And this time, when she moved that little bit closer, they were alone instead of being on a dance floor in a posh bar. This time, there was nothing to stop him kissing her. Nothing to stop him brushing his lips against hers, tasting and teasing until she opened her mouth to let him deepen the kiss. It made him dizzy, so he held her tighter, almost drowning in the sweetness of that kiss.

When Nathaniel broke the kiss and pulled back slightly to look at her, his pupils were huge.

'Rebecca,' he whispered. 'Right now, I really want you.'

She knew what he was asking. Part of her was scared; it had been years since she'd made love, and even longer since she'd made love with anyone except Lucas.

But she wanted this, too. It had been building up for ages: every time they went out together and he held her hand, or wrapped his arm round her, or kissed her goodnight, she'd wanted him a little more. And, if she was honest with herself, it was why she'd agreed to go back to his flat for a nightcap. She hadn't wanted a drink. She'd wanted *him.*

Common sense nudged its way in. Just. 'I don't have any condoms,' she said.

'I do.' There was a slight flush of colour along his cheekbones. 'Not because I'm taking you for granted, and not because I sleep around, because I don't actually sleep with that many women—but I'm a midwife. I know it's sensible to be prepared for every situation.'

This first time was going to be messy and hopeless; they'd have no idea what each other liked, or where each other liked being touched or kissed or stroked. Part of her really didn't want to disappoint him. But the greater part of her couldn't resist him. 'OK. But I'm rusty,' she warned.

'That doesn't matter.' He held her gaze. 'Are you sure about this?'

'I'm sure.'

'Then,' he said, 'let me show you the rest of the flat.'

She let him lead her through to his bedroom, where the curtains were already drawn.

The room was small but impeccably neat. A double bed with a black wrought-iron headboard took up most of the space, and the duvet cover was in masculine shades of blue and grey.

He cupped her face in his hands and kissed her. 'Is there a clever fastening?' he asked, looking at her little black dress.

'There's a zip at the back,' she said, turning round.

He undid the zip, drawing it down slowly, his fingers brushing against her skin as he revealed it. Then he kissed the nape of her neck, his mouth moving slowly down her spine, and she gasped. 'That feels amazing.'

He turned her round to face him again; she slipped the dress off and folded it neatly before placing it on the floor.

He sucked in a breath. 'You're gorgeous. Stunning.'

'Thank you.' She felt the colour pool in her face. 'I feel ridiculously shy. I think it's because you're wearing too much.'

'Do something about it, then,' he invited.

She undid the buttons of his shirt; the cotton was soft but his skin was even softer. Her fingers shook slightly as she undid the buttons, and she fumbled a couple of them.

He stole a kiss. 'OK?' His eyes were full of concern.

She nodded. 'Just…it's been a while.'

'That's fine,' he said, brushing the pad of his thumb over her lower lip, and her mouth tingled with anticipation. 'I'm going to enjoy you exploring me.'

'I'm going to enjoy you exploring me, too,' she whispered, and pushed the soft material of his shirt over his shoulders. She liked the definition of the muscles on his arms and his pecs. 'Do a twirl for me?'

'A twirl?' He looked surprised.

'So I can admire your muscles.'

A corner of his mouth quirked. 'I'm not exactly the sort who spends hours pumping iron.' But he turned in a circle anyway, letting her look at him.

He really was beautiful. If she'd been artistic, she would've wanted to sculpt him.

'Your shoulders are beautiful,' she said.

'Thank you.' He kissed her lightly. 'Your turn for the twirl.'

'Me? But…'

'You made me do it,' he reminded her, 'so it's only fair.'

Feeling a bit gauche, shy and awkward, she turned in a circle.

'You have beautiful curves,' he said. 'Take your hair down for me?' He gave her a rueful smile. 'Horribly cheesy, but I'd love to see your hair loose.'

And that admission was so sweet and charming. She liked the fact that he could laugh at himself. Once she'd loosened her hair and put the pins on his dressing table, he said, 'And another twirl?'

'You first,' she said.

It was silly and teenagery and...*fun*. She couldn't remember the last time she'd done anything like this. And she was still laughing when he drew her back into his arms and kissed her.

She wasn't sure which of them removed which item of clothing after that, but the next thing she knew he'd pushed his duvet aside, picked her up and laid her down on the bed. The mattress was comfortable and the fat pillows were even more comfortable, and she luxuriated against them.

He caught a breath. 'Do you have any idea how gorgeous you look like that?'

The compliment felt genuine and it boosted her confidence to the point where she could smile at him. 'Thank you.'

She felt the mattress dip as he joined her, and turned to face him; she kissed him and stroked his hair back off his forehead.

He deepened the kiss, then shifted so he could dip his head and nuzzle the hollows of her collarbones.

She'd almost forgotten what it felt like to make love; part of her was nervous, but she remembered what he said about not overthinking it and pushed the thoughts away. Instead, she concentrated on the way he made her feel, the way his mouth and his hands were skimming across her skin and coaxing a response from her.

She tipped her head back against the pillows as he shifted back down the bed, kissing the hollow beneath her ankle bone and then stroking, kissing, teasing his way upwards; she dragged in a breath as he kissed his way along her inner thigh, and she couldn't help herself sliding her hands into his hair as his tongue stroked along her sex.

Need and desire spiralled within her.

'Now,' she whispered.

He reached across to the beside cabinet, took a foil packet from a drawer and ripped it open, then slid on the condom and pushed into her.

And then he stopped. 'OK?' he asked.

She appreciated the way he was holding himself back and thinking of her needs first, knowing it was a long while since she'd had sex and realising that it might feel strange.

'Very OK,' she said, and reached up to kiss him.

Then he began to move.

Rebecca had forgotten that it could feel like this. She couldn't think of anything now except the way he made her feel, the pleasure coiling tighter and tighter within her, and then that blissful moment of release flooding through her. She felt his body surge against hers and knew he'd reached his own release.

He withdrew. 'I'm going to deal with the condom, but please don't go anywhere,' he said, 'because I really want a cuddle.'

It was unexpectedly sweet and made her like him even more.

She snuggled back under the covers and waited for him. He returned with a towel wrapped round his waist, and she grinned. 'How can you be shy after what we just did?'

He grinned back. 'I'm not shy, but I was thinking about my manners. I didn't want to come back in and wave my bits around at you like a caveman.'

'How do you know cavemen waved their bits around?'

'A wild guess,' he said; then he dropped the towel and climbed back into bed with her.

It was nice just to lie there with her head pillowed on his shoulder and his arm holding her close, her own arm wrapped round his waist.

It felt warm and sweet, having Rebecca cuddled into him. There was no need to talk, and the silence between them was restful rather than awkward. If he was honest with himself, Nathaniel didn't want her to go, but he knew she couldn't stay the night.

As if she was reading his mind, she twisted her face round to drop a kiss on his shoulder. 'I really need to be getting back. Sas is babysitting and Jasmine's got her swimming lesson tomorrow.'

'I've had three cocktails tonight so I can't drive you home myself—but I know a reliable taxi firm,' he said. 'I'll call them for you. If you want a shower first, you're welcome to use anything in the bathroom and I'll grab you a fresh towel.'

'Thanks. That would be good.'

He called the taxi and got dressed while she was in the bathroom, and made a fuss of the cat while he waited for her to finish getting ready. When she joined him in his living room, she was fully dressed.

'The taxi will be here in five minutes,' he said. 'They just texted me.' He paused. 'I'll see you home.'

'You don't have to do that.' She shook her head. 'You said yourself they were reliable.'

'Yeah, but I want to snatch a few more minutes with you.' He was aware of how needy that made him sound, and groaned. 'That's pathetic. Anyone would think I was twelve, not thirty-four.'

'Actually, it's really cute.' She stole a kiss. 'And I kind of like the idea of you holding my hand in the back seat of a car, all the way home.'

The reality was even better. They didn't need to talk; they just sat with his arm round her, her head on his shoulder, and their hands linked on their laps.

Finally, the taxi pulled up outside her house.

'Thank you for an amazing evening,' she said softly.

'Thank *you*.' He kissed her lightly. 'I guess I'll see you at work. But maybe we can steal some time together next week.'

'I'm on an early on Wednesday,' she said.

'Me, too. If you can get a babysitter, we'll work out where we can go between now and then.'

'I'd like that.' She kissed him. 'Sweet dreams.'

He knew they would be. Because they'd be of her.

He asked the taxi driver to wait until she was inside before driving him back to his flat.

When he walked through the door, Leo greeted him with a quizzical purr.

'Yes, Leo, I had a lovely night,' Nathaniel told the cat. 'I like her. I *really* like her. She's special.'

And he just hoped she was starting to feel the same way about him.

CHAPTER TEN

IN THE MIDDLE of Wednesday afternoon, Rebecca was called down to the Emergency Department. 'Molly Davidson's waiting in the cubicle,' Ellie, the charge nurse, said. 'We've done urine and blood tests, and we've stabilised her with oxygen and fluids and given her some pain relief. She's thirty-four, and she's had single-sided abdominal pain for a couple of days now but assumed she was just having a worse than usual attack of endometriosis.'

Oh, no. This sounded familiar.

Rebecca damped down the memories. Not now. 'Did you do a pregnancy test?' she asked.

'Yes, and it's positive,' Ellie said. 'The baby wasn't planned and her periods aren't that regular, but we've worked out she's probably about seven weeks. She hasn't had any bleeding, but she felt a bit faint this morning, she's had shoulder-tip pain and she collapsed at work an hour ago. One of her colleagues called an ambulance, and I asked you to come down because I think we're looking at an ectopic pregnancy and a ruptured tube.'

'Sadly, it sounds as if you're spot on,' Rebecca said. And she knew exactly what that felt like.

'I've got the portable scanner on its way,' Ellie said. 'And we've called her partner. He's coming in now.'

'Perfect. Thank you,' Rebecca said.

'Let me introduce you,' Ellie said, and led Rebecca over to the cubicle. 'Miss Davidson, this is Dr Hart. I'm going to leave her to have a chat with you. Is that OK?'

At Molly's nod, Rebecca thanked Ellie as she left the cubicle. 'Ellie's filled me in on how you're feeling right now. I need to do a scan to confirm it, but it sounds to me as if you have an ectopic pregnancy. That means the embryo got stuck in your fallopian tube instead of travelling all the way down to your womb, so the egg's growing in the wrong place.'

It was so easy to say. All neat and tidy and fixable. But Rebecca also knew how it felt: a pain sharper than labour, and then the grief afterwards for a baby that didn't have a chance. The fear that things might never be OK again.

In her case, it was the baby she and Lucas hadn't known about. An unexpected last gift she hadn't been able to keep.

'I'm going to give you a scan but, because you're in such pain, I'm pretty sure your fallopian tube has ruptured and you're going to need an operation for me to repair it,' she said.

Molly's face was white. 'An operation.'

'I'll do it under general anaesthetic,' Rebecca explained, 'so you'll be asleep when it's carried out. I'll do my best to repair the tube, but if I can't then I'll need to remove it to stop the bleeding and to keep you safe.' Which was exactly what had happened to her.

'I had no idea I was pregnant. We tried for a couple of years and it never happened, because of my endometriosis, and we're on the waiting list for IVF.' Molly looked distraught. 'Isn't there anything you can do to save the baby?'

Rebecca took her hand. 'I'm so sorry. The only place an embryo can grow and get the nutrients it needs to survive is in your womb. Your health is uppermost for us now, so surgery is the only option. But the good news is I can do it by keyhole surgery, so you'll be able to go home in a day or so.'

Just then, Ellie came back into the cubicle. 'Molly, your partner's here.'

'Dan!' Molly collapsed into tears again while her partner hugged her.

Rebecca slipped out to grab tissues and a cup of water for her patient.

'Here. These might help,' she said gently.

'Dr Hart was saying that I need keyhole surgery,' Molly said.

'What does that mean?' Dan asked.

'It's still done under a general anaesthetic, but the incisions are much smaller so Molly will recover from the operation quicker,' Rebecca explained. 'Once you're under, Molly, I'll make some small incisions in your stomach and put a small flexible tube inside you which has fibre optic lights and a camera on the end. It sends me images of your abdomen so I can operate. Hopefully I'll be able to repair your fallopian tube, but as I said if I can't repair it, I'll have to remove it. Then I'll minimise any bleeding and stitch you up. It'll take between thirty minutes and an hour.'

'But if you have to remove the tube completely, does that mean I won't ever be able to have a baby?' Molly asked.

'Even with one tube, you'll still have a good chance

of conceiving naturally—roughly six in ten—though it's more likely that you might have an ectopic pregnancy in future,' Rebecca said. Stats she'd dully listened to her own surgeon telling her, too; it had felt as if she were hearing it all underwater, at slow speed, the words not going in.

Jasmine dearly wanted a little sister, she knew. But even if this thing with Nathaniel worked out, that ectopic pregnancy would come back to haunt her. She might not be able to give Nathaniel a child and Jasmine a sibling. And what then?

'I know you said you were on the waiting list for IVF, but I'd suggest giving yourself three months to recover before you start trying for a baby again. If it happens before you have the IVF treatment, I'd advise you to come and see us pretty much as soon as you know you're pregnant, so we can monitor you and keep a close eye on you.'

Molly bit her lip. 'Is it likely it'd be ectopic again, if I fell pregnant?'

'An ectopic pregnancy is more common if you've had one already,' Rebecca said, trying to damp down her memories again—her patient needed reassurance, not a meltdown. 'But I want you to know that there's still a good chance that it would be a normal pregnancy, next time.'

'If it was another ectopic pregnancy, would I lose my other tube?'

'Not necessarily,' Rebecca said. 'It depends what sort of symptoms you're having. Sometimes we just wait and see, and the pregnancy ends itself naturally. Sometimes we can give you medication to stop the pregnancy growing and avoid surgery.'

'Can't you give her medication instead of doing surgery today?' Dan asked.

'No. I'm afraid that only works if a woman has only mild symptoms, and I'm pretty sure there's a rupture—I'll know more when I've done the scan.'

Just as she said it, the portable scanner arrived.

And the scan itself confirmed everything that Rebecca and Ellie had suspected. 'I'm sorry,' Rebecca said. 'You've got internal bleeding, Molly, so I'm going to need to take you to Theatre.'

'Why did it happen?' Dan asked.

'We don't necessarily know why,' Rebecca told him. 'If you've had previous surgery on your fallopian tubes or a previous ectopic pregnancy, it increases the risk—but, in more than half the cases, there's no reason. Sometimes it's caused by pelvic inflammatory disease, sometimes there's a hormonal imbalance, or sometimes it's the way the egg develops.' She squeezed Molly's hand. 'It's not something you could've prevented, so don't blame yourself.' Though she knew what that devastation felt like. Even though her doctor's training told her otherwise, she'd had a moment when she'd wondered if she'd done something wrong or all the stress of losing Lucas had caused it. She knew it wasn't true, but it hadn't done much to ease the misery. 'It's absolutely *not* your fault. I'm going to introduce you to the anaesthetist, and then I'll scrub up and we'll get you into Theatre. Dan, I'm afraid you can't go in to Theatre with Molly, but you can be with her until she leaves, and wait in the waiting room.'

The operation was a success; once Molly was round

from the anaesthetic, Rebecca scrubbed out and took Dan to see her in the recovery room.

'Did you manage to save the tube?' was Molly's first question.

'I'm sorry, I'm afraid I couldn't,' Rebecca said. 'But the good news is your other tube looked healthy.'

A tear dripped down Molly's cheek. 'We're on the waiting list for IVF. We didn't think I could get pregnant naturally. And…' She choked. 'I can't believe I actually got pregnant and then this happened.'

'I'm so sorry,' Rebecca said. 'But you do still have a good chance of having a baby in the future.' The words echoed hollowly in her head. It was one of the things she worried about with Nathaniel. What if he wanted children and she couldn't have them?

'What happens now?' Dan asked.

'When the anaesthetist is happy, we'll take Molly up to the ward—the gynae ward, not the maternity ward,' Rebecca added swiftly. 'You might be in a bit of discomfort later, Molly, either in your shoulder tip or your abdomen, but we can give you pain relief for that, and the nurses will be there to help you.'

'I lost the baby,' Molly whispered. 'And I wanted a baby so much.'

'I know. We both did. But it'll be better next time,' Dan said, holding her tightly. 'It's going to be fine.'

Rebecca felt completely helpless. Their dreams had been smashed, and there was nothing she could do to fix it. All she could do now was to focus on the practical stuff. It was what she'd ended up doing herself—focusing on the practical stuff. Organising a funeral. Looking after her toddler. Putting one foot in front of the other and keeping going.

'The stitches should dissolve within a couple of weeks,

but don't put any talc or moisturiser on the wound. If you spot any redness or swelling once you go home, go to see your GP,' she said. 'The scars will hardly be visible in a couple of months.'

'When can I go home?' Molly asked.

'Tomorrow, if you feel up to it. Make sure you rest for at least the next couple of weeks, take some gentle exercise and avoid heavy lifting, and if you feel up to it you'll be able to go back to work in two to four weeks. Come back and see me for a check-up in six weeks, and if you're worried about anything I'm here.' She took a deep breath. 'I know this is horrible for both of you. I can organise some counselling, and I'd recommend getting in touch with a support group. It helps to talk to people who've been through it, too—people who've come out the other side and will have some practical ideas to help both of you through the heartache.' She almost—*almost*—told them she'd been through it herself and she was talking from experience, but right at that moment she needed to calm her emotions down again.

'Thank you,' they said, but she could see the devastation in their faces and it made her feel horrible. Just as bad as she'd felt when she'd lost the baby. And the guilt she'd felt later at thinking that maybe it had been for the best—how, as a young widow, could she have coped with a toddler and a newborn? And, if Lucas had survived the crash, their marriage definitely wouldn't have survived all the changes and compromises that a second child would have brought.

By the time Rebecca went back up to her office, she was drained. All she wanted to do was go home and hug her little girl tightly. She was so, so lucky to have Jasmine.

And she really couldn't face her night out with Nathaniel tonight. She needed to rebalance her equilibrium. Going out felt so trivial, so pointless, when such serious things were going on in other people's lives.

Nathaniel had already finished his shift and gone home, so she texted him.

Sorry. Need to call off tonight. Had a rough shift. It's me, not you.

That sounded as if she was dumping him, and she didn't want to give him that impression. Though she didn't want to explain either.

She added,

Maybe we can go out some other time. Just not tonight. R x

Nathaniel looked at the text on his phone. He wasn't aware of any difficult cases on the ward today, but maybe someone from the Emergency Department had asked Rebecca to treat a patient. He knew she'd been in Theatre when he'd left.

Theatre, and a rough shift. It sounded as if the baby hadn't made it—the kind of case they all found hard to deal with. He hated to think she was so upset about work but would have to go home and pretend that everything was completely fine, for Jasmine's sake.

Maybe there was something he could do to help.

The florists were all closed by now, but the big supermarket round the corner from him had a decent range of flowers. He chose a large bunch of bright sunflowers, waited until he was pretty sure Jasmine would be asleep, and drove round to Rebecca's house.

Ringing the doorbell might wake the little girl, so he texted her.

Got a moment? On your front doorstep.

Two minutes later, the front door opened.

'Nathaniel, I—' she began.

'I'm not staying,' he cut in. 'I know you've had a tough day. So I just wanted to give you a hug and bring you these, because I wanted to make your day a little bit better.' He handed her the sunflowers.

She looked at them, then him, and tears spilled over her lashes.

He couldn't leave her like this. Gently, he put his arms around her and ushered her back into the house. He closed the front door behind them and held her tightly, cradling her head on his shoulder and letting her cry.

Eventually, she lifted her head. 'I'm sorry for sobbing all over you. I hate these kind of days,' she whispered. 'The sort of days where I can't make a difference.'

'What happened?'

'The Emergency Department called me down to a patient who'd collapsed and they thought it might be an ectopic pregnancy. She had a ruptured tube. The baby wasn't planned, but she really wanted it—she thought she might have to have IVF treatment before she could have a child.' She shook her head. 'I couldn't save the baby or the tube. The poor woman and her partner were both devastated.'

He winced. 'That's hard. But you did make a difference, Rebecca. You operated and you saved her life. And you know as well as I do that you can't save an ectopic pregnancy.'

'Intellectually, I know that. But emotionally…' She dragged in a breath. 'I had an ectopic pregnancy. After Lucas died. I didn't even know I was pregnant. I'd only just started organising the funeral, and suddenly I had this terrible pain and collapsed. So I know exactly what that poor woman went through today.'

He held her closer. 'Is this the first ectopic you've had to deal with since?'

She shook her head. 'But it got to me today. Jasmine was telling me this morning over breakfast that her best friend at nursery is having a little sister. And then she asked me if she could have a little sister, too.' Rebecca swallowed hard. 'I managed to distract her, but it made me think. There's no guarantee I could have another child. The tube was ruptured, so I lost it. There I was this afternoon, telling Molly Davidson that she still had a good chance of having another baby, but…'

He knew what she was trying to tell him. That she came with complications. That, even if their relationship worked out, she might not be able to give him a child. And he'd told her he wanted a family.

He stroked her hair. 'None of us knows what the future holds. And if you want another child and your fallopian tube is a problem, you can always consider fostering or adoption.'

She looked at him, and he could see the question in her eyes. What did *he* want?

He'd always planned to have kids with Angie. After she'd dumped him, he'd vowed to be happy being godfather to his best friend's daughter and uncle to Charlotte's children.

But at that point he'd told himself he wouldn't have another serious relationship. Now… Everything was different. Rebecca might just be the one worth taking the risk with. Yet now she was telling him that having more children might not be a possibility for her.

He needed some time to process this. So he held her close again. 'You've had a horrible day, but your patient is still alive, thanks to you. If you hadn't operated, with a ruptured fallopian tube she could've bled out and died,' he said. 'Focus on the good stuff.'

'I'm sorry I called off our date at the last minute.'

'Nobody would want to go out, in your shoes. I'm not taking it personally,' he reassured her. Was that the way Lucas would have reacted?

He stroked her hair. 'I just wanted to make you feel a bit better, that's all. So I brought you some sunshine in flower form, and the plan was for me to give you a hug and go.'

'Thank you.' She pulled back slightly so she could look him in the eye. 'A bit of me wants to tell you to stay.'

'But Jasmine's asleep, you have work tomorrow—and we have all the time in the world,' he said. He couldn't resist stealing a kiss, brushing his mouth lightly over hers. 'It can wait. So can our date. And it'll be all the sweeter when it happens.'

There was a glimmer of a smile through her tears. 'Yeah.'

'You're a good woman, Rebecca Hart, and you're an amazing doctor. Don't you forget it.' He kissed her again. 'I'll see you tomorrow. Sleep tight. And if you're awake in the middle of the night, feeling miserable, call me.'

'I can't do that. You'll be asleep.'

He smiled. 'And you're one of the people I won't mind waking me. If you need me, I'm there.'

'That's…' She shook her head, as if lost for words,

and stroked his face. 'You're the nicest man I know, Nathaniel Jones.'

'You're not so shabby yourself.' One last kiss, and he dragged himself away before he begged her to let him stay.

Because Rebecca Hart was worth the wait.

CHAPTER ELEVEN

ON THURSDAY MORNING, Nathaniel thought about calling Rebecca before his shift; but he knew she'd be busy with the morning routine of getting Jasmine ready. It would be better to text her, so she could pick it up at a time that suited her.

How are you? Xx

The reply came quicker than he'd expected.

Better. And thank you for yesterday. xx

My pleasure.

He paused.

What shift are you on tomorrow? Xx

Late. xx

Perfect.

If you're not busy, I could do with some female advice. Involves shopping. xx

Shopping? Xx

Something to cheer up a grumpy, very pregnant and overdue sister. xx

You're on. Meet you at the Tube station after the nursery run? Nine fifteen OK? Xx

Nine fifteen it is. xx

Nathaniel's path didn't cross Rebecca's at work that day—he was in clinic and she was in Theatre—but he met her at the Tube station as planned on Friday morning.

'Hey.' To his relief, she hadn't gone shy on him as she greeted him with a hug.

'So what do you have in mind to cheer your sister up?' she asked.

'Starting with flowers; something girly—which is where you come in; and I thought I'd take her freshly squeezed orange juice and a bit of organic carrot cake and spend some time with her,' he said. 'There's no obligation for you to do any more than the shopping—and I'm very grateful for that—but if you'd like to come and visit her with me, you'd be very welcome.'

'I'd like that,' she said.

Funny, he'd always loathed shopping with Angela, dragging around the shops while she dithered and looked at everything six times before going back to the first shop again. But with Rebecca it was easy. She steered him into a shop which specialised in freshly made toiletries with hypoallergenic, natural ingredients. 'When I was pregnant, the thing I hated was getting puffy feet.

So I think a foot-soak and foot cream would be the perfect treat,' she said.

The assistant wrapped the toiletries in a pretty fabric wrapper for him. Once they'd picked up flowers, cake and juice, they were at Charlotte's house by half-past ten.

'For you,' Nathaniel said, and gave his sister a hug. 'You look as if you had a rough night,'

'I couldn't settle.' She wrinkled her nose. 'I must've eaten something that disagreed with me yesterday and gave me indigestion. I've been getting twinges all morning.'

Nathaniel and Rebecca exchanged a glance.

'Charlotte, your due date was last week. Are you sure you're not having contractions?' Nathaniel asked.

'Of course I'm sure.' She rolled her eyes. 'I had Braxton-Hicks last week, and they felt a lot stronger than this. I just ate something that gave me a bit of indigestion, that's all.'

'Have you taken anything for it?' Rebecca asked.

Charlotte nodded. 'That horribly chalky stuff the pharmacist said is safe for pregnant women to take for heartburn.'

'And it hasn't helped?' Nathaniel asked.

'What is this, twenty questions?' Charlotte asked irritably.

'He's just being a concerned big brother,' Rebecca said, clearly trying to pour oil on troubled waters. 'I'd ask the same, if you were my sister. And I'd also ask if you had any back pain.'

'A little bit,' Charlotte admitted, 'but probably because I couldn't get comfortable last night so I must've lain awkwardly. I walked it off round the kitchen.'

Nathaniel exchanged another glance with Rebecca.

The more his sister was saying, the more it sounded as if she was in labour. And she wasn't usually the irritable sort.

'Let me put your flowers in water for you,' Rebecca offered. 'Tell me where you keep your vases.'

'Kitchen cupboard. Come through,' Charlotte said.

Then she stopped in the doorway. 'Oh!'

'OK, sis?' Nathaniel asked.

'Stupid pelvic floor.' She grimaced. 'Even though I did all the exercises, it feels as if I've wet myself. I *hate* this. Look, I'm just going to the bathroom to clean myself up.'

'Charlotte, please don't think I'm interfering,' Rebecca said, 'but have you thought that might've been your waters breaking rather than a leak from your bladder?'

'They'd better not. Robyn isn't—ow!' Charlotte grabbed the doorway.

'With my professional hat on, I'd say your indigestion was the first stage of labour,' Rebecca said, 'and your waters have broken. Would you let me examine you, or would you rather we called Robyn and an ambulance now?'

'You can examine me if you really want to, but I'm not in la—' Charlotte doubled over.

'I'm calling Robyn,' Nathaniel said, and speed-dialled his sister-in-law while Rebecca helped Charlotte over to the kitchen table and spread clean tea towels over it before helping Charlotte up to examine her. 'Robyn? I'm at your place with Rebecca. We think Charlotte's in labour.'

'Oh, my God. I'm coming now. Are you taking her to hospital?'

'Are we taking her to hospital?' He looked at Rebecca, who shook her head. 'No. We're calling an ambulance. I'll keep you posted on what's happening.'

'I'm leaving now. I'm getting a taxi. Tell Charlotte I love her.'

'I will,' he promised, then called the ambulance while he grabbed a pile of clean towels from the airing cupboard.

'Why have you got towels?' Charlotte wanted to know.

'Just call it a midwife's instinct,' he said.

'You think I'm having the baby *now*? No way. They said in antenatal classes that a first labour takes an average of twelve hours, and those were the first contractions I felt,' Charlotte protested.

They might've been the first ones his sister had felt, but he was pretty sure they weren't her first actual contractions. And he wasn't sure how to break it to her that some babies took an awful lot less time than twelve hours to arrive.

'When did the ambulance say they'd be here?' Rebecca asked.

'Twenty minutes,' he told her. 'Robyn says she loves you.'

'I hate to tell you this, Charlotte,' Rebecca said gently, 'but I've been timing your contractions. I agree with Nathaniel. I don't think you'll make it to hospital.'

'But I'm not in labour,' Charlotte protested, shaking her head. 'Ow!'

'Your baby has other ideas. I reckon my niece is planning on a fast labour and a home birth,' Nathaniel said. 'So having an obstetrician and a midwife with you might be useful.'

'A home birth? What, right now?' Charlotte went white. 'But—I can't. Not without Robyn here.'

'Robyn's on her way and I'm keeping her posted,' Nathaniel said. 'In the meantime, did you hire that TENS machine and is it in your labour bag?'

'No. You made me pack that bag weeks ago,' she grumbled. 'I was going to pick up the machine tomorrow.'

No pain relief, then. But there was an ambulance on the way and an obstetrician right beside him. They could do this.

'Let me examine you again,' Rebecca said.

Nathaniel held his sister's hand while Rebecca examined her.

'Eight centimetres dilated,' she said. 'This baby definitely wants to make her arrival soon.'

'But I can't be,' Charlotte said.

'You've probably been in labour all night,' Rebecca said gently. 'That indigestion and backache were contractions. You just didn't feel them the way you expected to.'

'Oh, my God.' Charlotte looked shocked. 'Robyn didn't want to leave me to go to work this morning, but I chugged some of the chalky stuff and told her I'd be fine, it was just indigestion.' Her eyes filled with tears. 'I'll never forgive myself if she misses our baby being born.'

'Relax,' Nathaniel said. 'It's all going to be fine. She's on the way right now. She'll be here before the little one arrives.'

'And we'll be here to support you and help you breathe until she gets here,' Rebecca said, exchanging a glance with Nathaniel.

Between them, they encouraged Charlotte to breathe and to walk around the kitchen.

'I'm going to put the heating on and close the doors and windows, so it's nice and warm in here for the baby,' Nathaniel said. 'Which room do you want to give birth in?'

'I'm going to make a right mess of the carpet,' Charlotte said.

Nathaniel smiled. 'No, you won't. If you want to go into the living room, I'll put some bin liners down to protect the carpet, a sheet over that, and some towels so it's comfy for you. Give me a few minutes, and we'll sort it.'

'Light a candle so you've got nice scent in the air, and put some music on—you don't have to throw your entire birth plan out of the window,' Rebecca added.

He busied himself making the living room comfortable for his sister, then came back in to help Rebecca support her through to the living room.

'Squeeze my hand whenever you need to,' he directed. 'Whatever makes you comfortable. You've got this. Just a few more minutes until Robyn's here. You can hold on. You can do *anything* for just five minutes.'

It reminded Rebecca of the way he'd talked her through the abseil. She'd thought then how good he'd be with mums going through an uncomplicated labour, and this proved her point.

She was timing the contractions, which were getting closer together.

'How far apart?' Nathaniel mouthed.

'Two minutes,' she mouthed back.

Charlotte puffed. 'I can't...'

'It's fine, sweetheart. Tell me what you need,' Rebecca encouraged gently.

Charlotte's face reddened. 'If I do a poo in front of my little brother...'

'It won't matter in the slightest. Forget the fact he's your little brother. He's a qualified midwife and he's really good at what he does. He's seen it all before and so have I,' Rebecca reassured her. 'We don't care about any of that. We just want you to be comfortable and relaxed.'

'Breathe for me,' Nathaniel said. 'Then start to bear down when you need to push.'

'OK.' Charlotte was close to tears.

Just then, there was a rattle at the door and Robyn rushed in. 'Charlotte!'

'I didn't think you'd make it.' A fat tear rolled down Charlotte's cheek.

'She's here now, so let Nathaniel and me examine you,' Rebecca said. 'Robyn's taking over hand-holding duties.'

She quickly examined Charlotte. 'Ten centimetres,' she said in a low voice.

'Remember your class about birth positions?' Nathaniel asked.

Charlotte nodded. 'I was going to kneel.'

'That's fine. I'll get you a chair,' Nathaniel said.

Once he'd brought in the chair, he and Robyn supported Charlotte so she was kneeling and holding on to the chair.

'I need to push,' Charlotte said.

'Breathe, and we'll be here to guide the baby,' Rebecca said. She and Nathaniel knelt behind Charlotte, and she examined Charlotte. 'Crowning,' she mouthed to Nathaniel. 'Charlotte, I want you to stop pushing. I need you to blow little short breaths out of your mouth.'

'Just like we practised,' Robyn said, and demonstrated.

The head was born slowly and gently.

'Another push with that next contraction,' Nathaniel said. 'You've got this, Charlotte. Nearly there.'

Another push, and the baby's head turned to the side.

'Now do some more of those short breaths,' Rebecca directed, while Nathaniel supported the baby's head and checked that the cord wasn't wrapped round her neck. 'That's brilliant. Keep going.'

'Another push,' Nathaniel said, and the baby's first shoulder slipped out. A second, and the other shoulder came out and the baby slithered into Nathaniel's hands.

'She's here!' Nathaniel said. 'And she's perfect.'

The baby cried, to Rebecca's relief, then started to pink up nicely. 'Let me wipe her face,' she said.

Robyn handed her a clean cloth, and Rebecca wiped the baby's face and wrapped her in a clean sheet.

'We want to keep the baby warm, so we're going to help you shift round, Charlotte. Then I'm going to put the baby on your chest and wrap a towel over both of you,' Rebecca said.

'What about the cord?' Robyn asked, looking anxious.

'It's long enough to let the baby be on Charlotte's chest, and hopefully the ambulance crew will be here with clamps and sterile scissors very shortly,' Nathaniel said. 'Though we might have to improvise.'

'If you can put a hat on the baby, Robyn, that'd be great,' Rebecca said. 'Charlotte, let the baby nuzzle your breast—it'll help your body produce the hormones so you can deliver the placenta more easily.'

Just as soon as Charlotte was settled with the baby, the doorbell went.

Rebecca went to answer it and led the ambulance crew into the living room. 'I'm afraid the baby had other plans, so you've missed the exciting bit,' she said with a smile, 'but we could do with some sterile clamps and scissors.'

Robyn cut the cord, and Nathaniel helped Charlotte to deliver the placenta.

'Congratulations, both of you,' Rebecca said, smiling as Charlotte and Robyn cuddled their baby.

* * *

Delivering babies was one thing; delivering his niece was beyond anything he'd ever experienced, and Nathaniel was moved to tears.

'Hey, Uncle Nathaniel. I'd better get to work. I'll call the boss on the way and get some cover for you,' Rebecca whispered, and gave him a hug.

'Cover?' He looked at her, too dazed to take in what she was saying.

'You just delivered your sister's baby.'

'*We* delivered her,' Nathaniel corrected.

'In your shoes, I'd want to stay here with my family for a bit.'

'I do,' he admitted.

'Leave it to me and I'll sort it out.' She smiled at him. 'I'd better be off. See you later.'

'Thank you for everything you did. You were amazing.'

'*Charlotte* was amazing,' she said. 'Go be with your family. They'll need you to take them in to be checked over properly.' She hugged Robyn and Charlotte. 'Congratulations. Your daughter's beautiful.'

'Delilah,' Robyn said.

'Great name.'

After Rebecca had gone, Nathaniel took Charlotte, Robyn and Delilah in to their local hospital for a check-up with their own midwifery team.

It was while he was in the waiting area that it hit him. Everyone around him was part of a family. There were couples on their own, glowing with the thrill of their first child. Couples with smaller children, clearly wanting their older child to be there for the scan. Single mums with a sister or a mum or a friend supporting them.

In his own department, he saw families of all shapes and sizes every day. He'd thought by now that he would have children of his own. If it hadn't been for falling off that roof, he would've been married to Angela, and with luck they would've had babies.

But all the dreams had shattered into smaller pieces than his bones, after his fall. It had taken only days for Angela to decide he wasn't enough for her. So what made him think he'd be enough for Rebecca?

Yes, they'd been getting on well, and he was starting to fall in love with the serious obstetrician who had a sweet, playful side she kept hidden. And yes, he could imagine making a family with her and Jasmine. They could be a unit, just like his sister with Robyn and Delilah.

That was what he wanted. A family. Himself, Rebecca, Jasmine and maybe a little brother or sister.

But what if it wasn't what *she* wanted?

The voice in the back of his head—the one he tried so hard to silence—wouldn't shut up. It kept telling him he was a fraud. He hadn't been enough for Angie, and he hadn't made any of his subsequent relationships work—because he hadn't wanted to commit his heart, only to have it broken again. What if he wasn't good enough for Rebecca, either?

She'd already been in one relationship where she hadn't been happy. She'd had the courage to plan to leave Lucas; maybe in a few months, when she realised Nathaniel wasn't enough for her, she'd leave him, too.

And that, he realised, would shatter his heart even more than Angie had.

So maybe he should stop now. Save himself the heartbreak.

It took him ages to find the right words.

Thank you for what you did today. I've been thinking—I think it's better that you and I are just good friends. Sorry to let you down. N x

He stared at the message for a while, and finally hit 'send'.

If only things could've been different.

But they weren't. He would never be enough for her.

Rebecca stared at the words on her phone screen.

Thank you for what you did today. I've been thinking—I think it's better that you and I are just good friends. Sorry to let you down. N x

What?

He was ending it?

But...they'd delivered his sister's baby together. She'd met his family and got on well with them. He'd met Jasmine and she'd adored him. They'd been planning for him to meet her mum and dad and Saskia.

Why would he end it?

She didn't understand. Everything had been going fine.

Or maybe she'd been fooling herself all along. Maybe she'd made exactly the same mistake that she'd made with Lucas, and she'd fallen for someone who didn't want commitment.

Given that Nathaniel could end this so casually, by text rather than bothering to tell her to her face, he clearly thought she and Jasmine were easily dispensable.

And it hurt. It hurt so much.

It made her ribs feel as if they'd just cracked, because

her heart had swollen in misery, and her skin felt tight and prickly. She'd been close to declaring her feelings, and she'd actually let him into Jasmine's life as well as her own: and this was how he'd treated her. As if she was worthless.

Just like Lucas had made her feel.

Well, she wasn't going to beg someone to love her when he clearly didn't. She'd been there, done that—and it seemed that she'd been stupid enough to do it all over again.

This was the last time she'd make that particular mistake.

And she'd have a quiet word with the head of department to see if she could change her shifts, so her path wouldn't cross that much with Nathaniel's in the future.

He'd made it clear that he didn't want to discuss it, and in any case she didn't know what to say. All she could do was send back a message.

OK.

And that was it.

Over.

CHAPTER TWELVE

THANKFULLY NATHANIEL WAS on duty over the weekend and Rebecca wasn't, so she didn't have to face him. She managed to avoid him on the ward at the beginning of the week, but on Wednesday, she was in clinic when Amara knocked on the door. 'Dr Hart, I'm sorry to interrupt, but it's urgent.'

The midwife looked worried, and Rebecca's breath caught. What was wrong? Had something happened to Jasmine? To her parents? To her sister? 'Excuse me, please,' she said to her mum-to-be. 'I'll be back in a moment.'

She stepped outside the room. 'What's happened?' she asked.

'Jasmine's nursery rang. There's been an accident.'

Rebecca went cold all over. 'What sort of accident?'

'She fell off a climbing frame. She's been sick and she's got a headache. The ambulance is bringing her in to the Emergency Department now.'

Rebecca wrapped one arm round herself, shivering. A fall, and a head injury enough to cause symptoms. Fear flooded through her, worse than the moment when she'd had the call from the Emergency Department about Lucas. She'd gone to the hospital, waited while the team tried desperately to resuscitate him. Supposing this was the same?

Supposing her daughter, too, went to the Emergency Department and never came back?

'I need to go to her,' she said. She dragged in a breath. 'But my patient…'

'I'll get Tan to take over,' Amara said. 'It'll be fine. Jasmine will be fine, too.' She placed a hand on Rebecca's arm. 'You know it's standard procedure to take a little one with symptoms of concussion to be checked over.'

But what if it was more than just concussion? Rebecca knew the statistics: traumatic brain injuries were most common in children aged four and under. *Jasmine's age.*

Please, no.

She couldn't lose her daughter the way she'd lost Lucas, waiting for news in the Emergency Department.

She pulled herself together. Just. 'Thanks, Amara.' On autopilot, she went back into the consulting room. 'I'm sorry, Mrs Fraser. There's been an accident and I need to go to my little girl. One of my colleagues will be in to see you very shortly.' She forced herself to smile reassuringly, then headed for the Emergency Department at a run.

All she could think of was that when she'd kissed her little girl goodbye this morning at nursery it might have been the last time.

Please don't let it have been the last time.

Intellectually, she knew Amara was right: if a small child had a head injury, was sick and complained of a headache, then you would take that child to the Emergency Department to get checked over.

But what if it wasn't just concussion?

Supposing it wasn't the most likely thing that had happened to Jasmine, but the rare thing? They said that lightning didn't strike twice, but that wasn't true. Lucas had died of a head injury. Supposing their daughter did the same? Supposing it was a subdural haematoma?

The nearer she got to the Emergency Department, the more her fears grew, and the more she wished she'd called her parents or her sister to be with her. Most of the time, she could cope with being a single parent; but right now, in the middle of a crisis, she needed someone to lean on. She'd started to think that Nathaniel might be that someone. But then he'd backed away and she realised how wrong she'd been.

The receptionist did a double take when she saw Rebecca in the Emergency Department. 'I'm not used to seeing you this side of the department, Dr Hart. Is everything all right?'

No. It was very far from all right. She tried to stay calm. 'My daughter's on her way in with the paramedics. Jasmine Hart.'

'Hang on, I'll see what's happening.' The receptionist checked on the computer. 'It says here she's just been brought in and she's being assessed. Do you want one of us to take you through?'

Rebecca shook her head. 'Just tell me which bay and I'll find her.' Then she realised how snappy she must have sounded. 'Sorry. Thank you. Sorry, I didn't mean to be rude. My head's all over the place.'

The receptionist's face was kind. 'Don't worry, it's every mum's worst nightmare, being called to hospital for your little one. I hope everything goes OK.'

So did she. *Please, please, let Jasmine be OK.*

'Thank you,' she said.

'She's in Bay Four.' The receptionist buzzed her

through, and Rebecca hurried to Bay Four. Jasmine, looking pale and still, was lying on the bed, and sitting next to her was Bethany French, Jasmine's key worker from the nursery.

'Mummy, my head hurts,' Jasmine whispered.

'I know, baby, but you're safe now,' Rebecca said, holding her hand. 'Everything's going to be fine. I'm here.'

'I'm so sorry,' Bethany said. 'One minute she was on the climbing frame, and the next she was on the floor. It happened so fast.' She bit her lip. 'She was sick, but she wasn't unconscious. We called 999 and when the ambulance came they decided to bring her in. I came with her so she'd have someone she knew with her and wouldn't be scared.'

'Thank you,' Rebecca said. Even though she was terrified, she couldn't let this poor woman think it was all her fault. 'And it wasn't your fault. I know what Jas is like with the climbing frame—she'd be on it all day if she could. It was an accident.'

'The doctor was here a minute ago,' Bethany said. 'You know—oh, she's here now.'

Rebecca glanced at the doctor walking in to the cubicle and almost sagged in relief. It was someone she knew: Hayley Price, one of the consultants, whose oldest child was the same age as Jasmine and went to the same nursery. 'Haze. Hello. Sorry. I'm all over the place.' She shook her head, trying to clear it. 'I'm…'

She'd never been the inarticulate sort, but right now she couldn't think straight. Panic and relief were clashing in her head, drowning everything else out.

'Hi, Rebecca,' Hayley said. 'Obviously you're frantic—anyone would be, in your shoes—but she's doing OK.

We've checked her blood pressure, heart rate and respiration, and they're all fine. Her GCS is fifteen. She can't remember falling off the climbing frame, which as you know is pretty common after a bump to the head, but she didn't lose consciousness. She's got a bit of a bump, but otherwise she's fine. We've checked her pupils and her limb movements, and I'm happy with them, but I want to send her for a CT scan as a precaution because she was sick.'

'Uh-huh.' CT scan. The last CT scan Lucas had had… Fear gripped her again.

'I'm pretty sure it's simple concussion,' Hayley said gently. 'You know we're always cautious with little ones.'

'Thank you.' Rebecca reminded herself to breathe and not spiral back into panic mode.

'Can we call anyone for you?' Hayley asked.

'No. I'll ring my mum myself. But I'd like to be there for the scan.'

'Of course. Though obviously you'll need a lead apron.' Hayley looked at Rebecca. 'And from your own Emergency Department training you know the rules.'

That a parent could go in with their children for a CT scan, unless the mum happened to be pregnant. This was obviously Hayley's way of asking the question without breaching her privacy. 'I do, and it's fine,' Rebecca confirmed.

'Can I come, too?' Bethany asked.

'If that's OK with you, Rebecca?' Hayley asked.

'Yes.' Rebecca thought Bethany could do with some reassurance, plus it would be good to have someone waiting with her. 'I'll call my mum while you take Bethany through the consent and privacy stuff, Hayley,' she said.

She stepped into the corridor and called her mum. Caroline, as always, was unflappable. 'It's probably a precaution. I'll drive over—if she's allowed home, you'll need transport with a child seat.' And Rebecca's parents kept a spare child seat for the car at their house.

'Thanks, Mum.'

'She's going to be fine, Bec. It's not going to be like Lucas,' Caroline added softly. 'I'll be with you soon.'

The CT scan seemed to take for ever, but finally they were back in the Emergency Department, Caroline had arrived, and Rebecca was holding Jasmine's hand and reassuring her.

'Good news. It's clear,' Hayley said when she came back into their cubicle.

Clear. *Not* the subdural haematoma Rebecca had half-convinced herself it was.

Relief flooded through her so fast that, if she hadn't been sitting down, she would've fallen.

'I know you know what to look out for, but it's always different when it's one of your own,' Hayley said, 'so I'm giving you the head injuries leaflet to take home. It's an awful lot easier to look at something written down than to rack your brain to remember your training when it's someone you love who needs care and you're inwardly panicking.'

Rebecca knew that Hayley had already been through a similar nightmare herself, when her firefighter hero husband had been killed. 'Thank you.'

'We'll give her infant paracetamol for the headache, and then you can take her home,' Hayley said. 'Just check her every hour for the next twenty-four hours. Any worries, bring her straight back.'

Rebecca nodded. 'Will do. And thank you.'

'I'll drop you back at the nursery on the way back to Rebecca's,' Caroline said.

'Thank you. They'll all be so glad to know Jasmine's all right,' Bethany said.

Rebecca called her boss to arrange to take off the next week as unpaid parental leave, then carried Jasmine to her mother's car.

Nathaniel hadn't been looking forward to his afternoon shift, as he knew Rebecca was the one he'd have to call if there were any problems on the labour ward. It would be the first time they'd be in the same room since they'd split up, and it was going to be really awkward. But when he went to the office about a baby whose tocography results concerned him, he saw Tanvir at the desk.

It looked as if Rebecca had changed the rota so she could avoid him. Not that he blamed her.

'Tan, can I ask you to come and check one of my mums? I'm not happy with the baby's heart rate.'

'Sure,' Tanvir said.

'I thought Rebecca was on this afternoon.' The words were out before he could stop them.

'She was. Didn't you hear?'

Nathaniel frowned. 'Hear what?'

'Amara took the call. Jasmine had an accident at nursery and she was brought into the Emergency Department.'

Nathaniel stared at Tanvir in horror. Having that sort of call would be a nightmare for any parent, but it would be even more of a nightmare for someone in Rebecca's shoes—someone whose husband had died in the Emergency Department after an accident. Rebecca must be worried sick.

'Is Jasmine OK?'

'I don't know,' Tanvir said. 'Though I do know Rebecca's off for the next week on parental leave.'

So it was serious.

Nathaniel's first instinct was to drop everything and go to Rebecca—to be there for her, support her emotionally as well as practically.

And then it hit him.

He loved her.

He loved Jasmine, too, and he wanted to be a family with them. And, even though he'd convinced himself that he wouldn't be enough for Rebecca, he realised that actually he *could* be. From what she'd let slip, he was pretty sure that Lucas would've found excuses to avoid sitting with a sick child or making his wife dinner while she sat with Jasmine; but Nathaniel could do all that.

More than that, he *wanted* to do it. He wanted to be with her. Needed to be with her.

Somehow he got through to the end of his shift—the baby still hadn't made an appearance, but the tocograph showed that his heartbeat was stable and Nathaniel was happy to hand over to the midwife on the next shift.

At the hospital entrance, he stopped at the shop for long enough to buy something for Jasmine and flowers for Rebecca, then headed straight to Rebecca's house.

When the doorbell rang, Rebecca answered the door and was shocked to see Nathaniel standing there.

'Tan told me what happened to Jasmine,' he said in answer to the question that filled her head but wouldn't come out of her mouth. 'How is she?'

'OK,' she answered warily.

'And how are *you*?'

She lifted her chin. 'I'm fine.'

'Are you?' he asked softly. 'You got a call to go to the Emergency Department, for someone you love very much. It must've brought back a lot of tough memories for you.'

It had. 'I'm fine,' she said again.

His expression said that he didn't believe her, but she wasn't going to rely on him for support. He'd made it clear that he didn't want her, and she didn't need his pity.

'I got these for you.' He handed her a gorgeous bunch of flowers.

'Thank you,' she said automatically. She remembered the last time he'd done that—the evening when she'd had a shift that reduced her to tears. When he'd been kind and thoughtful and supportive.

But he'd shown his true colours the day she'd helped deliver his sister's baby. The day he'd dumped her. By *text*. A man who didn't want commitment.

This time, she spoke the question aloud. 'What are you doing here, Nathaniel?'

'I wanted to see you. I was concerned about you and Jasmine.'

Concerned? He hadn't been that concerned about them when he'd sent her that cool, curt text. 'There's no need,' she said stiffly. 'We're fine.'

He huffed out a breath. 'I know I'm an idiot and I did something very, *very* stupid last week. I wouldn't blame you if you never spoke to me again. I know I don't deserve it, but please would you hear me out?'

Part of her wanted to tell him to get lost, but she was too tired to argue. 'Come into the kitchen. Jasmine's asleep in the living room.' Though she was still hurt and angry enough with him not to offer him a drink.

He followed her into the kitchen and she used the excuse of putting the flowers in water not to look at him.

'I brought Jasmine a present.'

A shiny, glittery pink bag that Rebecca knew her daughter would be instantly attracted to.

'It's a penguin.'

Her favourite animal. He'd clearly remembered that from their day on the river. And she really couldn't work him out. Was Nathaniel Jones a kind, lovely man; or was he a cold-hearted, callous bastard?

'Thank you, but she doesn't need presents.' It was just the sort of thing Lucas had always done, letting her down and then buying her a flashy present to make up for it and promising not to do whatever it was again, when they both knew that of course it would happen again. Presents weren't important. Being there for someone was what really mattered. And Nathaniel had proved to her that he wasn't reliable.

'I'm sorry. What I did was wrong. I didn't mean to hurt you.'

'But you did hurt me,' she said. 'I thought we were getting on fine. We'd dated. I'd met your family. You'd met some of mine. We had *sex*, for pity's sake.'

He flushed. 'Yeah.'

'I don't sleep around, Nathaniel. That night meant something to me.'

'It meant something to me, too.'

'Really? Because, if it did, why did you dump me with no warning?' That wasn't the only thing that rankled. 'And we delivered your sister's baby together. You didn't even tell me how they were.'

'I'm sorry. They're doing brilliantly, really settled into being a family. Delilah's put on weight and Charlotte's blooming.' He grimaced. 'As for your next question—I'm an idiot. A mess. We *were* getting on fine. I was looking forward to meeting your family.'

'So *why* did you dump me?' Hurt made her voice sharp.

'Because I panicked. We'd just delivered Delilah. I looked at Charlotte and Robyn, and I thought about what it must be like to be a new parent, how amazing it must be.'

'And that was your cue to dump me? How?' She shook her head. 'And you didn't even do it in person.'

'I texted you. I know. Which is about the worst way anyone could break off a relationship. I'm so sorry I hurt you.' He took a deep breath. 'I panicked. I thought about how I'd been looking forward to getting married and starting a family—and then the accident happened and I found out the hard way that I wasn't enough for Angela. And then it made me wonder: how could I know that I'd be enough for you?'

That was exactly how she'd felt after her marriage had started to crumble. If Lucas hadn't had the accident, Rebecca knew she wouldn't still be married to him because she hadn't been enough for him. She'd have tried her hardest to make it work, but deep down she knew she wouldn't have been enough.

'You could have talked to me about it,' she said.

'That's exactly what I should've done,' he replied. 'But the more I thought about it, the more I tried to work out what to say, the worse it got and the more I panicked. So I thought the fairest thing to do would be to end it.' He closed his eyes briefly. 'Stupid.'

'Yeah.'

'I was sitting in the waiting room while the midwife

was checking them over. Everywhere around me I could see families—everything I wanted. And this voice in my head reminded me that I wasn't enough for Angela—and back then I'd been in a senior role as a site manager. How can I be enough for you now, when I'm only a junior midwife and you're a senior doctor?'

She stared at him. 'You seriously think I'm that shallow? That I'm worried about how junior or senior you are?'

'No. That's not what I mean. You're not shallow at all.' He took a deep breath. 'I just feel like a fraud. I haven't had a serious relationship since Angie.'

'Because you can't commit.'

'Because I haven't *wanted* to commit,' he said. 'Until you.'

She stared at him. Could she believe him?

'I know it's a big ask,' he said, 'but would you give me a second chance?'

'I come as a package. I can't take chances.' She shook her head. 'I opened my heart to you—I let you into my life, into Jasmine's life—and then you dumped me without any warning. It's like Lucas all over again, happy with the thrill of the chase and then losing interest,' she said. 'And that's not what I want—for me or for Jasmine. What if I give you a second chance and you change your mind and back away from us again?'

'I won't,' he said.

'How can you be so sure?'

'Because,' he said, 'today I heard about Jasmine's accident, and all I wanted to do was to come and find you, be right by your side and support you both through this. It made me realise what an idiot I was being—and that I really want to be a family with you and Jasmine. I love being a godfather, I know I'm going to love being an uncle—and I really, really want to be a dad.'

Something she might not be able to give him. He was worried he wasn't enough for her—but would she be enough for him? It was too important to leave this for later. She had to face the issue. Now.

'Do you mean you want a baby of your own? Because that,' she said, 'might be a problem. I told you about my ectopic pregnancy. What if I have another and lose my other fallopian tube? What if I can't give you children?'

He looked at her, his dark eyes brooding as he thought about it. 'We'll have Jasmine—and I hope in time she'll come to regard me as her dad. I'd never do anything to push Lucas's family out, but I want to be there for Jasmine. And I believe there's more to being a parent than just biology. I want to be your partner and Jasmine's dad. If we're lucky enough to have more children, that'd be wonderful. If not, then we'll still be a family. Just the three of us. Or we could consider fostering or adoption. Families come in all shapes and sizes.'

He wanted to be her partner and Jasmine's dad.

'I want to believe you,' she said. 'I really want to. But.' Could she really trust him? She couldn't quite bring herself to ask the question, knowing how barbed it was.

'I don't blame you for being wary,' he said. 'You had a rough time with your first marriage, just as I had a rough time with my ex. I find it hard to trust, so I'm guessing you do as well—and I've already let you down once.'

Yes. He had.

'After Angela, I never wanted to get involved with anyone again. And then I met you. I tried to think about you as just a colleague—but everything changed, the moment you kissed me after the abseil. I realised I was falling for you.' He gave her a wry smile. 'You're the first of my girlfriends since the accident who's met my family. And you fitted in, Rebecca. The way you were with them made me think that I'd fit with your family, too.'

'You would,' she admitted. 'Our families are very similar.' And whereas Lucas hadn't had the patience to spend time with her family—or his own—she'd thought Nathaniel was different. A family man. He'd already shown her that, the day they'd spent on the river.

'So give me a chance to prove I won't let you down again.' He paused. 'Just so we're clear on this, you're enough for me.'

'You're trying to tell me you're not Lucas,' she said. 'In some ways, you're not. You don't have that restlessness and you pay attention. You notice things. You talk to people because you're interested in them, not because you're trying to work the room.' She dragged in a breath. 'But there are some ways where you *are* like Lucas. You're charming. People like you. And if I let myself admit that I love you, I'm scared it's all going to go wrong, just like it did last time. That you'll change. That… That you'll let me down and I'll still be alone but with a broken heart on top of it.'

If I let myself admit that I love you…

The words gave him hope.

She loved him, but she was as scared as he'd been. And no wonder—because he'd already let her down. So now all he could do was tell her exactly what was in his heart. 'I fell in love with you weeks ago. When you were standing on the edge of a building, really scared, but you were going to do it because you'd made a commitment and you don't back down. You see things through.' He waited a beat. 'And so do I. I love you, Rebecca Hart, and I want to be a family with you and Jasmine. I want family afternoons in the park and at the beach and in the garden. I want to bake brownies for school fundraisers. I want to do my share of the nursery run and the sleepless nights and mopping up—just as I want my share of cuddles and home-made cards and bedtime stories. I want family barbecues where your dad and mine spend hours sorting out the music together, and reminiscing, and having a competition to see who can tell the most terrible jokes. And, most of all, I want you. I want to wake up every morning with you in my arms and know that it's going to be a good day because you're the first thing I see.'

He'd opened his heart and told her how he felt. He couldn't do any more. He just had to hope that he would be enough for her.

All he could do now was wait.

Nathaniel loved her.

Rebecca thought about it.

He wanted to be a family with her and Jasmine.

He wanted to wake up with her every morning.

He wanted to take his share of the tough stuff as well as the fun stuff; he was under no illusions that being a parent was easy, and he was prepared to put in the work.

If she let herself believe him, if she trusted him and said yes, she wouldn't be repeating her mistake with Lucas. She could go into this with her eyes wide open. The light-hearted, charming midwife who made the world a brighter place—and who'd still be there when things were difficult. He'd been there when she'd had a rough day and made her feel better. Yes, he'd hurt her, but he regretted it and she really believed he wouldn't do it again. Because she understood now why he'd backed away: she had the same fears for not being enough for someone.

He wasn't sweeping her off her feet; he was standing beside her, an equal partner.

And he'd made it clear that she was what he wanted. That she'd be enough for him. And she knew he was enough for her.

'You love me. You want to be a family with me and Jasmine,' she checked, just to be sure.

'I do.'

His beautiful dark eyes were wary. He'd taken a risk. Trusted her with his heart. And, even though he'd got it wrong, he'd admitted it and taken the blame squarely.

That gave her courage to trust him with her heart, too. 'That's what I want,' she said. 'You. Our family. Everything.' She took a deep breath. 'I love you.'

And it was as if the sun had come out from behind thick clouds. He stood up and wrapped her in his arms. 'I love you, too. And our family. For ever.'

EPILOGUE

One year later

'READY?' SASKIA MADE a last-minute adjustment to Rebecca's veil. 'Perfect.' She bent down to the two smaller bridesmaids' level; Jasmine and Nathaniel's goddaughter had hit it off from their first meeting and were both thrilled to be bridesmaids. They were even more thrilled that they'd been allowed to choose their dresses, and that they'd chosen the same ones. 'You look lovely, too.'

'So do you, Aunty Sas,' Jasmine said. 'And Mummy looks like a princess.'

'She certainly does. Come on, girls. Let's give her a moment.'

'Are you sure you're ready for this?' Caroline asked.

'I'm sure, Mum.' Rebecca hugged her mother. 'This is going to be the perfect day. Our families, really joined. For ever.'

'You look radiant,' Caroline said. 'And not just bridal radiance.'

'Second trimester radiance,' Rebecca said with a grin. She and Nathaniel had had a few days of worry when they'd realised she'd fallen pregnant, but the early scan had reassured them that it wasn't an ectopic pregnancy, this time round. 'Nathaniel's still finding books to persuade Jas that she won't mind if she ends up with a little brother rather than a sister.'

'The cars are here, Bec!' Saskia called from downstairs.

It felt like the blink of an eye between settling the girls in the car and arriving at the register office. Then finally she was walking down the red carpet towards Nathaniel on her father's arm, Saskia and the girls following her, and Nathaniel's dad singing 'Happy Together' and playing an acoustic guitar.

The room was full to brimming with their closest family and friends. Nathaniel was there waiting for her, his face lit with sheer joy. Rebecca turned round to her bridesmaids and gave them a wink as Mark launched into the chorus of the song, signalling that now was the time to do what they'd been practising for weeks—and then together the bridal party danced and sang their way down the aisle to Nathaniel.

His dark eyes glittered with love and happiness as she drew nearer. All that worrying that they wouldn't be enough for each other: this last year had proved to them both that they were definitely enough. After the accident, Nathaniel had done his share of checking on Jasmine every hour until she'd recovered from her fall, and he'd been there in the park to encourage her to overcome her fears and climb on the bars again, making sure she was safe.

Over the months, Nathaniel had been there for bedtime stories, the school nativity play and Sports Day. He'd been there when Jasmine had woken from a nightmare or been laid low with a bug. And Jasmine had shyly asked him of her own accord if she could call him Daddy.

Leo had adjusted happily to moving from Nathaniel's flat to Rebecca's house, and he spent as much time curled on Rebecca's lap as he did on Nathaniel's.

Nathaniel bought flowers with Jasmine for Rebecca every Friday evening and made her mugs of tea exactly how she liked them; Rebecca had learned from Jason's mum how to cook Nathaniel's favourite dishes, and she'd become close to his sister and parents.

Their lonely struggles had turned into a warm, close, loving family—for both of them.

As she reached him in front of the registrar, Nathaniel greeted her with a kiss. 'My beautiful bride. My for ever family. I love you,' he said.

'I love you, too,' she replied, and the registrar began the service.

* * * * *

A NURSE, A SURGEON, A CHRISTMAS ENGAGEMENT

ALLIE KINCHELOE

MILLS & BOON

To all the brave doctors, nurses,
and other medical personnel who risk it all each day.
You've inspired me.

CHAPTER ONE

SCALPEL IN HAND, Dr. Dexter Henry made his initial cut through the abdomen of his patient. As the skin parted, the ringtone he reserved for his mother began to play. His muscles tightened with dread, but before he could open his mouth to tell the nurse handling messages to ignore that one, she read it.

Out loud.

Where everyone in the operating room could hear.

"Dr. Henry, your mother is texting. It says: The Wicked Witch of Westfield will be riding her broom back into town for your brother's wedding. Thought you should know ahead of time. How would you like me to reply?"

Hand frozen over the fresh incision, Dex struggled to maintain focus. The synapses in his brain blasted off like a Fourth of July fireworks display. Jessie had finally resurfaced. For some time now, Dex had managed to put the woman who'd quite literally left him standing at the altar out of his mind. Hearing that she'd returned opened a Pandora's box of memories he'd rather not relive.

Heart beating faster, negative thoughts flashed by one by one like an old film strip in his mind showing him the low points in his relationship with Jessie. It took more effort than he wanted to admit to shove down the moment of panic temporarily overwhelming him. Surgeons with a patient's life in their hands could not afford to let their minds drift off in the middle of a procedure to times—and women—best left forgotten.

"Dr. Henry?" the nurse questioned.

"No reply yet. I'll take care of it when I'm finished here." Dex sighed. Why couldn't his mother have waited until he was out of surgery to text that information?

"Well, now I'm even more curious," the nurse said as she laid his phone back down. "Is there more to you than we know, Dr. Henry?"

Ignoring her question, Dex said, "Suction, please. I need better visualization."

While Dex was trying to put the text and the woman in question out of his mind, the overly eager young resident couldn't seem to let the matter drop. Practically a prodigy when it came to medicine and surgery, the young man had no people skills, and his bedside manner needed work. With his lack of ability to read people squarely on display, the resident pushed for more information despite how Dex had clearly tried to shut the topic down. "Oh, come on, Dr. Henry, you can't leave us hanging like that! Who is the Wicked Witch? Where is Westfield? And most intriguingly, why is it important that you know she's coming to the wedding?"

As the words left the resident's lips, everyone in the room seemed to nod in unison. A chorus of "Mmm-hmm" and "That's right" followed.

Dex closed his eyes briefly. While snapping at the doctor in training might make him feel better temporarily, it certainly wouldn't help this uncomfortable situation. Finally, he decided to give them a very clipped version of his past while keeping his tone ice-cold to discourage further discussion. Still, his secrets would be on the lips of every nurse and carried through the entire hospital on excited whispers by the end of the day. Gossip traveled through a hospital faster than a virus, and he'd rather it be the truth than let them draw their own conclusions from his mother's words.

"Her real name is Jessie. And it's important because she hasn't been back to our hometown since she disappeared on our wedding day."

Only the blips on the monitors and the occasional rustle of paper broke the silence in the OR. The familiar noises seeped into his soul, and he let them soothe the ragged edges that voicing his secrets had exposed. The quiet should have been unnerving, considering everyone in the OR was currently contemplating his confession, but instead he found it comforting. When the silence continued, Dex put his head down and got back to work.

"You know, if you need a date, all you have to do is ask," Belinda finally spoke up.

Who else would make such an offer? Her support brought a smile to his face. Fifteen years his senior, Belinda had taken him under her wing when he'd first arrived at Metro Memorial Hospital with the cocky greenness of residency still permeating his every interaction. She'd taken him down a notch or two. There was no one else at the hospital who he respected more.

"Ah, but, Belinda, I'm already in love with you. Taking you back home to Westfield would just tempt me for things I know I can't have." He winked at the older woman. He didn't worry that his favorite scrub nurse would misunderstand his flirty words as an actual come-on. They didn't have that kind of relationship, just a teasing dynamic that allowed them both to let their guards down with each other.

Belinda stared at him over her mask. "If she's coming, then you need a date."

"It's you or no one, B." Even as the words slipped past his lips, the truth in her words sank in. He did need someone to go home with him for the wedding. Not Belinda, but someone to get his mother off his back. From the moment his brother Tommy had announced to the world that Jill had accepted his proposal, their mother had been on a one-woman mission to find Dex a new love.

His grip tightened around the scalpel in his hand. He'd rather stab himself with it than give Westfield something else to gossip about. He had only been home once since his ill-fated trip to the altar, and it had been awkward to say the least. In a single week at home, his mom had stuck every single woman in town under the age of forty in his path in hopes that he'd finally move on from Jessie. Awkward? Nah… What could be awkward about a parade of women he wasn't remotely interested in?

He had, though.

Moved on, that is. Even if his mother was having trouble believing that.

He dated. Quite frequently, even. But no one seriously enough to bring home. He only dated to have a little adult companionship on occasion. A physical release, not an emotional connection. No risk for either party. In fact, he told anyone he dated from day one just what he was willing to give, and he always made sure to end things before anyone got hurt. None of the women he'd dated recently would work for this half-hatched plan, either.

He wouldn't want to lead someone on, after all. Taking someone home for a family wedding during the holidays implied so many emotions that Dex almost shuddered in revulsion at the thought. Asking a woman to be his date to a family wedding at Christmas implied that a box with a diamond ring sat under the tree. And he'd never take that step again.

No, he planned to stay single forever. He had zero interest in long-term commitment, and he'd hesitate to do anything that might give any impression otherwise. After his trip down Matrimony Lane had dead-ended with him standing at the altar alone, his entire hometown watching as he got dumped from afar, Dex could live the rest of his life without putting himself into that sort of situation again.

"Taking a date would save me from more than a few matchmaking attempts and a fair bit of pointed stares. But finding someone on such short notice would be nearly impossible. It's a Christmas wedding," he added aloud, his thoughts running with how much more difficult the timing made things.

Getting someone to pretend to be his new girlfriend in June would have been easy. He'd just spring for a few days at a luxury beach resort and voilà, instant girlfriend. But with the wedding planned for the holidays, it made it ten times trickier to find someone to go along with a fake relationship scheme.

"Ah…so you need someone to go home with you, pretend to like you, and for the holidays no less. That will be hard to find." Lena's green eyes sparkled and he thought he might be able to see a hint of a smile behind her mask. "Who would have thought that a handsome young surgeon would have to resort to a fake Christmas girlfriend?"

"Are you volunteering?" He eyed Lena. She would

be perfect. Just his type—long brown hair, more than a few curves and enough sass to keep him on his toes. And even more, Lena intrigued him.

He'd actually asked her out when she'd first started working at the hospital a few months back and she'd turned him down cold. Women didn't tend to ignore him or say no to him. If anything, they usually came to him, leaving him to be the one to let them down easy. But not Lena. She'd looked him up and down, shook her head and said, "I'd rather empty bedpans." Ever since that day, she'd dodged him outside a surgical suite whenever she could.

When she didn't immediately answer, Dex returned his gaze to his patient. "Can I get more suction?"

For the next while, Dex gave his patient and the surgery his full attention. He ensured the patient was taken care of before he returned his attention to Lena.

Making eye contact with her, he murmured, "You never answered me."

Word around the hospital called Lena an ice queen—a brilliant and reliable nurse, but cold and limited in her friendship. He didn't know her story, had no clue why she had icicles in her eyes, but she'd certainly frozen him out. In his eyes, that made her a perfect candidate for a fake girlfriend. She'd never want or expect a proposal under the mistletoe.

Lena tilted her head and stared at him for a moment, her eyes seeming to reach deep into his soul as she considered his question. Scrutinizing him for some time, she finally asked, "How close to Christmas is it?"

"Christmas Eve." He rolled his eyes. "My future sister-in-law is a nut for Christmas. I think she'd have gone with Christmas Day if the pastor at the church would have allowed it."

The smallest laugh came from Lena at his words. "Is she really that bad?"

"You have no idea." Jill lived and breathed Christmas year-round. It had come as no surprise to anyone in the family when the wedding date had been declared as Christmas Eve. No one had blinked an eye since it had been expected from the moment she'd said yes to his brother's proposal. "When you meet her, you'll see."

"When I meet her… When?" She raised an eyebrow and he had to actively force himself not to flinch under the intensity of her gaze. "You're awfully sure of yourself, aren't you? I haven't agreed to anything yet."

"Wishful thinking?" He flashed her a hopeful smile. "It would really help me out."

"Are you willing to return the favor? I have a…thing in Los Angeles on New Year's Eve that would go much more smoothly for me if I had a successful surgeon at my side."

"Are we talking New Year's Eve party or decapitating the one who wronged you?"

Hearty peals of laughter rang out at his dark joke, and an awareness shot up in him like he'd been injected. He shook it off and focused on her words.

"The former. I might have to take you up on the latter, though. It's a fundraiser gala, black tie, of course. My father runs a hospital out there, and lately my mother spends her time doing his bidding and raising money for various charities. If I tell them I'm coming alone, it will be, uh, very strongly suggested that I take my father's current protégé as my date. And if there's anything I want less than attending this gala in the first place, it's attending it with *that* guy."

"Well, I do happen to own a tux. I suppose we should coordinate the details sometime before then." The dark-haired surgeon glanced over at her, and she thought he might be smiling beneath his mask. "It wouldn't be good if my fake Christmas girlfriend missed the wedding because I didn't give her the right directions."

Thank god for surgical masks that hid the blushes that her body seemed determined to produce any time he glanced her way. What was wrong with her? The man made her crazy. She couldn't be in the same room with him without wanting to strangle him, so why did she find herself glancing in his direction every few minutes and growing warm whenever their eyes met?

"So, who here is skipping the hospital Christmas party on Saturday?" the anesthesiologist asked. "I'm on call so I'll have to be here even though I hate the Secret Santa crap. Who needs another Christmas candle or a gift card in a lesser denomination than you brought? Or worse, a polo shirt that's three sizes too large, like I got last year."

"I'm skipping it," Lena and Dex said at the same time.

"Ooh… You two have a hot date?"

"No." Again, they spoke at the same time. Dex looked over at her and their gazes locked over the patient. A hint of amusement crinkled the laugh lines at the corners of his eyes.

When she met his eyes, though, her heart grew erratic. Dr. Dexter Henry had eyes a woman could spend the rest of her life lost in, with thick, dark lashes that framed them perfectly. But more than being captivating, those eyes held a level of emotion Lena wasn't used to seeing. A hint of mirth sparkled over his little joke, but behind that lingered a shadow. Had the ex-fiancée put the darkness in his gaze? And what would it take to banish the ghosts of his past and brighten his eyes back to their true brilliance?

"Uh-huh." The anesthesiologist laughed. "It would be more convincing if the pair of you weren't sneaking heated glances at each other every few seconds and practically finishing each other's sentences."

Lena shook her head, unable to form words at that moment. If other people were noticing, she must have been looking at Dex far more than she'd realized. Embarrassed tears welled up in her eyes and she blinked rapidly, determined to keep them from spilling over. *Crap.*

Gossip had been the motivating force behind her leaving LA, and she'd been in Nashville less than six months before finding herself right back in the middle of it. The one-year contract was supposed to give her the breathing room she needed to decide what to do with her life. Nashville had started to feel like home. Despite its lack of sand and ocean views, she could see herself making a life there. Away from California and her overbearing parents. She'd found a calm in Tennessee, but the anxiety and fears that the fresh start had quelled came rolling back in with a vengeance when she found herself the topic of conversation again. She swallowed hard. She hoped no one noticed the big, shaky breath she took while trying to gain control over her emotions.

"Leave it alone, Jason," Dex warned, his voice low and firm. "Worry about our patient, not my personal life."

"Come on, Dex, I'm just having a little fun. Don't get your scrubs in a knot."

"It's not fun for me, and I don't think it's fun for Lena. So knock it off."

An inexplicable urge to hug him rose up, and she had to squash it before she made an even bigger fool of herself. Past experience had taught her that men got close to her for one reason—to get close to her father for his connections in the medical field. She had never had a guy stand up for her just for her own sake, and it gave her this warm, fuzzy feeling deep down inside.

She tried to avoid looking at him and only spoke when necessary while they finished up the gallbladder removal. The puzzle of how Dex benefited from standing up for her rolled around in her mind unsolved.

The more she'd thought about it, the more she worried there was too much at risk. And she was the one who stood to be hurt. She'd been told how he'd dated half the nursing staff. A doctor could do that, though, whereas a nurse could not. She needed to put a stop to this before they reached a point of no return.

After surgery, she found herself alone in the scrub room with Dex. They washed up next to each other without speaking. She dried her hands and stepped away.

Lena took a deep breath and glanced at the door. She should really make her escape before she got sucked deeper into this ill-fated charade and the man at the center of it. Something about Dex had drawn her like a moth to a flame when she'd moved to Nashville. Handsome, of course, charismatic even, but something more about the young surgeon called to her. A confidence in his gaze that pulled her in like gravity and made spending time with him a risky endeavor.

After one surgery with him where she'd had to stand tucked at his side, arms brushing as they moved for several hours, she'd known they'd be physically compatible if nothing else, so when he'd asked her out, she'd shut him down hard. Getting involved with him was a risk that she just was not willing to take.

She'd heard the rumors about him. According to hospital gossip, Dr. Dexter Henry got around. His motto seemed to be love them good and leave them quick. His type was *exactly* why she'd uprooted her career and moved across the freaking country, after all. She'd fallen for the playboy once and still had the scars on her soul as souvenirs. Swallowing hard, she pushed those thoughts to the far recesses of her mind.

Lena couldn't take the risk of real involvement. Not after the things she'd seen when a relationship went wrong. So despite the surface-level attraction she felt to Dex, she'd never let it become more. Ever. After the fallout that had followed when the truth about her relationship with Connor had surfaced, Lena's entire foundation had been shaken. Her career had nearly collapsed back in California. The negativity had invaded all aspects of her life and convinced Lena to stay single for the rest of her life. Unfortunately, her parents were not on board with Lena's plan for an eternity of lone wolf status.

Statement of fact—she needed a good-looking, successful doctor to go home with her. Bringing home a date who looked like Dex might be the only chance she had of getting her parents off her back when it came to dating Martin. They'd been pushing that angle since about ten minutes after the scandal about Connor broke, and she'd love to avoid it if she could. Her dad had deemed his protégé to be perfect son-in-law material, while Lena herself would rather gnaw her own arm off than to marry, or even date, that balding schmuck with his fake tan. Her mother wanted her to settle down with Martin because it would force Lena to return to LA because of his career.

Dex presented a nearly perfect solution to the Martin situation. With just one problem…

"I'm not sure how nosy your family will be, and maybe with the wedding taking some of the focus off, we can get by with your family easily, but my family will expect me to know you if we are dating. Really know you. I don't bring a lot of guys home, so—"

"What do I need to know?" Dex interrupted her to ask.

Visions of Dex being the guy to make Martin disappear and get her parents off her back vanished with the delivery of that single question. As the only daughter of William Franklin, an egotistical plastic surgeon turned hospital administrator who thought himself better than every female in his acquaintance, Lena had spent much of her life being treated like her voice was nonexistent. Connor had been the same, but she'd been so stupidly in love with him that she'd overlooked his every fault. It wasn't until they'd broken up that she'd decided she'd never voluntarily spend time with a man who didn't have enough respect for her to allow her to finish speaking again, and she didn't plan to change her mind now. Even if Dex was the most likely candidate for helping her to avoid her parents' attempts at marrying her off.

"First of all, I absolutely cannot stand being interrupted like that. So if you aren't going to let me speak or if you are going to insist on talking over me, then we should both find someone else." Lena's eyes narrowed as she glared at him. With her fists balled at her sides, she added through clenched teeth, "You will be respectful enough of me to wait until I have finished my sentence or you can try your best to find another woman willing to pretend to be your girlfriend for this wedding, are we clear?"

Satisfaction rushed over her when Dex gaped at her for a moment. "Yeah, I'm sorry."

Lena's head moved side to side dismissively. "Why do guys do that? Do you even *realize* that you do that?"

"I'll try to be more mindful."

Tiny little wrinkles appeared on his forehead as he seemed to sink down into his thoughts. They made Lena wonder if anyone had ever pointed out to him that he talked over them. Or maybe she had merely projected some of her frustrations onto him. Either way, she kind of liked seeing that she'd gotten his attention. It had made him think at least a little about how he treated women. She'd never managed to accomplish that with her father or Connor.

"Okay, so as I was saying," she continued. "I don't bring a lot of guys home. My parents will assume that we are fairly serious if I have brought you home for the gala. Because of that, they will expect that you know things about me, things a dating couple would know. More than we can cram into a couple of plane rides. The best I'll be able to tell my family is that you are right-handed but prefer to keep your tools on the left for some unknown reason and that your favorite sandwich seems to be the turkey club since you've had it three times a week since we met. We need to spend some time together and learn these things."

"Are you asking me on a date, Lena?" The confusion on his face had cleared. In its place sat a self-satisfied smirk.

And there it was.

That unbearable arrogance that all the surgeons she'd

ever met possessed. Her father had it in spades. Connor had thought far too much of himself too.

Was it issued to them along with their medical license?

"Ugh!" Her hands flew up in irritation. "Why did I ever entertain this idea?"

Annoyance flashed through her, white-hot and simmering on the cusp of anger. Dexter Henry made her crazier than anyone had in a long time.

"Because you know we'd be perfectly suited to take care of each other's needs." Not a question. There was an undercurrent to his words that took that phrase from simple statement to sensual promise. His gaze moved over her body before he made eye contact once more, making her one thousand percent certain that he'd meant his words to have multiple meanings.

Her skin heated under the scrutiny of his gaze and she swallowed hard.

She couldn't do this.

No way. She could not spend two weeks with an arrogant man who changed women more than a lot of nurses changed their scrubs, but worst of all, made her want him to take off his scrubs and see if he could live up to the masculine sexuality he projected. Even if he won in every category when compared to Martin—better hair, nicer smile, sexier… Nope, she wasn't going continue that line of thought. Shaking her head, Lena took a step back.

"This is a bad idea."

Or a very good one...

"Hear me out before you reject the idea entirely."

She waited for him to speak, crossing her arms over her chest. He'd need a good pitch to get her sold on this idea. He was far too much temptation for her otherwise.

"We both need a significant other to get us through the

holidays unscathed by the cupid wannabes in our families, right?" He raised an eyebrow and waited for her to nod before he explained, "As far as I can see, neither of us has another solid lead on that."

"Having you with me would help me avoid yet another matchmaking attempt." She sighed. "Like I said, though, my family will expect us to know things that dating couples would know."

Not having to be partnered with Martin for another fundraiser would save her feet a great deal of pain, though. Her parents had insisted that she attend a gala with him at the local children's museum. The clumsy plastic surgeon not only had two left feet, but a complete inability to recognize his lack of skills. He'd nearly crippled her before she'd thought of a plausible excuse to leave early. But dancing with Dex would be dangerous for other reasons. She wasn't sure she could keep her distance from him if she had to step into his arms. And getting close meant risk. Her goal was to get through the New Year's Eve gala with as little risk as possible.

"So, we tell them that we only met a few months ago, which is the honest truth, but then tell them we started dating fairly recently but things are getting serious fast. That will help us with the not knowing enough details about each other. No one will expect us to know everything there is to know after only a couple months of dating."

"I don't know." She chewed on her lower lip. Dex's plan made a lot of sense, but she worried about spending so much time with him.

"Come on," Dex coaxed, his voice lowering as he tried to sway her decision. "What do you say? You go to the wedding with me, I'll go to the gala with you, and then we conveniently break up a few weeks into the new year. No one in either family is the wiser for it."

"Okay," she found herself saying. She almost couldn't believe she would be taking a man home to meet her parents that she'd barely had a conversation with. Remembering how her dad had grilled Connor the first time she'd brought him home, Lena shuddered. "There may be a pop quiz, though."

Not that her father's interrogation had sidetracked Connor's plans... He sold himself to her father with the same charisma he'd used to charm her. Lena had fallen for him quickly and her parents had been just as taken. It was only once Connor had gotten what he'd wanted—her father's influence to gain a promotion—that his true colors began to show.

"Luckily, I'm a good test taker." Dex winked at her, causing her stupid heart to somersault inside her chest.

Dex Henry is not datable. She repeated the little mantra to herself. *Dex Henry is not datable.*

"This isn't a joke." Lena put her hands on her hips and frowned at him. She tried to focus on the frustration she felt for Dex, not the attraction, but the hint of a smile that played on his lips distracted her more than she wanted to admit even to herself. "I don't know why I'm agreeing to this if you aren't going to take this seriously."

"I'm very serious, Lena. You know what? I think I'm going to have them leave you on my service through Christmas. It will keep us together during the days and give us some legitimate things to talk about. The fewer lies we have to keep straight, the better, right?"

"True." He certainly had a point on keeping things as close to the truth as possible.

"How about some dinner? We can discuss the finer points of our agreement." He raised a brow in question.

She shook her head. "No, if we are doing this, we are keeping it quiet around here. I do not want to be counted as the next notch on your well-whittled bedpost."

"Okay then. I've got patients to check on." He looked a little hurt by the brusqueness in her words, but recovered quickly. He stepped past her without another word.

CHAPTER TWO

"GOOD AFTERNOON, MR. CLEMONS." Lena moved into a patient's room, pushing a medication cart. "Looks like you should get to go home later today, according to your notes. I've got your afternoon meds, and if everything goes okay for the next couple hours, you are out of here."

The old man in the hospital bed perked up at her voice. "Ah, but my beautiful Lena, when I go home, I won't have anything so lovely to look at as your smiling face."

"Flattery will get you everywhere. You want an extra Jell-O? Some ice cream? I'm your girl." She smiled at the patient as she scanned his wrist band for the medications. "Now, here are your meds. I have a painkiller and an antibiotic."

His age-spotted hand shook as he took the tiny cup. "Ice cream does sound good."

"Take your meds first and I'll get you some in just a few." She watched as he tossed the pills into his mouth and chased them with some water from a Styrofoam cup. She made a note that he had taken the medications. "Chocolate or vanilla?"

"I've always been partial to chocolate. Are you married, my love?"

"I'm not, never found a man like you." She patted

his arm. His chart said he was single. "What about you? Ever married?"

"No, I never did. I came close once, probably quite a few years before you were born, but..." He trailed off. He shook his head and a wistful look came into his eyes. "Eh, you don't want to hear this old man's tales of woe and despair."

Lena pulled up a chair. "If you want to tell me, I do."

She'd learned years ago that sometimes the most important thing a nurse could do for a patient was to listen to them. Even if it didn't seem relevant to their current condition, or medically related at all, the act of engaging in a meaningful conversation created a bond, a trust, that encouraged the patient to be honest. And that was most certainly relevant.

"It was a long time ago. Her name was Betty. She had blond hair and the prettiest smile I've ever seen—I'm sorry, my love, but even prettier than yours—and after our first date I knew that she was the only woman I'd ever give my heart to. After our third date, I bought an engagement ring. That was two weeks to the day after we met."

Lena laughed. "Whirlwind romance, huh? Do you really think you can know that fast if something is meant to be?"

He took her hand in his. "My dear, if you don't know by then, you aren't with the right person."

Lena let that statement sink in. She'd never felt that before. Even with Connor, who she'd been in love with. And she thought they'd moved fast; after all, it had only been a month after they'd started dating that he'd been pushing to meet her parents and talking about forever...

A forever that was never meant to be.

"So, what happened with Betty?"

He sighed. "That third date was a double date with my best bud and his girl. I dropped Betty off at home and went and bought a ring. Even woke the jeweler up so I could get it—there weren't any twenty-four-hour-type places back in those days. I called her the next morning to try to set up another date, and her mother tells me that Betty had run off to get married."

Lena's jaw dropped. "What?"

He looked out the window, the slightest hint of tears shining in his eyes. "Seems she liked the look of my buddy more than she did me. They eloped. Married forty-eight years when she died last year."

"Oh, Mr. Clemons, I'm so sorry." The bulge in her throat was hard to choke down. This was why she didn't date anymore. Why she didn't trust. Even when someone was supposed to love you, so many times they were just waiting for a chance to hurt you. She'd learned that lesson the hard way.

"I never met another who made me feel half of what I felt with her."

What would it be like to trust someone enough to feel twice what she'd felt for Connor? It was unfathomable to her. Connor had thrown her life into such turmoil. And the lack of familial support in the matter had caused her to shut down even further. If you couldn't even trust your own parents, well, what was the point in sticking around? Hearing her dad side with Connor after the breakup had been the final straw.

After months of dating, months of hearing her father praise Connor and not so subtly put her down in the same sentence, Lena really should not have been surprised when her father continued to treat Connor like his future son-in-law, despite all that he'd put her through. When she'd told her parents that things were over with Connor, neither offered her any condolences. Instead, she was questioned on what she'd done wrong to lose him. After all, a surgeon like Connor was a stretch for a mere nurse like herself. So it must have been her fault.

If there was one thing Lena knew, it was how to be alone. Even if some of her "alone" had been when in the midst of her family. Her heart hurt for the sweet old man sitting here. No wife, no children. He hadn't even had a visitor that she'd seen. "So you've been alone all this time?"

"I've lived a long life. I had a long and accomplished career. I've just outlived everyone in my life." He patted her hand. "Don't be sad for me. I'm not sad for myself."

She couldn't help but be sad for him, though, and sad for herself. Even if they'd both made the choice to live their lives without anyone else involved, loneliness wasn't an easy cross to bear. Tears pricked her eyes and she blinked furiously, determined not to cry in front of a patient.

"I'll be right back. I promised you a chocolate ice cream, didn't I?"

Before leaving the hospital for the evening, Dex wanted to check on his patients. He had residents whose job it was to follow up after surgery, but he liked doing it. Many of his patients he barely saw before taking them into the OR. He whistled a low tune as he walked up the hallway toward his first patient's room.

Lena was coming from the other end of the hall, talking to another nurse. He was really baffled by her. Normally, women liked him. But not her.

She challenged him. And he liked it.

An alarm sounded at the nurses' station and Lena and the other nurse ran toward one of the rooms.

Over the PA system came a call for help. "I need a crash cart and the code team to Three North. Code team to Three North. Code Blue."

Dex wasn't on the code team, but he moved to the room in question. He grabbed gloves and pulled them on. "How can I help?"

Lena and the other nurse were moving around the patient. Lena pulled the pillows from beneath his head and lowered the bed to a flat position. The heart monitor showed a very weak, irregular pulse—V-fib—and the blood pressure monitor beeped to alert to the patient's low pressure.

Not one of his patients, Dex was relieved to see.

The other nurse began chest compressions. "Can you intubate him?"

Lena pulled out an intubation kit and handed it to him. She laid an Ambu bag out next to the man's side.

The patient's eyes were closed, his skin already showing the graying of lack of oxygen. The only movement to the man's body was from the compressions of the nurse.

Dex moved quickly, inserting the tube in the man's throat so that they could breathe for him. As soon as he removed his hands from the tube, Lena connected the Ambu bag and started squeezing it, forcing air into the man's oxygen-deprived lungs.

Still the monitors remained chaotic. The heart rate did not change. In fact, it seemed weaker. CPR continued.

The code team rushed into the room, slamming the cart into the wall in their rush. The doctor running the code took over. "I'm Dr. Clark. I'm leading this code. How long's he been like this?"

"About two minutes, Dr. Clark. Should we give him epi?" Lena asked.

Dex couldn't help but admire her professionalism in the chaos of the room. While people were darting quickly here and there, Lena was a calmness in the eye of the storm. She alone seemed unflappable in the moment.

"Yes. One milligram of epi." Clark reached for the paddles. "Charge the defibrillator. We are going to have to shock him and see if we can get his heart back into rhythm."

A moment later, the beep indicating the defibrillator was ready sounded. "Okay, everyone clear. Shocking."

The heart monitor went from jagged spikes to a total flat line.

"Asystole," Clark said, even though everyone in the room could read the monitor. "Push another round of epi."

He charged the defibrillator once more. "Okay, everyone clear."

The man's body jerked from the power of the shock. Still, the monitor showed only a flat line. No peaks, no valleys. This man wasn't coming back. And to keep trying would only be a waste of time and resources.

Clark hung the paddles back on the crash cart. He checked for corneal reflex. Tried for a pulse. And last took his stethoscope and listened for breath sounds. Shaking his head, he said, "He's gone. Time of death: six twenty-one."

Clark and his team left the room as quickly as they had entered. And in the space of a breath, the chaos from before was gone.

Lena switched off the machines one by one. The room fell into silence. There was a calm that seemed odd when contrasted with the flurry of noise and movement just moments before.

The other nurse laid a hand on Lena's shoulder. "I'll make the calls."

Lena shook her head. "There's no one to call. No family, no friends. He was all alone."

"Funeral home then." The other nurse shrugged and left the room.

Lena took the Ambu bag and tossed it. She removed the tube from the man's throat that Dex had placed. She started cleaning up the paper wrappings and remnants of trash left from the code. She pulled the electrode pads from the man's skin and put them in the trash too.

Dex wasn't sure she realized he was still in the room. She looked utterly heartbroken. The strong, unshakable nurse he'd been admiring during the code had been replaced. Now the woman in front of him looked like she might burst into tears at any given moment.

"Mr. Clemons, this wasn't how today was meant to end. You were supposed to be going home." She sniffled. She smoothed the old man's hair back. "I thought we were going to have ice cream together. I even brought your favorite—chocolate."

"Are you okay?" he asked.

She jumped at the sound of his voice. "I thought you'd left with the others."

"I wanted to be sure you were okay first."

"Of course I'm okay." The paleness in her face disagreed with her words, though. "We lose patients all the time. He's not my first, and I know that unfortunately he won't be my last."

"You look shaken by this one, though," Dex argued.

"If I'm ever not shaken when I lose a patient, that's

the day I quit, because I will have lost more than my patient." She started disconnecting all the monitors and IVs attached to the now deceased patient.

"Shift's almost over. Have dinner with me?" She looked so upset about losing this patient that he didn't think she should be alone tonight. He'd always thought of her as this ice queen, too cold to feel, but seeing her like this made him wonder if maybe his preconceived notions about Lena were entirely wrong.

Lena looked like she might argue, but then she nodded. "Okay. Dinner sounds good."

"I'll meet you out front in twenty?"

CHAPTER THREE

AT A FEW minutes after seven, Dex rolled to a stop in front of the main entrance of Metro Memorial to wait for Lena. He bumped the heat up so that it would still be warm inside the car after she'd opened the door. The mid-December day had been crisp and cold. The freezing chill and icy wind that cut straight through a person made him glad he'd sprung for the upgraded package when he'd bought the SUV. Those heated seats were worth every extra penny.

Lena came out the door wearing only scrubs, rubbing her hands briskly up and down her bare arms. Puffs of her breath rose in front of her in the frigid evening air.

What is she doing out in these temperatures without so much as a sweater?

He pulled up right in front of her. Lowering the window slightly, he called over the wind whipping around the buildings and cars, "Hey, Lena, I'm here. Come on, get in out of the cold."

Hurrying over, Lena climbed inside. "Hi," she said, her teeth chattering as she shivered.

"Where's your jacket?" He reached over and turned her heated seat on. "It's freezing today. You're going to get hypothermia."

"I, uh, don't have one yet."

He stared at her, unable to speak for a moment while he tried to process her statement. Her eyes were puffy like she'd been crying. He wanted to ask if she was okay, but he didn't want to overstep. So he decided to focus on the immediate concern she'd presented him with.

"It's December. What do you mean you don't have a jacket?"

"It's my first winter here. I wasn't sure what the climate would be like. And I didn't know it was going to go from shorts weather last week to snow flurries almost overnight. Isn't Tennessee supposed to have four seasons?"

Dex snorted. "Yeah, it does. Winter, pollen, suffocating heat and fall."

"I missed fall."

"It was only three days this year. You might have worked through it."

"Winter wardrobe is on the list for my next day off." She shrugged as she put her seat belt on. "I never understood why so many cars had heated seats, but now I'm thinking they should be standard equipment."

"You came from LA, right? Is that where you grew up?"

"Oh, yes. My father runs a hospital now, but he spent years as the most sought-after plastic surgeon for the stars. My mother spends all her time working charity events and fundraising." Melancholy tinged her soft sigh. "My first boyfriend was a celebrity's son, and we broke up when he asked me why I didn't ask my dad to 'do my tits' for my birthday because he found mine a little disappointing."

Hearing the indignation and more than a little hurt in

her voice, Dex glanced over to Lena. She had her arms crossed across her middle, unintentionally pushing her chest up. He grunted. “He’s an idiot. I see nothing that would disappoint me. I hope you told him that he should see your dad for a bit of enlargement action of his own because he was the disappointment.”

She chuckled. “There may have been comments along that line. It was our last date.”

“Jessie was my first girlfriend.” The confession tumbled past his lips.

“The ex-fiancée?”

“Yeah. That’s the one.”

“How long were you together?”

“Almost nine years.” And now they’d been apart almost as long.

“Wow.”

Pity permeated that single syllable. The same pity he’d heard in every single condolence after Jessie had disappeared. It had pervaded the looks in people’s eyes and filled conversations that stopped when he walked into the room. His hand clenched around the steering wheel.

Swallowing hard, he gave Lena more details than his brief admission in the OR had provided. “I found out she left the state while I was standing in the church, greeting the guests we had invited to our wedding.”

“She left you at the altar? That’s harsh.”

“Yeah.” He hadn’t been in love with Jessie for a long time now. But man, that punch to his pride was hard to get past. “After our rehearsal dinner, I kissed her goodbye. She got into her mother’s car and drove away. Sometime during the night, she disappeared.”

The cracks in their relationship had shown before that fateful night, though. Dex had just been too stubborn to see it. Jessie had struggled with the hours he'd put in during med school and had for some reason convinced herself that he'd be done as soon as he graduated from medical school. They'd fought over his hours a lot—she accused him of being a workaholic, when really he'd passed up surgeries and procedures in an effort to spend more time with her and avoid even more fights. She'd never understood his need to be a doctor, but seemed to like the idea of being a doctor's wife. He'd thought they'd be okay once he got through his residency. They didn't make it that far.

"Did she ever tell you why she changed her mind?"

He shook his head. They'd shared a lot of dreams that Jessie had walked away from without a backward glance. The swift way she'd cut all ties to him told him all he'd needed to know about their relationship, or lack thereof, really. After all, a person in love didn't ghost the person they were in love with, so clearly Jessie hadn't been in love.

"Nope. I have some assumptions, of course, but we actually haven't spoken since that day."

"I can't imagine spending nearly a decade with someone and walking away like that."

Dex puffed out a breath. "She doesn't seem to have looked back. But that's the past. Can we please discuss something besides how my first love ripped my heart out and tap-danced on it in front of literally every single person that mattered to me?"

Lena seemed to shrink back a bit from the vehemence that leaked into his voice. "So, where is Westville?" she finally asked.

"Westfield," he corrected, far more gently than he'd spoken to her before. "I'm sorry if I'm snappy about Jessie. Every time I go home, my mom starts trying to pair me up and bore witness to me being left at the altar. That wound is still a little raw."

"The breakup or the embarrassment over it?"

He didn't have to think about that answer. "The embarrassment, for sure. Jessie and I would have never lasted, even if we had gotten married that day. The pain of the breakup itself is long gone. I'm not pining for her, if that's what you are wondering, but the embarrassment just never seems to fade."

"Gotcha," she said softly. "So, taking me home with you is about more than blocking a matchmaking attempt. It's about showing all your old friends and neighbors that you found someone new."

"Yeah," he agreed. That was exactly it. Every time he spoke to someone from Westfield outside his family, inevitably they brought up the fact that he'd been left at the altar. It had become a never-ending horror story. "So, Westfield is a few hours' drive east of here, a small town nestled in the Smòky Mountains. Population about eight hundred."

"Wow." Lena snorted. "My graduating class had over nine hundred people. I'm not sure I've ever even been to a town that small."

"City girl," he said with a teasing tone.

"You have a little accent when you say *girl*," she said, poking his arm playfully. "Did you realize?"

A laugh rumbled up from deep in his chest. "Honey, if you think I have an accent now, wait 'til I'm around my family for a few days. All the *y'all*s and dropped letters will seep back in and I'll sound like the biggest hick you've ever laid eyes on."

"Don't call me honey."

"If you don't like being called honey, you moved to the wrong state." He pulled into a parking space in front of a steak house that wouldn't raise an eyebrow at Lena's scrubs. "Is steak okay? We can go somewhere else if you prefer."

"Steak's good."

He turned the ignition off and hopped out. The concrete walkway glistened with thousands of little ice crystals. Before he'd made it to the front of the SUV, she came up next to him, shivering. He slipped his blazer off and draped in over her shoulders.

"When we get to Westfield, I'm going to need you to sit in the car and wait for me to open your door. My mama raised me to be a gentleman and I'll catch hell if you don't let me treat you like a lady. Now, watch your step on this sidewalk, it's a little icy."

She raised an eyebrow at him and pulled the blazer closer. "You gave me your jacket. Isn't that gentlemanly enough?"

Stepping forward to open the restaurant door for her, Dex laughed. "Only someone not raised in the South could say something so naive. According to my mama, a man can never be gentlemanly enough."

Lena stepped through the door, her eyes twinkling with amusement. "I don't know if I'm the right fit for you to be bringing home to *mama*, then."

He told the host they needed a table for two before turning back to his conversation with Lena. "Why the negative emphasis on 'mama'?"

"I've never heard a grown man call his mother 'mama' in conversation like you just did. Most people of my acquaintance would say 'my mother' or 'my mom.' And I know no one who is grown and still says 'mama.'"

"Men of your acquaintance. Do you know how prissy that sounds?" He waited while she slid into the booth and then sat across from her. "It's a Southern thing, I guess. If I call her 'Mother,' she's going to tell me to stop sassing her and maybe box my ears for me."

Lena held the menu up, her eyes scanning down the list. "If I called mine anything but 'Mother' she'd give me a lecture about how my informal attitude could create negative impressions of our family. And nothing upsets Vivienne Franklin more than negative impressions." She slammed the menu down on the tabletop. "Unless it's my father creating that negativity. And then she will ignore it as if it never happened."

"Guessing there's a history there?"

"My father—" The server came over and Lena cut off her answer midsentence.

After they'd placed their order and were once again alone, Dex prompted her, trying to get her to tell him what she'd meant about her dad. Her actions said there was a story there, one that would be important for him to know.

Anger flashed in her eyes when she looked up at him and confirmed his suspicions. "I don't want to talk about it."

Frustration welled up within him at her words. They were here because she said they needed to get to know each other. And now she didn't feel like talking?

"Hmm..." Dex leaned back against the padded back of the booth and stretched his legs out, trying hard to project a calmness he certainly didn't feel at that moment. "So, what do you want to talk about? Getting to know each other better was *your* idea, after all."

"I know. And I'll tell you about my father before we

go to LA, I promise, but for now, can we just start with something lighter? That conversation will simply make me angry, and I don't want to be angry tonight."

"One last question and I'll leave it alone." He waited until she nodded. "Why do you feel so obligated to go back for this gala? Seems like it would be less stress to just skip it."

"Family obligations. Now, can I please change the subject? Today has been—" she paused and seemed to roll a few words around before deciding on the right one "—hard. So, we should probably set some guidelines about this, right?"

"Probably. My brother's wedding is Christmas Eve. It's been strongly suggested to me that I arrive at least a couple days before and stay through the holiday. How's that work for you?"

"I'm off from December 19 through January 6. I had the dates put into my contract because I knew I'd never get the holidays off otherwise, and my mother will make life unbearable for me if I don't attend the gala."

"And the gala is on New Year's Eve?"

She nodded. "I think we can both agree that we need to keep the PDA as minimal as we can, stick as close to the truth as feasible, and once we get back from LA this is done. And I think the fewer people at Metro Memorial who know about it, the better. Neither of us needs anyone to think that we are hooking up."

"Simple enough," he agreed. "Should we shake on it?"

Wrinkling her nose, she ignored his outstretched hand. "I don't feel that's necessary. Less physical contact is probably the best course of action, don't you think?"

"Okay, then." He didn't quite agree, but he let her have

this one. "And I think no emotional attachment is a pretty obvious one. Anything else?"

When she shook her head, he brought the conversation back to getting to know each other by asking, "So, what brought you to Nashville?"

Lena grumbled low enough Dex didn't catch her words.

"What was that?"

Her fingers traced little designs in the condensation on her water glass, and he thought maybe she was going to blow off another answer, when she finally did speak. "A relationship gone horribly wrong and my freaking father's inability to be faithful to my mother—both of which ruined not only my personal life but spilled over into my professional life as well."

"That sounds like a loaded topic."

Her bottom lip quivered a bit and she sucked in a shaky breath. But thankfully, she didn't burst into tears. He wasn't so great with tears.

"He makes me so angry I can barely think straight."

"Your dad or your ex?"

"Both." She shrugged. "My ex only dated me because I was the medical director's daughter and being with me got him closer to the man who could—and did—advance his career."

"How long ago did that end?" The wound still seemed raw from his perspective. He just wasn't sure which man had caused her the most pain.

"April."

Less than a year. Considering the timeline, Lena was doing far better than he'd been at the same point. Jessie had broken him for a long while. He could relate to a relationship gone wrong if she'd just open up and tell him about it.

"And your dad?"

"My father, well, other than repeatedly cheating on my mother with women half his age—including my best friend while I was dealing with the worst breakup of my life, by the way? He's a cold, overbearing jerk who expects total obedience and has standards so high that an Olympic high jumper couldn't reach them."

Clearly any conversation about her family would be a touchy one. He couldn't quite decide if she was more angry or hurt by father, but their relationship wasn't good. What sort of dad slept with his daughter's best friend? And for that matter, what sort of friend slept with their best friend's dad? Was the friend climbing the career ladder by climbing Lena's father? He'd ask, but Lena had made it crystal clear that she was ready for happier topics.

He'd struck out on trying to start a conversation twice. Maybe the third time would be the charm and he'd finally get some insight into what made her tick.

"Are you an only child?"

She nodded. "I am. What about you? I know you have a brother since you need a date for his wedding. Is it just the two of you?"

Her answer was exactly what he'd expected to hear. The familial obligation he'd only seen with only children. People with siblings, in his experience, were more likely to tell their parents when they needed to back off and would even walk away if it became necessary.

"Oldest of three boys, actually. The one closest in age to me, Tommy, is getting married to the literal girl next door. And I should probably go ahead and tell you that Jill is my ex's younger sister."

Lena raised a brow in surprise.

"Small town." He shrugged.

"Does that bother you?"

Tommy had asked him the same thing before he'd ever asked Jill out the first time. He couldn't blame Jill for Jessie's actions, though. That wouldn't have been fair to her. "Nah. Jill is nothing like Jessie. And if my brother is happy, then I'm happy."

"You said there were three of you?"

"My baby brother, Wade, is a senior at the University of Tennessee this year."

"I always wanted a brother or a sister." Wistfulness softened her voice. "But apparently I did so much damage to my mother's figure that she was unwilling to do that again."

Dex desperately wanted to lighten the mood. He tried a little joke. "You can have one of mine. I have a spare."

She snorted at his offer, and he could see she was trying desperately to hold back a smile.

The laughter in her eyes contradicted everything he thought he knew, and she was quickly becoming a code he was determined to break. Behind the laughter, there was a sadness that lingered in her eyes, and she often looked like she held the weight of the world in her slim fingers.

He wanted to make her smile for a bit. To chase the shadows out of her gaze and hear her laugh while she relaxed in his arms.

Lena shifted and her leg bumped into Dex's under the table. Even sitting in a booth, he had managed to spread himself out and take up so much space. The way his shoulders filled out those navy-blue scrub tops had fueled more than a few fantasies since she'd moved to Nashville. She fought against a blush as the memory of one of those fantasies popped into her mind.

Even in scrubs, Dex oozed masculinity. Tonight, in khakis and a button-down shirt, an air of power surrounded him, not unlike what she'd come to associate with her father and her ex-boyfriend. But with Dex, she didn't feel like being female made her less.

She'd have to examine that thought in more detail when Dex didn't sit so near she could barely breathe. She'd been hoping to find something about him that she hated. Some little detail that confirmed her suspicions of him being too much like her father, maybe. Or anything that reminded her of Connor allowing her to push him firmly back onto the "men she'd never date" list.

Dex was in line to be head of general surgery when the current head retired. It was common knowledge at Metro Memorial that Dr. Miller had been grooming Dex to take his place by letting Dex take a leadership role within the department. Like her ex, Dex would be in a position of power. In a decade, he'd be running a hospital, just like her father. Powerful men caused powerful problems for the women in their lives. Lena could not allow herself to forget that.

But here he sat, smiling that gorgeous smile of his, doing something incredibly sweet by offering to share his siblings with her. While he surely meant it in a teasing way, she couldn't help but find the gesture endearing.

What was wrong with her?

"It's so kind of you to share," Lena deadpanned.

Dex laughed. "Consider it self-care. If he has someone else to pick on, then I get a break."

The delicious sound rolled over her, tempting her to

want things that a fake relationship could never provide. Lena swallowed hard, fighting to regain her control and perspective. Fake meant she walked away unscathed. Real meant the consequences were equally as real. And she refused to do real.

"Which brother are you talking about?" She needed to get the conversation on something light, something that wouldn't be too tempting, because she couldn't take much more tonight. If he pushed her one way or the other, she might break.

"Both." He shrugged. "Either. You'll see when we get to Westfield."

"Tell me about them. Or about your parents," she suggested. Dex didn't seem to mind talking about his family. Starting there meant she didn't have to open up just yet. She'd left LA to get away from the embarrassment of everything that happened with Connor and her father and to escape his influence, and bringing them up and talking about their actions felt like tempting fate and potentially destroying even more of the peace she'd found here in Tennessee.

While they ate, Dex launched into a lively description of his parents and his hometown, and Lena had to squash down the envy. His narrative portrayed the idyllic childhood she'd only seen on television. From hiking in the Smoky Mountains with his parents, to trying all the touristy attractions in the area, every story spoke of a family with a solid and loving commitment to each other.

By comparison, her family had been a dysfunctional mess hidden behind a cosmetic front of perfection. Their family vacation spots were chosen for their exclusivity and her parents' enjoyment, never her own. Memories of her parents involving her in any sort of family-style entertainment slipped through her mind like wispy clouds pushed by a stiff breeze. When none cemented into a solid recollection, she released a deep sigh.

"You don't have a single bad story, do you?"

Dex had the type of family Lena had always wanted. When Dex talked about his family, love warmed his voice like a perfect cup of hot cocoa, and Lena had never had that. Might never have that if she couldn't find it in her to trust a man enough to have a family.

"Uh… Nothing much. We've had our squabbles through the years, but what family doesn't? Nothing we couldn't work out." He grinned at her. "There was this one time that my dad and I…"

Dex launched into a story about how he and his dad had pulled a series of pranks on his younger brothers, and her heart hurt. She'd be willing to bet that his father would never have slept with a woman under his employ, nor ruined the woman's career when the relationship went sideways. And from his description of his mother, she'd bet Mrs. Henry would not have ignored being cheated on and certainly would never have just gone on with her life as if it never happened. The man sitting across from her would never have to fear what his own father might do to his career, and he'd certainly never have to move across the country to get away from his father's influence.

But the worst part, the part Lena was really struggling to reconcile, was her dad sleeping with her best friend. During the absolute worst months of her life, she'd had no one to talk to. Her mother turned her away, dismissing her and her emotions like an unwanted telemarketer. And her best friend, the girl she'd grown up with and trusted with all her secrets, had slept with her father until he tossed her aside like yesterday's leftovers. And so then Lena had lost her best friend as well. It had been a long and lonely spring for her and she'd jumped into the travel nurse gig without a second thought—anything to get her away from California and the negativity that abounded there. Her memories weighed heavy on her, her heart aching like she'd been stabbed.

Swallowing hard, she blinked hard at the tears that all the thoughts of her upbringing and more recent turmoil had brought up. As she blinked, a tear dripped from her eye and slid down her cheek.

She should have canceled this fake date. Her nerves were already on edge after losing Mr. Clemons this afternoon, and her emotions couldn't handle being this close to a man like Dex—completely her opposite in so many ways and yet somehow drawing her in like waves to the shore.

Despite a smooth surgery with Dex, her day had been a roller coaster full of unexpected twists and emotions. A sweet elderly man had come through surgery yesterday looking like a champ, only to code that afternoon on her watch. He'd been alone, never married, no children, and it had hit Lena hard that she was staring down her own future. The thought hit her again that she might never have a child of her own, and her lower lip quivered.

"Hey, are you okay?" A warm hand covered hers.

Embarrassment washed over her. She met his gaze, feeling super self-conscious about how he caught her mired in the depths of her thoughts. "Yeah, sorry. I got lost in my own head for a minute."

Worry highlighted the gold flecks in his dark eyes. The weight of his hand over hers was warm and solid. Comforting. And when he spoke, his soft tone soothed her more than the teasing words themselves could have ever done. "I've never bored a woman to tears before."

"Well, you can't say that any longer." She laughed as she swiped at the stray tear on her cheek.

"Wanna talk about what's really bothering you?"

She searched his face, surprised to find genuine concern there. "Not at the moment," she finally answered. "Your childhood sounds perfect."

"I was lucky." His thumb rubbed circles on the back of her hand until she pulled away. That simple touch sparked a far too tempting awareness that radiated from the skin on her hand all the way down deep into her core. The attentiveness he showed was quite honestly the most irresistible feature she'd seen in a man in a long time now.

She needed a distraction. Something to take her mind off how every nerve in her body stood up and took notice of his touch. A television mounted to the wall behind him played a professional basketball game. She focused her gaze on the screen while she tried to pull herself together. Usually she could stare at something from a distance and put her emotions in check in the process. But this time, it wasn't working. Not even a little.

"I'm sorry. Could you take me back to my car?" She covered her plate with her napkin. She had to get out of there before she lost all control over her emotions. "I'd really like to go home."

Shock briefly crossed over his face before he schooled his expression back to neutral, but to his credit, Dex didn't question her decision to end their evening. He merely waved the server over and asked for the check. Within a couple minutes, they were out the door and on the way back to the hospital.

Several times, she saw him glance in her direction as

he drove. He had to be thinking she was a nutjob. But she was on the verge of tears and she did *not* want to break down in front of him. And if she didn't get away from him soon, that's exactly what would happen.

"Where are you parked?" he asked as he turned his SUV into the parking garage.

"Exit side of level three."

When they got to her level, she pointed out her car and he slowed to a stop near her trunk.

"Thanks for dinner," she murmured, reaching out to grab the door handle.

"Hang on a second." Dex hit the lock button to keep her door from opening.

"What are you…?" She stared over at him in confusion.

"I thought tonight was going well, but then you just shut me out." His frustrated sigh filled the SUV. "What happened back there? Did I do something wrong? Say something that upset you?"

Lena shook her head, trying hard not to cry.

"I'm trying to wrap my head around how this went downhill so fast. This isn't going to work if you don't talk to me. We go see either of our families like this and it's gonna look like we've been fighting the whole trip."

"I know. I just…" She choked back a sob. If she started crying, she might not be able to stop. Holding it together until she got away from him was the only hope she had to keep from embarrassing herself beyond recovery. "I can't tonight, Dex."

"Okay, well, if you aren't in, if you can't stand to be around me for even a single evening, then let me know, sooner rather than later, because I need time to come up with a new plan before Tommy and Jill's wedding." When she nodded, he unlocked the doors. "Good night, Lena."

She moved to shrug out of his blazer and he stilled her with a hand on her shoulder.

"Keep it until you get your own. You need it more than I do right now."

She got out of the SUV and closed the door. Dex waited until she'd gotten in and started her car before he pulled away.

Sitting in her car, she sucked in several deep breaths. She tried to be strong, really, she did, but now that she was alone there was no stopping the tears. They burst out of her like water spilling from a dam, cascading down her face. She leaned her head against the steering wheel and let the sobs punch through the remnants of the walls she'd surrounded herself with.

Today had taught her something—she did not want to spend the rest of her life alone, even if she had argued that point with her parents more than once. She didn't want to be eighty and have no one to miss her when she was gone.

A rap on the glass sent her heart straight out of her chest and into orbit.

She trembled as she looked toward the window at her side.

Dex.

He yanked the door open the second she hit Unlock, grabbing her hand and tugging her out of the car and into a gentle embrace. "Tell me what I did to cause this. Lena, I really have no idea."

She swiped at her tears with the sleeve of his jacket. Great, not only was Dex witnessing her breakdown first-hand, he thought he'd caused it.

"That patient we lost today," she found herself confessing on a sob. "It was like looking at the Ghost of Christmas Future—no family, no friends, just him alone and dying at Christmas with no one to miss him when he was gone."

"That's not your future." Dex pulled her in closer. She sank into his warmth, her heart fluttering at his nearness. His touch made the world around them fade, and suddenly the future seemed less bleak. He murmured reassurances as he rubbed his hand up and down her back. "One day you will find someone who makes your heart skip a beat. He'll sweep you off your feet when you least expect it. You won't be alone. I know it."

Why did he have to be such a nice guy? Making it through the next two weeks at his side would be a lot less scary if he wasn't the antithesis of everything she'd assumed he'd be. Yes, he was arrogant and powerful. But he was also thoughtful and kind. He came back after dropping her off to make sure she was okay and if that wasn't a sign of true character, she didn't know what would be.

As a result, a single question currently dominated her mind—if Dex treated a virtual stranger like this, how would he treat the woman he gave his heart?

CHAPTER FOUR

A FEW DAYS LATER, Dex wandered around Green Hills Mall, looking for the perfect Christmas gifts for his family. He normally made sure to get his shopping done long before Thanksgiving and the nightmare of Black Friday, but time had gotten away from him this year and with less than two weeks before Christmas, he'd had no choice but to make another attempt at the mall in December. The memory of the little old lady who had not only snatched a sweater out of his hand but then smacked him with her purse for protesting held a spot in his mind any time he got near a crowded mall, even though years had passed since that incident.

Just stepping through those automatic doors sent his pulse pounding in his temples. His breathing grew shallow and rapid and he had to wipe his now sweaty palms on his pants leg. He could walk into a complicated surgery without an ounce of nerves, but a busy shopping mall sent him into an uproar.

Dex swallowed hard as a woman carrying multiple bags while talking very loudly on her cell phone walked right into him and shouted at him to watch where he was going. He bit back the retort that jumped to his lips because she moved on without a backward glance.

Why hadn't he just ordered everything online and had it delivered? He shook his head and kept moving. The thought that it wasn't yet too late to do that sprang up in his mind, at least not if he was willing to pay through the nose for expedited shipping.

"Dex?"

He spun when he heard his name called, but when he saw no one that he recognized, he returned his attention to navigating the crowd surrounding him. Only a few gifts, then he could go home.

"Dex!"

Once again he heard his name and stopped to look around.

"Dex! Look up!"

From the upper level, he saw a familiar face staring down at him. "Wait right there," she called. "I'll come to you."

"Lena!" He moved around a group of grandmothers toward the escalators, and he and Lena met next to some potted plants just out of the flow of foot traffic. "This place is a madhouse. Why would anyone come here?"

The smile on her face could have lit Westfield for a month with its brightness. "Oh, don't tell me you are a Scrooge!"

He narrowed his eyes at her. Beaming with happiness, Lena looked perfectly relaxed and much happier than the last time he'd seen her. The brightly patterned scarf draped around her neck would have looked tacky on him, but on her it was perfection. Christmas spirit vibrated off her palpably.

His future sister-in-law would love her.

"You are already watching all of the Christmas romance movies and listening to Christmas music all the time, aren't you?"

She motioned him closer.

When he bent down a bit at her coaxing, she tiptoed and mock-whispered in his ear. "It's the most wonderful time of year." Her lips brushed his ear on the last word and a shudder of desire sliced through him as sharp as a scalpel.

"Is it?" He rested his hand on her waist, his head still bent near hers. Tension sizzled white-hot between them and had him wondering if they could turn this time-limited charade into a time-limited fling. The physical novelty always wore off quickly for him and he lost interest in the women he'd dated after a few weeks. It would surely be the same with Lena, but they could still help each other out in the meantime.

Lena remained on her tiptoes. Their faces were millimeters apart. But just as he pulled her closer, someone jostled into them and Lena moved away. Her cheeks flushed bright pink.

"Um…" she began, but then trailed off.

The moment might have slipped away, but Dex didn't want to let her slip away. "Would you like to help me with my Christmas shopping? I'm sure you'll be much better at it than I am, and your presence will make this day far more bearable."

People moved past them, many chatting with a friend, some alone moving faster as if on a mission. Christmas music played loudly through speakers overhead. Dex only had eyes for the beautiful nurse standing within arm's reach, wearing his blazer with the sleeves rolled up.

Biting her lower lip, Lena looked at him as she seemed to consider his offer. "What if we run into someone from the hospital? I thought we were going to keep this on the down low?"

"So, I tell them I am a hopeless shopper and bribed you into helping me." He sweetened the offer. "Lunch is on me. We can discuss the next two weeks and work out any kinks."

"Deal." She stuck her hand out to shake.

As their palms met, Dex had to suppress the urge to pull her back into his arms. After how fast she'd shot away from him, he didn't think she'd be eager to fall right into his embrace. And he didn't want to scare her off after they'd seemed to make a tentative truce the other night. Something had changed after her emotional purge, and she'd started to open up to him the tiniest bit more, at least when she didn't realize she was doing so.

And if he frightened her away, then he'd have to go home alone for his brother's wedding. He'd never find anyone else this close to Christmas to pretend to be his girlfriend. According to his dad, there would likely be a repeat of the eligible ladies' parade if his mom had her way. And he certainly didn't want to have to face Jessie alone. That would be so awkward.

Not that he was still hung up on his ex.

At all.

Jessie had killed any and every feeling he had for her when she'd walked away without a word, leaving her father to come to the church and break his heart. To his dying day, he'd never forget the look on Ray's face when he'd told him Jessie had left town. "I'm sorry, Dexter, but her note only said that she wasn't ready to get married."

But he knew how it would look to the people of Westfield if he showed up alone. They would assume he still pined for her after all this time. They would assume that he had hopes of a Christmas reconciliation.

Nothing could be further from the truth.

In reality, he just hadn't found anyone he was willing to risk his heart on again. Getting left at the altar could really do a number on a guy—even if he had been the tiniest bit relieved once the shock wore off. He realized just what a bullet he'd dodged in being left at the altar; it was far better than marrying someone who really didn't want to be married and going through a bitter divorce later.

But falling in love with a woman gave her a power over a man that Dex wasn't sure he could ever give again. It wasn't that he didn't believe in love or anything as harsh as that. He just didn't believe that love was ever in his plans again. Short-term flings with no feelings involved kept him satisfied and his heart protected.

"So, what are we looking for?" Lena questioned, pulling his thoughts away from Jessie and the past. "I'm just looking for some winter clothes. As you reminded me, I'm not exactly equipped for a Tennessee winter." She plucked at the lapels of his blazer, her radiant smile giving him stirrings of thoughts toward the future. "And I thank you for the loan again. It came in handy in the just above freezing temperatures this morning."

"I bet it did," he said with an easy smile. "I think I might like how it looks better on you than me anyways."

The tiniest hint of pink brightened her cheeks again but she met his gaze. "I don't know if I'd agree with that, but it's certainly warm." She held up the bags in her hands. "I found some warm sweaters, but I haven't been able to find a winter coat yet that I like."

"Maybe you are just too picky?" he teased, loving the reactions he coaxed from her with a few words.

She wrinkled up her nose. "Maybe I just have more refined taste."

He took the bags from her hands and nodded in the direction of the nearest store. "Well, we won't find you a coat without looking. Have you been in there?"

"That was actually going to be my next stop."

She allowed him to guide her into the store, where she made a beeline for some ugly Christmas sweaters. Picking up a green one that was nearly the color of her eyes, she held it up in front of her. "We should get these for your brother's wedding! What do you think? Is this one me?"

"I think Jill would kill us. At least for wearing them to the wedding. But I might buy her one of these for a Christmas present. She'll love it."

Lena laughed, but stopped suddenly. She tilted her head, and her expression grew thoughtful. "You know, I never asked how fancy the wedding was going to be. Do I need something formal?"

Dex shrugged. "I have no idea. I was told to bring my black suit. And Jill has, apparently, picked out matching ties for us all."

"Yeah, men have it easy. A black suit is appropriate for anything casual to dressy. It's not so easy for us girls."

It couldn't be that hard. Dresses were the female equivalent of a suit, weren't they?

"Just wear a dress."

"Dresses come in various degrees of formality and to wear the wrong one would be a massive faux pas." The expression on her face said he might have been the one to make a massive faux pas. "What did the invitation say?"

"I didn't get an invitation."

She gaped at him. "Why are you attending a wedding you weren't invited to?"

"I'm not allowed to say no, so there was no need to waste money on an invitation for me."

"Then how am I supposed to know what would be appropriate for me to wear? I don't want to wear something casual and find out everyone else is formal, or even worse, wear something more formal than the bride herself." She shuddered in apparent horror.

"I could call my mama and ask her," he offered, trying to figure out what he needed to do to fix this before the entire situation derailed.

His offer seemed to be the right decision because Lena perked up as he spoke. "Have you told them you were bringing a date?"

"Not yet. I wanted to be sure that you were coming." He rubbed the back of his neck. Suppressing a shudder of his own, he let his mind wander to his family's reactions if she didn't go after he'd told his family she would be there. His brothers would never let him live down getting stood up again at a wedding, even if it wasn't his this time. His dad would just shake his head and possibly give him a talk about what to look for in a "good" woman. And his mom? She'd worry herself into a frenzy about him being alone for the rest of his life before launching herself into a mission to have him married off by May. "The only thing worse than showing up alone would be to say that I was bringing someone home with me and *still* show up alone."

"True."

"Have you told your family that I'm coming?" he asked, turning her question back around on her.

With a sigh, she shook her head. "No. Like you said, I wanted to make sure it was going to happen first."

"Well, I'm committed to you."

The words came out without thought and he almost apologized for the bluntness he'd put on the statement. It had sounded rather like an accusation instead of the motivational comment it should have been.

The din surrounding them almost drowned out her reply when she said softly, "I'm committed too."

Lena slipped into the fitting room to try on a few items of clothing while Dex called his mother to check on what exactly she should wear to the wedding. Through the slats on the door, she overheard every word of his conversation. His deep voice carried even over the Christmas music piped in from above.

"Hey, Mama," he said. "Yeah, I miss you too. I had a reason for calling actually."

He either paused or moved away.

Lena stopped moving with a pair of gray corduroy pants halfway up her thighs, listening carefully as she tried to catch Dex's next words. Eavesdropping unashamedly, she stood half-dressed in the fitting room without moving a muscle so that she could better hear Dex over the sounds of the store.

"No, I'm not calling to cancel just because Jessie is coming. I was actually calling to make sure it was okay if I brought my girlfriend with me."

The smile that sprang up on her lips at the word *girlfriend* surprised her. She yanked the pants up and looked at her reflection in the mirror. When she realized why she was grinning like a fool, the smile quickly became a frown. Being called Dex's girlfriend shouldn't make her smile.

It was fake. Their entire relationship was fake.

She shoved the pants off and roughly hung them back on the hanger. She didn't even try the pair of khakis on and just put her own jeans back on. Her desire to shop had fled with the realization that she'd really liked hearing Dex refer to her as his girlfriend. She had to get her head straight and remember that, even if Dex wasn't quite as bad as she thought, getting involved for real would ruin everything that she'd accomplished by leaving California.

She knew this with every fiber of her being.

So why was she having such a hard time remembering that when Dex was around?

Putting on the coat she'd picked out, she examined her reflection. It would do for now. She didn't have the luxury of waiting for the perfect piece of outerwear to come along.

Once she had dressed, she stepped out of the fitting room and almost walked right into Dex. He seemed to be pacing back and forth in front of the fitting rooms. Agitation deepened the frown lines marring the perfection of his face. A muscle twitched at the corner of his eye and a rigid grimace darkened his countenance.

"Mama, I told you, it has nothing to do with Jessie. I want you guys to meet Lena and—" He stopped suddenly like his speech had been interrupted on the other end of the line. After a lengthy pause he answered, "Yes, ma'am. No. She's right here if you want to talk to her."

Before Lena could squeak out a protest, Dex had shoved his cell phone into her hand. "I can't do it anymore. You talk to her," he grumbled before stomping away, his shoulders squared off in visible frustration.

"Hello, uh, Mrs. Henry," she said, hoping she wasn't about to get cussed out by some crazy Southern woman she'd never met. Getting told off before they'd even met just might be the icing on the cake of this charade they'd made inescapable when they involved his mother. She didn't expect his mom to love her, or anything of the sort, but if his mom hated her, it would make for a long and stressful week in Westfield.

"My son tells me you are coming home with him for Christmas and Tommy's wedding."

The voice on the other end of the line was as stereotypically Southern as any that Lena had ever heard faked out in LA.

"Um, yes, ma'am, I am. If that's okay with you, that's the plan."

Suck up.

She was totally and completely sucking up to his mother. What was wrong with her?

"Do you work at the hospital with Dexter? I know that son of mine and if you didn't meet at the hospital, then you'd have had to trip him at the grocery store to catch his attention."

Lena couldn't help but laugh. "Yes, we met at the hospital. I'm a registered nurse."

"I see. You don't sound like you are from around here."

"No, I'm from California."

Mrs. Henry snorted. "Well, I suppose I won't hold that against you. If Dexter's bringing you home, he must see something special in you. He hasn't dated anyone in years that was serious enough for him to bring home to meet the family."

"I… Um… I don't think I'm that special."

She knew the truth. Dex wasn't bringing her home

because he thought she was special. He was bringing her home because he needed a pretend girlfriend and she fit the bill. The hope she heard in his mom's voice hurt. They were going to get her hopes up that Dex was seriously in love with someone, and for what?

"Oh, well, Dexter thinks you are, and I trust my son. I'm so excited to meet you. Dexter has been alone far too long and it does my heart good to hear that he's found someone to love. Maybe we will have more than one thing to celebrate this Christmas!"

His mom seemed so genuinely warm and kind. And completely enamored with the idea of Dex settling down with a new love. A huge lump of guilt rose in her throat and Lena had to choke it down. Deceiving his family left a bad taste in her mouth, but she'd made a commitment to Dex to be his pretend girlfriend through the holidays and if she was anything, it was stubborn. She'd see this through or die trying.

Forging on out of sheer determination to keep her word, Lena continued the charade but changed the topic to something less likely to trigger more guilt. "I had asked Dex what I should wear and he sputtered something incoherent that I took to mean he had no clue. A few suggestions would be appreciated, if you don't mind?"

A short chuckle met her ear. "That boy wouldn't know a tea-length dress from a ball gown. The wedding isn't going to be very formal, though. They are going with a rustic holiday theme, complete with burlap lace. Anything dressy you feel pretty in that doesn't show off all the goodies God gave you would be appropriate. And the rehearsal dinner is going to be an ugly Christmas sweater party. So if you want to bring something hideous for that, my soon-to-be daughter-in-law will find that illogically delightful."

Another smile crept up on Lena's face at the revulsion she heard in regards to the ugly sweaters. She thought the gaudy Christmas sweaters were fun, but Dex's mother clearly did not agree. She nearly snorted when she pictured her own mother's face if anyone dared wear one of the Christmas sweaters to one of her charity events—it would be epic.

"Sounds great. I'm sure I'll find something appropriate for both the wedding and the rehearsal. Thank you for the tips. I look forward to meeting you soon."

"And the same to you, dear. Tell my son to call me later, would ya?"

"Of course."

Lena hit End on the call and looked around for Dex. He had stopped pacing and slumped down onto a bench outside the fitting rooms.

"Here's your phone back." She held it out for him to take as she stepped over to him. "Your mother wants you to call her later."

"Did she say why?"

"Well, she seemed to think I must be something special if you were willing to bring me home. Her exact words were, 'Maybe we will have more than one thing to celebrate this Christmas,' if that gives you some idea where she's taking this."

He threw his head back into the wall so hard Lena heard the thump. "She didn't," he said with a groan.

"Oh, yeah." Lena sat next to him and nudged his side with her elbow. "And she's so excited that you're in love again."

Dex huffed out a noise of disbelief. "I can't believe she said that."

Lena leaned against him, her shoulder pressed against his biceps. She looked at him out of the corner of her eye and couldn't resist a bit of a tease, hoping to get a rise out of him and distract him. "If you don't freak out and confess our plans, I think we really can pull this off."

"I hope so." Dex didn't take the bait. Instead, he took her hand in his and Lena squeezed his in solidarity.

"We got this." Trying a different tactic, she infused her voice with positivity. "We will go to Westfield and they will think we are so in love that we will be announcing our own wedding once it won't steal your brother's thunder."

With his thumb rubbing slow circles against the back of her hand, Dex exhaled long and deep. "And when the truth comes out, they will never forgive me, will they? What are we doing? Is salvaging a little pride for one day each worth potentially hurting both of our families?"

Worry and concern roughened his voice and gave her a minute's pause.

"Listen, we've already told your mom that I'm coming. If I don't show up now, I think that will make things worse for you, won't it?"

Dex murmured something noncommittal that could have been either an agreement or a disagreement.

"If they don't know our relationship is fake, it can't hurt them, right? Seriously, we just mention each other for a few weeks after the holidays and then casually say we broke up. No one gets hurt. That's what you told me, remember?"

Why did it feel like she was the one talking him into this mess now?

"Right." They made eye contact and a lingering spark in his gaze smoldered brighter as they continued to look at each other. Smack in the middle of a crowded shopping mall, with "Rudolph the Red-Nosed Reindeer" playing through the overhead speakers, a spark fluttered between them. The place buzzed with Christmas spirit, frazzled nerves and people going further into debt, but Lena's eyes seemed locked with the handsome surgeon's next to her.

"So, remember those sweaters we saw on the way in? We are totally buying those for the rehearsal dinner." Lena stood and held out her hand. "Come on. I'm starving and we have gifts to buy."

CHAPTER FIVE

THE WAY HER cheeks pinked up when he pulled out her chair made him want to do more for her. Something about that shade of pink made him think about what he could do in order to see it again. *And if that isn't crazy...*

Once they got through the holidays and this fake romance, Dex needed to find someone new. Someone who didn't want forever and who didn't look at him like he was a jerk for only wanting short-term. He hadn't had a deep connection since Jessie. In fact, he'd actively avoided making a connection that lasted longer than a month. But why did that seem less and less appealing?

"So, why did you become a doctor?" Lena asked as he rounded the table and sat across from her.

"I wanted to help people."

It wasn't the greatest of answers, but it was an honest one. Maybe a little bit of an oversimplification, but true, nonetheless.

She snorted. "Nice try, Doc. I'm gonna need a bit more info than that."

"Long story short, when I was ten, I witnessed a really bad car crash. And the paramedics, they were just brilliant. I watched them take these people that were so bloody, I thought they had no chance. And they pulled them out of this mangled heap of metal and got them in an ambulance."

She tilted her head and stared, eyes full of questions. "So why not a paramedic?"

"Honestly, that's what I wanted at first. I even did a couple ride-alongs, but it was a paramedic that convinced me to go to med school. He told me that surgeons were the ones who really helped the most people. So I got involved with this mentor program that let me shadow a couple surgeons for a day, and, well, the rest is history."

That conversation that day in the back of that ambulance had been life-altering for him. It had set him on a trajectory out of the tiny town of Westfield and into a life that he loved. Westfield had been a great place to grow up, but he'd had little problem leaving it behind.

She wrinkled her nose in disagreement. "Clearly that man has never worked with a nurse. Because all nurses know who really helps the most people as well as keep the hospitals running."

Dex laughed, both at the cockiness in her voice and the truth in her statement. Years ago, he'd learned that if a doctor got on the wrong side of the nursing staff it made for a rough work environment. Nurses definitely made the world go 'round and kept a doctor's arrogance firmly in check.

Still, he couldn't just admit that to her, could he?

"Yes, we know, nurses are the real rock stars. Yet how many nurses can perform something as simple as an appendectomy or save a person from a ruptured spleen?"

Lena rolled her eyes. "Point taken. We are all necessary."

"Anyways, so then I set my sights on being a surgeon. And that's my story." He paused and looked around the crowded restaurant. Red-and-gold tinsel hung from the rafters. Why did every place insist on burying their business under a rainbow of Christmas trappings?

When Lena didn't continue the conversation, he did. "Why did you become a nurse?"

"Because it angered my father." She snatched one of the rolls from the basket the waiter was setting down. "At least initially."

They quickly ordered, and Dex tried to steer the conversation back to her motivations for being a nurse. He straightened in his chair and leaned forward with interest to catch her answer. He'd known a lot of people who took jobs for various reasons, but to spite their parent? That was a new one.

"You chose a career simply to tick off your dad?" He held back the laugh that tickled against his lips because the expression on Lena's face was one hundred percent serious. Deep in his gut, he knew laughing now would be one of the worst mistakes he could make with the beautiful nurse sitting across from him.

She picked bits off the roll, smooshing the tiny bits of bread between her fingers. "My father is one of those doctors who thinks nurses are second-class citizens. You don't do it, but I know you've seen the kind I mean. That act like nurses are only there to do their bidding."

He nodded, pulling in a slow breath and releasing it even slower while he thought of the best way to respond. Lena was the definition of someone with daddy issues, that much was clear. She'd need to let go of all that if she wanted to truly move forward.

Lena continued without his response, though. "In my misguided youth, I thought that if I were to become a nurse, I could show my father that nurses were worthy of respect."

He let the statement settle and it felt heavy. The weight she carried around with that mission meant she was far stronger than he'd given her credit for. Every scrap of information he learned about her ticked his admiration up a notch or two.

"And how'd that work out?"

She laughed sadly. "Not well. But it was absolutely the best decision I've ever made. I love my job."

"You're really good at it too."

Her cheeks pinked up again but she met his eyes when she said, "Thank you."

Dex took a big gulp of water, swallowing hard. Lena was so much more than he had been expecting. Being around her made him oddly nervous. He worried she'd see his hands shake or realize that he had butterflies constantly flitting about in his stomach when he was with her.

He'd saved lives. Taken organs out of people's bodies. Sliced through layers of skin and muscle. He'd held a human heart in his hand during a cardiac rotation and massaged it back to life. Going on a fake date with a beautiful nurse should be as simple as pie.

Lena's heart raced as Dex complimented her. Knowing your skills and having them recognized by someone else were totally different. She wasn't sure she'd ever stop blushing when someone praised her. This was starting to feel a little like a real date, though, and she felt the need to rein it back in.

The waiter brought their food by and then once again left them alone.

Lena poked at her food for a minute, rolling ideas around in her head for how to begin this conversation. “So, um, we should talk about expectations.”

“Seems simple to me. You pretend to be my girl while we are in Westfield for a few days for my brother’s wedding. I’ll pretend to be your guy while we are in LA for your fundraiser thing.” He jabbed a fry in her direction. “No emotions. No risk. Simple enough.”

Lena patiently took a large drink of her water. “I meant the finer points of the agreement. Logistics, travel dates, lodging.”

He popped the fry in his mouth and chewed, his eyes never leaving hers. “I figured I’d sort out the details for my thing, you’d sort them for yours. But I really like your concern for our sleeping arrangements.”

The air between them seemed charged with that hint of this being more. His voice wrapped around her and sent zings of electricity up and down her spine. She swallowed hard, trying to put the picture out of her mind of them sharing a bed.

“While I think that’s an acceptable start, I’m really going to need more details. I need to know where I’ll be staying while we are in Westfield.”

“With my parents, of course. My hometown isn’t exactly set up for out-of-town visitors. It’s more of an idyllic haven in the midst of a tourist area. There are no hotels in town, only some rental cabins. The closest are down the mountain in Gatlinburg.”

“With your parents?” She gulped.

“Yeah. But it’ll be fine. They have a spare bedroom and I’ll be in my own room next door.”

The odd feeling the settled in her chest in that moment took Lena some time to identify. It was a mixture of relief and disappointment. How bizarre that she should feel disappointed about the idea of her own room.

"Unless you'd rather share," he said with a wide grin.

She took a large bite and chewed slowly while digesting that line of thought. The blatant flirting she could deal with, but she didn't like how her body reacted to it. Not giving in to the temptation that Dexter Henry presented was going to be a big challenge.

It was hard to keep her eyes off the handsome surgeon sitting across from her. And when he flirted, it made her think about things she had no business even imagining. Dex could break her heart if she wasn't careful. But she was done being this submissive nothing, catering to the whims of surgeons who thought themselves better than her.

And she wasn't going to give him the chance to hurt her.

Even if they had so much chemistry that she found herself daydreaming about just how much Dexter Henry was her type. Because she didn't have a type anymore. That implied she could trust someone enough to let them in.

And the last thing she was willing to do was to trust another surgeon.

"No, my own room is an inflexible requirement. My parents have several spare rooms, if you want to stay at the estate. I'm happy to foot the bill for a hotel while we are in California, though." She took the emotion out of her tone. This was a business transaction, nothing more.

"You decide. I trust you." He leaned across the table as he said it, taking her hand in his.

Lena's breath shook when she inhaled sharply. "I think we need to keep the PDA to a minimum too."

He held on when she tried to tug her hand away. "We

have to be comfortable touching each other, Lena. We'll be in close proximity and under scrutiny. Even if we say minimal touching, there has to be some. Or we will be fast outed as fakes."

Shifting uncomfortably in her seat, Lena still tried to tug her hand free. "Maybe so, but do we have to do this now? I could eat easier if you weren't holding my right hand hostage."

"Fine." He squeezed her hand before letting it go. "But you know I'm right."

"Do you worry about them finding out that this is all fake?" She changed the subject, refusing to discuss the idea of them touching further in that moment. "My family will be critical, examining for weaknesses in our story and cracks in our relationship, in hopes of it not working out so that they can continue to push me toward marrying a man of their choice."

Dex leaned back and shook his head. "Why would you let them tell you who to marry?"

Lena stared down at the melting ice in her glass. "You don't understand the pressure. Sometimes it's easier to give in than to fight and fight only to lose anyways."

"Some things are worth fighting for." He reached out and ran a finger down her arm gently. "Like love. You can't help who you love, Lena. And you sure can't let someone else decide that for you."

"Oh, believe me, love is not a factor in their decisions."

"Well, my mom's just going to be happy that I'm seeing someone. She won't expect perfection."

"I feel a little guilty deceiving everyone." Lena sent him a wry smile. "Don't you?"

He shrugged. "Maybe a little. But it benefits both of us,

and if we do this right, it's not like they will even know. No one needs to know, and that way no one gets hurt."

She nodded an agreement, but couldn't help but think that the person most likely to get hurt in all this was her. Sucking in a deep breath, she focused on the positives.

"We did manage to get a lot of shopping done today. How about a wrapping party to get all these gifts ready for our trip?"

"Whatever makes you happy," Dex said, staring her down.

Lena licked her lips under his scrutiny. She could think of a lot of things that might make her happy right now, and every single one of them involved a certain dark-haired general surgeon.

She was in so much trouble.

CHAPTER SIX

DEX RECLINED BACK on the couch, feeling the tension ease from his muscles. He flipped on the hockey game and tossed his phone onto the table out of reach. He was half-asleep when a loud banging came from the door.

It sounded like someone was kicking it?

He answered the door and his jaw dropped. "Uh, how did you know where I live?"

"Belinda told me." Wrapping paper and ribbon filled Lena's arms. From the various angles her rolls projected from her grip, it looked like she had a very precarious hold on the colorful load. She was grinning from ear to ear and her cheeks were as bright a shade as the paper in her hands. "Are you going to let me in or not? I'm about to drop all this all over your doorstep if you don't."

"Yeah, of course." He jolted into movement and pushed the door open wide, motioning for her to come in out of the cold. "Can I help?"

"I think if you try to take any of it, I'll drop it all." She stepped over to his coffee table and squatted down. She carefully dropped all the festive trappings across the wooden surface. A spool of silvery ribbon bounced off the table and rolled across the carpet to his bare foot.

"What is all this?"

She waved a hand vaguely at the mess she'd just made of his coffee table as if that was explanation enough. "We're wrapping presents tonight. I told you this."

"I got it covered." Dex gestured toward the hearth where a stack of gift bags sat beside the presents he'd purchased with Lena's help. He didn't wrap presents. Gift bags were made for a reason, the reason being that wrapping paper was an unnecessary annoyance created to annoy people who weren't overflowing with Christmas spirit.

"I have presents in my car too. I couldn't carry everything at once. Since you don't have shoes on, I'll get them myself."

"Lena…"

But she had disappeared out the door before he could verbalize another thought.

She came back a moment later with several bags in her hands. She set her bags on the couch before turning to him, hands on her hips. "Did you forget that I was coming over tonight?"

"I didn't think you were serious!" Dex protested against the accusatory tone in Lena's question. He'd thought she was joking when she'd said she'd be at his door with bells on to wrap the gifts they'd bought before they left for Westfield in a couple days. He never expected her to actually show up with wrapping paper and ribbons.

"I'm always serious when it comes to Christmas!" Spinning around, Lena's eyes took in the minimalistic decor. A measure of shock shone brightly on her face. "Why don't you have a Christmas tree?"

Dex huffed. "Because I'm a busy surgeon who lives

alone and won't even be in town for Christmas? What's the point?"

She looked so affronted by that he decided not to tell her that he'd never once had a Christmas tree in this house. She might implode. At the very least, it would launch her into another rant about Christmas spirit and the importance of the holiday season.

The last tree he'd put up had been with Jessie the Christmas before their disastrous attempt at a wedding. She'd moved from Westfield to live with him in Florida while he finished med school. He'd hoped that by removing the physical distance between them, the emotional one would close too. Their relationship had been splintering even then, but he'd stubbornly tried to patch it like a crumbling gingerbread cookie. The thought of losing her had propelled him into proposing, and her acceptance had been half-hearted at best. He'd been too bullheaded to even allow the idea that Jessie didn't want to marry him into his head. In hindsight, he'd lost her before that Christmas, and all the Christmas traditions and wedding planning had only pushed her farther away.

He'd spent every waking moment of that December planning a wedding with a woman who'd been apathetic about the idea at best. It should have given him pause, but no. He'd prodded and planned while she seemed more interested in watching breakup movies and going out with her new friends without him. Reflecting back, he couldn't remember why he fought so hard to keep their relationship intact when it had been clear she was pulling away. Or why he had let it get so far without addressing it at all.

Instead of communicating concerns, he'd pushed her to get married, somehow thinking a ring would be the glue that held them together. He'd ignored the hard signs of trouble, how her eyes constantly drifted to other men, how she never wanted him to touch her, how she had zero interest in planning their wedding. She'd wanted the world and he'd been working as hard as he could to try and give her those dreams.

Looking back, he could pinpoint his being matched to the residency program in Nashville as the final straw for her. That notification had come in the week before their planned nuptials and she'd actually cried. For the first time in a while, Jessie had shown emotion. She'd wanted him to request a different residency program. Preferably something on a beach, she'd begged, but anything that got them out of Tennessee. The signs had all been there. He'd just been too stubborn to see them.

A poke to the belly brought his focus back to the present and the woman standing in front of him. "Well, where's your tree? We'll put it up."

He rubbed the back of his neck and winced as he said, "I don't have one."

At her gasp of horror, he struggled to hide a smile. Maybe celebrating Christmas again wouldn't be so bad if it meant getting a reaction out of Lena. Her face was so expressive that he wanted to keep pushing her, to see if her eyes sparkled with anger like they did with amusement.

"We will just have to go out and buy you one. Where are your shoes?"

"Tonight we are wrapping presents, right? We won't have time to do that and go get a tree and decorate it. I have to be at the hospital at five in the morning for back-to-back surgeries, so I need to get some sleep at least."

Although she wrinkled her nose, and he could tell she wanted to protest, she finally agreed. "I want it noted, though, that wrapping presents without the presence of a decorated tree might be against the rules of Christmas."

"There are no rules to Christmas."

"Of course there are rules to Christmas." She rolled her eyes. Pulling her phone out of the back pocket of her jeans, she pulled up a music streaming app. When a Christmas carol blared out of the device's tiny speakers, she sat the phone on the table next to the ribbons. "Like, you have to play Christmas music while you decorate. Also when gifts are being wrapped. Preferably with eggnog?"

He shook his head. "No eggnog either."

"You have to have eggnog." She strode into the kitchen and flung the refrigerator open. The sigh she released as she stood in front of his open refrigerator sounded frustrated. "Not even boiled custard? You really are the Grinch in human form."

"You know the Grinch didn't actually hate Christmas?"

Crossing her arms over her chest, Lena faced him down, clearly ready to hand him his opinions chopped on a platter. "How can you even argue that?"

The fire in her eyes made him want to get to know her more. Her spirited responses intrigued him in a way no woman ever had. It made him want to piss her off just to see her reaction.

"He didn't care about Christmas until the singing disturbed his peace. He just wanted to make the noise stop." Dex shrugged, knowing the casual reply would get her worked up. "I kinda relate to the guy. I used to have this nice, peaceful life where I went to work and came home to the serenity of this house, but then this adorable sexy nurse started ordering me around, and before I even knew it had happened, she replaced my quiet with Christmas carols and the crinkle of ribbons."

"Are you calling me bossy?"

With as much innocence as he could muster, Dex said, "*I* was just telling a story. What meaning *you* derived from it is entirely on you."

"You are calling me bossy!" She stepped up to him and poked him right in the chest. Hard. "I am not bossy."

He laughed, resisting the urge to rub the spot on his chest where she'd just poked him so hard he might have a bruised lung. "Says the woman who barged into my house carrying her body weight in gift wrap while telling me exactly how we are going to spend my night off."

Her eyes narrowed at him. "We talked about—"

She broke off with a squeak when he threw her over his shoulder and carried her back into the living room, where Christmas carols still played from her phone.

"Dexter Henry, you put me down this instant!"

"If we are going to wrap gifts, let's get to it." With a smirk, he set her back on her feet. He faked a bow. "Where do we begin, Taskmaster?"

Grabbing one of the shopping bags sitting by his fireplace, she shoved it against his chest. Anger sparkled in her eyes like he'd hoped it would. His plan was working out just as he'd hoped.

"Start with this one. It's small. Surely you can handle wrapping it."

Again, he laid on the innocent act, nice and thick. "But that's my gift to you. You're not meant to see it until Christmas."

All of the irritation drained from her face. With eyes wide, she stared up at him. "What?"

"You heard me." He flashed her a shy sort of smile

when he saw how much the wholesomeness was getting to her. "I can't wrap your gift in front of you."

"When did you...?" She trailed off, eyes filled with wonder that had him curious about when she last had an unexpected gift. "Why would you...?"

"After you left me at the mall, and because you are my girlfriend."

"Fake girlfriend," she corrected.

Shrugging his shoulders, he said softly, "I can't take you home as my girlfriend and not have a gift for you to put under the tree. As you said about your family, my family will also have certain expectations, and believe me, it will not end well for me if I don't put something under the tree for you."

Her eyes were bright and she blinked rapidly as if blinking away unshed tears. "I didn't think to get you anything."

"Then it's a good thing you have a few days before we leave," he teased, trying to lighten the mood. Had he taken things too far with teasing her?

When she didn't smile back, Dex took her hand in his. His touch was warm and welcoming and a million other little things that she should not be thinking of about a man only meant to be her fake boyfriend for a few short weeks. The logical plan would be they'd get through the next few weeks without either of them doing something stupid like falling for the other.

But nothing about the way she felt in that moment was logical.

Her heart beat faster as Dex tugged her closer. The skin-to-skin contact should have been nothing. They were barely holding hands. Should have been... From this close, she got a nice view of the jagged little scar on his chin that she'd always thought was a natural cleft. She wanted to kiss it and—

Oh, no.

Her lips could not meet any part of Dex's body, not even the scarred cleft in his chin. Swallowing hard, she took a giant step back from him. Hopefully with some physical distance between them she could get herself under control.

"You know what? I bought myself a new sweater that still has the tags on it," he said. "We can wrap that up as your gift to me. You'll even know that I'll like it and that it fits because I picked it out myself."

Being near him made her crazy. If she wasn't wanting to throw herself at him, she wanted to cry at his thoughtfulness.

This man… He had bought her a gift. Maybe it was part of the ruse to fool his parents, but she couldn't help but be touched by the gesture. It hadn't even occurred to her that she should get him something. And now he added an offer to let her wrap something he'd bought for himself? She wasn't quite sure how to handle that, but one thing for sure was that she couldn't accept that last offer.

"I can't give you a gift you bought yourself after you bought me something. What sort of price range am I spending?" She fought back a sniff. His considerate nature brought her nearly to tears.

"You really don't have to get me anything."

The last dregs of tears dried up with the frustration his non-answer had sparked. She was sprinting through all the emotions tonight. All of them. For so long, she'd refused to allow herself any sentimentality. She kept people—men especially—at arm's length, afraid she'd end up hurt again, but somehow Dex dug his way under her skin and seemed determined to drown her in her own pent-up emotions.

"What price range?" she repeated through clenched teeth.

A weighted silence settled over them, thick and palpable in the room. Their eyes met and the air between them charged with an invisible battle of wills as Lena and Dex sized each other up.

After a few long seconds, Dex broke the stare and Lena did a little internal dance at the win. Dex exhaled his resignation.

"I spent about a hundred bucks on yours. But don't feel obligated to spend that much on me. I know I make significantly more than you, plus you just paid for a cross-country move and a new place."

Dex had no idea that she'd inherited more money than she'd ever spend from her maternal grandfather. She hadn't even heard the words "trust fund" since moving to Tennessee. One of the upsides to living in Nashville, really. She nearly snorted at his concern for her financial status, but stopped it at the last second. The fewer people in Tennessee who knew about her trust fund, the better.

"You want to put this one up to wrap later, then?" She held the small bag out to him with the slightest shake. Lightweight. And it didn't have a noticeable rattle or rustle other than the crinkle of the nondescript white paper bag. It didn't even have a logo on it to identify what store it came from. Curiosity piqued, she tried to run options through her mind as to what the little bag might contain. When he reached for it, she pulled it back out of his reach. "Or maybe I should just take a little peek?"

"Or maybe you should hand it over before I have to take it from you?"

Laughter bubbled out of her at the mischief shining in his eyes. "If you think you are man enough, come get it."

"Is that a dare? You're gonna regret that." Dex grabbed up the spools of ribbon and started pelting her with them.

"Oh, you are going to get it now!" she squealed. The decorative onslaught sparked a war of competitiveness within her. He was going down! Snatching up a roll of wrapping paper, she swung it into his side like a bat. The paper made a lot of noise as it crumpled against his side. "Ha!"

Faster than she could blink, Dex seized the improvised weapon in her hand and pulled her in closer to him. His deep, delicious laughter sent her heart on a jog as he tugged her closer.

And closer.

Dex held tight to the now bent wrapping paper roll with one hand and used the other to brush her hair away from her face. Tucking a lock behind her ear, he cupped her face with his hand.

Lena leaned into his touch. The subtle scent of his cologne wafted over her, its notes reminiscent of the ocean and fresh air. Her eyes fluttered closed as she anticipated his lips on hers.

But then he moved away.

She opened her eyes in confusion.

Dex took another step back, wagging the shopping bag holding her gift back and forth in front of her. He kept walking backward through the open doorway, a wide grin on his face. "I'm going to put this in the bedroom for safekeeping."

"Well played," she grudgingly admitted when he returned. Making her forget she held her own gift took some skill. She'd been too focused on that almost-kiss to notice his actions. The sneak had lifted it right from her distracted and unsuspecting fingers. "I admit defeat. You win that round."

"This is all crinkled up now," he said, picking up the roll of wrapping paper they'd fought over. The red paper was bent nearly in half with creases and wrinkles radiating out from where it had impacted against his body. "I think we need to use this for my brothers' gifts. They won't appreciate pretty paper anyway."

She scoffed. "We can't use wrinkled paper. That's trash now."

"Another Christmas rule?" His brow raised.

"Of course." She gathered up the undamaged supplies and sat down on the floor to get started. Not a single gift had been wrapped. They really needed to get to work if they were going to get everything wrapped in a single evening.

He sat next to her and reached for the pack of bows. "How about you wrap and I'll decorate?"

"I don't think so, Doc. That's not an equal division of labor," she protested as she watched him open the package. "We aren't ready for those yet."

"Shh..." He leaned over and stuck one of the bows to the top of her head. "I'm wrapping my own present."

"Dex." Her heart barrel-rolled in her chest as the implication of his words crashed hard over her.

"I keep trying to ignore the chemistry between us, but it's hard to do."

Oh, they had chemistry all right. Enough chemistry for six couples and then some, but that didn't mean starting something up would be a good idea. Just chemistry alone wasn't enough to risk a relationship on. Not in her opinion, anyway.

"A meth lab has real chemistry, but it's still hazardous to my health."

Dex's laughter was a laughter that she felt in her own lungs, so deep and joyful that it took her breath away. It erased the concerns and worries she'd had a minute ago and replaced them with a hope that somehow this wouldn't end badly.

"You are a stubborn woman, you know that, Lena Franklin?"

"Says the player who is hitting on me." A giggle rose up and turned into a snort, causing Lena to flush with embarrassment. She dearly loved to laugh, but hated the sounds she made when she did. She argued back, playfully, "It's a lost cause. I'll have you know I have a boyfriend."

"An imaginary one."

"You are not imaginary." Lena laughed until her sides hurt. She had to swipe at a tear trekking down her cheek. "But that's beside the point. I'm not interested in guys who change girls more than I change my scrubs."

"Fair enough. I'll give you that one." He leaned back against the couch, his pose deceivingly relaxed for someone who'd just been shot down hard. "So, what's your story? Who hurt you, Lena? I'm hoping that I'm wrong, but if I was a betting man, I'd put money down that some idiot male screwed up so badly it sent you running across the country to get away from him."

Was she that obvious? Somehow, she'd hoped that her secrets wouldn't follow her, but it didn't seem like she'd been that lucky. Telling Dex about Connor and how much he'd deceived her, how gullible and naive she'd been in the search for love, was too much to bear, though.

She tried to change the subject back to something

lighter. “I’m going to make you wrap your own presents if you don’t behave.”

Dex reached over and took her hand in his. Bending his head, Dex brushed his lips against the back of her wrist, his lips soft and warm against her skin. “I already wrapped the only thing I want.”

He stared at her for a moment. The heat radiating up her arm from his touch made her think about things she couldn’t have. Things she wouldn’t let herself have. Lena swallowed hard. “We should get these presents wrapped.”

Coming here tonight might have been a mistake. They’d had such a good time shopping together and she’d learned so much about him in that single day that she’d thought spending more time together would make things easier. But the attraction between them kept things from getting easier. In fact, being near him without giving in to the physical need his touch inspired within her was far harder than she’d anticipated.

“Okay.” With one last swipe of his lips over the bare skin of her wrist, Dex released her hand. His intense gaze delved straight into her soul as he said, “I’ll back off. For now. What do you want to wrap first?”

CHAPTER SEVEN

In the days since their wrapping paper adventure, something had changed between them. Dex just couldn't put his finger on exactly what. A good change, though, he thought. Lena was relaxing her guard around him, ever so slowly, and opening up with bits and pieces about her past. But whenever he made a move physically, the walls came slamming back into place. Slow and steady was going to be the name of the game with her. He had to ease into this so as not to spook her.

Lena had been all smiles when he'd picked her up for the drive up to Westfield. Her suitcase was nestled in the back of his SUV between his own luggage and the brightly wrapped Christmas presents for his family. Her smile of satisfaction at seeing all the gifts piled in there when he'd put her luggage in had made fiddling with all that ribbon worth it.

"Penny for your thoughts?" Lena asked, tapping him on the arm.

"Just thinking of the other night and how much I enjoyed spending the evening with you."

The colorful paper had been all Lena's idea, but the memory of the evening they spent with rolls of shiny colored paper, curls of ribbon and togetherness would forever be a happy one for him. He hadn't laughed that much in a long time. And Lena softening up to him was a major bonus.

"How can such a gifted surgeon not manage basic gift-wrapping?" She shook her head. Exasperated disbelief filled her voice. "You are hopeless, you know."

"I missed that skills lab," he deadpanned.

The little joke made her laugh. The sound of her laughter was quickly becoming an addiction for him. The more he heard those happy noises, the more he wanted to hear them. She'd told him how she hated her laugh, but for him, it was bright and cheerful, like the mountains around his home covered with fresh snow. There was an imperfect perfection to it and he couldn't get enough.

Dex merged onto the interstate and they began the longest part of the journey home to Westfield. They had a good four hours on the interstate before they got to Gatlinburg and then would begin the windy mountainous trek to the small town of Westfield, Tennessee.

The excitement of going home was building. There was nothing better than Christmas in the Smoky Mountains. Most of the tourists would be gone after the last of the fall color had faded away for the season, leaving locals and a few random people seeking a quiet country holiday with a view.

He hadn't been home for Christmas in far too long. He'd told his parents he'd had to work because of being the low man on the totem pole. It had always been, "Next year should get better, and I'll come home then." The real truth was that he'd volunteered to work so that he could have a reason to avoid celebrating Christmas. That last Christmas with Jessie had spoiled him on the season.

Then he'd met Lena. Her infectious Christmas spirit

had managed to seep into his soul, and he found himself actually looking forward to Christmas this year. He glanced over at the woman in his passenger seat.

Lena shifted around a bit as she found a comfortable position for the long drive. She dug a bag of pretzels out of her purse. "So, what do your parents do? I'm not sure you've ever said."

"My dad is the manager of the town bank and my mom runs the Westfield tourism board. They are pretty involved in all the local issues as a result. You want town gossip, ask my mom. And my dad knows the credit score of everyone in town, probably better than they do. They were so excited when I got into medical school."

"Were?" Lena caught his slip of the tongue and he groaned. He'd revealed more than he'd meant to.

"Are."

"Mmm-hmm." The palm of her hand settled over his forearm. "How much did it disappoint them that you didn't come home and work in Westfield?"

Telling his family that he was not coming back home after med school and residency had been one of the hardest things he'd ever done. His family had always been super close. Tommy had graduated college and moved right back to teach science at the local high school. Jill, his future sister-in-law, had gotten a job at the insurance agency while still in high school, went full-time a minute after graduation and never left town. His youngest brother, Wade, would be right back in Westfield after graduating the next spring with his degree in finance, where his plans were to work at the bank and eventually take over from their dad.

He had been the only one in the family who didn't see a future in the cozy little town. And while his family had never really commented about it, he could see the look in their eyes that said they were hurt he didn't come home to stay, and in the way his mom bit her tongue sometimes when they talked about the future, or his dad stopped midsentence and backtracked.

No matter how much they wanted him home, he couldn't return. It boiled down to one simple fact—there was no place for a general surgeon in his hometown. Westfield didn't even have a proper hospital. It had an emergency room only, no inpatient rooms. It was really for stitches and broken arms. Any actual emergencies were taken to Gatlinburg or Knoxville.

"They thought I would go into family practice and set up shop right on Main Street. But that was never what I wanted." Exhaling slowly, he continued, "From the moment I decided on med school, I wanted to be a surgeon. I put off telling them, though, because I knew how they'd take it."

"I understand going against parental expectations." The pressure her parents had put on her echoed in her words, and he truly believed she did understand.

His parents had hoped he'd come home, yes, but they'd never pressured him to do so. And he knew they never would. However, he didn't think Lena had the same on her end.

"You don't have the best relationship with your parents, do you?"

"What gave it away?" she snarked in reply. "The number of times I've bit your head off for mentioning them or the fact that I hate talking about them?"

"Both?"

A snort came from Lena's direction. "Well, now you know why I wouldn't want to date a guy who is just like my dad, then. I won't become my mother, standing in a man's shadow, lapping up the tiniest scrap of his attention like a sun-starved plant would bask in rays of sunlight. I made that mistake once and refuse to go down that road again."

He looked briefly in her direction. Solid determination masked any other emotion her face might have shown. It told him a lot about who Lena was deep down.

"I don't see much chance of that, as outspoken as you are."

Lena reached over and took his hand in hers. Her fingers tangled with his. "I'm going to take that as a compliment."

"I meant it as one." He rubbed his thumb over her hand. "I told them the truth on how we met, by the way. Well, I said we met at work shortly after you moved to Tennessee."

"That was true. We had that impossibly long surgery with all the peritoneal adhesions about two weeks after I moved here. We stood elbow to elbow for a good eight hours that day."

He remembered that day with perfect clarity. The surgery had taken a good three hours longer than he'd anticipated because of the patient's condition, but he hadn't really minded the extra time because he'd been fascinated by the sharpness of the new nurse at his side who'd known nearly as much about the surgery as he had. She'd impressed him. And when he sought her out later that day, he'd found out that not only was she intelligent, but beautiful as well.

"I asked you out after that surgery."

"Ugh." She scrunched up her nose. "I remember."

"The idea of me asking you out is that distasteful a memory?"

That hurt. He shoved down the initial burst of anger that popped up. His ego was taking a real hit as they rehashed how wrong he'd been about asking Lena out.

"Actually, I was pretty interested." As she continued, her voice grew more confident. "Then I remembered the hospital gossip about you. I can't be one in a line of bed partners for a cocky arrogant surgeon who doesn't care for anything beyond his own needs. Been there, done that, got the heartbreak to prove it."

"Ouch." He wanted to deny her description of him, but there was a grain of truth to her statements. He squeezed her fingers to remind her that she'd taken his hand in hers earlier. "And yet here we are, hand in hand anyways."

"We need to be more comfortable touching each other if we are going to pull this off," she snapped and snatched her hand away. She rubbed it on the thigh of her jeans like he'd contaminated her. "That was your idea, if you remember."

After whatever idiot she'd been involved with had hurt her, prickliness had become her default setting. Each time he pushed too close emotionally, she bristled up like a cactus and went straight into defensive mode.

When he glanced over at her, she was staring out the window and had that stubborn set to her jaw that he was quickly learning meant he wasn't going to win.

"For the record, Lena, I wasn't complaining about holding your hand. In fact, it's been the highlight of my day."

Her cheeks pinked, but she ignored the compliment like he'd expected she would. Trees and exit ramps rolled by as the SUV moved down the interstate. Their conversation trailed off a little, but when he switched on the radio and tuned it to a station playing only Christmas carols, Lena began to hum along.

They passed a sign for a rest area and Lena perked up. "Do you mind if we stop?"

"I could stand to stretch my legs myself." Flipping his blinker on, Dex moved the SUV into the right lane and then onto the exit ramp. He eased to a stop in front of the rest area.

They climbed out of the warm SUV into the brisk December air. A shiver coursed through him and he yanked his zipper up on his jacket to protect himself from the wind.

A woman with two small children—a little girl skipping next to her with a doll in one hand and a tiny boy in head-to-toe blue who was barely keeping up—came out of the building housing the restrooms. They headed toward the parking lot.

Dex nodded toward them. "Look how adorable they are. In case it comes up, someday I do want to have a couple kids."

"Me too," Lena replied softly. A sadness in her voice when she'd said she wanted children pulled him up short.

But before he could ask her why the thought of having children made her sad, Dex saw the toddler trip and could only watch in horror as the little guy fell face-first onto the concrete walkway.

The thought of how beautiful a baby with Dex's eyes would be sprang to mind, but the image vanished when he suddenly sprinted away from her side. Where was he going in such a rush? She looked in the direction he'd run. The little boy he had just pointed out lay unmoving on the concrete walkway, blood just beginning to pool next to his face.

"He's unconscious," Dex shouted. "Grab the first aid kit from the back of the SUV."

Digging her phone out of her coat pocket, she dialed 911 as she ran back to the car. When the operator answered, Lena quickly gave them what information she could remember. "We are at the rest stop on I-40 between Nashville and Knoxville. I don't know the mile markers. A little boy about two years of age fell face-first onto the concrete walkway here at the rest stop. He's unconscious with some apparent facial injuries based on the amount of blood."

When Lena ran back over, Dex sat on his knees next to the boy. He was trying to explain to the mother why she couldn't pick the child up, because it could worsen his injuries. Despite how much it must be going against her natural instincts, the woman finally just sank to the ground crying. She pulled her daughter into her lap, and her sobs cut sharper than the cold winter wind swirling around them.

"The ambulance is on the way." Lena squatted next to him, opening up the first aid kit and pulling out a roll of gauze.

"What can we do?" His eyes looked tortured as he met her gaze.

"Slow the bleeding." She took the gauze and pressed it to the gaping wound on the child's head. "Here, hold this. We have no equipment. No facilities. All we can do is keep him as warm and as still as possible."

Dex shrugged out of his coat and covered the child with it.

Lena leaned close to the child's chest and listened to

his breathing. "Airways seem clear. Breathing is a little rapid." Her fingers felt along the boy's throat. "His pulse is strong and color is still good despite the cold and blood loss."

The little one woke up and started moving, fighting their attempts at helping him and ignoring all their warnings to stay still. He wanted his mother and only barely tolerated them holding the gauze to his wound. It seemed an eternity before they heard the wail of sirens and the ambulance finally pulled up. The paramedics hopped out and hurried over where they took over the boy's care.

Lena and Dex stepped back out of their way.

In moments, the paramedics got the boy loaded into the ambulance, while the boy's mother followed behind with her little girl clinging to her, tears on both their faces.

Dex went to run his hands through his hair as he watched the ambulance drive away, but Lena stopped him.

"You should wash your hands first."

He looked down at his hands, at the blood now drying on his skin. "Good idea."

"Meet you back out here in five?"

He nodded and stomped toward the door with the Men sign hanging overhead.

Lena went the opposite direction to the ladies' room. Random emotions and feelings swirled through her, whipping past her like that icy wind outside. Some fleeting, others lingering, like the desire to see Dex with his own child.

When she was young, she'd dreamed of what it might be like to have a family. To be the mom she'd always wished she'd had, the kind of mom who made messes in the kitchen baking with her kids, and put soccer games before board meetings. And she'd pictured the father of those children as the kind of dad who would build forts and have snowball fights and teach his kids to fix things, not dismiss them to play another round of golf.

Then she'd grown up and babies had become a "someday" thought for her, pushed off even more by the realization that a family meant trusting someone enough to risk a pregnancy. She'd almost considered it with Connor, but then he'd shown his true colors and she'd locked even the hope of ever having a child away in that "never gonna happen" box. But today, seeing the tender way Dex cared for that little boy had kicked the hint of wondering about what his children might look like into a full-blown need to mother the man's children.

After splashing some water on her face, she looked up at her reflection in the mirror. "Pull yourself together. You need to calm down before you go back out there and jump him in the parking lot." She took several deep breaths and tried to put the idea of seeing Dex holding their child out of her mind.

She walked outside, still trying to talk herself out of creating those imaginary babies right then and there. They would make beautiful babies, but she and Dex were so not to that point. She was barely tolerating a fake relationship. She didn't trust him enough to go on a real date. Something was clearly wrong with her given her current line of thought.

Dex hadn't noticed her yet. She walked behind him, a few paces back, and the tight fit of his shirt across his shoulders and the snug way his jeans molded to his backside did not help her clear her mind.

Why would that thought not go away?

Dex picked up his jacket from the ground where it had been tossed aside by the paramedics. He shook it and bits of dirt and dust flew off it, floating away on the crisp breeze.

Lena stopped next to him, nodding toward the blood-stained jacket in his hands. “Pretty sure that’s ruined.”

He shrugged. “Maybe. Have to take it to the dry cleaner in the morning and see if they can do anything with it. I’m just glad it looks like the little guy will be okay. He had me worried.”

“Me too.” She quickly stuffed the packets of medication she’d thrown out of the way while looking for gauze back into the first aid kit. She rolled the loose unused gauze into a ball to toss in the trash. “You’ll need to refill this soon. The rest of that gauze is unusable thanks to this wind.” She closed the plastic container and looked up at him carefully. “Are you okay to drive?”

With a nod, he held a hand out to her. “Guess we need to get moving after our non-rest stop, don’t we? It’s going to be late by the time we get to Westfield now as it is.”

They walked back to his SUV hand in hand. He tossed his jacket into the back before taking the first aid kit from her and placing it inside. Closing the back, he guided her around to the passenger side and opened her door. She was still getting used to the idea that he wanted to open doors for her. But it was another thing she had found that she really liked about Dexter Henry.

“You were amazing out there. I was floundering, trying unsuccessfully to determine where to start outside of a sterile operating room. And you…you just stepped right up and took charge.” He brushed a strand of hair back away from her face. “I haven’t been this much in awe of someone's medical skills since my first day of medical school."

His admiration sparked a fresh wave of interest in him. It had been a long time since anyone had given her such genuine, heartfelt praise and it felt really, really good. Before she could second-guess the impulse, she moved against him and wrapped her arms around his neck. Tugging his head down to hers, she rose up on tiptoe and pressed her lips to his.

She might have initiated the kiss, but Dex controlled it. His lips moved over hers with a barely reined-in passion. His arms worked their way beneath her coat and behind her back. He held her close, his touch gentle but firm. The kiss held a realness, a promise of something yet to come. Any hint of the relationship being fake flew away on the wind for the duration of their embrace.

When he broke the kiss, they stared at each other, silent for a moment. His breath warmed her cheek. Her hand rested on his throat and his pulse beat beneath her fingers, rapid and strong.

"Why did you do that?" he asked. "And that's so not a complaint."

"I thought we should have our first kiss before we had to potentially kiss in front of your family." A completely made-up answer slipped from her lips because she couldn't—wouldn't—admit to him that she'd been thinking about having his babies or that his compliments had been enough for her to throw caution to the wind for a brief moment. That would go over well, wouldn't it? *Sorry, I'm scared to date you but I can't wait to see how adorable our children would be.* He'd call her a lunatic.

"One hell of a first kiss."

That was an understatement if she'd ever heard one.

She'd known they had a strong physical attraction and she'd still been totally unprepared for the intensity of his lips pressed against her own. Her racing heart served as proof of that, still pounding against her ribs.

He nuzzled against her throat. "How about a second? Wouldn't want to look like amateurs, would we?"

Before she could formulate a coherent response, his lips were on hers. His tongue asked for access and then delved into her mouth when she parted her lips in permission. He wasn't just kissing her, he was savoring her.

When they broke apart for the second time, he rested his forehead against hers while they both gasped for air. The chemistry between them had been exactly why Lena had been hesitant to get involved with Dex. Nothing short of magical, his kiss made her think stupid thoughts. Things a rational woman shouldn't be thinking. Long-term, family planning, scary sorts of things.

She swallowed hard, needing to put some distance between them and regain her perspective. "We should go before your mama sends out a search party."

Dex groaned and stepped back. "Way to kill the mood, Lena."

The mood had not been killed for her. But she was trying her best to murder it because Dexter Henry was a temptation she no longer wanted to resist.

No!

She had to resist. This relationship was meant to be fake. Falling into anything with Dex would only lead to heartache. No lust, no beds, and definitely no love.

She climbed into the SUV and leaned her head back into the seat. This thing was spiraling out of her control and she had no idea how to stop it now. She had to remind him that this was fake and she had to keep her distance. Simple as that.

A moment later, Dex was in the driver's seat next to her and they were back on the interstate heading to his hometown. Dex remained quiet as he maneuvered the SUV through the holiday traffic.

As the mile markers flew past, Lena tried to pull herself together. She just needed to get through the next two weeks and then they'd be back in Nashville, back to their normal lives, where they could go back to only seeing each other at the hospital and only talking about patients. That had always been the plan. A few kisses didn't change that.

Kissing Dex was definitely at the top of things that she should have never done, but couldn't bring herself to regret. She'd moved to Tennessee for a fresh start, though, and she wasn't going to mess that up because of a surgeon with enough passion in his kiss to make her knees weak. She just needed to make it through the holidays without falling for Dex.

Even if that seemed like an impossible task at the moment.

"We're here." Dex pulled to a stop in front of his parents' house just before midnight. Christmas lights and decor covered the log cabin that nestled into the edge of the forest. The eaves were outlined in colorful lights, while white lights outlined the shape of reindeer and a sleigh next to the sidewalk. The holiday adornment gave it a very festive feel.

As they walked up the sidewalk to the front door, she grabbed his hand and tugged him to a stop. The need to put them back on level ground overwhelmed her. "Despite how intense those kisses were, we need to remember that this is fake."

"Is it though?" His thumb rubbed temptingly along the back of her hand.

"It has to be," she said with a conviction she didn't quite feel anymore. "We can't get too carried away and forget that this is all for show."

His stare sliced straight to her soul. The hint of a grin on his lips said he didn't believe her. "If you say so."

"I do." She'd told him how things needed to be. She'd just keep her distance as much as possible and that way she'd be sure to get through this unscathed. Lena told herself these things even if she wasn't quite sure that she even believed them.

When the door opened, she came face-to-face with Dex's mother for the first time. Lena put a smile on her lips as they reached the top of the steps. She could only hope her smile didn't look as fake as she felt.

CHAPTER EIGHT

"DEXTER, GET OVER HERE!"

"Hey, Mama," Dex said, dropping his suitcase as soon as he reached the porch so that he could give his mom a hug. "What are you still doing up? We could have let ourselves in."

"Oh, you know I couldn't sleep 'til I knew you were home safe."

When his mom pulled him into a warm hug, his guilt spiked. He had to spend the next week lying to his parents. As much as he'd wanted to see his parents, he'd been hoping that their late arrival would buy him a few more hours free of lying. He'd even briefly entertained the thought of faking an emergency and heading back to Nashville before his parents woke up in the morning, of letting them see Lena for only a moment before disappearing back to Nashville with her and making an excuse for why she didn't make it back for the wedding.

"Where on earth is your coat? It's freezing out here." His mom released her hold on him enough to back up to arm's length. She held on to his biceps and looked him over critically. He could almost see the calculations in her mind as she examined him. "Are you eating enough? You look too skinny."

Lena laughed from beside him and he caught the note of disbelief. With a single brow raised, he glanced over at her in question.

She brushed his question off with a wave of her hand. "It's nothing."

"It's not nothing. I heard that tone."

Rolling her eyes at him, she said, "Laughs don't have tones, Dex."

"Yours do," he argued.

Lena sighed, but her jaw wasn't set in stubborn refusal. If he had to put an emotion on her expression, he'd say she was a little sad.

"It's just… Well, your mom worries that you are too skinny. Next week mine will be lecturing me about how I need to watch my waistline and insisting that I must be eating too much. She'll probably even suggest I go in for a consult about liposuction."

"Hmmph." His mom reached out and pulled Lena toward her. "Come over here in the light where I can see you better." Mrs. Henry clicked her tongue, her head shaking as she did. "Why, you aren't as big as a minute, and if your mama can't see how beautiful you are then she needs to get her eyes checked."

Lena's shocked expression made his heart hurt. She seemed genuinely surprised that his mom thought she was beautiful. He didn't think she had a clue just how gorgeous she was. If only she could see herself the way he saw her.

His mom put her arm around Lena and ushered her toward the door. "Now you two get in here out of the cold before you freeze solid and I turn you into lawn ornaments for the rest of the winter. I made some chili earlier and I can heat you some right up." She looked over her shoulder at him, concern darkening her eyes. "You need something warm in you after being out in that cold, and without a coat. For such a smart boy, I wonder about your common sense some days, Dexter. You're gonna catch your death being out in this wind without even a sweater on."

Like most of the single-family homes in Westfield and the greater Gatlinburg area, his parents' home was a rustic log cabin. Even the interior was filled with dark wood, from the walls down to the hardwood floors. Being more at home on a hiking trail than in a fancy restaurant meant that his mom didn't care for frills and lace, though. No, her style was more handmade quilts, cozy plaids and soft blankets. This house he'd grown up in was a cozy family home, but it wouldn't win any decorating awards. Dex was sure it wasn't what Lena was used to, but hopefully she'd feel at home here.

"Wow," Lena said as she took her coat off in the living room. She spun in a slow circle and looked around. "This place is amazing. It reminds me of a cabin we rented in Aspen one year when my parents wanted to ski for Christmas, but with far less dead animals hanging on the walls. Thankfully. All those eyes staring down at you is creepy."

His mom reached out and squeezed Lena's hand in commiseration. "Oh, I'm right there with you on that, honey, and I promise you, there are none of God's creatures preserved in an unnatural state under this roof. Not while I'm alive. Let me get you all that chili."

"You ski?" Dex asked Lena while his mom walked away. Lena didn't seem like the skiing type to him, so hearing that she'd spent a Christmas on the slopes in Aspen was a surprise.

"Not at all." Lena shook her head and gave a little laugh, almost a snort. "*They* spent the week on the slopes. My much older nanny hated the cold, however, so she and I spent a lot of time at the clubhouse having hot chocolate and working jigsaw puzzles."

Even though she laughed, it sounded forced and pain laced her words. It gave him more insight into her relationship with her parents and helped explain why they weren't close. What sort of parents ditched their only child at Christmas? His heart hurt as he envisioned a tiny Lena hanging out at the clubhouse with an old lady, her face pressed against the window watching while the other kids were out on the slopes with their parents, or worse, watching her parents ski away without a backward glance.

"Was that a typical Christmas for you then?" he asked, taking her hand and pulling her over to the couch.

She sank down next to him, leaning into his side, and he felt more than heard the sadness in her exhalation. "Being alone with the nanny somewhere adjacent to where my parents did something fun? Yes, that was a traditional Christmas for us. I'd be decked out in a fancy dress and paraded out whenever they wanted to prove they were parents. Sometimes I'd be forced to perform for them and their friends. But otherwise they did their thing while I stayed behind with the nanny."

Dex swallowed hard. "Perform?" he asked hesitantly. Given that she was finally opening up, he didn't want her to shut down again.

"Piano, sing, one year they put me in tap dance lessons before they realized I was far too clumsy to ever succeed at that." She smiled at him, a pitiful little grimace, really, that didn't reach her eyes. "It nearly turned me off Christmas entirely."

He gaped at her, dumbfounded. "You love Christmas so much, though."

"Now I do." Lena shrugged and pulled one of the throw pillows into her lap. She fidgeted with the decorative trim around its edge. "Our house never decorated for Christmas when I was growing up because it wasn't like we were going to be home, so when I moved out on my own, the first year I went all out as a bit of rebellion, but then… Then going all out for Christmas became *my* tradition, ya know? Even if I'm alone, it's something that no one can take from me. While a lot of things are more fun with someone else, it's still nice to decorate a tree, or build a gingerbread house, or go look at Christmas lights."

It hadn't taken him long to realize that Lena isolated herself because connecting with people scared her. She wasn't really antisocial; she was anti getting hurt. And who could blame her for that after the upbringing she'd had? Everything he learned about her past made him think that her icy exterior was a veneer designed to protect her from the pain of involvement. He saw it in the hot-cold way she reacted to him. She warmed up until she realized how much she was letting him in, and then she took a step back to put that distance between them that would protect her heart.

Maybe he recognized it so easily because in a lot of ways he was just like her. He hadn't retreated within himself to the extent Lena had, but he guarded his emotional interactions with others and didn't freely allow people close because he knew what it felt like to have his heart shattered until he didn't recognize himself anymore. He knew the pain of loss.

But Lena had such a caring heart and truly beautiful soul that he hated to see her withdrawing from everyone like she had.

Squeezing her tight, Dex pressed a kiss to the top of her head. "New rule of Christmas, no more spending it alone."

Lena swiped at a tear trailing down her cheek, but she smiled at him through her tears. "You said there were no rules to Christmas."

He rubbed his thumb over the errant tear she'd missed. "Your rules are growing on me."

With Dex so close, still cupping her cheek gently, his hand warm and perfect against her skin, Lena did the only thing she could do. She leaned forward and pressed her lips to his. Unlike the kisses at the rest stop that were hungry and carried a sort of desperation, this kiss was gentle and comforting.

His lips moved over hers slowly, sensually. Each movement a caress. His thumb grazed her cheekbone as he moved it over her skin, mimicking the movements of his lips.

Lena sighed as she relaxed into his embrace.

A throat clearing in the doorway pulled them apart and Lena's cheeks heated. She pressed her face into Dex's shoulder, feeling like she could die of embarrassment, while he merely laughed.

"It's not funny," she whispered, which only seemed to make him laugh harder. "What's your mom going to think of me?"

His mom hadn't been gone but long enough to heat up

a couple bowls of chili and came back to them practically all over each other. They weren't setting themselves up for his mom to like her at all.

With her embarrassment now complete, Lena smiled shyly over at Dex's mom. "Hello," she said, without knowing what else to say.

This is going well, she thought sarcastically.

"I brought the two of you some chili. The corn bread's gone, but I have some saltines that'll be near as good." Dex's mother set a loaded silver tray on the coffee table in front of them. She raised a brow at Dex in censure. "I didn't expect to find the two of you making out like teenagers when I came back."

Lena cringed. Exactly what she'd been afraid of…his mom hated her and they hadn't been here an hour. Less than an hour had to be a new record.

Dex handled his mother in a way Lena would never have attempted—with a joke. "Well, you did say for me to come inside and warm up. What better way is there to warm up than in the arms of a beautiful woman?"

"Mmm-hmm…" Mrs. Henry shook her head at them, but there was a hint of a smile on her face. "Eat your chili while its hot. Dexter, you know where to find your room. The two of you keep it down, though. Your aunt Peggy is asleep in Tommy's room next door. And if your brother gets too loud with those video games, you remind him I said he better not wake anyone up cussing at some cartoon man on the television just because the poor thing ran off a cliff like he was told."

Lena suppressed a snicker. She doubted either of Dex's brothers played any sort of game that involved running a cartoon character off a cliff. Not at their ages.

Then a stressful realization dawned on her. His mother

had implied they were sharing a room. That was not in the plans.

Not at all.

She couldn't share a room—or a bed—with Dex. She swallowed hard. She just *couldn't*. Not if she wanted to make it through this unscathed. He'd assured her there was no need for a hotel room because his parents had a spare room. Had he planned this all along?

Whispering to Dex, Lena asked, "I don't suppose your room has two beds in it, does it?"

He gave his head one swift shake in the negative.

"Eat now." His mother tapped on the tray. "I'm going to bed and will see the two of you in the morning. That's soon enough for me to get to know this lovely girl you've brought home." She stood and rounded the couch to stand behind them. She enclosed them both in a loose hug, kissing Dex on the top of the head. "Don't stay up too late."

Lena watched as the older woman walked toward the back of the house. Lights flicked off until they were left in only the light of a lamp next to the couch and the light above the stairs across from them.

"I had no idea Aunt Peggy would be here or I'd have rented us a place nearby. There aren't any hotels in Westfield, but there are quite a few rental cabins. The last I'd heard, Aunt Peggy wasn't coming in for the wedding." Dex leaned forward and grabbed his bowl of chili. "I'll sleep down here on the couch. It'll be fine for tonight and we will see tomorrow about getting a rental for the rest of the week."

"What will your mom say?"

"Probably think we had a fight after she went to bed." Dex shrugged. "And she'll probably get her feelings hurt by us getting a rental, but she'll get over it. Eventually."

Lena closed her eyes and tried to wrap her mind around what the best course of action would be. If he slept down here, that left her sleeping in his bed alone. And the idea of upsetting his mother did not sit well with her. "I don't want her to think we are fighting, especially not on the first day we're here. And how would it look if we had a fight just minutes after she walked in on us kissing?"

"It would make us breaking up next month more realistic." Lifting one shoulder in a half-hearted shrug, Dex added, "Besides that, our options are pretty limited. I either sleep down here or I sleep with you."

"I guess you are sleeping with me tonight, then. It doesn't feel right to take your bed and kick you to the couch."

"I'd be more than happy to share a bed with you, Lena."

The passion behind those words made it far more than a simple tease. Ducking her head to hide the blush she felt creeping up her cheeks, Lena tried to put the idea of sharing a bed out of her mind and focused her thoughts instead on what he said about a fight making their breakup more realistic.

"We can stage a fight later this week, maybe. I don't want her thinking I'm totally wrong for you from day one and making the entire week miserable and tense. We'll have enough of that with my family, trust me."

"You don't want her to think you don't like her chili either." He waved his spoon at her bowl still sitting on the tray untouched. "Eat."

Lena picked up the bowl of chili. Steam no longer rose from the surface, but warmth flooded her fingers from the heated stoneware. The heady aroma of peppers and spices wafted up from the surface. "It smells good."

"Tastes even better."

She dipped her spoon in and hazarded a taste. "Ooh, that's spicy." She blinked rapidly as her eyes began watering. Wow. It was hotter than she'd expected.

"It's character-building. Put some crackers in it. That'll tone it down, city girl."

Lena dipped the saltine in the spicy chili and had to admit that Dex was right. The cracker calmed the heat down enough that she could tolerate it.

"What does me being a city girl have to do with thinking this chili is too spicy?" she asked as she tried to let some of the heat dissipate off her tongue.

Dex tucked a lock of her hair behind her ear and smiled at her, the dim light of the room throwing part of his face into shadow and making it hard to read his expression. "Not a thing. But you told me I can't call you honey anymore, so I'm trying to honor that."

"What's wrong with my name?"

"Not a thing."

He laid his hand on her jeans-clad thigh, and the heat from his palm sent her heart racing like she'd climbed the mountainous road into Westfield on foot instead of in the passenger seat of an SUV. She swallowed hard when he leaned close. Her breath caught in anticipation that he might kiss her again.

"You gonna eat the rest of that chili?"

"Oh, you..." She shoved the bowl into his broad chest. "You have it. I don't think I can take any more anyway. My eyes are boiling as it is."

With her nerves in an uproar at Dex's closeness, Lena tried to get a handle on her emotions and thoughts while he finished off the second bowl of chili. Over the last few hours, she and Dex had moved into dangerous territory for a fake relationship. She'd anticipated having to kiss him. After all, their families were meant to think they were serious enough to be meeting the family, and that meant the expectation of at least a low level of PDA. She'd even braced herself for the desire that washed over her at every touch of his hand.

But the way he placed his hand on the small of her back when he walked next to her? Or how those little lines appeared and crinkled just so at the corners of his eyes when he laughed? And most of all, the way his expression softened sometimes when he looked at her?

Those things she hadn't been ready for.

He tapped her on the nose. "Lost in thought?"

"Hmm..." Her cheeks heated with embarrassment at being caught staring at him. Hopefully in the dimly lit room he wouldn't be able to see the color surely darkening up her cheeks. "Just tired. It's been a long day."

"That it has. Wait here. I'll stick these bowls in the dishwasher and then we can get to bed."

Lena tried to relax while she waited, but the knowledge that in just a few short moments she'd be in the same bed as Dex had her too keyed up to manage it. Anticipation and dread warred within her and she wasn't quite sure which would win out in the end.

He walked back in and held out his hand. When he spoke, his words were loaded with innuendo and her heart beat so loud in her ears that it nearly drowned him out.

"Come on, city girl, let me take you to bed."

CHAPTER NINE

DEX NOTICED THE momentary panic in Lena's eyes before a wary desire moved in. Cautious interest he could deal with. Fear, not so much. He didn't want her to be afraid of him. She had to come to him willingly.

"You don't have to be afraid of me, Lena," he said with his hand still outstretched. He waited to see if she was going to take that step and put her hand in his. To see if she trusted him enough to move forward with him in this way.

After a moment where she nibbled her lips and he nearly closed the distance himself, Lena swallowed hard. But her voice was rock solid when she said, "I'm not afraid of you, Dexter Henry." She stepped away from him to grab her bag, and what she said next he didn't think she meant him to hear.

But he thought he heard her say, "I'm afraid of my reactions to you."

"I'm so tired I could sleep on these stairs, how 'bout you?"

"Exhausted." She looked up the steep stairs, slung her bag over her shoulder and sighed. "A hotel would have had a bellhop to carry our bags up for us."

"I can get it for you, if you need me," he offered.

"No, I can do it. You know, if we stay at my parents' like my mother wants, they have 'Robert,' who will carry them up for us." She used her fingers to make quotations around the name.

"Robert?" he asked, making air quotes like she had. "Why would you put air quotes around a person's name?"

Her expression was one of long suffering mingled with annoyed disbelief. It intrigued him how much she could say in a single glance. Her face expressed more emotions than people he knew. Or maybe he was just so intrigued by her that even her microexpressions couldn't slip past his scrutiny? He packed that last thought away for later examination.

"Because our butler's real name is usually not Robert. My mother just can't be bothered to learn any new names, so when someone gets hired there, they take on the mantle of Robert."

"I'm sorry, what?" Surely he had misunderstood what she'd just said. No one could be so egotistical as to rename their employees, could they?

"All our butlers are named Robert now, regardless of what their given name is." She shrugged. "Please don't judge me on this. I have no say in what my parents do."

"Wow. Just…wow."

"I know." She waved toward the stairs. "Can we…?"

"Oh, right." He took her bag from her hand. "I'll carry this. Consider me your own personal Robert."

She snorted. "I'm never going to live this one down, am I?"

"Probably not, city girl," he called over his shoulder as he led the way up the stairs. He walked into his childhood bedroom and dropped the suitcases at the foot of the bed. Looking around, he tried to see if anything too embarrassing still lingered in here. He hadn't stayed with his parents in years, after all, and never with a woman he cared about impressing. Nothing jumped out at first glance, at least.

Lena leaned against the open door frame. "Okay, so we need to set some ground rules before we get in that bed."

"Shh…" Dex pointed quickly toward the wall on his left. With his voice barely above a whisper, he continued, "You would think with ten-inch-thick log walls you'd have some privacy, but sound carries in this place like you were standing next to each other. The only privacy in this house is visual."

How sound carried in this cabin was his least favorite thing about his childhood home. His mom had always known exactly what kind of mischief he was up to practically before he started because she could hear everything he did. Everything he said.

Maybe even what he thought.

"Really?" She wrinkled her nose up and stared at the wall separating his room from the room where his aunt slept. "Strike log cabins off my list of future dream homes, then."

"For real." He rolled his eyes. He'd made that determination himself years ago. "And when I was a kid, my parents had the room next door. They didn't build the addition downstairs until I was in high school."

"Lovely."

Shaking his head at her, he said, "That's a word someone would use who was not regularly subjected to hearing just how much their parents still loved each other."

"That would imply that said person's parents actually ever loved each other." Wrapping her arms around herself, she grimaced. "I told you that love didn't factor into my parents' decisions. Pretty sure my parents are only together because they each had something to offer to the other. My mother came from old money. But my dad had the hotshot career and the more varied social connections that my mother desired. And after thirty years together, neither is willing to admit defeat or suffer the societal downturn that a divorce would entail."

"Surely they loved each other at some point. They had you, after all."

"No, they needed an heir to parade about as proof they were really married." The melancholy etched on her face cut straight to the depths of his soul. "I happened to be who they got stuck with. Both would have preferred a son."

Dex moved in front of her and tugged her into his arms. He wanted to soothe away her sadness and give her some happy memories. And that vulnerability in her gaze made him want to do whatever it took to protect her. He stiffened at that thought and rolled the idea around in his head. Protect her? Where did that come from? And why did it feel so natural?

"Dex, this isn't a good idea."

"I told you before, I'm a big boy and I know what *no* means."

Even though his voice was a low whisper, the hurt and frustration slammed into her like a wave pounding at the sand. This man had her emotional state sitting on a fault line that spanned her already fragile heart. She needed time to stabilize it before anymore seismic activity worsened it. But at the same time, if she continually hurt him with her actions, then she was no better than her father.

"When I'm tired, my emotions run closer to the surface, and I don't want to subject you to another potential meltdown," she admitted.

He took a step back and slid his hands down her arms, linking his fingers with hers. His voice was barely audible. "You know I'd never want to cause you pain, right? I know I have a bit of a reputation—"

"A bit?" she scoffed, interrupting him. "According to hospital gossip, you've slept with half the female staff under forty."

"Not even close. But even if I had, what's wrong with two consenting adults finding a few moments of pleasure with one another?"

"A few moments, huh?" She leaned closer, her lips grazing his ear. "Never pegged you for a two-punch chump."

The speed with which he moved surprised her and the next thing she knew, Dex had her pinned to the wall. His teeth nipped at her earlobe with a sharp warning. "If you don't want to find out about my skills in the bedroom, then don't tease."

In the span of a breath, the dynamic between them shifted from something awkward that still held a layer of falsehood to something far deeper. Swallowing hard, Lena put her hands up on his shoulders to push him away—which was the responsible thing to do, of course—but just as she did, he nuzzled his way down her throat, and the thought of rejecting his advances fled.

"Dex…"

"You want me to kiss you, don't you?"

"Mmm-hmm." She didn't trust her words in that moment. But yes, she wanted him to kiss her. More than she'd ever wanted anyone to kiss her.

"Well, well, well, what have we here?"

"Wade!" Dex spun around. "You saw nothing. You heard nothing. And if you tattle on me, then I'm going to hit you so hard you'll have a dent for a week."

"Dex, if you hit him that hard you'll break your hand and you might not be able to cut anymore. I've seen what happens when surgeons can't operate anymore. I don't want to live through that again." She shivered, despite the heat lingering from Dex's touch. "Maybe kick him instead?"

When her father had lost the full use of his hand after a car accident, their lives had been nearly destroyed by the man's own self-pity. Once he'd moved past the initial depression, he'd thrown all his energy into trying to mold Lena into his replacement. But she'd never been interested in plastic surgery. She'd disappointed him when instead of pre-med she'd chosen nursing. It was only after he'd accepted the medical director position that things had slowly got back to normal, where he'd mostly ignored her and worked constantly again.

"Lena, this is Wade, my youngest brother." Dex waved a hand in Wade's general direction, then waved toward her. "Annoying baby brother, this is my girlfriend, Lena."

Her heart skipped a beat as her referred to her as his girlfriend again. She hadn't quite solved the mystery of why her body liked that term so much. Was it the way the word rolled off his tongue in that sexy Southern accent he tried so hard to squash?

Or, and she hated to even admit this to herself, was it because Dex was the first man ever to make her feel valued? And he did it so effortlessly.

"Hello," she said, flashing a smile at Wade. So that's what Dex had looked like in college.

Wade had the same dark hair and the same broad shoulders, but there was something about him that seemed lesser. Maybe a lack of maturity? She couldn't quite put her finger on it.

Dex and Wade started talking and she moved into the bedroom without either of them being aware. They moved down the hallway into another room, their quiet conversation carrying just barely through the space.

She sighed when she sank down on the bed. Flopping back, she closed her eyes against the burn of tears. Having Dex's brother interrupt was frustrating, of course, but it had also kept them from potentially taking things a step too far. A step they weren't really prepared to take.

At least with Dex down the hall catching up with his brother—and judging from the occasional laughter and unending conversation, he might be a while—she had the room to herself for the moment. And that was a relief.

Sitting back up, she went into the attached bath and got ready for bed. Dex was still down the hall when she flipped off the lights and climbed under the covers. If they were both lucky, she'd be sound asleep by the time he had finished reminiscing with his brother. Because if she was awake, they might find themselves in a situation that didn't get interrupted.

And she wasn't sure if that would be a good thing or not.

CHAPTER TEN

THE ALLURING AROMA of coffee tickled at his awareness. Dex rolled over and reached for Lena, his hand coming up empty, and the sheets on the other side of the bed were cold.

"Lena?" He sat up, rubbing at his eyes.

With the bathroom door standing open, he could be sure she wasn't in the en suite. She'd fallen asleep while he and his brother had caught up. He'd been tempted to wake her up and finish what they'd started before Wade's interruption, but she'd looked so peaceful that he'd let her sleep.

She'd been in his arms when he'd fallen asleep. Now where the heck was she?

A few minutes later, after he'd got dressed, he made his way down the stairs. Soft feminine laughter carried through the cabin from the kitchen. He stopped in the doorway to see what he was walking into.

Lena stood in the kitchen wrapped in one of his mother's oversized aprons, her hair piled loosely on top of her head. She focused on a bowl of batter before her on the island countertop. Concentration wrinkled her forehead as she scrutinized the batter. "Is it meant to be so lumpy?"

"You never made pancakes before?" Dex asked in disbelief.

Lena waved a whisk with clumps of flour clinging to it in his direction. "Hush, you. I told you I don't know how to cook much."

"Does 'Robert' make your pancakes, then?"

She rolled her eyes at him. "Butlers do not cook. Robert would be insulted if asked to make pancakes. He could be sent to ask Chef to do so, however."

"You have a butler?" his mom asked with disbelief. "Stir that batter a little more. It shouldn't be quite that lumpy, but a few lumps are okay."

Lena stirred the batter slowly and carefully, her attention focused on it. "My parents have a butler, not me. They have a butler, a chef, a housekeeper and a gardener. Robert, the butler, is in charge of the others as well as being my father's personal assistant. When I was younger, they had my nanny as well."

"Your parents must be busy people." His mom tried to be diplomatic, but he could see on her face how she really felt. She'd never tell Lena that she thought people with that many servants were ridiculous, because she wouldn't want to hurt Lena's feelings. But they'd had a lot of arguments just getting his mom to accept help with even occasional housekeeping. She was old-fashioned and believed a woman should take care of her own home and family.

"You won't hurt it if you stir a little more vigorously. Give it a good stir." Dex stepped closer and put his hand over Lena's.

"Busy? Sure." Lena's sigh reached deep and held frustration as she came back to his mom's question. "My father had his practice and later the hospital to run. Mother had her charities."

"And what did you have?" Dex questioned, noticing she'd left herself out of that explanation. He wrapped his arms around Lena from behind and pressed a soft kiss to the side of her throat. There was a naturalness to the move that settled over him. Holding Lena in his arms felt right.

"Paralyzing self-doubt, endless anxiety and so much fear of commitment that I could be my own Halloween attraction?" Lena gave him a raw, honest answer, deeper than she meant to give if the blush that soared up into her cheeks was any indication. "Forget I said that, please," she murmured.

How could he forget what she said when she'd just given him so much insight into her history? He held her closer. "That's why you turned me down at first, isn't it?"

"She did what?" his mom interrupted, sounding really surprised. "Turned you down? When?"

"Shh..." He shushed his mom. "Lena and I have moved past it, so don't think on it."

Lena sighed and leaned back against his chest. "After surgery that day, when we'd spent all that time side by side, and just talking, you know, I got to thinking, maybe I could get lucky and find someone who would really see me and want to be with me. Not because of who I was related to, or the connections I could offer them, but the real me. But, well, I let the gossip get into my head. So, yes, my parents were part of why I turned you down, but I let other people convince me that you were like *him* and I couldn't—"

Dex spun her around. "I'd never—"

Lena cut him off with a sound. He pressed his lips shut and waited for her to finish her thoughts.

"I couldn't risk it. Not 'til I got to know you better. And the more I get to know you, the more I realized that the only thing you have in common with my father and Connor is that you are all surgeons." Lena reached up and cupped his cheek. "I've also realized that I'm going to have to accept the loss on these pancakes. I think I'll go get a shower now."

He watched as Lena took the apron off. She folded it neatly and placed it on the island before heading upstairs.

With a deep sigh, he sank down onto a stool.

"Trouble in paradise?" his mom asked. She nodded in the direction of the stairs. "I'm having a hard time getting a feel on her. She flutters from friendly to frosty faster than a honeybee in your Nana's flower garden."

He shrugged. "I'm hungry. You got any pancakes made?"

"You just gonna ignore my question?" Her brow rose as she looked him over, scrutinizing his face while waiting for him to answer. Ignoring her was never an option. She'd hound him until she got the answers she wanted out of pure stubbornness.

"No, ma'am, I'm not ignoring you. I was just trying to think of the right way to phrase what I need to say." The need to protect Lena rose up again. He wanted to defend her to his mom, but he didn't want to overshare something Lena might have said in confidence either.

"How many pancakes you want?" His mom lifted the cover on the cake plate where she'd stacked up the pancakes she'd made.

"Three's good. Thanks." He took the plate of pancakes offered. "Lena had a far different upbringing than I did. She wants to be friendly, really, she does. She's not used to sharing feelings and such like she just did. When she does, and she realizes how much she shared, it scares her. Then she frosts over and retreats. Give her a little time and she'll be right back down here with a smile."

"Oh, that poor girl." His mom looked toward the stairs. He recognized that look—Lena just became his mom's new project. "Well, we will make her fit in here and she'll know she can trust us."

"It would mean the world to me if you did." He popped a bite of pancake in his mouth, chewing slowly while he considered the implications behind that. Those agreed-upon boundaries were starting to get a little fuzzy for him and he wasn't sure how he felt about that. If she wasn't starting to feel the same, he could be setting himself up for a whole world of heartache.

Since his disastrous engagement, he'd kept his relationships short and sweet. A few weeks, maybe a month, max, and then they parted ways. He didn't stick around long enough for there to be drama. He'd already invested more time in getting to know Lena than he had in his last three relationships. And yet, he didn't regret a moment of it.

"Does Lena make you happy?" his mom asked, rubbing his back.

"She does. I can see a real future with her."

"Oh!" She nearly squealed and pulled him into a big, tight hug. "You have no idea how long I have been waiting to hear you say that! It does this old heart good to hear that."

Saying that had maybe taken this fake relationship a step too far toward real. He had never been good at lying to his mother. She'd always seen through any charade he'd attempted and had known his every transgression as a child almost before he'd done it. How he would make it through the next few days without spilling his guts and admitting the truth, he wasn't quite sure. But was he really lying to her this time?

That was the real question, wasn't it?

"While Lena's upstairs, I wanted to ask…" His mother paused for dramatic effect.

And his heart stopped. The pancakes he'd just eaten sat heavy in his stomach, a gluttonous brick weighing him down. He pushed away his half-finished breakfast, having suddenly lost his appetite. She always saved "the pause" for when she was about to call him out for the transgression he'd thought he'd gotten by with.

"How are you really feeling about Jessie's return?"

"Jessie?" His heart started up again with an odd lurch. She wanted to talk about Jessie? "I…uh… Well, I'm sure Ray and Mary will be happy to have her home."

He'd always liked Jessie's folks. They'd been like a second set of parents to him when he'd been with their daughter. He'd hated the role he'd played in separating them from their daughter, even if it was unconsciously done.

"But how are *you* feeling about it?" His mom clucked her tongue at him. "I know they're happy to see her. But she isn't my concern. You are. And I'm worried about what seeing her is gonna do to you."

He opened his mouth to tell her that the idea of seeing Jessie again hurt, but then it dawned on him that it really didn't. He closed his mouth without speaking as he rolled that realization around in his head. The knowledge that he was going to see the woman who left him standing at the altar actually didn't hurt.

Had he really and truly moved on, then?

"Dexter?" His mom put a hand on his shoulder and he

looked up. Her eyes were clouded with concern. "I knew I should have found a way to keep them from inviting her. This is too much for you."

"No. It's fine. Really." The way to explain it finally came to him. "I realized just now that it no longer bothered me that I might have to see Jessie again. I know… I know… I've been saying for a while that I was over her. But I don't think I was. At least not fully."

"And you are now?"

He hadn't known hope could be audible until that moment, but he heard the hope in his mother's voice as she asked that.

"I am," he confirmed, flashing her a real smile. "I really am."

"Lena is more than just good for you, then," his mom said, her voice no longer concerned but now filled with a happiness he hadn't heard directed at him in years. "I think I'm going to love that girl."

He was going to have to burst that happiness bubble like a bully would pop a younger child's balloon when he told her that he and Lena "broke up" after the holidays. And he stubbornly shoved away the thought that maybe, just maybe, Lena's presence in his life was why he finally felt completely over Jessie. Accepting that would make things with Lena far too real.

Lena paused outside the doorway to the kitchen as she overheard the tail end of Dex's conversation with his mother about his ex. Hearing him say that he was completely over Jessie sent a warmth running through her entire body that made her giddy. She wanted to find some pompoms and do a cheer. Or clap like a lunatic until she burst into awkward laughter.

She wasn't ready to acknowledge why Dex's confession made her so happy she could skip. But it really and truly did.

Taking several deep breaths, she tried to wipe the smile from her lips that would clue him in that she'd overheard his conversation.

Making sure to make her steps heavy, she took the final few steps into the kitchen. She poured herself a cup of coffee and walked over to him. She couldn't stop herself from wrapping her arms around his waist and giving him a tight hug from behind.

"So, uh, what's the plan for today?" she tried to ask nonchalantly. Like she hadn't been eavesdropping on their conversation from the hallway. "I know the rehearsal dinner is tomorrow, but is there anything on the schedule today?"

"We are having lunch with the soon-to-be newlyweds and her parents," Dex's mom said. A pained look crossed her face and she added, "And some family from each side."

"What my mama is hinting at, unsuccessfully, is that Jessie is likely to be there."

"I see…" Lena leaned against Dex, trying to work out how she was supposed to feel at the thought of meeting the ex before the wedding. "Do I have anything to worry about with her?"

"Of course not," Dex protested, stiffening up beneath her touch.

"Then bring it on. I'm looking forward to meeting the rest of your family, at least. I thought there'd be more people here this morning, even."

Namely, Dex's father and the aunt from the next room they'd had to be quiet for to avoid waking. When she'd come downstairs in search of food and coffee this morning, she'd found only Mrs. Henry sitting and staring out over the most beautiful sunrise Lena had ever seen.

"David and Peggy went into Gatlinburg for the morning. Every time Peggy is here, she insists on having a morning with just the two of them, and they usually end up at the Donut Friar to get her cinnamon bread fix in."

Dex laughed. "But it's so good that I can't even blame her for that. Lena, I'll take you if we have time before we leave."

Seeing his comment as the perfect way to reinforce his mom's belief in their fake relationship, Lena laid her head on Dex's shoulder. "If not this time, maybe we can do it next time, then."

His mom had been kind this morning, but she'd gotten the impression that the older woman wasn't completely buying that they were in love. Not even after walking in on them kissing last night. She was very perceptive and had a way of looking at a person that made them want to spill every secret they'd ever heard.

They'd have to up their game to make it through this week without being found out. But Lena was up for the challenge. She'd handled twenty-seven years under her parents' scrutiny. One week under the watchful eye of the Henry matriarch would be a breeze.

Meeting the ex was what she was more worried about. This Jessie had dated and loved Dex for years, so she'd know his tells and mannerisms. If anyone was going to out them as fake, it would be her.

"Where are we meeting everyone for lunch?" Dex asked.

"Down at Westfield Steak House. Roy and Mary reserved their party room. And tomorrow morning we will head over to the church and get all the decorations up before having the rehearsal and that awful ugly sweater party that Jill insists on."

Dex and his mom talked about some of the people who might be there, with Mrs. Henry filling Dex in on what had happened with them regularly.

The mention of Jill's parents brought questions to mind for Lena. Even if they managed to pull the fake relationship off for the entire week here, Dex would have to deal with his ex being around for the rest of his life with his brother marrying her sister. What would he do next time? Find another fake girlfriend? She mentally noted to bring this up with him when they were alone.

Wade stumbled into the kitchen just then, half-asleep and half-dressed. "I'm hungry."

Mrs. Henry looked him up and down without a word.

Lena knew there was something being said with the older woman's gaze, she just wasn't sure what. Wade must have understood though, because he left and returned a minute later fully dressed.

When he sat next to Dex, a plate of pancakes was placed in front of him. He tucked in like he'd never eaten before. Like Dex, his appetite surprised Lena.

"Wow, I can't imagine what your grocery bill was like when all of your boys were at home."

Mrs. Henry laughed. "More than a mortgage payment for years. Are you hungry? I think that batter you made is salvageable. I can make you up some pancakes if you don't think you can wait for lunch."

"No, but thank you." Lena shook her head. If she ate even a third of what she'd seen Dex put away, she'd be sick. "I'm good to wait."

"Lena..." Wade said with a grin. "You look more

beautiful in the light of day. You know, you could move across the hall and get to know the better Henry man."

Dex slugged him in the arm. "Hey! Back off."

Lena couldn't help but laugh. "I'm afraid I can't take you up on that, but it was, uh, sweet of you to offer."

"Sweet? You think he's sweet?" Dex shot her a look of pure disbelief. "There ain't nothing sweet about Wade."

"Is this why you wanted to give him away?"

"Give me away!" Wade gasped in faked outrage. "How dare you? Dex, I'm hurt."

"Lena's never had a sibling." Dex shrugged nonchalantly, but the look he shot his brother was one hundred percent mischief. "I told her I had a spare."

"Well, Dexter, I'm not sure which is worse, giving Wade to Lena because she was an only child or selling Tommy for a potato."

Lena nearly spit out her coffee. "You sold him for a potato?"

The slightest hint of a blush crept up into Dex's cheeks, but he met her gaze defiantly. His eyes crinkled up in that happy way she loved. "In my defense, that potato was shaped like a duck. Wade's proof that a kid can have another baby brother, but how often do you find a potato that looks like a duck?"

"You need a little more backstory before you judge my son too hard on this. He was only two, after all. And Tommy had the worst colic. That child…he didn't sleep for more than a few minutes at a time and I usually had to be walking the floors with him to get him to doze off then."

"That sounds rough."

"Dexter had been so excited to get a baby brother." A soft smile lit her face as she reminisced about Dex as a child, and Lena could see hints of Dex in the crinkles around her eyes. "I think Tommy was a bit of a disappointment since all he did was cry and puke. My daddy had just retired and had a big garden that year. He used that garden to keep Dexter busy for me so that I could focus on Tommy. When Dexter dug up that duck potato, he wanted to keep it. Well, Daddy told him he had to pay for it if he wanted to keep it."

"To be fair, my first offer was my fire truck. But then I tripped and broke the duck potato." Dex stretched, his shirt pulling tight across his muscular chest. "And I couldn't trade a perfectly good fire truck for a broken potato. So I offered him a broken baby brother."

"Wow."

"Yeah, as you can see, it's been three whole decades and I still haven't lived that one down. I'll be hearing about it until I'm old and gray." Dex grinned at her and she could tell he wasn't upset in the slightest by his family's teasing.

In fact, she thought he might like it.

There was a warmth in this room that had nothing to do with the heating and entirely to do with the love shared by the people in it. It seeped in through the soft smiles and was reinforced with the patted shoulders. It was something Lena had absolutely no experience with.

She'd never had her mother look at her with the kind of indulgent tenderness that Mrs. Henry did her sons. Her mother had never made her a single meal and certainly wouldn't have gotten up early just to have a moment alone before doing it.

What would it have been like to have been surrounded by pure affection her entire life?

A longing rose up in her chest. She wanted what Dex

had with his family. The fondness and caring, even the teasing, made her yearn for the impossible.

Sitting in that kitchen, surrounded by Dex and his family, in that instant, it felt very possible. If Dex ever attempted something long-term again, that is.

But even more, would she ever be able to live up to the expectations of a family like this? She had no experience with what a healthy, loving relationship looked like. Romantic or platonic.

A shrill song pierced the moment and Lena blinked several times while she tried to focus on where the sound was coming from. Finally, she dug her cell phone out of her pocket and winced as the caller's name flashed on the screen.

Of course. The woman had a sixth sense for knowing when happiness crossed Lena's path and her instinct was to burst that bubble. Fast.

Lena put the phone to her ear. "Hello, Mother."

CHAPTER ELEVEN

LENA SCHOOLED HER expression to a calm facade, but Dex had spent enough time with her to catch the frustration and hint of fear. Talking to her mother scared her?

For a split second, he wanted to jump up and pull her into his arms, reassure her that she wasn't going to have to face her parents alone. Then common sense returned and the recollection that this was entirely a farce washed over him with a grim reality.

He wouldn't be there beyond this single visit. And he couldn't let himself forget that simple fact.

She met his gaze and then motioned toward the door. At his nod, she stepped out onto the back deck to take her call. Through the windows, he watched her pace, tension in her frame visible through the glass.

"She doesn't get on well with her mama, does she?" Wade asked around a bite of pancakes.

"That's an understatement." It wasn't his place to share all of Lena's secrets, but the answer to Wade's question was pretty obvious. "So, what's going on today in Westfield?"

Changing the subject to the town's Christmas traditions was as much a tactic to distract himself as Wade. He didn't want to accidentally share something Lena might have told him in confidence.

"Oh, you're in luck. They are having a gingerbread house contest over at the library at four, and I believe the Mason lodge has a craft fair going on." His mom pursed her lips in thought. "At least, I think they do. You'll have to drive by the lodge and see. I might have the dates mixed up on that one."

"I thought I'd take Lena out and spend some one-on-one time doing something Christmassy after lunch. I already have tickets for the High Bridge in Gatlinburg. I want to show her the lights later tonight."

"Just the two of you?" Wade whistled low and slow. "That sounds romantic. You aren't about to pop the question too, are you? I'm not even ready to be the only Henry man left single."

Propose?

Oh, man. He hadn't thought out the implications of taking her to the High Bridge alone at night. While he knew Lena would not be expecting a proposal that evening, he hadn't considered how it would look to his family for him to take her to one of the most romantic spots in the area. He glanced over at his mom and she'd perked up at the conversation. Her eyes were lit with excitement that he had to crush.

"Uh, no. I was just thinking that since she loves Christmas so much, she'd like to see the lights over Gatlinburg and the mountains. We haven't been dating that long and we aren't at that point yet."

"You said you saw a future with her, though?" his mom questioned. "Why wouldn't you propose?"

"Yeah," he said, gesturing vaguely. He swallowed hard. Fake dating was one thing, but he refused to propose. That was too far. "In the future. Don't rush it, Mama. I've known her less than a year."

"I knew your father was the man for me after our first date." His mom smiled at him knowingly. "He proposed on our third date. By the time we'd known each other a year, we were married and expecting you."

"If you follow their timeline, I'll be an uncle by next Christmas." Wade grinned at him, mischief filling his face. "'Uncle Wade' has a nice ring to it."

"Hush."

"Seriously, though, if you don't mind taking her someplace with a lot of, uh, old memories, the ice rink has open skate this afternoon."

Dex snorted. "If I only took her to places in Westfield where I'd never taken Jessie, I could only take her to places built after the breakup. It's a small town. Jessie and I went everywhere here, especially if it was even slightly romantic."

As high school sweethearts, he and Jessie had probably found every niche and alcove in the town where they could share a few kisses and fumbled fondles. They'd had more than a few dates at the ice rink in town, but it held no special significance to him. No major firsts had occurred there, unlike the little theater down by the courthouse, where he'd had his first ever kiss, or the church they'd be standing in for Tommy and Jill's wedding, where she'd left him at the altar. He couldn't avoid memories of Jessie in Westfield. He could only make new ones here with Lena.

"Maybe I'll just see what Lena wants to do today. Give her the options and let her choose." He pushed back from the counter. Standing, he put his plate and coffee mug in the dishwasher. "Thanks for breakfast, Mama. I'm going to take Lena's coat out to her before she freezes out there."

Grabbing her jacket—and one of his brother's jackets for himself since his own was covered with blood—he stepped out on the deck and caught a snippet of Lena's conversation.

"Yes, Dex will be attending with me. I did RSVP for myself and a plus one for a reason."

She smiled up at him softly when he wrapped her coat around her shivering shoulders. She mouthed a *thank you* at him before rolling her eyes at something her mother must have said.

"I know that, Mother. And believe me, I am fully aware of the expectations that you and Father have for my behavior. I trust Dexter to behave in an appropriate manner." Her lips thinned out to a barely visible line. She grew silent and while he couldn't make out the words, he could just make out that her mother was lecturing on the other end of the call.

The seriousness on her face and the formal way she spoke to her mother struck him as unacceptable. Today was supposed to be a fun day and he didn't want to let her mother ruin that for her. The witch had already stolen the sparkle from Lena's eyes. Needing to see her smile, Dex stuck his thumbs to his ears and wiggled his fingers while making a cross-eyed face.

Lena snorted and spun away from him. "Of course I wasn't laughing at you. That was a sneeze."

She looked back over at him and grinned. Her shoulders shook in silent laughter, and her eyes once again contained a glint of delight.

Mission accomplished.

"I'm sorry, Mother, but I really do need to go. We are

attending a luncheon with his parents and it would be unacceptable for me to be late."

She ended the call and stepped up to him, pressing her face against his chest. His heart thudded against his rib cage as she wrapped her arms around his waist.

"Thank you for that," she murmured, her voice muffled. "She drives me crazy."

"I could tell."

"Lecturing me about behaving in a manner befitting a Franklin while I'm here as well as at the gala, as if I hadn't attended dozens of formal events at their sides throughout the years. I think if I'd told her you were standing next to me, she'd have given you a lecture on expectations as well. Actually, you should probably expect one once we get to California."

The loud sigh of resignation Lena gave sank deep.

"Well, if she gives me a lecture, I promise not to hold it against you. We really do need to head out soon to get to the restaurant on time, but you have time to change if you want."

"Is my outfit unacceptable?" Lena stiffened against him.

Open mouth, insert foot.

"You look amazing. I did *not* mean to imply otherwise. I have this condition where my mouth works faster than my brain. It gets me in trouble a lot." Squeezing her close, he pressed a kiss to the top of her head. "After lunch, what do you say to a craft fair or ice skating?"

"Changing the subject from your gaffe?"

"Trying to." He tipped her head up to his and met her eyes. "You really do look stunning. This isn't going to be anything formal, so jeans and a sweater are perfect."

"Mmm-hmm."

"So, will you spend the afternoon with me?"

"Are you asking me on another fake date?" Mischief brightened her expression.

"Who said it was fake?"

The pull to put his lips to hers nearly got the best of him. He'd been aching to kiss her since he walked into the kitchen to find her with flour on her face. When her arms slid up around his neck and she rose up on tiptoe, he groaned. Tightening his arms around her, he pressed his forehead to hers. His voice was low and ragged when he said, "We kiss and this is real."

Lena stiffened. She dropped down from her toes and moved to step back. "Didn't you say we had somewhere to be?"

"Hmm… I think the lunch is optional." He tried to bring her back into his embrace, but she was too evasive.

"Nice try." Lena stepped away from him, and this time he allowed the separation. "I'm pretty sure that as the best man, your presence is expected."

"But I get some alone time later, right?" he negotiated, knowing she was right. He had to attend. Not attending would get him strung up by his ears. But in this moment, he wanted to convince Lena to take a risk on him. Only then could he get her out of his system. "An actual real date?"

Smiling at him a little shyly, Lena nodded. Her voice was soft when she said, "I think I'd like that."

A short while later, Dex ushered her to his SUV so they could head into town. Butterflies fluttered about in her stomach and she couldn't decide if it was in remembrance of the embraces on the Henry's back deck or worries about meeting his ex-fiancée.

Westfield was a twisty maze of narrow streets that flowed along the side of the mountain. And the curves did nothing to settle her stomach.

"Are you sure we have to do this?" Dex slowed to a stop to allow a group of kids to run across a brick cross-walk to the playground on the opposite side. "It's not too late to make a break for it and head back to Nashville."

"Ha!" Lena poked playfully at Dex's arm. "Only if you tell your mother face-to-face, because I don't want the fallout of her finding out after the fact that you snuck out of town like the paparazzi are hiding behind every bush."

Groaning, Dex turned right. "This is going to be hor-rendous."

"I hate to see what you'll think of my family dinners, then. Your family is nothing compared to mine. Trust me. We got this."

She tamped down her nerves. Promises had been made and she wouldn't go back on them. Turning her gaze to the view outside the car window, Lena focused on the uniqueness of the little town. City planning seemed lax and every building appeared to have been borrowed from a different architectural era. Somehow, it fit together as a beautiful and cohesive patchwork.

Dex pulled to a stop in front of the steakhouse. "Not sure I'm ready for this."

"Seeing her again?" Lena asked, placing her hand over his.

"Yeah." He winced. "Sorry, I guess I shouldn't have said that since I have you here as my date. I didn't mean..."

"I know you didn't mean anything by it. I'm not sure I'll ever be ready to see Connor again." She sighed. A century would be too soon, but there was a good chance he'd be at the New Year's Eve gala, and that thought was sobering.

Taking her hand in his, Dex brought it up to his lips and pressed a soft kiss on her wrist. "He didn't deserve you."

"I know."

Dex laughed. "Good to see you found a little of your self-esteem, at least."

At barely more than a whisper, she confessed, "It's only because I'm with you. You make me feel like I'm really worth something."

"Good." His gaze was hot and intense. "I really want to kiss you right now."

She cupped his cheek with her palm. "I'm not stopping you."

With a groan, Dex leaned across the center console to kiss her but stopped a breath away from their lips meeting when there was a tap on the glass. He muttered a curse under his breath before straightening up.

An older version of Dex stood outside the vehicle, grinning from ear to ear.

"My dad," Dex explained unnecessarily. He turned the SUV off and got out, hugging his dad and laughing.

Why can't I have that?

Again, Lena found herself envious of his relationship with his parents. Her dad would never hug her like that in public. He barely offered the occasional hug in private. They just didn't have a lovey-dovey relationship.

When—if—she ever had children, she'd make sure they knew they were loved and wanted from the moment of conception, and not merely because she wanted an heir. She wanted them to have the same carefree joy that Dex must have had in childhood to have such a warm personality and loving relationship with his family. The more she got to know him, the more she saw the truth of the man inside. And the more she liked. Oh, boy, did she like what she saw when she looked at Dex.

Sighing, she reached for the door handle just to have the door opened before she could touch it. Another Henry male stood in the opening. Same dark hair, same broad frame, but this one had a beard darkening his jawline.

"I'm guessing you are Tommy," she said.

Grinning down at her, he nodded. "And you must be Lena. I've heard so much about you."

She glanced toward Dex. "Oh?"

"You've really gotten to him, you know. And from that smile on his face, I'd say that's a very good thing." Tommy held a hand out and assisted her out of the vehicle. "It's good to see him happy again."

Smiling back at Tommy, she said, "He makes me happy too."

The thoughts of her and Dex making each other happy flooded her mind and sparked a boatload of questions. Was Dex a good actor? Or was he really and truly happier than he had been the last time his family had seen him? And if he was happier, then what part did she play?

Before the landslide of emotions tied to those questions took her out, Lena let a tease slip from her lips uncensored. "Did the sale fall through once the potato was gone or did your grandfather return you as defective merchandise?"

"Ha!" Tommy chuckled, loud and deep. His laugh had a similar sound to Dex's but it didn't affect her like his brother's did. "They told you about that, huh?"

She eyed him up and down. "I'd have sold you for a snow cone."

Tommy laughed harder. His eyes watered and he was gasping for air before he could get his breathing under control. “I bet you don’t take any sass, do you? You couldn’t be more perfect for Dex if you tried.”

Tommy’s words warmed her heart. She smiled over at Dex, who was still on the other side of the SUV talking to his dad, and he winked when they made eye contact.

She loved the way he seemed aware of her, even when he wasn’t right at her side. It made her feel loved, more than she’d ever had with Connor or anyone else she’d dated.

Oh, no.

Closing her eyes, she swallowed hard. She couldn’t start loving things about Dex! That wasn’t part of the plan. This was spiraling out of her control. And she’d already agreed to go on a real date with him later today. Nervous energy washed over her. What had she gotten herself into?

“Hey, you okay?” Dex asked, putting a hand on her shoulder. “You just got really pale all of a sudden.”

With a forced smile, she nodded. “I just need to eat, I think.”

Wrapping his arm around her waist, he leaned in close. Whispering softly in her ear, he asked, “Are you sure that’s all? You could tell me if there was something bothering you. I’ll find a way to fix it.”

He’d come around the vehicle in seconds once he’d noticed her reaction. How could she not fall for a man who cared enough to watch her expressions like Dex did? He was so observant. Now more than ever, Lena couldn’t believe any woman would be stupid enough to leave him standing at the altar.

She leaned her head against Dex's chest and inhaled his scent. "I'm okay. Really."

But was she?

She was falling in love with Dexter Henry, playboy general surgeon. Despite the warnings and initial red flags, Dex was a genuinely good man. That's what made him so easy to fall for. He was kind, considerate, and had a smile that could unlock the most guarded of hearts. But Dex had made it crystal clear that he was only looking for short-term. She had no doubts he'd be interested in kicking their fake relationship up to a full-blown sexual relationship for the duration of the holidays, but it was the concern about what happened when they went back to Nashville in January that gave her pause.

If they got involved and then he stuck to his love 'em and leave 'em pattern, she'd have to look at him every single day at work. She'd gone that route with Connor and the fallout had sent her fleeing across the country when the full details of their unfortunate affair reached the lips of the rumor mill. Where would she go if things with Dex blew up at Metro Memorial?

She sighed and snuggled in closer to his chest. Which was the exact opposite of what she should be doing… She took a deep breath and his scent filled her nostrils. This would be so much easier if Dex didn't feel and smell like home.

He whispered in her ear, "Are you ready to do this? I'm not sure I am, but I feel like I can face her finally with you at my side. You give me strength."

Heart slamming into her ribs, Lena tried not to read too much into his words. Really, she did. But his words gave her hope that he was starting to think long-term, and maybe, just maybe, falling for her like she was falling for him. Hope led to excitement. If he was feeling the same, maybe they could make this more than a holiday fling.

Filling her lungs with Dex-scented air, Lena straightened her spine and pulled her courage around her like a protective cloak. Her mother and her grandparents before her were pillars of Los Angeles society, and Lena could fake her way through an awkward dinner with the best of them.

“Absolutely,” she said, pleased to hear that there was not even a hint of a quiver in her voice. “Let’s get this meeting over with and get some food. I’m hungry.”

CHAPTER TWELVE

Dex led Lena inside the restaurant, guiding her with his hand on the small of her back. He wasn't sure what had upset her outside, but something had. She seemed to have put it out of her mind, though. She had a smile on her face and held her head high as she walked by his side. Still, something about the way her eyes shifted around the restaurant was less curiosity at new surroundings and more nervousness.

Tommy motioned them toward the back room where the party was being held. He hadn't stopped smiling today. Tommy had found his perfect match and Dex had never been happier for him.

He steeled his resolve as they stepped through the doorway into the reserved room. His mom sat at the end of the table just inside the door talking to Mary. Mary had a cell phone in her hand, swiping through what looked like a series of beach pictures. His future sister-in-law, Jill, was at the far end of the room. The smile on Jill's face was as big as the one on his brother's as she stood there talking to his aunt Peggy. He recognized one of Jill and Jessie's aunts sitting with Ray.

But the one person he'd expected to see wasn't there.

He looked around, thinking somehow he'd missed her,

but no. Jessie wasn't there. A wave of frustration washed over him. He'd been ready to see her, ready to get this first meeting over with, and it was a letdown to find that she wasn't there.

"Dexter!" Ray saw him and came over. The older man started to give him a hug, but then switched it at the last second to an awkward handshake. "It's been a long time. How have you been?"

Years ago, Ray would have hugged him, no question. Now, though? It was awkward. The pain of that resonated deep in his gut. He and Ray had always had a good relationship. Jessie had broken that too.

Okay, maybe he'd contributed by vanishing to Nashville and barely returning, but Ray hadn't reached out to him, either.

"I'm good, Ray." He took Lena's hand in his. "I'd like you to meet my girlfriend, Lena." He made the introductions and some small talk with Ray for a few minutes. He wanted to ask where Jessie was, but he didn't out of respect for the woman at his side.

Ray began to look uncomfortable. He shifted from one foot to the other and didn't make eye contact when he asked, "Uh, Dex, you did hear that Jessie's coming home for the wedding, right?"

Just the opening he needed.

"I did, actually. I'm glad to hear it. I can only imagine how much you and Mary have been missing her. You haven't seen her since our rehearsal dinner, have you?" He rubbed his thumb along Lena's hand, hoping to keep her aware that he was grateful for her presence.

"Not once. She didn't even call us for the first year or so." Ray sighed, rubbing the bridge of his nose. "But she's promised Jill and Mary that she'd be here for this wedding."

He didn't look happy about that fact. And Dex didn't blame him. They'd always been such a close family. It had to be eating at them that she'd abandoned her family like that.

"Ah, well, then the wedding's serving a dual purpose?"

With a wry smile, Ray shrugged. "I'll believe she's coming in when I see her. She called and said they bumped her flight back until tomorrow night. She's still supposed to be here in time for the wedding, though."

So he had another day without having to face her. He could live with that. "At least you'll have her home for Christmas this year."

"True, true." Ray smiled at Lena. "I hope we aren't upsetting you with our conversation about Jessie. I'm sure she's the last thing you'd choose for a topic."

Lena handled his concerns with aplomb. "No worries at all. Dex told me about his relationship with your daughter. It's only natural that you'd speak of the connection. Now, it's your youngest daughter that's marrying his brother, is that right?"

The smoothness of Lena's transition from Jessie and the past to Jill and the present made Dex smile. Ray seemed impressed as well. How could he not be? Lena was poised and confident, not to mention beautiful.

Her composure held as he introduced her to the rest of his family. She kept that smile on her face even when stories were told of his past with Jessie. When they had a moment of relative privacy, he questioned her about it.

"I can't believe it doesn't bother you at all when they bring up my past. I know if your family starts telling stories of you and your ex, I'm going to be a jealous mess. What's your secret?"

She leaned close and her lips brushed his earlobe as

she answered. “We have her to thank for our chance at being together. If she hadn’t crushed you, you’d have never needed me to come home with you. So thank her, don’t hate her.”

Thank her, don’t hate her.

Those five words changed everything for him. He looked at Lena, and it dawned on him that his future really was sitting next to him in a soft blue sweater. Not just a short fling, but a real future. And the thought scared him senseless.

He wasn’t looking for forever. He wanted fun and easy and low risk. But if that was true, then why was Lena tempting him to throw all those wants to the side and risk it all?

Lena made him feel more alive than he’d felt in years. The protective walls he’d erected around his heart were being cracked open, and the desire to knock them down entirely so that he could give Lena his whole heart was getting hard to resist.

Mary and his mom called for everyone to sit. All the tables had been pushed into one huge table that took up most of the vast space. Dark cloths covered the table, and several bright flower arrangements were placed at evenly spaced intervals along the table. Servers started bringing in food, family style.

He found himself seated between his dad and Lena, who seemed to hit it off instantly. At one point, he just reclined back to make it easier for them to continue their discussion. Usually his dad’s financial discussions ended up a little over his head, but Lena had a surprising knowledge of finances. From the gleam in his dad’s eyes, Lena had won him over in that single conversation.

Watching her banter back and forth with Wade brought

a smile to Dex's face. She was holding her own against his annoying little brother, and even more, she seemed to be enjoying it.

Seeing her fit in with his family felt so strange. He'd convinced himself that Lena was such a city girl that his family would make short work of her and he could use that as justification for why they "broke up" in a few weeks. Somehow, he'd really thought this week would be easy justification for why their relationship ended. Yet Lena was not only getting along easily, but she was even bonding with them.

He wanted to have her bond with him. He rubbed the bridge of his nose. Jealous of his own family? That was a new low for him. And maybe a hint of warning that he was getting in over his head with Lena. But rather than reinforcing the walls around his heart, he reached for her hand and their fingers interlocked. She smiled softly over at him before returning to her conversation with his dad and brother.

Shortly after they'd finished eating, he leaned over and asked her quietly, "You wanna get out of here? How's ice skating sound?"

She nodded.

Within five minutes, they were back in his SUV and heading down to the local ice rink.

"I haven't been ice skating since I was a teenager," she said with a laugh. "And not even regularly then. I'm not sure I'm going to be any good at this, but I'm game to try it."

He wanted to pull her close and hoped that skating would give him the opportunity. "All you have to do is hold my hand, and I promise, I'll never let you fall."

"On the ice or in life?" she asked.

He wasn't sure he had the words to communicate everything he was feeling. Slipping his hand over hers, he squeezed gently. "I want to be with you, Lena. I want to see where this could go between us."

"For how long, though?" She pulled her hand away and tucked it into her coat pocket.

While he wasn't completely sure, he thought she was saying she wanted something long-term. He knew she'd hated how he bounced from relationship to relationship, and she'd said she didn't want this to be real. But occasionally she said something that made him think she'd be open to more if there was the possibility of a commitment.

Even a day ago, he'd have sworn he wasn't the commitment type anymore.

But how long did it take for a woman to change a man's mind?

A month? A week?

The breadth of a kiss?

Lena's muscles tensed as Dex pulled her around the ice rink. She clung to his hands like he was her lifeline, her only defense against another bone-jarring crash into the ice at their feet. Her savior—he'd rescued her from a few hard falls. His protective nature and gentle coaxing as he'd tried to teach her to ice-skate had given her a glimpse at the type of father Dex would be, if he could ever open his heart up to a long-term relationship again.

"I think you are starting to get the hang of this," Dex encouraged as he skated backward, holding both of Lena's hands in his own. He glided across the ice with a grace she envied.

"Ha, you're only saying that because the last time I

fell I didn't take you out with me." Unlike the time before where she'd slammed him into the wall so hard that a hockey ref would have called a penalty on her for boarding. She'd managed to knock the breath out of them both in one embarrassing moment.

"That might bear a slight resemblance to the truth." He laughed. The chill of the ice rink had added color to his cheeks. "Are you having fun, at least?"

"I'm freezing cold and have bruised far more than my pride, but surprisingly, yes, I am having fun." Her right skate hit a divot in the ice and she pitched forward into his chest. "But I swear this skate has it out for me."

Thankfully, he had enough balance for the both of them and kept them from tumbling onto the ice again. His arms wrapped around her, keeping her upright. "I'm sure it's the skate's fault. You want me to give it a good talking to?"

"If you think it will help," she murmured from her position against his chest. "I think I'll sit this lap out and maybe get some hot chocolate. Not sure my bottom can handle another hard landing."

A group of teenagers skated past, laughing. Cheeks pink from the cold, they seemed far surer on those tiny strips of metal strapped to their feet than Lena could ever hope to be. She watched one of the girls do some fancy loop or axel—Lena wasn't sure of the proper terminology. Even a child had more technical ability on the ice than she did.

"She's good," Dex said.

Lena looked up at him in question. How'd he know what she'd been thinking?

"You've been watching her. If she's who I think she is, her grandparents own this rink, so she's practically grown up here." He brushed Lena's hair back and tucked it behind her ear. "She's been skating as long as she could walk, so of course she's good."

"So, what you are saying is that I shouldn't feel bad that someone who is half my age is a better skater than me?"

He whispered in her ear, "I'm sure there are a lot of things that you are far better at than that kid is."

She blushed at his comment, feeling the heat rising up into her cheeks at the innuendo in his words. "Shh… what if the kids hear?"

He shrugged. "So what if they do? You are a great nurse. None of them would be of any help at all in surgery. Most of them probably barely know basic anatomy."

Pushing against his chest, she moved away from him, wobbling on her skates. "That's not what you meant."

"If anyone overheard me, it is exactly what I meant." The broad smile on his face was as innocent as it was genuine. "I'll defend that position to the end too."

Lena grabbed for the rail when her skate decided to go off on its own again. "How 'bout that hot chocolate?"

Answering physically rather than verbally, Dex led her off the ice and over to the food counter. He ordered them a couple hot chocolates, and they went and sat on one of the benches overlooking the rink. It was a little warmer off the ice, at least.

"I'm so cold I think my blood has frozen." Cupping her hands around the warm cup of chocolate, Lena sighed. "And don't even lecture me on how that's impossible. I may not have a medical degree, but I know how I feel. And that's nearly solid ice."

He wrapped an arm around her shoulders and leaned in close. His breath was warm and delicious against her cheek. "If you didn't insist on sitting on the ice so much, you wouldn't be chilled through."

"We don't have winter where I'm from!" she protested. "Even the coldest days are warmer than it is in here. How'd you do the last time you went surfing?"

A loud, harsh laugh burst out of him and drew the attention of some of the people around them. "I've never attempted to surf, so probably worse than you did skating. Do you surf?"

"I used to." There was a longing in her voice. Man, she missed the rush of being out on the waves. The freedom that came with being out on the water. But when Dex picked up her hand and held it in his own, she missed it a little bit less.

"Well, I know just the thing to cheer you up. It's not surfing, but I'm sure you going to love it anyway." He squeezed her close and pressed a kiss to her temple. "Way better than ice skating, I promise."

Her heart raced at that tiny display of intimacy. "What do you have planned?"

"If I tell, it ruins the surprise." He stood and offered her his hand. "Do you trust me?"

She gazed up at him while she considered the question. Did she trust him? He had such an earnest expression on his face in that moment that not taking his hand had to be a crime. Gingerly, she placed her hand in his.

"I'm going to trust you for the evening."

A wide grin spread across his face. "You won't regret it."

Leading her out of the skating rink, he had her tucked into the passenger seat of the SUV before either of them uttered another word. When he turned the SUV out of town and back down the twisty road they'd traveled when they came in from Gatlinburg, she had to speak up.

"Where exactly are you taking me?" She gasped as they passed several white-tailed deer standing right on the side of the road. "Did you see them?"

"Everyday occurrence around here." He glanced over at her. "You look shocked. Have you never seen deer before?"

Lena scoffed. "Not outside a zoo or nature preserve. City girl, remember? We don't exactly have deer running past the hospital in LA. I mean, in some of the parks and on the outskirts, yeah, but not where I'm from."

"Don't look to the left now if deer shock you."

"A bear!" She spun in her seat and her excited exclamation filled the cab. Staring out the window, Lena could barely believe her eyes as Dex drove slowly past the large black bear who seemed to be in no hurry as she lumbered down the road. "Don't bears hibernate? Why is it just ambling down the road right now instead of sleeping?"

"Ah, see, that's what most people think. But where it stays warmer here, our bears don't spend months straight hibernating like northern bears do. They do sleep for extended periods, of course. But they are also very easily awakened. And when they wake up they usually go searching for food and stay up for a little while before they return to their den or sometimes find a new one."

"I had no idea." She tried to sneak a topic change in while he was in a talkative mood. "So, where are you taking me for our first real date? It's getting dark now."

"We are almost there." He reached over and squeezed her hand briefly. "Did skating not count as a real date? By my count, this should be date number two."

"Nice try. Same day, same date."

His mention of this being a real date sent her heart out for a jog. Dating for real made her nervous, and excited, and a thousand other emotions all at once. Lena's mind raced as they passed by tourist attraction after tourist attraction. "Are we doing a dinner theater show?"

"Nope."

"Can I get a little hint?" Christmas lights competed with attraction signs in every direction. Twinkling lights lit all the trees along the sidewalks, and most of the businesses had lighted displays garnishing their windows, filled with Santas and reindeer-pulled sleighs.

"Nope."

"Are we buying moonshine?" She laughed as they drove past a second distillery. "I've never had moonshine but I'm not opposed to trying it."

"That's not why we are here, but we can stop in to one of the distilleries on the way back if you like."

"Hmm…" She scanned the signs along the street. "I don't think it's the aquarium."

"Nope." He pulled into a public parking lot. "We have to walk a bit to get where we are going."

Interest piqued, Lena climbed out of the SUV and wrapped her scarf tighter against the cold wind. "Is it indoors?"

Dex gave an awkward sounding chuckle. "Not exactly, but give it a chance, okay?"

They walked a block or so down, with Lena completely fascinated by the red lifts going up the side of the mountain into the darkness. Above them, a suspension bridge hung, covered in Christmas lights.

"Are we going up there?" she asked, her voice as filled with wonder as a small child's on Christmas morning.

"Yeah, we are. I hope you aren't afraid of heights."

He showed their tickets to the attendant and they were soon seated in the next lift chair. The attendant tucked the safety bar down into place and they began the slow trek up the mountain.

"This is amazing, but cold!"

Dex's arm settled over her shoulders and the weight brought with it a delicious warmth much welcome in the crisp evening air. "Does this help? If not, I can think of a few other ways to warm you up."

The words sounded like a flirtatious challenge as they rolled off his tongue, but Lena didn't want to run away from something with Dex anymore. Being with Dex, spending time with him and seeing how he was when with his family, had changed her opinions on giving a relationship a chance.

She loved him. Loved spending time with him.

Love...

She swallowed back the realization that she'd somehow allowed herself to fall in love with Dex. No longer falling, she was head over heels, beyond the point of rescue. She laid her head on his shoulder. What would come next? How on earth did she proceed with a fake relationship when she was in real love with the surgeon at her side?

When they reached the top and got off the lift, employees ushered them inside to warm up. Dex bought them each a hot chocolate, and they sat up on the second floor, staring out over the town below them.

"This place is gorgeous." Wisps of steam rose from the mug in her hands and warmed her wind-chilled cheeks. "I'd love to see the fall color from up here."

"Maybe next fall. My mom would love to show you all the touristy places around Westfield too. It's kinda her thing, after all." Dex sipped at his own drink. "But there's one more part to this evening and I think it will be your favorite."

Confidence abounded in his voice. The wind had put color in his face. Women from across the room eyed him and not even discreetly. In jeans today, or scrubs at the hospital, Dex was a man who drew attention with very little effort. It felt really good to have his attention focused on her.

When she finished her hot chocolate, Dex took her hand.

"Come on, one last thing before we head back down the mountain." He led her outside and over to the suspension bridge she'd been in awe of from down in town. "You ready for this?"

The suspension bridge seemed to extend forever. Christmas lights lit up the railings and some of the cables all the way across the valley, it seemed. Bright reds, greens and blues twinkled in rows above their heads and at their sides. As they stepped out onto the bridge, Lena gaped at the glass panels at their feet and the rows of lights below them too.

"Dex, this is…wow."

When they reached the center of the bridge, Dex stopped her. "I thought you might like to see Gatlinburg lit up for Christmas from the best view in town."

"It's beautiful."

His arm slipped around her waist and moved her into his embrace. Tilting her chin up, he leaned in close. "So are you."

Lena couldn't fight the attraction anymore. When her arms snaked up around his neck, Dex responded as she'd hoped. His lips brushed hers, innocently at first, teasing. He tasted of chocolate and mint and hope.

This kiss was unlike the ones in the parking lot at the rest stop. This kiss held more than simple attraction. Lena projected her love for him into the embrace and hoped Dex could sense that she wanted, no, needed more.

He eased back on the kiss, but kept her contained within the circle of his arms. “Do you think we can give this a real try? I’m game if you are.”

CHAPTER THIRTEEN

AS THEY ENTERED the church, Dex waited for the dread that he'd been sure would come when he walked through that vestibule, but it never came. The last time he'd been in this sanctuary, he'd been left at the altar. The grin that spread across his face was from the realization that being here didn't hurt.

"It's about time the two of you showed up. I was thinking I might have to send a scout out and make sure you were alive," his mom called out. She glared down at them from above, perched on the top of a ladder where she was wrapping a string of lights around one of the stained-glass windows.

Dex glanced down at his watch. "It's only nine, Mama. You act like we rolled in at noon. Should you be up on a ladder? Maybe I should do that."

"We've got two locations to decorate. Mary and I have been here for ages already, unlike some of you lazy bones who couldn't be bothered to roll out of the bed until the sun had been up for hours." The Southern accent came out stronger with the censure in her tone. Jabbing a finger toward the opposite side of the church, she directed, "There are bows to go on the ends of each pew in a box over there. You two start with getting those put up. And don't give me any sass about being on a ladder, I know my own limitations."

"Yes, ma'am," Dex and Lena echoed. Their eyes met and they shared a small laugh. Today wouldn't be the day to test his mom's patience, and he was glad Lena seemed to be picking up on that.

The interior of the church was warm, so they shed their coats and scarves and tossed them onto the last pew. Dex guided Lena over to the overflowing box of red bows his mom had indicated.

While Lena pulled one of the bows from the box, Dex wrapped his arms around her from behind. "I'm sure I'll be as good at this as I was wrapping presents."

Leaning against his chest, Lena sighed. "You were so bad at that."

"At least we get to spend the day together."

She snickered and waved a hand toward his mom and Mary. "With a pair of sixty-year-old women as our chaperones."

No sooner than the words were out of Lena's mouth, his mom barked out an order for them to hang the bows. He muttered under his breath, "You heard the general, hang the bows."

He took a step back from Lena and snatched one of the bows out of the box. They hung several without speaking, but that didn't mean they weren't saying anything. As each bow came out of the box, his hands brushed against hers. Their eyes met and lingered on each other as each bow was placed. With each graze of their hands, Dex wanted to clasp his fingers with hers and find somewhere private to see where those teasing touches might lead. Sharing a bed the night before without taking things beyond a few kisses had been akin to torture, but he was determined to do things right with Lena. She wanted to take the physical side of things slow, and he would honor that. But each touch of their skin, each kiss, made that harder.

When Tommy and Jill came in a little while later, they brought with them an excitement that filled the church. The smiles on both of their faces energized Dex, and he found himself humming a Christmas carol.

"What's this? Ebenezer Scrooge actually knows Christmas music? I am shocked." Lena poked him, grabbing a bow and hurrying to the other end of the pew.

He grinned and grabbed a bow before following her. "I know a lot of Christmas music, actually."

Tommy strolled over, still smiling broadly. "So, the way I hear it, the two of you had quite the romantic evening last night. Even went up to the High Bridge? You aren't trying to steal my thunder, are you, big brother?"

Dex grinned at him. He took Lena's left hand in his and brought it up to his lips just to tease his brother. "So what if I am?"

He considered—briefly—allowing the misunderstanding to continue, but he didn't want to scare Lena. It was less than twenty-four hours ago that they'd move out of the fake zone and into reality. From the moment he'd taken her hand and led her out onto the High Bridge, he'd known that one day he would be proposing to her, though. It just wasn't that time yet, but before he could correct his brother, Jill squealed and ran over.

On the eve of her wedding, she was even more bubbly and bouncy than usual. He'd have never guessed it was possible for her to get more excitable, but he'd just been proven wrong.

"Oh, my God, did you really propose to her last

night? Tommy said you wouldn't, but I told him that you wouldn't have brought Lena home with you unless you were dead serious about her."

The excitement on Jill's face was overwhelming. Dex swallowed hard at the onslaught of energy coming his way. Her words rushed over him and crashed into his mind. Knowing that one day he'd propose to Lena and having everyone think that was this day were miles apart. He'd just came to terms with the idea of another serious relationship and having a future with someone. It was starting to feel like commitment was crowding in far too quickly, like a flash flood rushing up over his heart.

His voice cracked when he spoke. "We haven't been dating that long yet, guys. This Christmas is all yours. We aren't engaged."

There was an awkwardness to Lena's laugh, but she backed him up with her own confirmation that they weren't ready for that step. "Yes, we are so not to that point yet."

Slipping an arm around her waist, he leaned close and whispered, "I like that you said 'yet,' though."

"Why would you think we were engaged?" Lena asked, and he had to admit it was a very good question. He should have thought to ask that one himself, because he thought he'd quashed that line of thought from his family the previous morning.

Jill looked at them with a cat-that-got-the-canary grin. "I'm guessing that you haven't seen the photos that High Bridge put up on the tourism page we help your mom run, have you?"

Dex shook his head, forehead wrinkling as he considered her words. "No?" he finally ventured cautiously.

Jill pulled out her phone and tapped a few times before holding it out to him. Her smile was now ear to ear. "That was some kiss. They even tagged it with 'I think we just had another proposal. #perfectproposalspot.' So if you didn't propose last night, you really missed your opportunity, and you'll have to work extra hard to find a better one now."

Pink tinted Lena's cheeks as they viewed the photographic evidence of last evening's embrace together. She grabbed another bow and busied herself attaching it to the next pew. Clearly an avoidance tactic, he thought.

Not that he blamed her. He'd really like to change the topic himself, but Jill and Tommy seemed to want to press the issue. Probably because they were so deliriously happy with each other that they wanted to infect everyone within reach with the matrimony bug.

Personally, Dex thought the matrimony bug felt a bit like the start of a nasty stomach bug in that moment. His stomach churned with a nervous anxiety, and a deep desire to change the subject rose up from his core. "Drop it, please," he entreated. "Focus on decorating for your wedding."

Focus on anything but embarrassing Lena further…

Anything but marrying him off to the first woman he'd been serious about in years…

Anything at all.

He grabbed a bow out of the box and passed it to Lena. Looking back at Tommy and Jill, he asked, "Don't you have some decorations to put up, or are you just expecting us to do everything for you?"

After spending the day decorating both the church and the reception hall for Tommy and Jill's wedding, Lena was ready for bed. Unfortunately, they still had several more hours of wedding-related activities to go. She was used to being on her feet all day, but Dex's mom had kept them going nonstop for hours. She'd followed behind, tweaking half the decorations they'd put up, obsessing over making everything absolutely perfect.

It was as heartwarming as it was frustrating.

Lena couldn't imagine her own mother hanging a single item of decor. Micromanaging the wedding planner or interior decorator hired to do the job? Absolutely. But she'd never be hands-on like Ruth Henry had been.

"You ready to go get through this ugly Christmas sweater rehearsal dinner mess?" Dex asked, holding the car door open for her.

"I'm as ready as I'll ever be." She reached out and straightened his sweater. "That color looks as good on you as I thought it would."

"It will look better off."

"Shh..." Fighting against the blush she knew was rushing up her cheeks, Lena admonished him. "We are going to be late for this thing if we don't get inside soon. Put those thoughts right out of your mind."

He grumbled good-naturedly, but took her hand as she stepped out of the car. "My vote is still for skipping. We could leave a note saying we were heading back to Nashville to elope. They'd never even question it."

She rolled her eyes at him, trying her best to stick to that same joking tone. "After you spent the entire day arguing that we weren't engaged. Sure."

The thought of marrying him was far from distasteful, though. In fact, she could imagine a future where she and Dex were married. She could see them in a house in the suburbs of Nashville, a little boy, a little girl and a dog. They'd make trips to see his family regularly, so that their kids knew what a grandparent's love felt like. Having seen just how quickly they welcomed her into their loving arms, she had no doubts they'd move the world for their grandbabies. Being around Dex and his entire family had been easier than she'd thought possible. Actually, it felt really right. Being part of a real family was a novel experience for her, one she found herself deeply longing to hang on to, and the very last thing she wanted was to go back to her solitary existence in Nashville.

She was getting ahead of herself. She and Dex had shared a single date and she was imagining their children. Exhaling quickly, she pushed the thought of that imaginary future out of her head. "Should we go in?"

"Let's get it over with." He opened the door to the church and they stepped in out of the cold. From the looks of things, they were the last to arrive.

His mom made a quick motion to him to join them at the front of the church. Lena followed up the aisle more slowly and sat next to Dex's aunt Peggy.

Jill wore a simple veil with what Lena could only assume was a custom-designed ugly Christmas sweater that had the words Bride-to-Be knitted into the Christmas pattern. It was hideous, but Jill's radiance overcame the sweater's deficiency. The way the young bride stared at her groom-to-be, clad in a matching Husband-to-Be sweater, sent a pang of longing through Lena's heart. She wanted what Jill had—a Henry man standing at the altar next to her with a goofy grin on his face.

Shifting her glance to Dex, she found him staring back at her. He winked at her before turning his gaze back to the pretend ceremony in front of him. Even the obnoxious sweater couldn't detract from how handsome he looked.

As she sat waiting for the rehearsal part of the evening

to be over, she wondered, was this the church where Dex had been left at the altar? He had never said, but she reasoned that it was possible, even likely. She searched his face for signs of upset, but all she could detect was happiness as he watched his brother and future sister-in-law practice their ceremony.

Soon, the rehearsal was done and they moved to a large room at the back of the church for the ugly sweater part of the evening. At the back of the room stood a table loaded down with finger foods and appetizers.

Lena's stomach rumbled at the sight. Lunch had been so long ago. She and Dex made their way over to the food and filled their plates quickly. They took a seat at one of the round tables placed along one side of the room. After getting something in her stomach, she let her eyes scan the room. She'd expected a small party, given that the wedding was tomorrow, but there was actually quite a crowd.

Suddenly, Lena stood. Her heart jerked as her eyes and brain tried to process what she was seeing. *Who* she was seeing. Blinking hard, she tried to clear what had to be a hallucination from her mind. There was no way that her lying, cheating ex-boyfriend could be standing in front of her. The man turned and she swallowed hard when she realized it wasn't Connor. Of course, it wouldn't be Connor. Why would he be in Westfield, Tennessee, of all places?

"Lena?" The concern in Dex's voice brought her back to a state of calm. "You look like you've seen a ghost."

"I thought I saw someone I recognized and had a momentary panic. I'm okay now." She waved vaguely at the man talking to Tommy. Now that she got a better look at the man, she could see he only bore a faint resemblance to

Connor and not nearly enough that she should have panicked. "I am going to step out and get a little air, though."

"I'll come with you," he offered.

"No." She laid a hand on his forearm. "You are needed here. And I'll only be a moment."

Leaving him standing alone, Lena grabbed her coat and stepped out into the crispness of the winter night. Though the frigid air pained her lungs, she inhaled deeply several times. Looking up, she focused on the constellations shining bright in the clear, dark sky.

"What am I doing?" she said aloud.

"Hiding out to avoid giving me a real answer, if I had to guess." Dex's voice came from behind her.

Spinning to face him, she grimaced. "That could be at least partially true."

"I'm a good listener though, I promise. And whatever it is, we can talk about it. We can get through it." With a gentle hand, he brushed his thumb along the edge of her lower lip. "And if it's about Jessie, you don't need to worry about her."

"It's nothing. Completely stupid."

"Your reaction said that it was something." His eyes searched her face. "Every drop of color left your face."

Breath puffing out visibly in the cold, Lena closed her eyes for a moment. "I thought I saw Connor."

"Your ex?"

"Yeah." Looking up at him, she shrugged. "It's completely irrational. He'd have no reason to be here, and yet I thought I saw him."

There was a harshness to his inhale, noticeable in the quiet. "You looked afraid. Did he hurt you?"

"Not physically." She shook her head and moved away from his touch. Staring out at the sky, she continued, "But yes, he hurt me. He was the first man I ever said 'I love you' to. And I found out too late that he'd been playing me from day one."

"Ouch."

"Yeah. He only wanted me because of who my father is. He wanted to be department head. Looking back, I ignored a lot of warning signs. The tan lines where he'd had a wedding ring, the nights when he ignored my calls, the way he never wanted me at his place and insisted on coming to mine."

"He was married." Dex's words weren't a question.

"Yeah. Oh, he told me he was separated and in the process of getting a divorce. And then weeks after my father promoted him to head of Cardio, he and his wife decided to work things out. Later, I found out they'd never actually been separated and she had encouraged him to pursue a relationship with me so that he could get in good with the medical director."

"Your father?"

"Got it in one. Connor's actions told me who he truly was, but I didn't want to see the truth because I had fallen hard for him. Or at least I thought I had."

"Thought?" Dex moved toward her quickly, his gaze intense.

Her lips turned up in a hint of a smile. "My heart's been telling me a little something different lately."

"I know exactly what you mean." His arms circled her waist and pulled her into his chest. "It's crazy, isn't it, that we could find something so strong in such a short time?"

"Mmm…" With her arms wrapped around his neck, she tiptoed up. "Are you going to kiss me or not, Doc?"

"Definitely going to kiss you, Nurse," he murmured against her lips.

Every kiss with Dex became this magical experience. Undeniably fierce, yet layered with an unexpected tenderness. Comforting, when she let her guard down enough to let him in.

And every moment, every kiss, she trusted the man who held her a little more.

CHAPTER FOURTEEN

DEX TOOK HER hand in his as they entered the church and he seated her with his aunt before leaving to find his brother. As best man, he couldn't stay in the sanctuary with Lena, even if she'd have vastly preferred that. So she settled in next to Peggy and they made a little small talk while they waited for the ceremony to begin.

Most of the guests were already inside and seated when Tommy came in and took his place at the altar. A goofy love-struck grin screamed to the entire church just how happy he was in that moment.

Dex followed right behind him. The matching grin on Dex's face warmed Lena's heart. The candlelight glow and remnants of sunset streaming in through the stained glass created this moody, intense lighting that highlighted all of his best features. Clad in dark reds and pine greens, the wedding party gathered at the front of the church to await the moment when Tommy and Jill would exchange their vows.

Crisp garlands of flowers mixed with shiny ribbons and ornamented wreaths. At the back of the altar, a large Christmas tree rose tall just beneath the cross. Christmas had never looked more romantic.

Lena struggled through the ceremony to keep her

focus on the bride and groom. Even as Jill made her way up the aisle, as lovely as she was, her gaze kept drifting over to Dex. And given how often their eyes met, she knew he shared her struggles. As the pastor started the ceremony and even through the vows, Dex kept sneaking peeks at Lena.

He even missed the cue to pass Tommy the rings and had to be prompted.

"Looks like our best man has been distracted by that lovely young lady in the second pew," the pastor said with a teasing tone. The man's words sent a wave of tittering laughter through the church.

Lena's cheeks heated but she couldn't control the smile on her face. It took all the self-control she possessed to avoid rushing up there and throwing herself into his arms.

Peggy nudged her and whispered, "I do think that boy is in love with you."

Her eyes darted back to Dex and their eyes met again. His smile widened and her heart swelled. In his expression, she found hope. It radiated out and soothed the wounds talking about Connor had left jagged. It left her optimistic that the future would be bright.

"Relationships take love and they take work. Tommy, Jill, you've vowed to always love each other before all these witnesses, but it will also take commitment to stay dedicated to each other and to uphold what is best for your marriage." The pastor paused to allow the impact of the moment to build. "With that said, this is the moment where I have to ask those who have joined us here today for this momentous occasion to also make a promise—a promise to stand by this couple, to remind them of their vows if necessary, and to set the example of what love is and what family is. If you agree to this promise, please now confirm with your own 'I do.'"

The entire crowd yelled out, "I do."

Holding up a hand, the pastor waited for the sanctuary to grow quiet again. Finally, the last of the stragglers stopped chorusing their agreements and silence filled the church.

"Tommy and Jill, this room is filled with people who have pledged their support to you. You will be starting your marriage strong and—"

He was interrupted by the sound of the sanctuary doors slamming open.

"Oh, I'm so sorry to interrupt! Don't mind me. I'll just find a seat." In walked a tall woman in a dress that was more appropriate for a night out at a club than a church wedding. Her long hair was styled in big curls that bounced around her as she strode forward on stiletto heels. She walked up the aisle like she owned the place, her steps sure and confident. Instead of taking a seat, though, she stepped up to Jill and hugged her tight. "Sorry, Jilly! I didn't mean to interrupt, really."

Lena knew without anyone saying that this was Jessie—the runaway bride, Dex's ex-fiancée. That thought was confirmed when the other woman blew a kiss to Dex.

"Hey, Dex. Maybe we can catch up after?" Jessie sashayed down to sit next to her parents, exaggerating her movements and keeping her eyes on Dex.

Dex had this totally gobsmacked expression on his face that Lena couldn't quite decipher. His gaze kept drifting over to where Jessie sat, the hem of her bright red dress creeping higher on her thighs.

Maybe it had been inevitable, but Lena had really

hoped they could avoid Jessie. The way the other woman had looked at Dex, though, the desire and want shining brightly in her eyes, oh, her intentions were crystal clear. Jessie had realized what she'd lost and planned to rectify that mistake, no matter who she trampled in the process. A trickle of fear shimmied down Lena's spine.

Her heart hurt at the realization that once Jessie walked in, Dex had hardly spared her a glance. As Dex's first love, Jessie had a power over him that Lena did not. With their relationship being so very new, Lena wasn't sure that what they had was strong enough to withstand Jessie wanting him back.

The pastor came out of his shocked stupor and finished the ceremony, finally pronouncing Tommy and Jill as man and wife.

After the ceremony, Dex had to walk the bridesmaid out and stand for pictures. It looked like it might be some time before Lena would be able to reconnect with him. A little while longer before she found out once and for all where things stood between them. He sent her a quick wave and mouthed an apology.

When Jill grabbed Jessie and pulled her in for pictures, it sent another jab of panic running down Lena's spine. Jessie laid her head over on Dex's shoulder for one of the photos and they looked like a couple. Knowing that continuing to watch Jessie make a play for Dex was only torturing herself, Lena sighed and stepped away.

She made her way over to the reception alone.

"I finally escaped from that photographer. I think Tommy and Jill will grow old together getting their wedding photos taken." He kissed his aunt Peggy on the cheek. "Have you seen Lena?"

He needed to reassure her that seeing Jessie changed nothing for him. The stricken look on Lena's face when she had realized just who had made such a dramatic entrance to the wedding was seared into his brain. He had to make sure she knew how he felt before Jessie somehow made things worse.

For a horrible moment, Dex could imagine just what Lena had looked like when the truth about Connor had surfaced. Lost and vulnerable, she'd looked like she was seeing her world implode before her very eyes. He'd wanted to pull her into his arms, close that physical distance, and kiss her until they had to break for air or suffocate. The desire to do just that had been palpable, but he'd had to dismiss it. Jessie had already interrupted Tommy and Jill's wedding enough. He'd had to avoid looking at her for the remainder of the ceremony because if he'd seen even a hint of tears, he couldn't have remained standing next to his brother.

"Dexter, that young woman of yours is remarkable," his aunt Peggy said. "I do hope you know that you've found a keeper this time and don't let that painted-up tart ruin this for you like she nearly did Tommy's wedding."

"I hear you, Aunt Peggy. But first I need to find Lena."

Blowing kisses at him in front of an entire church full of people? Jessie couldn't have been more obvious if she'd hung a sign around her neck that said Property of Dexter Henry. After all this time, just when he was finally happy again, Jessie had to pull this crap. Why now? Was it just another way of torturing him?

"They are going to start dancing soon. You should go find your girl, because you two lovebirds don't want to miss out on that." Peggy jabbed his arm. "I hear rumors that destination weddings are what's going to be in style for next year. White dress, white sand, sounds like what's right to me, don't you?"

"Hint heard and noted."

"This one's worth fighting for. Don't you let her walk away." She winked at him before disappearing into the crowd. She wobbled slightly before righting herself. He considered that before continuing his search for Lena.

When his little brother entered the room with his new bride, Dex paused his search for Lena momentarily and joined in the applause that spread throughout the room. Tommy and Jill held hands, both smiling like lunatics, as they made their way to the head table. When Tommy kissed her before they sat down, someone cheered.

"We want to thank you all for being here to share this day with us. It means the world to us," Jill said. "Now let's dance!"

He scanned the crowd, looking for Lena. Their eyes met from across the room. He took one step toward her and someone screamed.

"Dexter!" his dad shouted.

Moving away from Lena with regret, he headed in the direction his dad's voice had come from. The crowd on the dance floor parted to let him through. His aunt Peggy lay sprawled out next to a chair along the edge of the room.

"What happened?" he asked, already reaching for her throat to take her pulse. Her heart rate was rapid and felt irregular under his fingers.

His dad looked on anxiously. "We were walking toward the dance floor and she said 'Oh, I think my blood sugar's crashing.' She walked away and fell before she got to the table."

"I should have followed up when I realized she was

unsteady on her feet," Dexter said. "I should have read the signs."

Lena had hurried over from the opposite direction. She pulled a glucose monitor out of Peggy's purse and was checking her numbers already. The machine beeped and flashed a number that was far too low.

"She's had a hypoglycemic crash." Lena pulled an autoinjector syringe out of the purse. "Glucagon. She must be prone to this sort of thing."

"She's never passed out before that I know of." Dex's dad paced around next to them. The entire crowd was focused on them.

"You can't give her that. We don't know she needs it."

"This wasn't in her purse for no reason," Lena argued. "She needs it, and I'm giving it to her now." She pulled Peggy's sleeve up and pushed the autoinjector against her skin. Dex watched as she pushed the button and the clear liquid in the pen was dispensed into his aunt's arm. "We should roll her onto her side. This can sometimes cause vomiting."

"Has anyone called 911?" Dex asked as he rolled his aunt over.

"She also has glucose tablets and hard candies in her purse. I'm guessing her glucose plummets frequently." Lena put the purse down next to him. "She should wake up within a few minutes once this kicks in. I'm going to get her some food. Keep an eye on her."

Lena disappeared from his sight.

He brushed Peggy's hair away from her face and checked her pulse again. It was stronger and not quite as fast as earlier.

Swallowing hard, he couldn't help but be grateful that Lena was with him. He'd done rotations in general medicine, of course, but his knowledge of hypoglycemia was limited to it being a potential postsurgical complication that the nurses dealt with. Lena would have vastly more experience with this condition than he did.

Peggy started to stir. She muttered something incoherent and tried to sit up.

"Shh. We got you, Aunt Peggy." Reassurances slipped from his tongue. He helped ease her into a seated position. "Try not to move too much."

Lena came back with a small plate and a cup of soda. "Hey, Peggy. You think you could sip at this soda for me? I've got some of those tiny sandwiches for you too once you feel up to that."

Peggy's hand was shaky as she reached for the soda, but she managed to get it to her lips without spilling. After a few sips, she set it down and took one of the little sandwiches.

Paramedics came in then.

"Oh, you didn't have to call them. I'm fine," Peggy argued in a weak voice.

"You were unconscious. Yes, we did," Dex countered. Stubbornness ran in his family. She was not going to give in easily, that's for sure. He took a step back to give the paramedics a little breathing room.

Just as he turned to look for Lena, Jessie ran into his chest. Her arms snaked up around his neck.

"Oh, Dexter, I was so scared. You saved her. You actually saved her!" Jessie gushed. "My hero!"

Opening his mouth to argue that actually Lena deserved that credit, he froze when Jessie's mouth pressed against his and her tongue slipped past his parted lips. He struggled to comprehend exactly what was happening.

He put his hands on her hips and pushed her back away from him.

"Jessie, please don't do that again." Extracting himself from her clutches felt like trying to get away from the world's clingiest octopus. "What were you thinking?"

"I screwed up before, baby. You are my past, my present and my future."

Jessie really hadn't changed, though. After the time and the distance between them, he could see what a self-centered person she was. She still needed to be the center of attention, no matter who she hurt in the process. She'd never been anyone that he could have had a real marriage and a real future with. That was a lesson that had been driven home like a hammer pounding a nail into his thick skull. He'd left their wedding alone, his heart hollow and empty. And it wasn't until Lena came into his life, pelting him with shiny balls of ribbon, that he'd even realized how much he'd isolated his heart.

The carefree playboy persona he'd adopted after Jessie's betrayal had been scattered into the crisp winter wind after that mind-altering kiss he shared with Lena at the rest stop. Or maybe even before then. He couldn't be sure.

A few things he was sure of. One was that he'd never go back to Jessie. Two, quick hookups with no feelings would never be enough for him again. And most important, if he couldn't be with Lena, then he'd rather be alone.

He stepped back and she followed.

"Jessie, stop. You and I…never going to happen. Not again. I'm with Lena now."

Jessie flipped her hair over her shoulder, a sign he recognized as her doubling down on her efforts. He'd seen that exact motion many times during the years they were together. "I refuse to accept that."

"You'd better learn to accept it. Jessie, you are my past. And, honestly, you leaving me at the altar was the best thing that you've ever done for me. If it hadn't been for that, I'd have never ended up where I did, and I'd have never found Lena—the woman I intend to spend my future with."

Smirking at him, Jessie waved a hand. "You mean the girl who ran off when I kissed you. Some future."

Ran off?

He scanned the room. No sign of Lena.

His heart started racing. Jessie had ruined him in this very church once. Had she done it again? He had to find Lena, fast, before it was too late.

Lena watched as Jessie threw herself into Dex's arms. As they kissed, her heart shattered into a million pieces. When Dex's hands moved to Jessie's waist, she couldn't bear to watch.

She left the reception and found herself in the sanctuary. In a town like Westfield, she couldn't just call an Uber. Especially not on Christmas Eve.

Maybe Wade could be persuaded to get her out of town.

She sank down behind the Christmas tree, wanting a little privacy for the breakdown that seemed inevitable at the moment. Tears lurked just behind her lashes, waiting impatiently for her to lower her guard and allow them the freedom to roll down her cheeks.

Dex had chosen Jessie. Just like Connor had chosen his wife. What was it about her that made men only want her when she had something to offer them?

For Connor, a promotion.

For Dex, a way to avoid matchmaking and potentially a way to make his ex-fiancée jealous.

She swallowed hard and wrapped her arms around her knees. She'd trusted Dex too. Let him in, like she'd sworn she'd never do again. Little by little, he'd broken through the layers of ice around her heart and warmed her clear down to her soul.

And while she'd cared about Connor, and the end of their relationship had destroyed her, it never hurt this much. Seeing Dex kiss Jessie had felt like her heart and lungs had been ripped violently from her chest.

Gasping for air, she tried to remember how to breathe. This was what true heartbreak felt like.

"Lena?" Dex called from somewhere at the back of the sanctuary.

Sinking lower, she made herself small, hoping to avoid seeing him. How could she face him now? Knowing he had just been kissing Jessie after claiming to be all in with her?

She couldn't bear to look at him.

"Lena?" He called again from much closer. "Where are you?"

The door to the sanctuary banged open again, the sound of music growing louder until the door swung back closed. Lena breathed a sigh of relief.

"Dex, why are you in here alone when we could be dancing?"

Lena stiffened. She wasn't alone after all.

"Go away, Jessie." Agitation made Dex's voice rougher than usual. "I'm looking for my girlfriend."

"I'm standing right here, baby."

"Not you."

Lena peered through the tree at the hostility she heard from Dex. He was standing a few feet away, glaring at Jessie.

"But—"

"No *but*s. No *if*s. No us. Jessie, you left me standing at that altar in a tux. You disappeared without a word and didn't resurface for years. Surely you didn't think you could just come back and we'd pick up like nothing had ever happened?"

Lena watched as Jessie shrank back from his vehement tone.

"I hoped—"

"No." Dex ran his hands through his hair. "I love her. Don't you see? I am in love with Lena. And you might have screwed that up. Can't you just let me be happy?"

Lena's heart raced. *Dex loves me?*

A wisp of hope hummed through her, rising and thickening as she watched Dex crush Jessie's reconciliation plans. She choked back a sob, stuffing her fist to her mouth to muffle the sound.

But it was too late. Dex had heard.

He came around the tree, sank down next to her, and pulled her into his arms. "Lena, you have to know, you are the only woman I want. Getting back with Jessie has never once been a consideration for me."

"I'm standing right here," Jessie whined from the other side of the tree.

"And you can feel free to leave any time unless you want to hear me professing my love to another woman." Dex looked at Lena and rolled his eyes. "She never has been good at taking a hint."

Jessie huffed loudly and stomped out of the sanctuary.

When the door closed behind her, Dex sighed. "Okay,

so, elephant in the room. I know you saw her kiss me. I didn't kiss her back. Admittedly, I didn't stop her immediately, but I panicked. My brain couldn't seem to process what was happening or how to make it stop."

"I saw tongue."

"Hers!" he insisted. "I swear. Honestly, that was what seemed to jar me back into action. It was only once I'd managed to detach her—have I mentioned she's a major clinger?—that I could see you had left."

Her heart wanted to believe him.

"I won't be the other woman again."

"You've been the only woman I've looked at for months. Don't you know that?" Snorting, Dex squeezed her tight. "Since the day I asked you out and you shot me down so hard, you have been making me crazy."

"I don't believe that."

"Believe it." He captured her lips in a fiery kiss. Cupping the back of her head with one large hand, he held her as his lips roamed over hers and his tongue coaxed her lips to open. When it dawned on her that they were in a church, she pushed him back.

"Dex…" she started.

"I need to say something. Will you just hear me out before you reject me?" He stood and held a hand out to her. "Please?"

"Okay," she agreed. Putting her hand in his, she let him help her up off the floor.

Leading her around the tree, he stopped in the spot where his brother had stood earlier that evening. "A few long years ago, I stood right here in this very church and waited for someone who never showed. A few short weeks ago, I just wanted to get in and out of this church with some of my pride intact."

"Where are you going with this?"

"Shh… Let me finish." He took a step back. "A few hours ago, I stood right here looking at you and realized that I wanted to be the groom. I wanted to be someone's husband. Your husband." He dropped to one knee in front of her. "I don't have a ring. I don't have some elaborate proposal planned. But I love you. Will you marry me?"

CHAPTER FIFTEEN

One week later

THE FIRE CRACKLED brightly as Dex put another log on the flames. "Now, this is my idea of how New Year's Eve should be spent," he said as he walked back over to the couch and pulled the blanket back up over himself. "Just me and the love of my life, tucked away in a honeymoon cabin nestled in the Smoky Mountains."

They were only a few miles from his parents' house in Westfield, but this single-bedroom cabin afforded them the privacy that a newly engaged couple desired. They'd spent most of the week between Tommy's wedding and New Year's Eve with his family. Instead of staying for the party his family had planned, they'd decided to end the year snuggled up in front of a fire, just the two of them.

Lena placed her hand on his chest. She admired the way the shiny diamond Dex had slid on her finger on Christmas morning sparkled in the firelight. "I think when we do get married we should come back here. This place is perfect. I've never been happier than when I'm here with you."

"I haven't upheld my end of the bargain though. You

met my family, dealt with all the drama with my ex, and we skipped out on going to LA for the gala to come here instead." He pressed a kiss to her temple. "I feel a little guilty about that."

"You have nothing to feel guilty about." She ran a single finger along his jaw. "It was my decision not to go to California and subject you to the scrutiny of my parents."

He shrugged. "I have to meet them someday."

"Why?" She saw no reason to force him to meet parents who had never put her best interests at heart. "You actually deserve the credit for the decision. If you didn't love me so much, and hadn't taken me home to show me what a real family looks like, I would never have known just how bad my family dynamic really was. You gave me the confidence—no, that's not the right word—the *courage* to stand up to them and refuse to accept their treatment of me any longer."

"You deserve so much better than that."

Dex gave her a newfound respect for herself that she hadn't known possible. For years, Lena had only been sure of herself when clad in scrubs and within the walls of a hospital. Outside, she was a different person, and when with her parents, she was even less than that. Her family's constant scrutiny and relentless inquisition made her a shell of a person.

But with Dex's love, she felt strong. Like she could face anything, and even stand up to her parents. She'd called them and told them she was engaged and while they were still screaming about that fact, she'd informed them that she was not only not attending the gala, but that she wasn't moving back to California either.

"And I found something...someone better."

Dex cupped the nape of her neck, which felt just right. The gentleness of his touch sent a warm tingly feeling down her spine. "Have I told you how much I love you?"

"I don't mind hearing it again."

If they lived to be one hundred and he told her one thousand times a day, it would never be enough. His lips brushed hers in the lightest ghost of a kiss. Her heart beat faster at the feel of being in his arms. Like breathing, she needed him close. His kiss fed her soul like oxygen fed her lungs.

"It's hard sometimes for me to believe how much my life has changed in less than a year."

He tickled her side. "Try less than a month."

"You're right about that." She laughed. "And to think, I almost didn't agree to your initial proposal. If I hadn't agreed to be your fake girlfriend, I'd have never become your real fiancée."

That was a truth that she hadn't managed to wrap her head around yet. She'd been so close to passing on an amazing man simply because she'd been scared. It was a hard thought to accept that she might have missed out on all this because of fear.

A slow, easy smile lit his face and brightened his face like the fireplace brightened the room. "Imagine how things would have turned out if I'd brought Belinda home as my fake girlfriend instead. I could have been engaged to a woman who came to the relationship not just with kids, but grandkids as well. I could have been a grandfather. I gave that up for you."

Lena laughed. "Well, you're mine now. Belinda will have to find her own surgeon to marry."

"Is that right?" he asked, and his gaze dropped to her lips. "So, getting back to the idea of that wedding and honeymoon, when did you have in mind?"

* * * * *

MILLS & BOON

Coming next month

HIS BLIND DATE BRIDE
Scarlet Wilson

Ivy took another bite of her cake. It was going down well. 'What do you think would have happened if we'd actually gone on that blind date?'

She could have kept things simple and stuck to chat about work. But she didn't want to. If she wanted to work easily with Travis, they had to deal with this.

There was no one else around so they wouldn't be disturbed. It was just her and him in her cabin. It was now or never.

Travis made a little choking noise as his cake obviously stuck at the back of his throat and Ivy burst out laughing, 'Sorry, did I make that go down the wrong way?'

He laughed too and shook his head, leaning back in her chair. 'You just like to keep me on my toes, don't you?'

There it was. That teasing tone. The one that had completely drawn her in, whether it was spoken or in texts. The thing that had made Travis King something more than a potential blind date. Even if that had never been her intention.

She gave an easy shrug. 'Why not?' She held up her hands. 'It's not like there's much else to do around here.'

She was joking, and he'd know she was joking. But shipboard life was so different from being back at home where bars, cinemas, open air and long walks could easily fill her life.

Travis sat his tea on her desk and folded his arms. 'I think,' he started as he raised his eyebrows, 'if we'd gone on a blind date before meeting here, it would have been an absolute disaster.'

Really? What was it with this guy? Had none of his sisters taught him the art of talking to a woman? The words were like being hit with a tidal wave of icy water.

'Okay, then,' she said shortly, feeling like a fool, because in her head their blind date would never have been a disaster.

He held up one hand. 'No, wait, you didn't let me finish. Let me tell you why it would have been a disaster.'

She swung her legs off the bed. 'I don't need microscopic data on why we're a never-happened,' she said, pushing her 'not good enough' feelings away again.

He reached over and put his hand on her knee. His voice was low and throaty. 'Our date would have been a disaster, Ivy Ross, because one meeting would have had me hooked. Who knows what might have happened? It keeps me awake enough at night just thinking about it.'